PENGUIN BOOKS

Sign of the Cross

'One of those rare finds: a chilling tale told by a true craftsman. Whether for the superb writing or the non-stop, what-was-that-noise-in-the-other-room suspense, this one will keep you up at night. Daring in both plot and style, *Sign of the Cross* is a winner!' Robert Liparulo, author of *Comes a Horseman*

'Chris Kuzneski is a remarkable new writer, who completely understands what makes for a good story: action, sex, suspense, humor and great characters. I can't wait for the next Jonathon Payne novel!' Nelson DeMille, #1 *New York Times* Bestselling author

'Harrowing, but always suspenseful, *Sign of the Cross* makes you wish it would never end. Chris Kuzneski writes as forcefully as his tough characters act' Clive Cussler, #1 *New York Times* Bestselling author

'Chris Kuzneski writes with an energy that is contagious! Action, suspense, mystery, and a biting thread of humor . . . what more can you ask of a novel?' James Rollins, *USA Today* Bestselling author

'One of those perfect bookstore finds. I was hooked at the first sentence – literally – and from then on, it was one continuous wild ride. Chris Kuzneski flawlessly and seamlessly combines truth and fiction to create a wonderfully entertaining story. He's the real deal' John Gilstrap, author of *At All Costs* and *Six Minutes to Freedom*

'An immensely inventive and rewarding thriller packed with
enough fascinating information and international intrigue to
keep the reader's brain cells spinning long after the last page
is read' Lewis Perdue, author of *Daughter of God*

'*Sign of the Cross* starts with a bang and twists masterfully
through a maze of truth, lies, betrayal, and hope. An
intriguing blend of fact, fiction and theory propel this unique
story to a tense and exciting conclusion' Allison Brennan,
author of *The Kill*

ABOUT THE AUTHOR

Chris Kuzneski attended the University of Pittsburgh, where
he played football, wrote for three newspapers, and passed
most of his classes. He earned a master's degree in teaching,
then taught English for five years before pursuing a career in
writing. His first novel, *The Plantation*, introduced the characters of Payne and Jones, and received rave reviews. To learn
more, please visit his website www.chriskuzneski.com

Sign of the Cross

CHRIS KUZNESKI

PENGUIN BOOKS

PENGUIN BOOKS

Published by the Penguin Group
Penguin Books Ltd, 80 Strand, London WC2R ORL, England
Penguin Group (USA) Inc., 375 Hudson Street, New York, New York 10014, USA
Penguin Group (Canada), 90 Eglinton Avenue East, Suite 700, Toronto, Ontario, Canada M4P 2Y3
(a division of Pearson Penguin Canada Inc.)
Penguin Ireland, 25 St Stephen's Green, Dublin 2, Ireland (a division of Penguin Books Ltd)
Penguin Group (Australia), 250 Camberwell Road, Camberwell, Victoria 3124, Australia
(a division of Pearson Australia Group Pty Ltd)
Penguin Books India Pvt Ltd, 11 Community Centre, Panchsheel Park, New Delhi – 110 017, India
Penguin Group (NZ), 67 Apollo Drive, Rosedale, North Shore 0632, New Zealand
(a division of Pearson New Zealand Ltd)
Penguin Books (South Africa) (Pty) Ltd, 24 Sturdee Avenue,
Rosebank, Johannesburg 2196, South Africa

Penguin Books Ltd, Registered Offices: 80 Strand, London WC2R ORL, England

www.penguin.com

First published in the United States of America by The Berkley Publishing Group 2006
First published in Great Britain in Penguin Books 2007

12

Copyright © Chris Kuzneski, 2006
All rights reserved

The moral right of the author has been asserted

Set in 11.75/14 pt Monotype Garamond
Typeset by Rowland Phototypesetting Ltd, Bury St Edmunds, Suffolk

Printed in England by Clays Ltd, St Ives plc

ISBN: 978-0-141-03084-5

Acknowledgments

Writing a novel is a difficult task but not nearly as tough as raising a son who wants to be an author. Therefore, I'd like to start off by thanking my mom and dad. There's no way I would have a writing career if it weren't for them. They've been the key to *everything*. Somehow they always figured out what I needed (love, support, free food, etc.) and provided it for me. Seriously, I can't imagine having two better parents.

Professionally, I'd like to thank Scott Miller, my agent at Trident Media. How we teamed up is a remarkable story. He bought a self-published copy of *The Plantation* (my first Payne & Jones novel) in a Philadelphia bookstore and liked it enough to e-mail me. At the time, I had a folder with over one hundred rejection letters from literary agents, yet the best young agent in the business bought my book (at full price) and contacted me. Not only did I get a royalty from his book sale, but I also got the perfect agent. Amazing!

Of course, Scott doesn't work alone. I'd also like to thank Claire Roberts, who handles all my foreign sales, and the entire staff at Trident Media. You've done a remarkable job!

Speaking of jobs, I'd like to thank Berkley for paying me to do something I love. No, not watching football in my boxers. I'm talking about writing books. A huge thanks to Natalee Rosenstein for taking a chance on me. I'm so fortunate to work with an editor who is looking beyond my current project. Instead, she's hoping to build my career.

On a day-to-day basis, Michelle Vega is the person who I deal with most often at Berkley, and she's a superstar. In my opinion, she'd make a great game show host because she has the answers to all my questions. Then again, I shouldn't be surprised. Everyone I've ever dealt with at Berkley has been wonderful.

Next, I'd like to thank Pat LoBrutto, Joyce Kuzneski, and Joe Golden for their editing expertise. They helped shorten my 711-page first draft into something readable. Oh, and I'd be remiss if I didn't mention Ian Harper for answering all my late-night research questions, and Randy Raskin for his computer expertise. You guys are great friends.

Finally, I'd like to thank the dozen or so fans I already have. The first version of *The Plantation* came out a long time ago, and since then I've heard from many of you – mostly to tell me to get off my lazy ass and write another book before Payne & Jones die of old age. Man, I wish it was that easy. Unfortunately, the publishing world is a hard one to break into. Over the years, I've learned a few *lessons* (inside joke) and taught a few, too. In the end, I'm hoping *Sign of the Cross* was worth the wait . . .

Knowledge is the enemy of faith.

—translated from a stone marker
discovered in Orvieto, Italy
(circa 37 AD)

Central Europe

- Liechtenstein
- Vienna
- Austria
- Zurich
- Switzerland
- Küsendorf
- Milan
- Venice
- Florence
- Adriatic Sea
- Ligurian Sea
- Italy
- Orvieto
- Rome
- Naples
- Tyrrhenian Sea

N

0   100
miles

I

Monday, July 10
Helsingør, Denmark
(thirty miles north of Copenhagen)

Erik Jansen was about to die. He just didn't know how. Or why.

After saying a short prayer, he lifted his head and tried to regain his bearings but couldn't see a thing. Salt water burned his eyes and blurred his vision. He tried to wipe his face, but his hands were bound behind him, wrapped in thick layers of rope and attached to the frame of the boat. His legs were secured as well, tied even tighter than his arms, which meant there was no hope for escape. He was at their mercy. Whoever *they* were.

They had grabbed him as he left his apartment and forced him into the back of a van. Very quiet, very professional. No time for him to make a scene. Within seconds they had knocked him out with a narcotic. He awakened hours later, no longer in the bustling city but on the open sea. Day was now night. His freedom was now gone. His life was nearly over.

Jansen was tempted to scream but knew that would only make things worse. These weren't the type of men who made mistakes. He could tell. If help was nearby, they would've gagged him. Or cut out his tongue. Or both. No way they would've risked getting caught. He had known them for less than a day but knew that much. These men were professionals, hired to kill him for some ungodly reason. Now it was just a matter of time.

When their boat reached the shore, Jansen felt the rocks as they scraped against the bottom of the hull. The sound filled the air like a primeval wail, yet none of them seemed to care. It was the middle of the night, and the coast was deserted. No one would come running. No one would come to save him. It was in God's hands now, as it always was.

Suddenly, one of the men leapt over the side and splashed into the icy water. He grabbed the boat with both hands and eased it onto the narrow beach, just below a footpath. The other three followed his lead, and soon the boat was hidden in the trees that lined this section of the island.

They had traveled over a thousand miles but were just getting started.

Without saying a word, they loosened the ropes and lifted Jansen from the boat, placing him on their broad shoulders for the journey inland. Jansen sensed this might be his last chance to escape, so he flailed back and forth like an angry fish trying to break free of their grasp, yet all he did was upset them. In response they slammed his face into the jagged rocks, breaking his nose, shattering his teeth, and knocking him unconscious. Then they picked him up and carried him to the place where he would die.

One of the men cut off Jansen's clothes while the others built the cross. It was seven feet wide and ten feet high and made out of African oak. The wood was precut so the planks slid into place with little effort. When they were finished, it looked like a giant *T* spread across the freshly cut grass. They knew most people would be confused by the shape but not the experts. They would know it was authentic. Just like it was supposed to be. Just like it had been.

In silence they dragged Jansen to the cross and positioned his arms on the *patibulum* – the horizontal beam – and put his legs on the *stipes*. Once they were satisfied, the largest of the men took a mallet and drove a wrought-iron spike through Jansen's right wrist. Blood squirted like a cherry geyser, spraying the worker's face, but he refused to stop until the nail hit the ground. He repeated the process on Jansen's left wrist, then moved to his legs.

Since Jansen was unconscious, they were able to place his feet in the proper position: left foot on top of the right, toes pointed downward, which would please their bosses no end. One spike through the arch in both feet, straight through the metatarsals.

Perfect. Simply perfect. Just like it needed to be.

Once Jansen was in place, out came the spear. A long wooden spear. Topped with an iron tip that had been forged to specifications. The largest of the men grabbed it and without blinking an eye rammed it into Jansen's side. No empathy. No regret. He actually laughed as he cracked Jansen's ribs and punctured his lung. The other men followed his lead, laughing at the dying man as blood gushed from his side. Laughing like the Romans had so many years before.

The leader checked his watch and smiled. They were still on schedule. Within minutes, they would be back on the boat. Within hours, they would be in a different country.

All that remained was the sign. A hand-painted sign. It would be nailed to the top of the cross, high above the victim's head. It was their way of claiming responsibility, their way of announcing their intent. It said one thing, one simple phrase. Six words that were known throughout the world. Six words that would doom Christianity and rewrite the word of God.

IN THE NAME OF THE FATHER.

2

El Presidio de Pamplona
(Pamplona Penitentiary)
Pamplona, Spain

The frigid water slammed the prisoner against the stone wall and held him there like it was made of Velcro. That is until the prison guard turned off the fire hose and watched him fall to the floor.

'*¡Hola, Señor Payne! ¡Buenos días!*'

'*Buenos días*, my ass.' He had been locked in a cell since Friday, and this was the third morning in a row that they'd used the hose to wake him up.

'What is wrong?' the guard asked with a thick accent. 'Not happy to see me, eh?'

Jonathon Payne climbed off the floor and stretched his six foot four frame. He was in good shape for his mid-thirties, yet all the training in the world couldn't stop the years from adding up. Throw in some old gunshot wounds and a few football injuries, and getting out of bed was his least favorite part of the day. 'Oh, it's not you. I *love* seeing your two teeth every morning. The thing I can do without is your wake-up call. I go to sleep in Spain and wake up in Niagara Falls.'

The guard shook his head. He was slight of build and ten inches shorter than Payne, but the thick iron bars gave the guard courage. 'Just like a spoiled American. I go out of my way to shower you in bed and you do nothing but complain. Tomorrow I might skip the hose and wake you with my bullwhip.'

'Damn, Ricardo. You're one kinky cop.'

'What you mean *kinky*?'

Payne ignored the question and walked to the front of the cell. 'Sorry to disappoint you, but your boss promised me a phone call today. That means the embassy will be here long before you show me your bullwhip and matching leather thong.'

'Yes, I sure they will drop everything to save you and your friend.' The guard laughed as he walked down the corridor. Pointing to another inmate, he said, 'Hey, *hombre*! You an *americano*, no?'

'Me?' the prisoner asked with a twang. 'Yes, sirree. I'm from Bullcock, Texas.'

'And why are you in jail?'

The man blushed slightly. 'I was caught whizzin' on one of your streets.'

'That is right! The Pisser of Pamplona! How I forget about you?' Laughing harder, the guard pointed toward the man's crotch. 'And how long have you and your little *señor* been in here?'

'About two weeks.'

'For pissing in public?' Payne growled. 'And the embassy hasn't helped you yet?'

'I'm still waiting for 'em to show. They're down

in Madrid, and we're way up here in Pamplona. I reckon they don't come this way too often.'

'Son of a bitch,' Payne mumbled. He had assumed that he and his best friend, David Jones, would be given their release once the weekend was over. Or, at the very least, someone would explain why they'd been arrested. But his confidence was slowly waning. If the Texan was correct, Payne realized he might have to do something drastic to get out, because there was no way in hell he'd rot in a cell for much longer. Especially since he didn't do anything wrong.

Three days in jail and still no charges. Three goddamned days.

It had started last week. They were in Pamplona for the *Fiesta de San Fermín*, better known as the Running of the Bulls. They'd been in town for a couple of days, drinking and sightseeing, when they were ambushed at their hotel. Completely overwhelmed by a surprise attack.

Payne was getting cleaned up for dinner when someone kicked in his door. The local cops. A lot of them. They were there en masse to arrest his ass. They kept mumbling in broken English about something he'd done long ago. Way before his recent trip. None of it made any sense until he glanced down the hall and saw Jones in handcuffs, too. That's when he realized this *must* have something to do with their former careers. Their military careers. And if that was the case, then they were screwed. This would become an international incident.

The duo used to run the MANIACs, an elite counterinsurgency team comprised of the best soldiers that the Marines, Army, Navy, Air Force, and Coast Guard could find. Whether it was personnel recovery, unconventional warfare, counterguerilla sabotage, or foreign defense, they'd seen more shit than a proctologist. And caused their share of it, too. Clandestine operations all over the globe. Missions that no one else could handle. Or be entrusted with. When they got an assignment, it came straight from the top brass. Right from the Pentagon. And the reason was simple: the less people who knew about the MANIACs, the better. They were the government's secret weapon. The boogeymen the U.S. wouldn't admit to. *Couldn't* admit to.

And that's what had Payne worried. If he'd been arrested for something he'd done with the MANIACs, would the Pentagon come to his aid? Could they afford the negative publicity?

So far it had been three days and still no word.

Three days and counting . . .

3

Orvieto, Italy
(sixty-two miles northwest of Rome)

Dr Charles Boyd dropped his hammer and searched for his canteen. He was in decent shape for a fifty-eight-year-old, but the heat from the floodlights was brutal. Sweat poured off his scalp like rain.

'Good heavens!' he complained.

Maria Pelati smiled but kept working. She was half her professor's age and possessed twice the energy. And while he suffered in the traditional garb of an archaeologist – khaki pants, cotton shirt, hiking shoes – she wore a T-shirt and shorts.

They'd spent the past few days together burrowing into the 900-foot plateau that lifted Orvieto high above the vineyards of the Paglia Valley, a location so impenetrable that it was used as a safe haven by the popes of the Middle Ages. Papal documents prove that the Italian popes transformed Orvieto into the *vacation Vatican*, their home away from home during the most tumultuous era in the history of the Roman Catholic Church. Sadly, papal scribes were banned from describing any specifics for fear that their descriptions could be used by their enemies to plan an attack. Still, that didn't stop rumors from spreading.

According to legend there was supposed to be a city built *underneath* the city – the Catacombs of Orvieto – which was used to store the Church's most important documents and protect its most precious artifacts. Most experts dismissed the Catacombs as a fairy tale, the creation of a drunk monk from the fourteenth century. But not Dr Boyd. Not only did he believe in their existence, he used all of his free time to search for them.

'*Professore?* When I was little, my father used to speak of the Catacombs, though he never talked about them in real terms. He always considered them to be like Atlantis.' Pelati took a deep breath and brushed the hair out of her eyes, something she did when she was nervous. 'Well, sir, I was wondering, why are you sure that the Catacombs exist?'

He held her gaze for several seconds, then eased the tension with a half smile. 'Trust me, my dear, you aren't the first person to question me. I mean, who in their right mind would waste their time searching for the Catacombs? I might as well be fishing for the Loch Ness Monster.'

She laughed. 'Just so you know, it's probably cooler near Loch Ness.'

'And just so you know, I'm not the least bit crazy.'

'I never said that you were.'

'But you've considered it. You'd be crazy if you didn't.'

She brushed the hair out of her eyes again. 'There's a very fine line between genius and insanity, and I've never seen you cross that line . . . Of course, you *are* rather elusive. You still haven't told me about the Catacombs yet.'

'Ah, yes, the Catacombs. Tell me, my dear, what do you know about the Roman Empire?'

'The Roman Empire?' she asked, puzzled. 'I know quite a bit, I guess.'

Without saying another word, he handed her a series of documents from his fanny pack, then took a seat in the shadows of the rear wall, waiting for the reaction that he knew would come. *'Santa Maria!'* she shrieked. 'This is Roman!'

'Hence my question about the Empire. I thought I made that rather clear?'

Pelati shook her head, then returned her attention to the documents. At first glance they seemed to illustrate an elaborate system of tunnels that were hidden underneath the streets of Orvieto, yet it wasn't the maps or the illustrations that perplexed her but rather the language itself. The document was handwritten in a form of Latin that she was unable to translate.

'Is this authentic?' she demanded.

'That depends on your perspective. You're holding a photocopy of a scroll that I found in England. The photocopy is obviously fake. The original is quite real.'

'In *England*? You found the scroll in *England*?'

'Why is that so surprising? Julius Caesar spent some time there. So did Emperor Claudius.'

'But what does that have to do with the Catacombs? I mean, the popes came to Orvieto a thousand years after the fall of Rome. How could this be related?'

Pelati knew that Pope Gregory XI died of natural causes in 1378, leaving a vacancy that was filled by Pope Urban VI. Many cardinals claimed that he was improperly selected, and they demanded a second election. When the next outcome differed, the Catholic Church severed, splitting into two factions, with each supporting a different pope. Italy, Germany, and most of northern Europe recognized Urban VI, while France and Spain supported Clement VII.

This rivalry, known as the Great Schism of the West, divided Catholicism for almost forty years and in the process put the papal courts in danger – not only from outsiders but from each other. For that reason, the Italian popes spent much of their time in Orvieto, which was virtually impervious to attack because of its location on the plateau. And it was there, in the depths of the tufa stone, that the legendary Catacombs were supposedly built.

Boyd smiled at the confused look on his pupil's face. Refusing to make it easy on her, he said, 'Tell me, my dear, have you ever been to the Roman ruins in Bath?'

She growled in frustration. 'No, sir. Why do you ask?'

'Ah,' he sighed, remembering the quaint town on the River Avon. 'There you are in the middle of the English countryside, yet you're surrounded by relics from ancient Rome. It seems so surreal. Do you know what the most amazing thing is? The baths still work. The warm springs still bubble up from the ground, and the architecture still stands proud. Ancient pillars rising to the heavens from the magical waters below. It is somewhat amazing, if you think about it.'

Confused by his tale, Pelati grimaced. 'Not to be rude, but what are you implying?'

'Think about it, my dear. The popes of the 1300s used the Catacombs for protection. However, that doesn't mean that they *built* them. The ancient Romans were well ahead of their time. Correct? I figure if they were able to build bathhouses that still work two thousand years later, then they certainly could've built some tunnels that were still standing seven hundred years ago.'

'Wait! So that's why there were no records of their construction. They were already in place when the pope came to town?'

He nodded, pointing to the documents in her hand. 'When I found the original scroll, I assumed it was a hoax. I mean, how could it possibly be real? Then I had it tested, and the results were conclusive. The scroll predated the Schism by more than a thousand years, proving once and for all that the Catacombs actually existed. Furthermore, they *weren't* built for the popes of the Middle Ages. They were built by the ancient Romans.'

'A date,' she demanded. 'Do you have an exact date for the scroll?'

'As you know, carbon dating isn't *that* specific. The best I could come up with was an era.' Boyd took a sip of water, trying to prolong the suspense. 'According to my tests, the Catacombs of Orvieto were built during the life of Christ.'

4

Nearly 300,000 tourists flock to Kronborg Castle every year, but none of them had ever seen this before. And those that saw it wished they hadn't.

By the time Erik Jansen was discovered, his torso was grayish white, and his legs were light purple, caused by postmortem lividity. Birds dined on his flesh like a country buffet.

A group of students spotted Jansen across the courtyard and assumed that he was a historical exhibit. So they walked closer, marveling at all the wonderful little details that made him seem life-like: the color of his flesh, the horror on his face, the texture of his sandy-brown hair as it blew in the wind.

They crowded around him, begging to have their picture taken with the display. That is until one of them felt a drop. A single drop. That was all it took. One drop of blood and chaos erupted. Kids were wailing. Parents were screaming. Teachers scurried for help.

The local police were called to the scene but were in over their heads. They were used to car accidents and petty crimes, not murders. Certainly nothing of this magnitude. Yet that was to be expected in a quiet place like Helsingør. It sat on the northwestern coast of Sjaelland Island across the øresund from Hälsingborg, Sweden, away from the city life of Copenhagen. The last time anyone was brutally killed here was back in 1944, and *that* had been done by the Nazis.

Still, they shouldn't have made the mistakes that they made. Some of them were inexcusable.

The first squad arrived by boat, landing on the same shore as the killers. Since the castle's beach was private, the cops should've cordoned off the area, protecting all the information that was scattered in front of them. Clues about the murder. The number of assailants. Their approximate sizes. Their time of departure. All of it was there in the sand, just waiting to be found. But not for very long, because the commanding officer failed to think ahead, opting to sprint across the beach like a soldier at Normandy, soon followed by the rest of his men.

In a flash, the evidence was buried.

Of course, their next error was far worse. The type of screwup that occurs when people are crying, sirens are blaring, and there's no time to think. When the cops reached the body, they heard the story about the dripping blood and assumed that Jansen was still alive. His temperature should've told them otherwise. Same with the color of his skin. But as it was, they ripped the cross out of the ground, hoping to bring him back to life with CPR, yet all they managed to do was destroy evidence. Crucial evidence.

The kind of evidence that could've stopped the killers before they could strike again.

Ironically, their effort to save a life *guaranteed* that others would be killed.

Nick Dial was an American, and that made him very unpopular in certain parts of the globe. So did his career. He ran the newly formed Homicide Division at Interpol (International Criminal Police Organization), the largest international crime-fighting organization in the world, which meant he dealt with death all over the globe.

Simply put, he coordinated the flow of information between police departments anytime a murder investigation crossed national boundaries. All told he was in charge of 179 different countries – filled with billions of people and dozens of languages – yet had a budget that was dwarfed by an American school district.

One of the biggest misconceptions about Interpol is their role in stopping crime. They rarely send agents to investigate a case. Instead they have local offices called National Central Bureaus in all the member countries, and the NCBs monitor their territory and report pertinent information to Interpol's headquarters in Lyon, France. From there the facts are entered into a central database that can be accessed via the Interpol's computer network. Fingerprints, DNA, terrorist updates, the works. All of it available twenty-four hours a day.

Unfortunately, that wasn't always enough. Sometimes the head of a division (Drugs, Counterfeiting, Terrorism, etc.) was forced to hop on a plane and take control of a case. Possibly to cut through red tape. Or to handle a border dispute. Or to deal with the media. All the things that Nick Dial hated to do. He figured in his line of work the only thing that really mattered was *justice*. Correcting a wrong in the fairest way possible. That was his motto, the creed that he lived by. He figured if he did that, then all the other bullshit would take care of itself.

Dial arrived in Helsingør in the late afternoon. He didn't know much about the case – other than someone had been crucified and the president of Interpol wanted him there – but that was the way he preferred it. He liked forming conclusions based on personal observations, instead of relying on second-hand information.

Most investigators would've rushed to examine the body, but that wasn't the way Dial worked. He preferred to understand his surroundings before he dealt with the crime, especially when he was in an unfamiliar country. If the murder had been committed in France, he would've gone right to the corpse because he had lived there for the past ten years and knew how French people thought.

But here, he was a little unsure of the landscape. He needed to understand Denmark – and Danes in general – before he could understand the crime. So instead of studying the victim, Dial headed down a long corridor and searched for someone to talk to. Not to interrogate, but someone to chat with. Someone to give him the lay of the land. It took three attempts until he found someone who spoke English.

'Excuse me,' he said as he flashed his Interpol badge. 'May I ask you a few questions?'

The man nodded, half intimidated by Dial's credentials and half by his stare. Dial was in his early forties and had a face that looked like it was chiseled out of granite. Clean lines, thick cheekbones, green eyes. Short black hair with just a hint of gray. Not overly handsome, yet manly as hell. Black stubble covered his features even though it wasn't enough to conceal his chin. His massive, movie-star chin. It sat at the bottom of his face like a tribute to Kirk Douglas.

'So, what's a guy have to do to get a cup of coffee around here?'

The man smiled and led Dial into a tiny office. Work schedules and pictures of Kronborg decorated the walls. A metal desk sat in the corner. Dial took a seat just inside the door and was handed a mug of coffee. 'So, I take it you work here?'

'For over forty years. I'm the senior tour guide.'

Dial grinned. He had hit the jackpot. 'You know, I've traveled all over the world to every continent on the globe, but I've never seen a country like this. Denmark is simply gorgeous.'

The man beamed with pride. 'It's the best-kept secret in Europe.'

'Well, if I promise to keep my mouth shut, will you tell me about it?'

Their conversation went on for ten minutes, filled with the facts and figures about the area. Dial spoke every once in a while, gently steering the conversation in the direction he wanted, but for the most part kept quiet. 'Out of curiosity,' he asked, 'what type of tourists do you get?'

'Mostly people between the ages of forty and sixty, equal mix of men and women. Though we tend to get a lot of students during the school year.'

'What about nationalities? Are most of your tourists from Denmark?'

He shook his head. 'Just the opposite. Most of them are from the surrounding countries. Sweden, Germany, Austria, Norway. We get a lot of Brits because of Shakespeare.'

'Shakespeare? What does he have to do with anything?'

'You mean you don't know?'

Dial shook his head, even though he was *very* aware of the Shakespearean connection. Of course he wasn't about to tell the tour guide that. Better to play dumb and get the story from him.

'Shakespeare's *Hamlet* takes place in the castle at Elsinore.'

'Elsinore? Is that somewhere around here?'

'You're *in* Elsinore! Elsinore *is* Helsingør. *Hamlet* took place here! Sometimes we even give performances in the courtyard. You should stop by and see one.'

Dial grimaced. 'Nah. I'm not much of a theater fan. More of a sports guy myself ... But for the sake of my investigation, let me ask you something. Does anyone die in *Hamlet*?'

'Good heavens, yes! The whole play is about murder and revenge.'

'That's kind of interesting, considering recent events. I wonder if there's a connection?'

The man looked around, paranoid, then lowered his voice to a whisper. 'Of course there's a connection. There *has* to be. Why would someone dump a body here if there wasn't?'

Dial stood from his chair, finally ready to examine the crime scene. 'That's what I need to figure out.'

5

Maria figured it was an illusion caused by poor lighting. All of that changed when she put her hand on the stone. Its texture was too perfect to be natural. '*Professore?* Do you have a minute?'

Boyd crossed the grotto, stepping over the tangle of power cords and dusty tools that were scattered about the floor. Maria was staring at the wall, so he turned in that direction. In an instant he knew what it was, and the realization made his knees buckle.

Over a span of three feet, the cave went from rough to smooth to rough again, like someone had taken a giant piece of sandpaper and rubbed it against the wall. He reached out, half afraid, worried that the floodlights were playing tricks on his weary eyes. The sleek surface proved that they weren't. 'Quick! Hand me my gun.'

The *gun* was Boyd's nickname for his handheld blower, a small archaeological device that he used during excavations. Approximately the size of a cell phone, the gun contained a small cartridge of oxygen that blew dirt out of the tiny crevices and did less damage than a sharp tool. Boyd cleaned the surface of the wall using a paintbrush in one hand and his gun in the other. Rubble fell to his feet like heavy rain, causing tiny wisps of dust to float into the air. A few minutes later the outline of a three-foot square began to take shape in the middle of the cave.

'Yes, I do believe you have found something.'

Maria squealed with delight. 'I knew it! I knew that rock looked different!'

After clearing three sides of the seam – upper, left, and right – Boyd was able to measure the stone slab: thirty-seven and a half inches square by five and a half inches deep. Maria dragged one of the lights closer and tried to peer through the corners, but the cave wall had a back lip that prevented it.

'*Professore*, what do you think it is? It's too small to be a door, isn't it?'

Boyd finished writing in his binder. 'Drainage, perhaps? Maybe an aqueduct? Once we see what's on the other side, I'm sure we'll have a better idea.'

Boyd handed her a crowbar. 'And since you found the stone, I think you should have the privilege of removing it.'

'Thank you,' she whispered as she slipped the bar in the seam. 'This means a lot to me, sir. I actually feel like we're a team.'

'Now don't be surprised if you need my help. Stones like this can be rather stubborn. I recall one time in Scotland when –'

A loud thud echoed through the chamber as the massive rock crashed to the floor. The two archaeologists glanced at each other in disbelief, then lowered their gaze to the giant slab that sat at their feet. 'Good

Lord!' Boyd said. 'Have you been taking steroids?'

Confused, he dropped to his knees and examined the stone that had practically jumped from the wall. He tried to push the block on its side but was unable to budge it. 'Then how in God's good name did you manage that? This thing weighs a ton. And that's not a hyperbole, my dear. This thing literally weighs a ton!'

'I don't know. I barely put any pressure on it. I just put the crowbar in and . . . pop!'

Boyd realized engineers in ancient Rome were advanced for their time. However, he couldn't figure out why they would build a wall where one of the stones could be knocked out of place with such minimal effort. Perhaps, he thought, it was an escape tunnel.

'Excuse me, *Professore*?'

He blinked, then turned his attention to his assistant. 'I'm sorry, my dear. I was lost in thought. Did you need something?'

Maria nodded. 'I wanted to know if we could go inside now.'

Boyd's face turned a bright shade of red. 'Good Lord! How silly of me. Here I am, pondering the significance of this bloody stone when we're on the verge of . . .' He took a deep breath. 'Yes, by all means, let's venture inside.'

The passageway was narrow, giving them just enough room to enter. Boyd went first, then waited for Maria to pass him his equipment. When her arm finally appeared, he snatched the flashlight and struggled to find the power button. The powerful beam overwhelmed the blackness, shattering the sanctity of the holy grounds for the first time in years, exposing the high-arched ceiling and the colorful murals that adorned the smooth walls.

'My Lord,' he gasped in amazement. 'My sweet Lord!'

Seconds later, Maria squeezed through the hole while carrying a video camera. She had no idea what Boyd was gaping at but was determined to capture it on tape. At least that was the plan. But, the moment she stepped inside the chamber she was so overwhelmed by the artwork that she dropped the camera to her side. *'Santa Maria!'*

Stunned, she spun in a small circle, trying to soak in everything at once. The vaulted roof was typical of the ancient Roman era, allowing the majority of the ceiling's weight to be supported by the chamber's four walls. Despite this classical approach, the chamber still utilized a series of four Tuscan columns, one placed in each corner for architectural decoration.

In between each pillar, starting just below the arched ceiling, was a series of four religious frescoes, each depicting a different scene from the Bible. The showcased piece of the group appeared to be the life of an unknown saint, for it was twice as large as the others and was centered on the right wall directly behind a stone altar.

'What is this place?' she whispered.

Boyd continued to gaze around the room, amazed that he'd found the mythical vaults. 'The basic design looks similar to many buildings built during the peak of the Roman Empire, but the paintings on the walls are much more recent – perhaps fifteenth or sixteenth century.'

He paused, staring at the frescoes. 'Maria, do they look familiar to you?'

She strolled forward, studying the colorful scenes as she moved about the chamber. She had no idea what he was referring to, but that didn't stop her. She carefully eyed the paintings, trying to find the common thread that would unite them. 'Oh my Lord! I *have* seen these before! These murals are in the Sistine Chapel.'

'Exactly!' Boyd applauded. 'Adam and Eve, the flood, Noah's ark. The three main subjects of Michelangelo's ceiling. In fact, these frescoes look remarkably similar to his.'

Maria glanced from picture to picture. 'They *do* possess his flair, don't they?'

'I almost hate to say this without any tangible proof, yet . . . I wonder if Michelangelo actually did these himself.'

Her eyes doubled in size. 'You're joking, right? You actually think *he* painted these?'

Boyd nodded. 'Think about it, Maria. This place served as a second Vatican for decades. When the Great Schism occurred, the Italian popes came to Orvieto for protection. At the time the Church was in such disarray the papal council actually considered moving the Vatican here permanently. They felt this was the only place that could offer them adequate protection.'

Maria grinned. 'And if the Vatican was going to be moved, the popes would want the right decorations for the new home of the Catholic Church.'

'Exactly! And if the pope wanted Michelangelo to do the decorating, then Michelangelo did the decorating.' Boyd chuckled as he remembered a story about the famous artist. 'Did you know that Michelangelo didn't want anything to do with the Sistine Chapel? Rumor has it that Julius II, the pope at the time, bullied him into doing the project. Once beating him with a cane, and once threatening to kill Michelangelo by tossing him off the scaffolding . . . Not exactly the type of behavior you'd expect from a pope, is it?'

She shook her head. 'Do you think he forced Michelangelo to do these, too?'

Boyd considered her question. 'If my memory is correct, the last pope to stay here was Pope Clement VII during Spain's attack on Rome in 1527. I believe Michelangelo did the Sistine Chapel about twenty years before then, meaning he would've had plenty of time to duplicate his scenes on these walls before his death.'

'Or,' Maria deadpanned, 'someone could have done these first, and Michelangelo might have copied them back at the Vatican.'

A flash of excitement crossed Boyd's face. 'My dear, you have a bloody good point there! If these were done before the others, then the Sistine Chapel would be nothing more than an imitation. Goodness me! Can you imagine the flak we'd get if we proved that Michelangelo was a forger? We'd never hear the end of it!'

Maria laughed, knowing her dad would have a stroke if she were involved in something like that. 'That does have controversy written all over it. Doesn't it?'

Although the concept was controversial, it paled in comparison to things that they were about to discover deeper inside the Catacombs.

While Maria filmed the artwork, Dr Boyd crept down the three stone steps on the left side of the chamber. At the bottom he turned to his right and peered into darkness.

Amazingly, he saw a series of open tombs so great in number that they faded into the depths of the corridor beyond the reach of his light. The ceiling soared above him to a height of over fifty feet and was lined on both sides by an intricate system of niches, built to hold the skeletal remains of the dead. These *loculi* were cut into the tufaceous walls in straight rows, each rectangle measuring six feet across – just big enough for a body.

'This is stunning,' he gasped. 'Simply stunning!'

Maria hustled after him and focused the camera

on one of the unmarked graves. She hoped to get a better view of the long passageway, but it was far too narrow for her to slip past Boyd – no more than three feet from wall to wall.

'Tell me, Maria, what do you see?'

She smiled. 'I see dead people.'

But Boyd missed her reference to *The Sixth Sense*. 'So do I. Don't you think that's strange?'

'What do you mean?'

'Why can we see the bodies? Per custom, most *loculi* were sealed with tiles and mortar after the dead were placed inside. Others were covered with a marble slab. But I've never seen this before. Why would they leave the bodies exposed?'

She frowned, thinking of the Catacombs of Saint Callixtus in Rome. They were built by Christians in the middle of the second century and encompassed an area of ninety acres, with four levels and more than twelve miles of galleries.

When she was ten, she toured the ruins on a school trip, an experience that she loved so much that she rushed home and told her parents that she wanted to be an archaeologist. Her mom smiled and told her she could be whatever she wanted as long as she worked hard. But it was an answer that didn't set well with dad. When he finished laughing, he stared Maria in the eyes and told her, in all seriousness, to give up her dreams and concentrate on finding a husband.

It was a moment that she'd never forget. Or forgive.

'Correct me if I'm wrong,' she said, 'but aren't the Christian tombs at Saint Callixtus open-air as well? I remember seeing a lot of holes in the walls.'

'You saw holes, but no bodies. It was the custom of early Christians to wrap their dead in a shroud before they sealed it inside the *loculi*. The holes that you're referring to were cracked open by looters and scholars. But that's not the case down here. If you look –'

Boyd stopped in midsentence, his attention suddenly focused on the passageway ahead. Something was wrong. The corridor stretched into the darkness, snaking through the stone like a black viper. He tried to see the end of the hall but couldn't. Shadows danced around him, cast by human hands that dangled from their graves like they were reaching for his light. As though his presence had somehow stirred them from their centuries of slumber. In a moment of panic, he stepped backward into one of their outstretched hands and felt icy-cold fingers against the back of his leg. Terror sprang from his lips, soon followed by a shriek from Maria.

'What happened!' she demanded. 'What's wrong? Did you see something?'

Boyd took a deep breath and laughed, completely embarrassed. 'I am *so* sorry . . . I just scared myself silly.' His face turned a shade of red. 'I didn't mean to scare you. Truly I didn't. I'm just jumpy. That's all . . . I just bumped into a hand, and it startled me.'

'A hand? You bumped into a hand? Good lord, *professore*! You almost gave me a stroke.'

'Trust me, I know the feeling. I almost had one myself.'

Maria put her hand on her chest and closed her eyes. Her heart felt like a jackhammer pounding against her rib cage. She took a deep breath, trying to cope with the rush of adrenaline. 'You're sure you're all right?'

He nodded sheepishly. 'Yes, my dear, I swear.'

'Then let's get moving. I need to burn off all this energy.'

They traveled together for several seconds, passing grave after unmarked grave, never stopping to examine the bodies. They were still too jumpy to do that. Thirty yards later, the corridor split in two. The path on the left led to a stairwell that slowly curled into the darkness below. The hallway on the right continued forward past hundreds of more bodies.

Boyd turned to Maria. 'Lady's choice.'

'Let's go downstairs. I hear there's a wonderful gift shop in the basement.'

He nodded, then started down the steps. They were no more than six inches deep – perfect for the feet of yesteryear but small for the modern-day traveler – which forced Boyd to lower himself sideways. To steady his descent, he used the jutting stones in the walls as a handrail.

At the halfway point, he stopped and turned

toward the camera. 'I believe we're under the upper hallway now, more than twenty feet down. What an incredible achievement, carving this much rock yet keeping it hidden from the outside world. Simply remarkable!'

She asked, 'Do you think the Empire built these stairs, or was it done in the Middle Ages?'

He paused, soaking in everything – the vaulted ceilings, the high arches, the colors, the smells, the sounds – before he answered. 'My guess would be the Empire. The shallowness of the steps is the first clue, followed by the basic design. It's very typical of the ancients.'

Smiling, Boyd continued forward at a methodical pace. Normally he would've zipped down the stairs at top speed, but the heat of the outer chamber had sapped his strength. Combine that with a lack of food and sleep, and he was lucky to be standing.

'*Professore?* What do you think is down here?'

He was about to answer when the hallway came into view, stretching out before him like an arroyo. No crypts, no graves, no doors. Just an empty corridor for as far as his eye could see.

'Strange,' he mumbled. 'I feel like we're in a different world down here.'

Maria nodded. 'It looks like it was decorated by the Amish.'

Boyd ignored her comment and crept down the hall searching for clues. Fifty feet later, he spotted a stone plaque on the left-hand wall. Its color was the same shade of brown as the rest of the passageway, yet its surface was remarkably different. Without saying a word, Boyd ran to it, immediately placing his hands on its cold surface. Then, like a blind man reading, he slid his fingers across it, probing the shallow grooves with slow, tender strokes.

Maria stood back, confused by his strange behavior. She wanted to ask him what the hell was going on, why he was acting more bizarre than he normally did, but all it took was a single glance and she knew the answer. One look at his face and everything made sense.

Her mentor, the one man she actually trusted and believed in, was hiding something.

6

Walking to the shore near the rear of the castle grounds, Nick Dial realized the Danish police would never solve the case. Unless, of course, there was a witness that he didn't know about or a security camera that had inadvertently taped the crime. Otherwise the cops' methods were too sloppy to nail anyone. No pun intended. Not only had they moved the body, but they had done very little to protect the integrity of the crime scene.

In a perfect world, they would've sealed off the entire area, building temporary barriers that would've kept people out and cut down on the gusts of wind that blew in from the sound. Instead, officers strolled across the beach like they were on vacation, kicking up sand and blatantly ignoring the rules of evidence.

'Excuse me, are you Mr Dial?'

Dial turned to his right and stared at a well-dressed woman who was heading his way. She pulled out her badge and held it up for him to scrutinize.

'Yeah, I'm Dial,' he finally said.

'I'm Annette Nielson from the NCB in Copenhagen. I was the agent who phoned in the initial report this morning.'

Dial shook her hand and smiled, half surprised

that the local field office had sent a woman to handle such a high-profile case. Not that he had anything against female investigators, because he didn't, but he knew most executives at Interpol were far less open-minded than he. 'Nice to meet you, Annette. Please call me Nick.'

She nodded and pulled out her notepad. 'I'm so glad you're here. I've been trying to get the local chief to talk to me. He keeps making excuses, though.'

Typical, Dial thought to himself. 'What can you tell me about the victim?'

'Caucasian male, mid-thirties, no tattoos or piercings. Death occurred sometime this morning, probably around dawn. Puncture wounds in his hands, feet, and rib cage. Severe damage to his face and mouth. Leads us to believe that he was beaten into submission.'

'Do we have a name?'

She shrugged. 'The locals took his prints, but I don't know if they have the results yet.'

'Point of access?'

'Best guess is the beach. The front of the castle is well-lit and guarded. So is the interior. Unfortunately, by the time I got here, the locals had covered any footprints with their own.'

'Number of assailants?'

'Multiple. The cross is too heavy for just one.'

'Anything else?'

'They left a note.'

'They left a *what?* Show it to me.'

She led him to the cross, which sat in the lawn near the edge of the sand. The body was nowhere to be found. 'The note was painted on a walnut sign and affixed to the top of the cross with a long spike driven vertically.'

Dial read the message aloud. 'IN THE NAME OF THE FATHER.'

He kneeled next to the sign for a closer look. The letters were five inches high and hand-painted in red. Very neatly done. Like the killer had taken calligraphy lessons in his spare time. Right before his advanced course in woodworking. 'I'm assuming this isn't blood.'

'Red paint,' she concurred. 'We're tracking down the shade and the manufacturer. Who knows? We might find a bucket of it in a nearby Dumpster.'

'I doubt it. This sign wasn't made around here. The killers brought it with them.'

'Why do you say that?'

Dial put his nose next to the board and took a whiff. 'Three reasons. One, the sign is dry, which wouldn't be the case if they'd painted it this morning. There's too much moisture along the shore for anything to dry quickly. Two, if they'd painted it around here, they would've made a mess. The wind would've been whipping across the beach causing sand to stick to the paint like a magnet. No way they did it out here. It's too neat.'

'And three?'

He stood from his crouch and grimaced, knowing

that this was the first of several victims yet to come. 'The sign was just the icing. The killer's way of taunting us. His real work of art was the victim, the way he killed the guy. That's the thing we need to focus on.'

The sound of clapping emerged from behind, followed by a mock 'Bravo!'

Dial took a deep breath and turned. There was no doubt in his mind that it was the local chief of police because he had dealt with this type of idiot many times before, and it was always the same. They taunted Dial because he was an Interpol big shot who was infringing on their so-called turf. Then, once they got it out of their system, he made a phone call to their immediate supervisor, and they were forced to kiss Dial's ass – usually in a very public ceremony – and cater to his every whim for the rest of the week.

But Dial just wasn't in the mood today. Not for some dipshit who didn't know how to run a crime scene. So instead of letting the guy speak, Dial whirled around as quick as he could and charged toward him like an angry rhinoceros. 'Where the fuck have you been? I've been looking for you for the last half hour, but you've been too scared to show yourself.'

'Excuse me?'

Dial whipped out his badge and shoved it in the guy's round, bloated face. 'If you're the man in charge, then you're the guy who's been avoiding me.'

'No one told me –'

'What? That Interpol was involved in this case? I find that hard to believe since Agent Nielson has been here all morning. According to her, your staff has been anything but helpful.'

The chief looked at Nielson, then back at Dial, trying to think of something clever to say. But Dial refused to give him a chance. He had heard all of the excuses before and wasn't about to listen to them again. Time was too precious in a case like this.

'And don't even start with your jurisdiction bull-shit. The victim was brought in through the sound, and half of that water belongs to Sweden, meaning this is an international case. International means Interpol, and Interpol means *me*. You got that? *Me!* That means you need to get off your ass and tell me everything I need to know, or I swear to God I'll call every reporter in Europe and tell them that you're the reason that this case hasn't been solved yet.'

The man blinked a few times, stunned. Like he had never been on this end of an ass-chewing.

'Oh yeah,' Dial added, 'one more thing. Once I hop on my plane and get out of this godforsaken country, I expect you and your staff to treat Agent Nielson with the utmost respect. She works for Interpol, which means she's an extension of me. Got it?'

The chief nodded at Nielson, then returned his gaze to Dial.

'So, what have you got for me, Slim? You've wasted enough of my time already.'

The chief hemmed and hawed for a few seconds, searching for something to say. 'We got word on the victim. His name was Erik Jansen, a thirty-two-year-old from Finland.'

'Finland? That's a thousand miles away. Why in the world was he in Denmark?'

The chief shrugged. 'Our customs office has no record of him being here. Not ever.'

'Annette,' Dial said, 'call headquarters and find out where he's been during the last year.'

She nodded and hit the button on her speed dial.

'Chief, while she's on the phone, let me ask you a question. Where's the body?'

'We moved it to the morgue.'

'Before or after you photographed the scene?'

'Well,' he muttered, 'my men tried to revive the victim. And the quickest way to do that was to pull the cross out of the ground.'

Dial grimaced. 'Please tell me you took some pictures before you pried him off the beams?'

The chief nodded and ran off to get the photos; at least that's what he said he was doing. The truth was, he was looking for an excuse to get away from Dial and had no plans of coming back until he regained his composure. But that was fine with Dial because it left him in charge of the entire scene and prevented the chief from hearing a key piece of information that Agent Nielson had just acquired from Interpol.

'Rome,' she said. 'Jansen has been living in Rome for the past eight years, not Finland.'

'Rome? What in the world was he doing there?'

'Our victim was a priest who worked at the Vatican.'

7

The last time Payne had seen Jones was when they were being arrested. From there both of them were taken to the penitentiary in separate squad cars, stripped of their clothes and possessions, and locked in cells on opposite sides of the building. Mostly for the protection of the staff.

That was Friday, nearly seventy-two hours before.

Payne was on his cot, pondering his next move, when a team of guards interrupted him. They burst into his cell and chained his hands and legs together with a device that looked like it was from *Cool Hand Luke*. The men were of average size and training. That meant Payne could've gotten free if necessary. But he let things slide, allowing them to drag him to an isolation room where he assumed he was going to be interrogated. Or tortured. Or both.

In the center of the room was a metal table bolted to the floor. A large iron loop was fused to each side, used to restrict the movement of the prisoner. The guards locked Payne in place, taking extra precautions, making sure he was secure. They had to be careful with a prisoner like Payne. He was *that* dangerous. Once they were satisfied, they left the room without speaking. No words. No instructions.

Nothing. The only sound Payne could hear was the rattle of his chains and his own shallow breathing. The distinct smell of old vomit hovered in the air.

They left him like that for several hours, allowing him to sweat. Allowing him to think of all the horrible things they could do to him. Hoping it would make him break. Little did they know they were wasting their time. They could do whatever they wanted to Payne, and he wouldn't feel it. He was trained not to feel it. To join the MANIACs, soldiers were required to pass a rigorous torture test that had two basic parts: getting torture and giving torture. Payne excelled at both.

So instead of dwelling on what might happen, Payne focused on other things. Mostly events of the past few years. All the things that had led him to his current predicament.

Sadly, family duties had forced him to leave the military long before he was ready. His grandfather, the man who had raised him, passed away and left him the family business. A multimillion-dollar corporation named Payne Industries. In truth Payne wanted no part of that world. It was one of the reasons he had gone into the military, to avoid such obligations. He wanted to forge his own identity and make a name on his own. He wanted to be his own man. But all that changed when his grandfather died. Suddenly he felt obligated to come home and take charge. Like it was his destiny. His burden.

Payne Industries was an American success story. It was his duty to protect the legacy.

When Payne's grandfather was young, he scraped together his life savings and started a small manufacturing company near the Ohio River. The steel industry was booming back then, and Pittsburgh was its capital. The air was black and the rivers were brown, but he got tons of business. One minute he was a mill Hunky from Beaver County, the next he was a tycoon. The most successful Polish American in the history of the U.S.

Now everything – the company, the land, the wealth – belonged to the grandson.

Someone without experience.

Payne knew he was out of his element. So he passed his duties to his board of directors and focused all of his time and energy on charity work. His first charity? It wasn't actually a charity. It was more of an investment. He gave David Jones, who had retired from the military at the same time, enough start-up capital to open his own business. It had always been Jones's dream to run a detective agency, and Payne had the means to help. So he figured, why not? After his grandfather died, Payne knew the only family he had left was Jones.

Of course, since Payne was white and Jones was black, they looked nothing alike.

Anyway, the first year Payne was happy. He raised

money for the Mario Lemieux Cancer Fund and other Pittsburgh charities while Jones scoured the city for clients. Occasionally Payne gave Jones a hand on the juicy cases, but for the most part they did their own thing.

By year two, Payne started getting antsy. He loved helping good causes, but he needed more out of life than hosting golf tournaments and mingling at black-tie affairs. He missed the excitement of the MANIACs. The adrenaline rush he got when he risked his life. The thrill of getting his hands dirty. He couldn't get those things in the business world, not when the worst injury he could receive was a paper cut. So Payne compensated by helping Jones all the time. The two of them partnered again. Making a difference in the world. Albeit on a much smaller scale than before. They used to rescue hostages. They used to overthrow governments. Now they were tracking cheating husbands and looking for lost pets. It was a huge letdown for both men.

So they did what they could in their spare time, searching for *artificial* excitement wherever they could find it. Anything to get the buzz they used to feel. To help them keep their edge. To help them feel alive. Swimming with the sharks in Australia. Race car driving in Brazil. Skydiving in South Africa. Deep-sea explorations in Florida.

And lastly, running with the bulls in Spain. That's what had brought them to Pamplona.

Unfortunately, it's the event that led to their current predicament. Abandoned in jail. Alone.

They had come to Spain for adrenaline. They had found incarceration instead.

8

Maria had no proof, but she knew that Boyd was keeping something from her. *Typical man,* she thought. They never trusted women with the important stuff.

'Come on,' she begged, 'what does the sign say?'

Boyd laughed as he walked away from the stone plaque. 'You mean you don't know? Tsk, tsk, tsk. I could've sworn that Latin was one of your academic requirements.'

'Yeah, but that didn't look like regular Latin to me.'

'Perhaps because it wasn't. That sign was written in one of the earlier forms of the language, one that hasn't been used as a primary language in nearly two millennia.'

'See! That's why I ... Wait! Does that mean that this floor was built by ancient Rome?'

Boyd nodded. 'It appears that way. I doubt they would have used antiquated language on one of their markers, not in a tomb of this magnitude.' He pointed to a large archway that loomed down the narrow corridor. 'We'll know for sure in a moment.'

Made out of off-white masonry, the main components of the arch were exquisitely carved, each illustrating a different moment of Jesus Christ's crucifixion. The two lowest blocks, the *springers*, showed Jesus being nailed to the cross and being lifted above the ground by a team of Roman soldiers. The next series of stones, the *voussoirs*, depicted Christ as he hung from the cross, his life and stamina slowly slipping away. The crowns, the two stones that sat off-center from the top of the arch, revealed the events right before Jesus's death. First, when he was given a sip of wine vinegar from the end of a hyssop stalk – while flowers bloomed underneath him, possibly as a sign of rebirth – and the instant his head drooped to his chest in death.

Strangely, the keystone, the most important block of the archway, differed from the others. Instead of depicting Christ's resurrection or his ascension to the right hand of God, the middle stone of the arch was sculpted into the lifelike bust of a man. A *laughing* man. The intricate details of his face revealed his amusement in a number of obvious ways: the sweeping curve of his lips, the lighthearted twinkle in his eyes, and the arrogant protrusion of his jaw. For some reason, he was laughing at a most inappropriate time.

Maria raised the camera and filmed the arch. 'What is this place?'

'The plaque said it was a document vault. But after seeing this artwork, there's a good chance that its purpose has changed over the years, perhaps to something more religious.' Boyd placed his hands on

47

the archway and traced the contours of the lower stones. Finally, he said, 'Tell me, my dear, who killed Jesus Christ?'

The question was so unexpected it took her a moment to answer. 'The Romans in 33 AD.'

'And why was he killed?'

Maria rolled her eyes behind Boyd's back. Why did he have to make a lecture out of everything? 'Treason,' she replied. 'Many priests viewed him as going against the Roman way of life. They figured it was easier to kill Christ than put up with his flock of fanatics.'

'Did they know he was the Son of God at the time of his death?'

'Of course not. If they did, they wouldn't have crucified him.'

Boyd nodded, content with her answers. 'Then why are these carvings here? Why would the ancient Romans make a big deal about such a small event in their history? If they believed that Christ was a fake Messiah – just like dozens of con men who pretended to be the Son of God before him – why would they devote so much space to him in such a phenomenal work of art?'

Intrigued, Maria studied the images and decided that Boyd was onto something. 'Maybe this art-work was added after the Romans converted to Christianity? They could have commemorated Jesus's crucifixion in the mid-300s, still a thousand years before the Great Schism occurred.'

Boyd stared at the center carving, amazed at its vividness. It was so damn lifelike he could practically hear its laughter. 'If that be the case, why is the figure on the keystone laughing? Hmmm? The Romans killed the Son of God but eventually realized their mistake. Then, in a moment of atonement, they converted to the Nazarene's religion and commemorated his death by ridiculing it with a laughing statue ... Somehow I don't think that would be appropriate.'

'Probably not,' she admitted.

Determined, Maria focused her eyes on the archway and tried to uncover the connection between the bust and the images of Christ that surrounded it. To complicate things further, the longer she looked at the laughing man's face, the more certain she was that she had seen it before. '*Professore*, is it just me, or do you recognize his face?'

'I was going to ask you the same thing. He does look bloody familiar, doesn't he?'

Maria racked her brain, going over hundreds of historical figures in her mind. 'Could he be famous like Octavian or Trajan? Maybe even Constantine I, the first Christian emperor?'

'I'd need a guide book to know for sure. This could be anyone.'

She grimaced, realizing that Boyd was right. 'Oh well, it'll come to me. I might not be great with ancient Latin, but I never forget a face.'

'If you figure it out, be sure to let me know. I'd

love to understand the juxtaposition between the sculpture and the carvings. The subtext of the two truly baffles me. What in the world was this artist trying to say about Christ?'

As they moved forward, Boyd's light trickled into the colossal chamber, revealing an expanse that was nearly three times as large as the room they'd entered upstairs. Measuring over sixty feet by thirty feet, the massive space was filled with dozens of hand-carved stone chests of varying shapes and sizes, each one possessing a historical Roman scene. And the artwork didn't end there. The walls of the chamber were adorned with a series of first-century frescoes, each remarkably similar in theme and color to the paintings that they'd seen in the original room.

'My God!' Boyd gasped. 'Will you look at this place? The engineers of ancient Rome were truly ahead of their time. As I mentioned earlier, a large number of their structures remain standing today. Still, we're quite lucky this place was never disturbed by drilling, soil erosion, or even the shifting of tectonic plates. One small earthquake would've covered this site forever.'

Maria frowned at the possibility. 'What do you say I do some more filming before something like that happens?'

'That sounds great, my dear. That'll give me a chance to examine these chests.'

With the touch of a button, she began her work, documenting the chamber from left to right while slowly moving toward the back corner. She started with the frescoes, concentrating on one colorful image after another before shifting her focus toward the vaulted ceiling and the dozens of chests that filled the room.

Little did she know that one of them contained the most important discovery of all time.

A secret that would change her life – and the history of the world – forever.

9

Father Erik Jansen. From the Vatican. Crucified. At Hamlet's castle.

Nick Dial knew the media was going to have a field day with this story unless he was able to eliminate the Shakespeare angle right away. There was nothing he could do with the religious aspect – a priest being crucified was hard to explain – but eliminating Hamlet was a possibility.

Unfortunately, Dial didn't know much about literature, so he decided to call Henri Toulon, the assistant director of the Homicide Division. Toulon was a wine-loving Frenchman who had the ability to speak at length on every subject under the sun. Whether it was quantum physics, soccer statistics, or a recipe for fondue, Toulon was the man with the answers.

Dial said, 'Hey, Henri, it's Nick. Do you have a minute?'

Toulon answered with a hoarse, 'But of course.'

'Man, are you feeling all right? You sound a bit under the weather.'

'*Oui*, I'm fine. It was a late night. Again.'

Dial smiled, not the least bit surprised that Toulon was hungover. His late-night carousing was one of the main reasons that Dial had been promoted ahead of him. That plus Interpol's desire to have an American as the head of a division, a rarity in the European-dominated organization. 'Out of curiosity, how much do you know about Shakespeare?'

'More than his own mother.'

'And what about the Bible?'

'More than Dan Brown. Why do you ask?'

Dial filled him in on the case and told him what he was looking for. Why was Jansen kidnapped in Rome but killed in Denmark?

Toulon answered, 'Religion played an important role in Shakespeare's world, yet I can't think of a single character who was crucified. That would have been heresy back then.'

'Then ignore the crucifixion and focus on the murder. Besides the location, can you think of any connections to *Hamlet*?'

'The thing that grabs my attention is the sign above the cross. Whoever painted that was brilliant. Is "FATHER" referring to God, a character in Shakespeare's play, or the killer's actual father? At first glance, I'd assume it's referring to *Hamlet*. The plot follows Prince Hamlet as he avenges the death of the king – a son getting revenge for his father. Sounds perfect to me. Until you examine the method of execution. In my mind, crucifixion screams of Christ, not Shakespeare. If the killer cared about *Hamlet*, he would have chosen the sword.'

'So this is about religion?'

'Not necessarily. It could be about the killer's father or the victim's father. But that's why the sign is so brilliant. You'll have to track down all these possibilities, whether you like it or not. For all we know, the killer is simply messing with you.'

'Maybe. Or it could be about something else, something you missed.'

'Such as?'

Dial smiled, glad that Toulon didn't know everything. 'The victim was a priest. For all we know the sign could be about him. *Father* Erik Jansen.'

'Which only adds to the brilliance of the sign. It's memorable yet ambiguous. The perfect way to attract attention without giving anything away.'

'That's why I decided to call you. I figured I'd fight brilliance with brilliance.'

Toulon grinned. 'I'll tell you what, give me a day or two, and I'll see what I can find. Who knows? Maybe I missed something else.'

'Thanks, Henri, I'd appreciate that. Before you go, though, I have one more question, this one about religion. Do you have any idea what Jesus's cross looked like?'

Toulon took a deep breath and ran his fingers through his gray hair, which was pulled back in his trademark ponytail. He desperately wanted a cigarette but wasn't allowed to smoke inside Interpol, even though sometimes he did just because he was French and fuck them if they didn't like it. 'You'll be happy to know you're not alone. Most people are confused about his cross. Tell me, what kind of cross did they use in Denmark?'

'Wooden, made out of some kind of oak.'

'That's not what I meant. Was it Latin? Tau? Greek? Russian?'

'Honestly, I have no idea. They're all Greek to me.'

Toulon rolled his eyes. Why did Americans have to make a joke out of everything? 'A Greek cross is easy to spot. It looks like a plus sign. All four of its arms are the exact same length.'

'Not Jansen's. His looked like a capital *T*. The horizontal beam was way at the top.'

Toulon whistled softly. 'Then they got it right.'

'They got it *right*? What do you mean by that?'

'Most people think that Jesus was crucified on a Latin cross – one where the crossarm sits a third of the way down the vertical beam – but that's wrong. The Romans used tau crosses for crucifixions, not Latin ones.'

'Really? Then why do churches use the Latin cross?'

'Because Christian leaders adopted it as their symbol during the ninth century, a decision that sparked controversy, since it was originally a pagan emblem representing the four winds: north, south, east, and west. Yet Christians preferred that to the history of the tau cross, a symbol that meant death by execution to the ancient world. The death of criminals.'

Dial stroked his massive chin, wondering if Erik

Jansen was a criminal. Or had dealt with one in the confessional. 'Speaking of crosses, what can you tell me about the crucifixion? I mean, I'm familiar with the biblical version, but do we know what *really* happened?'

'I guess that depends on your perspective. If you're Christian, the biblical version is the way it really happened, right down to the last detail. I mean, the Bible is the word of God.'

'And if you're not a Christian?'

Toulon realized the subject was a powder keg. Groaning, he put an unlit cigarette in his mouth, just so he had something to suck on. 'The truth is we don't know what happened. Christian historians say one thing while Roman historians say another. Then there are the Jews and the Buddhists and the atheists. Everyone has a different opinion on what happened, and no one knows for sure because it happened two thousand years ago. We can't check the videotape and come up with something definitive. All we can do is sort through the evidence, read what our ancestors wrote, and try to reach our own conclusions, which are invariably tainted by our upbringing.'

'Meaning what?'

'Simply put, if your parents taught you to believe in Christ, you're probably going to keep believing in Christ. I mean, that's what faith is all about, isn't it?'

'And if you're a nonbeliever?'

'Well, I guess that depends on the person. Some

people keep their doubts to themselves in order to fit into this Christian world of ours. Others join the local synagogue or temple or shrine and start practicing non-Christian faiths. Then, of course, you have the third group. The wild cards. They're the ones who don't care what society thinks about them, the type of people who enjoy rocking the boat. And if I were a betting man, guess which category I'd put the killer in?'

Dial smiled, wishing that all of his questions were that easy. 'Thanks, Henri, I appreciate your candor. Let me know if you come up with anything else.'

'You got it, Nick.'

Dial hung up his cell phone and turned his attention to Agent Nielson, who was standing off to the side, smiling. 'You look happy,' he said. 'Good news?'

'I just got off the phone with Rome. Father Jansen had a small apartment near the Vatican. When he didn't show up for a meeting at nine p.m., they tried to call him but couldn't get through. In their mind it wasn't a big deal until he failed to show up for work this morning. That's when they decided to call the police.'

'And what about the Vatican? Do we know what Jansen did for them?'

'I'm still working on that. I'm expecting a call from his supervisor any minute. Hopefully, he can shed some light on it.'

'I wouldn't count on it. I've dealt with the Vatican

before, and they tend to be very tight-lipped about their business. Of course, who could blame them? I'd be secretive, too, if I had a billion-dollar art collection locked in my basement . . . What are the locals doing in Rome?'

'A forensics team is searching his apartment. They said they'll give me a call if they find anything of value. Otherwise, we'll get their report tomorrow.'

'Nice work, Annette. I'm impressed. Do me a favor, though, and stay on top of the Vatican. Just because they promised you a report doesn't mean you'll get one.'

In fact, Dial laughed to himself, it would probably take a miracle.

10

Maria strolled around the chamber, carefully filming the dozens of stone chests that filled the room. The gray containers, sitting in a series of straight rows, varied in size and shape – some had the dimensions of a VCR while others approached the mass of a coffin – but each of them had one thing in common: artistic brilliance.

Pictures of colossal battle scenes, marking the significant Roman victories of the early Empire, had been chiseled into the hard rock of several chests. Proud generals, standing in their horse-drawn chariots as legionnaires fought valiantly in the distant battlefield. Weary warriors, their faces streaked with blood from their fallen victims, continued to march forward, extending the boundaries of their homeland while bludgeoning anything that got in their way. And Roman heroes, their profiles etched into stone with such precision that –

'Oh my God,' Maria muttered. She quickly hit the pause button on her video camera. 'Remember the face on the archway that appeared to be laughing at Christ's death?'

He walked toward her. 'Of course, I do. That blasphemous image is burned into my mind.'

Maria pointed to the two-foot-high stone cube that sat at her feet. 'He's back.'

Boyd glanced at the box and realized that she was correct. It was him, all right, and his devilish grin was featured in great detail. 'I'll be flummoxed. What's he doing here?'

She ran her gloved finger over the carved face. 'I don't know. But he seems awfully happy.'

'Maria, while you were filming the artwork, did you see this man on anything else?'

She shook her head. 'I would've told you if I did.'

'What about his face? Do you remember where you've seen his face?'

Maria stared at the image. 'No, but I have to admit that it's been driving me crazy. I know I've seen him before. I just know it!'

Boyd stood and quickly inspected the other chests in the room. Even though they varied in size, he realized that every box carried a similar theme: They were adorned with pictures of war. All of them, that is, except one – the one with the laughing man.

'This man had to be an emperor. Or at the very least, a man of great power and wealth. He is the only person who is featured on his own cube.'

'Plus he was on the arch. They obviously held him in high esteem.'

'But why?' Boyd pondered the question as he wrapped his fingers around the box. After a brief pause, he carefully slid his hands over the edge of the crate's lid, making sure that it was sturdy enough to be moved without damage. 'I know this goes against many of the things that I told you earlier, but –'

Maria nodded in understanding. 'You want to see what's inside.'

'I have to. I can't help it. It's the young whipper-snapper in me.'

'That's all right. If you didn't remove the lid, I was going to get a crowbar and do it myself.'

It took nearly five minutes to ease the stone cover from its tight-fitting seam, but once they did, they were able to lift it with little difficulty. It was much lighter than they had expected.

'Careful!' Boyd begged. 'This stone could provide us with important clues about the identity of this man. I'd hate for anything to happen to it.'

The duo lowered the chiseled lid onto the floor, making sure they didn't scratch it. Then, once they were satisfied with its positioning, they rushed to the box to see what they had found.

'Bring the light closer. Quickly!'

Maria grabbed the flashlight and pointed it into the box. The bright stream of light overwhelmed the darkness, revealing the sole object inside: a slender bronze cylinder.

'What is it?' she asked.

Boyd smiled while removing the eight-inch bronze cylinder with his gloved hand. 'It's a twin, my dear. An identical twin.'

'A twin?'

'The documents that I found in England – the

documents that led us to the Catacombs – were stored in an *identical* bronze cylinder . . . Do you know what that means?'

'No! What?'

Boyd laughed. 'I have no idea, but I bet it's bloody important!'

Maria smiled, but in her heart she knew something was going on that Boyd wasn't talking about. She could sense it from the way he cradled the cylinder, treating it with a parental tenderness that was usually reserved for newborns. '*Professore?* May I look at it?'

He grimaced, reluctant to part with the artifact. 'Be very careful, my dear. Until we open it, there's no telling what may be inside. The contents could be quite delicate.'

She nodded, although she sensed that Boyd was being melodramatic. Nevertheless, she obeyed his wishes and treated the discovery with the utmost respect. 'Wow! It seems so incredibly light. Are you sure this is the same type of cylinder that you found in Bath?'

'Positive!' Boyd brought his flashlight closer to the object and pointed out a series of small engravings that could barely be seen. 'I'm not sure if this symbol can be translated, but I found an identical marking on the other one as well.'

Maria ran her finger over the triangular carvings, trying to probe the subtle indentations in the metal. The engraving on the cylinder was so shallow she could barely feel anything. 'Why is this so faint? I can barely see it.'

'I don't know,' Boyd admitted. 'It could've been worn down over time, or perhaps it was the style of the particular engraver. I'm hoping the contents of the canister will give us a clue.'

'That's if there's something inside.'

The look on Boyd's face proved that he wasn't amused. In response, he snatched the artifact from Maria's grasp. 'We don't have the correct tools to open this. I need to go upstairs to get them.' She winced, not realizing what had caused his sudden mood swing. 'While I'm gone, make yourself useful and finish filming this room.'

'Of course. Whatever you want, sir.'

'Well, that's what I want.' Boyd took two steps through the archway, then stopped abruptly. 'And don't touch anything while I'm gone. Just film!'

Maria watched as her mentor stomped down the stone corridor, the radiance of his flashlight getting dimmer and dimmer with every step that he took. Then, when he reached the far end of the hallway, Boyd turned up the narrow stairs and disappeared from sight, leaving her alone in the massive vault.

As Boyd made his way upstairs, he slowed his pace near the crypts, careful not to brush against any of the hands that reached into the corridor. His light danced along the walls as he walked, giving the corpses the illusion of movement. For a split second he could've sworn that one of the fingers twitched, like the skeletal remains were coming to life. He paused ever so slightly to examine it before stepping into the first chamber.

The bronze cylinder needed to be protected, he knew that, so he tucked it into his deepest pocket before he climbed through the hole in the wall. He opened his toolbox in a huff, tossing aside screwdrivers and wrenches, hammers and nails, even a small set of rock picks until it dawned on him that he had no idea what he was looking for.

He stood there pondering the question when he realized that the walls of the cave seemed to be shaking, actually vibrating with pulsating bursts of energy.

Whoosh! Whoosh! Whoosh!

He could feel the rocks trembling beneath his feet.

Whoosh! Whoosh! Whoosh!

Putting his hand on the wall, Boyd tried to determine the source of the tremors, but the entire rock face was vibrating at an even rate. Next, he placed his ear to the cool surface of the wall, hoping to establish the origin of the bass-filled pitch. Strangely, the strength of the sound actually seemed to diminish as he moved closer to the sides of the cave.

He quickly went through a series of calculations, attempting to figure out what could cause such a phenomenon. The resonance, the undulation, the energy. After a moment, it dawned on him that it was probably due to an external force. But what?

As he moved toward the site entrance, he noticed the drastic change in temperature. His body, which had grown accustomed to the underground climate, was now forced to deal with the hot Italian sun. Large beads of sweat surfaced on Boyd's brow, droplets that turned to mud as they streamed down his dirt-caked face and tumbled to the ground below.

His eyes, which were used to the dim light of the tunnels, suddenly burned in the afternoon sun. Its radiance was so intense that he found himself shading his face like a moviegoer leaving a matinee. And to make matters worse, the sound grew in intensity, forcing him to plug his ears while shielding his eyes at the same time.

'What is that hullabaloo?' he screamed over the noise. 'What in the world can that be?'

Oblivious to the commotion above her, Maria danced around the vast chamber, carefully filming the Roman chests. Even though it was a simple task, she knew her work would eventually be viewed by the world's leading archaeologists and scholars, a thought that made her ecstatic. Of course, that feeling would pale in comparison to the joy she'd feel when she told her father about her recent success. That would be the highlight of her life, for it would be the first time in memory that he'd have to admit that he was proud of her. The first goddamned time.

And it would actually involve something that she'd worked for, and trained for, and dreamed about for as long as she could remember. The first accomplishment in a career that her dad had discouraged from day one. A moment when her father, the great Benito Pelati, would have to admit that a woman was actually capable of making a mark in the world of archaeology.

A smile surfaced on Maria's face as she made her way to the back corner of the room. She gracefully sidestepped the largest crate while zooming in on an elaborate battlefield scene. Several seconds later she noticed a red light blinking on the back of her camera. The battery on the digital unit was about to run out.

'Damn! I don't believe this!' Maria glanced around the room, realizing there was no way she could finish her work with so little power. She'd have to go to the upper chamber to get her backup battery before she could finish the task.

The black helicopter hovered near the plateau, swaying in the strong wind. The pilot fought the air currents the best he could but realized he was in danger of losing control. 'Let me set her down, sir. The wind is swirling off the rock face. I don't know how much longer I can hold it.'

The lone passenger in the copter lowered the binoculars from his cold, black eyes. 'You'll hold it until I tell you otherwise. I have two men on that rock face, and my job is to cover them from an airborne position.'

The pilot argued, 'Well, I have a job, too. And it's impossible to do it in these conditions. I'm setting her down now!'

'If you do, I swear to God I'll have your ass.' The intensity of his glare proved that he was serious. He was willing to do anything to complete his mission. *Anything.* There was simply too much at stake. 'Give me five more minutes, and this will all be over.'

11

Piazza Risorgimento,
Rome, Italy
(fifty meters from Vatican City)

Buses filled with foreigners rumbled past him on their way to the main gate of the Holy City. People with cameras and unruly children strolled by his bench completely ignorant of who he was or why he was there. Their sole focus was on Saint Peter's Square and the Sistine Chapel and all the glorious artifacts in the Vatican museum, not the old man in the expensive suit or the two bodyguards who stood behind him.

Of course that was the reason that he liked to come here, the perverse amusement he got from watching so many people shell out their hard-earned cash for guidebooks and private tours. Meanwhile he sat on his bench knowing the vast majority of the Vatican's treasure lay hidden underneath the streets that they were walking on, everything protected in hermetic vaults that made Fort Knox look like a piggy bank. He smiled, realizing that none of them, no matter who they were or how much money they had, would *ever* see the treasures that he saw every day.

The contents of *Archivio Segreto Vaticano*. The Vatican Secret Archives.

Benito Pelati's official title was the minister of antiquities, a job he'd held for over three decades. Unofficially he was known throughout Italy as the godfather of archaeology, for he vowed to protect every relic found on Italian soil, even if that meant breaking a few laws in the process. Some critics looked down on him for his questionable methods, especially in the early years when he just started building his violent reputation. But the Vatican never did. They knew a man with his talents would be invaluable. Not only his academic knowledge but his willingness to do *whatever* he needed to get results.

Every organization, even one as sanctimonious as the Church, can use men like that.

Still, in the beginning it was Benito's expertise in the world of art, not his brutality, that got him noticed. Cardinal Pietro Bandolfo, the former chair of the Vatican's Supreme Council, was a childhood friend of Benito's and his biggest ally. Bandolfo understood politics better than his fellow cardinals and assured the Vatican the only way to protect its place in the modern world was to join hands with Benito, someone trained outside of the Church. Someone who could update their antiquated system. Someone who *wasn't* encumbered by papal law. Eventually, the Vatican agreed, and Benito was hired to update their way of doing things.

And his first project was organizing their most valuable asset: the Secret Archives.

Benito ran his fingers through his slicked-back gray hair and remembered the first day he was taken through the vaults. What an honor it was. Less than thirty men were privy to the contents of the Vatican's collections: the facility's curators, senior members of the Sacred Congregation of Cardinals, and the Curia. All of them devout Catholics who had dedicated their lives to God and were an established part of the Church. But not Benito. He was the first outsider to be given unlimited access to the vaults. Ever. And the experience made him tremble. Never before had he seen so many beautiful things in one place. Paintings, statues, and treasures filled room after room. Plus more than *forty miles* of shelves that held nothing but written documents: scrolls, parchments, and stone tablets for as far as the eye could see.

Unfortunately, once he got past all the beauty and started thinking about his job, he realized the Archives' filing system was a mess. Computers were still on the distant horizon, so everything in the vaults had been logged into card catalogs similar to those in a public library. Cards that could be moved, lost, or stolen. Adding to Benito's confusion were the curators themselves. Over the centuries the men in charge of the Archives had different preferences for recording their data. Some logged artifacts by year, others by country, others by theme. And one curator used a system Benito couldn't even interpret. To him it was amazing. He was staring at the most valuable collection in the world, yet one that was in complete disarray.

However, he was thrilled by the chaos. Not only because he had the honor of placing everything where he thought it belonged, but because he realized if the curators themselves didn't know what they had in the vaults, then neither did the Vatican. And if that was the case, there was no telling what he might find as he dug deeper into the bowels of the Church.

One day on the job, and he'd been given a ticket to the greatest treasure hunt of all time.

It was an opportunity that changed his life forever.

Dante was one of Benito Pelati's top assistants, a no-nonsense disciple who went out of his way to please the old man. He arrived on time and greeted Benito with a kiss on both cheeks. No words were said, no pleasantries exchanged. This was a business meeting, not a social call. They would save the chitchat for another day. If ever.

Dante was much larger than Benito and half his age. Yet their features were similar, especially the way their noses sloped away from their sunken eyes. Romans referred to it as *the look of the emperor*, though Dante didn't care about his face or his clothes or the make of his car. He didn't give a damn about those things because the only thing that mattered to him was his work. It was an addiction that ruled his life.

Minutes passed as Dante sat there, quiet, patiently waiting for Benito to speak because that was the way it was done in the Old Country. The old man had called the meeting, so he controlled the agenda, just like every time the two of them got together. Someday Benito would die, and Dante would move up in the organization. But until then Dante would sit there like a loyal dog, studying the people who poured past them on the busy street. Waiting to be briefed.

Eventually, the old man said, 'It's been a bad day for the Church.'

Dante remained silent, realizing details would come in short bursts, every statement measured before it left the old man's lips. As if Benito didn't know how to talk to him.

'A priest was found crucified . . . A warning was issued . . . The Council needs our help.'

In the power structure of the Vatican, the Supreme Council was second in command to the holy father. At least on paper. In reality, the seven cardinals who made up the Council – led by Cardinal Vercelli, the man who replaced Cardinal Bandolfo when he died less than a year before – were the most powerful men in the Catholic Church. They decided what the pope knew and what he didn't, protecting the papal throne from the bureaucratic issues of the day. To put it simply, their job was to keep the pope squeaky clean while they made the tough choices behind closed doors. The type of decisions that could soil the papacy and the Church.

And when these issues came up, Benito Pelati was usually part of the solution.

Finally, after several more seconds of silence, Benito turned toward Dante. 'I need you to go to Vienna . . . There's an excavation I need you to oversee . . . Something quite important.'

'In Austria?' Dante asked. 'Do we have permission to dig there?'

Benito stared at him until Dante lowered his head in shame. He should've known better than to question Benito's orders. 'Everything is ready . . . All you'll do is supervise . . . Once you're done, bring what you find back to me.'

12

Curiosity had a way of consuming Dr Boyd. Although he should've been focused on the bronze cylinder, he was more interested in the sound. The deafening roar of the outside world was too intriguing for him to ignore. 'Hello!' he called in his English accent. 'Is anybody out there?'

The rotor blades of the helicopter continued to reverberate like thunder just outside the entrance to the Catacombs.

'Goodness gracious! What is causing that tumult?' Boyd continued to ponder the question as he made his way to the mouth of the cave. 'People should have more consideration when –'

The sight of the massive machine, coupled with the overpowering roar of the turbines and the hurricane-like wind that enveloped him, was enough to take Boyd's breath away. He'd assumed the noise was probably a piece of equipment working on the plateau above but never expected to see a helicopter staring him in the face from more than 700 feet in the air.

The man in the passenger seat grinned, then ordered the pilot to rotate to the left. A split second later, the man's M501 sniper rifle was out the side window, and Boyd was in its crosshairs.

'Gentlemen,' he whispered into his headset, 'the Lord works in mysterious ways.'

The two soldiers stopped their ascent up the plateau and looked skyward, though their angle prevented them from seeing anything of value. 'What's going on, sir? Is everything all right?'

The man squinted as he adjusted his scope. 'It will be in a moment. One shot, and our biggest problem is history.'

They nodded in understanding. 'What should we do?'

He shoved the rifle's recoil pad against his shoulder and tried to compensate for the chopper's sway. 'Keep on climbing. I'll need you to deal with the girl and seal the site.'

Boyd shielded his eyes the best he could, but the mixture of dust and sunlight prevented him from seeing much. 'Hello!' he screamed. 'Can I help you with something?'

When he heard nothing, he figured he needed to alter his approach. So instead of shouting, he simply waved at the helicopter, hoping its passengers would wave back, then move on.

'Hold steady,' the sniper ordered. 'Steady!'

But it was an impossible task. The wind was surging off the top of the ridge like a waterfall, then

75

swirling on its descent to the rocky terrain below. The result was an aeronautical nightmare, a pocket of turbulence that literally chewed at the lift the helicopter was trying to produce. The pilot did his best to compensate, increasing and decreasing the pitch of the main rotor. But it made little difference. Choppers weren't meant to fly in these conditions.

'I'm losing it,' warned the pilot. 'I swear to you I'm losing it!'

With camera in hand, Maria strolled into the colorful first chamber, making her way directly to the Catacombs' exit. As she crawled through the narrow opening, she suddenly became aware of the noise and vibrations that had intrigued Boyd. *'Professore?'*

She continued up the slope of the rocky trail, trying to shield her eyes from the intense glare. With the exception of her hand, the only thing protecting her from total blindness was the figure that stood in the cave's entrance. And from his slender frame, she knew it was Boyd.

'Professore? What's making that noise?'

Before he could respond, she heard the unmistakable sound of gunfire, then watched in horror as Boyd turned from his perch and scrambled down the path. Without hesitation he buried his shoulder into her gut and tackled her to the floor, protecting her from the blitzkrieg. Skidding to a painful stop, he grabbed her hand and dragged her to the nearby corner, making sure they were out of the gunman's range. 'Are you all right?' he demanded. 'Are you hurt?'

Stunned, she took a moment to probe her body. 'No, I'm fine.'

Boyd climbed to his feet and peeked around the nearest outcropping. The roar of the chopper still thundered outside. 'I think we're in trouble. There's a helicopter out there.'

'A helicopter?'

'Yes! And it's got a nasty little passenger. All I did was wave, and he started shooting at me!' He peered around the rock, still unable to see. 'But that's not the worst thing. I saw a sign on the chopper that said *Polizia*.'

'What? Are you serious?'

'Of course I'm serious.' He grabbed her hand. 'Listen to me, we're in grave danger. But if you follow my lead, we'll survive.'

'We can beat an armed helicopter?'

'Yes! But we have to act quickly. If they land and come inside, we're going to be killed.'

'Wait! You want to fight a helicopter? With what?'

Boyd rushed to the corner and rummaged through their tools. 'Did we bring any rope?'

'Rope? Not with us. We left that in the truck.'

Quickly, Boyd turned the toolbox upside down and dumped its contents with a loud clatter. 'I guess this will have to do instead.'

She stared at him, confused. 'You asked for a rope

but settled for a toolbox? Do you mind telling me what you're going to do?'

'Watch and learn, my dear. Watch and learn.'

Boyd carried the box toward the entrance of the cave and studied the machine that threatened their lives. It hovered less than fifty feet in front of the opening, its occupants glaring out the front window of the craft. 'Maria, come here. Grab the camera and anything you want to take with us. Whether this works or not, I think it's best if we leave this place as soon as possible.'

'We're leaving?'

'Go!' he ordered. 'And be quick about it!'

She scampered to the rear while Boyd moved forward, boldly walking into the line of fire. He wasn't sure if his idea was going to work, but he figured it was better than being trapped inside the Catacombs without any weapons. 'Hello! Come and get me!'

He quickly repeated the phrase in Italian, just to make sure they understood his command. The chopper instantly moved closer, trying to reduce the angle between the sniper and target, hoping to avoid another misfire. But the maneuver was a tactical mistake. As the craft inched forward, Boyd extended the toolbox behind him, then tossed it underhanded as far as he could. The container sailed through the air until it floated into the path of the main rotor blades.

As the box closed in, the pilot suddenly realized

what was about to happen. He'd been so concerned about the gusting wind and the dangerous rock face that he never paid attention to Boyd or his toolbox. It was an oversight that would cost him his life.

Clank!

Metal struck metal in a sickening scream, shattering two of the four rotor blades on contact and sending shrapnel in every direction. With the sudden loss of lift, the chopper lurched forward, missing the rock face by inches before the pilot managed to pull the craft back. The sudden change in pitch couldn't be handled by the rear rotor, causing the vehicle to spin like a broken Tilt-A-Whirl as it tumbled toward Boyd's truck 700 feet below. Seconds later, the crunch of metal was masked by the powerful explosion that engulfed the side of the rock face, literally shaking the ground underneath Boyd's feet.

'Brilliant!' he cheered. 'Bloody brilliant!'

As the roar continued, Maria burst from the interior of the cave to see what had happened. '*Professore*, are you . . .' Before she could finish her question, she noticed the bright ball of fire. Orange and red flames shot high into the air as thick clouds of black smoke surged from the smoldering wreckage. '*Santa Maria!* You broke their helicopter. And our truck!'

He nodded, happy with his handiwork. 'Thank goodness we paid the renter's insurance.'

Normally she would've howled at his comment,

but Boyd didn't give her the chance. He grabbed her arm and pulled her back inside, where he started gathering his equipment. Unfortunately, he was forced to stop when he heard a distant rumbling.

'Maria? What is that? Is that another chopper?'

She grimaced, then took a few steps toward the mouth of the cave. Leaning back, she glanced at the cliffs above her. A slow trickle of rocks and debris were heading down the steep slope. 'Oh my God!'

In a flash Boyd knew what was happening. The impact of the explosion had forced the ground around them to shake, producing the last thing that he wanted. 'Avalanche!'

The duo burst from the tunnel entrance, running as fast as they could. Although it was a risky choice, they knew they'd rather face an onslaught of falling rocks than the sudden impact of a cave-in. Debris they could dodge. Collapsing tunnels they couldn't.

Grabbing Maria by the hand, he led the way along the narrow rock face, making sure they stayed together as they hugged the wall of the cliff. They scurried on the precipice for several seconds when they realized they couldn't outrun the falling debris. The footing was too unstable, and the stones were too constant for escape. They needed to find cover and hope for the best.

They scrambled under the first ridge they found, hoping the large outcropping would shield them from the debris. Unfortunately, as they stood underneath the slab, they realized that the ledge had several cracks near its base, flaws that might collapse when put under sudden duress.

'Please hold!' Maria begged. 'Oh God, please hold!'

The two soldiers stared in disbelief as the helicopter plummeted past them. Flames shot skyward like a geyser from hell, forcing the men to cower against the rock face for protection. But it wasn't the heat that they needed to worry about.

The landslide started with a trickle. First a pebble, then a stone, and finally a massive boulder. Before long, half the damn ridge was heading toward them, and they realized it was just a matter of time before they'd be joining their commander in the afterworld. The younger of the two men was the lucky one, for he died without suffering. A sharp piece of rock hit him squarely on the head, shattering his skull and rupturing his frontal lobe like a blow from a battle-ax. One minute he was by his partner's side, the next he was splattered on his face.

Soon his lifeless body was swept down the cliff face in a torrent of dust and stones.

The older man tried to ignore the gruesome scene, though it was impossible. Chunks of brain stuck to his face like scraps of sushi, while blood seeped into the corner of his eyes, stealing his ability to see. Despite this hindrance, he somehow managed to hang on, shaking off the falling stones that tore at his flesh, praying he could somehow survive this horror and scramble back to his squad in one piece. But it was not to be.

The rock that sealed his fate struck him squarely on the right shoulder, ripping his arm from its socket with a nauseating pop and shattering his clavicle like it was made of glass. He teetered on the edge for several seconds – just enough time to express his agony with a scream that rose above the roar of the fire below – before crashing to the earth.

One toolbox. Four dead.

The outcropping shook and trembled throughout the landslide. Maria watched nervously as stones plunged past her, but nothing, not even the tiniest of pebbles, managed to find them in their protective haven.

After the rocks and debris subsided, Maria said a short prayer of thanks, then turned to check on Boyd. His face was more pale than usual, but a smirk was etched on his lips. 'Are you OK?'

He took a deep breath. 'Brilliant. And you?'

'I'm fine.' Maria showed him the camera that she clasped in her hand. 'So is the video.'

'Oh, dear Lord! The cylinder!' Boyd frantically moved his fanny pack, hoping that the artifact had stayed in the pocket of his shorts during all the chaos. When he felt metal, he smiled, knowing they had lucked out. 'Well, my dear, it appears that things aren't a total loss.'

'No, but pretty close.' Maria pointed toward the Catacombs. Their entrance was now covered in debris. 'I don't think anyone will be using that door in the near future.'

Boyd grinned as he inspected the rubble. 'Good! In the meantime we can take our video to the authorities and use it as proof of our discovery. Then we can come back with proper protection and stake our official claim to this site!'

'Yeah,' she sighed, 'if there's anything left to claim.'

'Don't worry. I'm sure we won't leave Italy empty-handed.'

And Boyd knew that was true, for even if the Catacombs had been completely destroyed, he realized that he already possessed the object that he had come to Orvieto for.

The bronze cylinder.

13

Several hours passed before they came back for Payne. By then his legs were dead asleep, two lifeless limbs barely able to move. Still in handcuffs, he was dragged upstairs and shoved into a metal conference room where Jones, handcuffed as well, was sitting at the end of a long table. A large stranger in a dark suit sat on Jones's left. A second man, speaking on a cell phone, stood in the far corner of the room, watching everything with steely resolve.

Jones smiled when he saw Payne. It was the first time they had seen each other since they had been arrested. 'Hey Jon, you're looking well. How ya been sleeping?'

'Like a baby. Every morning I wake up wet.'

He nodded knowingly. 'Fuckin' hose.'

Payne took the seat across from Jones and studied the man to his side. He was roughly the same height as Payne but outweighed him by a hundred pounds. Muscle, not flab. Payne stared at him for five seconds, sizing him up, and in all that time he couldn't find his neck. Finally, to break the silence, Payne introduced himself. 'I'm Jonathon Payne. And you are?'

The yeti stared back at Payne but didn't say a word. He just let out a soft growl.

Jones, who was black and had the physique of a defensive back, laughed. 'Thank God he hates you, too. When he didn't talk to me, I thought he was a racist . . . Maybe he's just deaf.'

'Any idea what this is about?'

'Nope. And you?'

Payne shook his head. 'I was promised a phone call for today but never got to make it. Maybe these guys are from the embassy.'

'No,' blurted the man on the cell phone. 'We aren't from the embassy.'

'Oooooh!' Jones teased. 'They can talk!'

'Yes, Mr Jones, we can talk. But I promise this will be a short conversation if you continue to make comments at our expense. I will not tolerate lip from a prisoner.'

The guy was six foot one, in his mid-forties, and a total prick. They could tell that immediately. There was something about his demeanor that said, *If you fuck with me, I'll shit in your corn flakes.* Maybe it was his hair, which was high and tight, or his eyes, which were cold and reptilian. Whatever it was, he made it work because there was no doubt he was running things. 'So, should I leave right now, or will you shut up long enough to listen?'

Payne hadn't followed orders since he was in the military but got the sense that they had no choice. Either they listened to this guy, or they went back to their cells for a very long time. 'Sure, silence can be arranged. But only if you give us the courtesy of your name and rank. I feel that's the least we deserve.'

'No, Mr Payne, you don't *deserve* a thing. Not with the charges you're facing.'

The man took a seat at the far end of the table and removed a folder from his leather briefcase. Then he sat there for a minute, studying its contents. Refusing to say a word. The only sound in the room was the occasional rustle of paperwork. When he spoke again, the harshness in his voice was softer than before. Like he had reconsidered how to handle things. 'However, due to the circumstances of my proposal, I think it would be best if I remained civil.'

'Your proposal?' Payne asked.

'Before I get to that, let me honor your request. My name is Richard Manzak, and I'm with the Central Intelligence Agency.' He whipped out his identification and handed it to Payne. Manzak's partner followed his lead. 'This here is Sam Buckner. He's been teamed with me for this particular, um, situation.'

Payne studied both IDs, then passed them over to Jones. 'I don't understand. What do we have to do with the CIA? Shouldn't this be an embassy matter?'

Manzak grabbed his badge, then ordered Buckner to stand guard across the room. Payne found that kind of strange, since they were in the middle of a secure facility. Nevertheless, the big guy lumbered over there and leaned his ass against the door like a tired moose.

'This is well past an embassy matter,' Manzak assured him. 'The embassy tends to avoid crimes of this nature.'

'Crimes? What are you talking about? We didn't do anything. We came here as tourists.'

'Come now, Mr Payne. Both of us know the type of missions you used to run. I'm sure if you thought about it you could come up with a long list of activities that the Spanish government might disapprove of.' Manzak leaned forward, lowering his voice to a whisper. 'For now I think it would be best if we refrain from any specifics. You never know who might be listening.'

Payne thought back to his time with the MANIACs and realized they had passed through Spain on hundreds of occasions. Moron Air Base, located near Seville, was midway between the U.S. and southwest Asia, making it a prime spot to gather supplies and jump-start missions. Same with Naval Station (NAVSTA) Rota, positioned on the Atlantic coast near the Strait of Gibraltar. It gave them access to the Mediterranean Sea and assistance on amphibious assaults. Throw in Torrejon Air Base and all the other U.S. facilities scattered around Spain, and Payne shuddered at everything they might have on him and Jones.

Hell, every time they carried weapons off the base was a breach of regulations. So was crossing the border with nonmilitary personnel. Or flying through restricted airspace. In fact, just about everything the MANIACs did in Spain – even though it was always in the line of duty – bordered on a punishable offense. Not the type of violation that was *ever* pursued or prosecuted. The symbiotic relationship between the U.S. and Spain would not survive if the Spanish government started cracking down on active personnel in sanctioned U.S. missions. Still, the thing that worried Payne was the classified nature of his operations. How could he defend himself if he wasn't allowed to talk about anything he did?

Payne said, 'You know, you're right. This *isn't* an embassy matter. It's way beyond their scope. This is something the Pentagon will have to handle themselves.'

Manzak shook his head. 'Sorry, gentlemen, it's not going to happen. The Pentagon was notified by the Spanish government as soon as you were arrested. Sadly, in their eyes they have nothing to gain by getting involved. Can you imagine the public relations nightmare they'd face if they admitted to the missions you were involved in? Things *might* be different if you were still on active duty. Unfortunately, their desire to help is usually related to your current usefulness. And since you're currently retired, they view your usefulness as next to nothing.'

Manzak smiled crookedly. 'It's a cruel world. Isn't it, Mr Payne?'

Payne wanted to jump across the table and show

Manzak how cruel the world could be. Just to shut him up. But he knew he couldn't do that. Not until he found out why he was there, why the CIA was interested in his situation. For all he knew, Manzak could be his only ally. 'And what about you? Does your organization view us as *useful*?'

Manzak's smile widened. 'I wasn't so sure until I read about your trip to Cuba. Very impressive. In my mind, anyone who could do *that* is useful ... That mission still boggles my imagination.'

Payne and Jones looked at each other, confused. No one except the top brass at the Pentagon was supposed to know about Cuba. Not the CIA, the FBI, or even the president. As it stood, the Cubans didn't even know about Cuba, because the moment they found out, they were going to be pissed. Anyhow, the fact that Manzak knew about their trip told them a lot. It meant he was a heavy hitter with some serious connections. Someone who could cut a deal.

'Great,' Payne said. 'You've done your homework. Unfortunately, there's still one question you haven't answered. Why are you here?'

Manzak leaned back in his chair, quiet. Watching them squirm. Most people would've answered right away, but not this guy. He was cooler than that. Much cooler. The definition of self-control. Finally, when he sensed that they were about to lose their patience, he gave them an answer. 'I'm here to buy your freedom.'

Freedom. Neither Payne nor Jones knew how that was possible, but that didn't stop Manzak from sitting there, stoic, enjoying the power he had over them like an evil puppet master. He didn't smile, frown, or even blink. After several seconds of silence, he pulled out another folder, this one several inches thick and wrapped in a rubber band.

A single name appeared on the cover: *Dr Charles Boyd.*

'Gentlemen, I've been authorized by the Spanish government to make a once-in-a-lifetime offer. If you're willing to accept my terms, they won't keep you in jail for your lifetime.'

Jones grimaced at the pun. 'Great. Who do they want us to kill?'

Manzak glared at him. 'I'm not sure what you were used to doing for the MANIACs, but I can assure you that the CIA would never broker an assassination.'

Jones rolled his eyes. 'Please! I can name at least twenty cases where the CIA was involved in the death of a key political figure – and that's not even counting the Kennedys.'

'Whether you believe me or not is irrelevant. What is important is this: My proposal doesn't involve murder or illegal activities of any kind.'

Payne remained skeptical. 'Then what does it involve?'

'A missing person.'

'Excuse me? They want us to find a missing

person? And if we agree, they'll what? Let us walk?' Payne read the name on the manila folder. 'Let me guess, Dr Charles Boyd?'

Manzak nodded. 'That's affirmative. We'd like you to find Dr Boyd.'

Payne sat there, waiting for more information. When it didn't come, he said, 'And out of curiosity, who the hell is Dr Boyd?'

His question was intended for Manzak. But Jones stunned everyone by supplying the answer. 'If I'm not mistaken, he's an archaeologist from England.'

Manzak glanced at Jones. 'How did you know that?'

'How? Because I'm smart. What, a black man can't be intelligent?'

Payne rolled his eyes at the mock outrage. 'Just answer him.'

'Fine,' he sneered. 'I saw Boyd on the History Channel. Seems to me he's a professor at Oxford or one of those fancy-pants English schools. It might've been Hogwarts for all I know. Anyway, he was talking about the Roman Empire and how it influenced modern society.'

Manzak wrote a note to himself. 'What else did you learn?'

'I never knew the Romans had indoor plumbing. I always thought –'

He cut him off. 'I meant about Boyd.'

'Not much. They used his voice but he rarely appeared on-screen. He was just the narrator.'

Payne rubbed his eyes, trying to play catch-up. 'Let me get this straight. Dr Boyd is an English archaeologist, someone with enough credibility to teach at a world-famous university and narrate a special on the History Channel?'

Manzak nodded, refusing to give additional information.

'OK, here's what I don't understand. What's the big emergency here? I mean, why does the Spanish government want this guy so badly that they're willing to cut a deal with two prisoners? Furthermore, where does the CIA fit into this? Something just doesn't add up here.'

Manzak gave him a cold, hard stare, one that suggested he wasn't ready to lay his cards on the table. Nevertheless, Payne stared back, unwilling to back down. He'd been locked up for seventy-two hours and was sick of being jerked around. His aggressiveness paid off moments later when Manzak leaned back in his chair and sighed. A long, drawn-out sigh. A sound that told Payne he had backed his prey into a corner, and he was about to surrender.

Manzak stayed like that for a moment, like he was still trying to decide if it was the right thing to do. Finally, with reluctance on his face, he pushed the folder forward.

'Dr Charles Boyd is the most wanted criminal in Europe.'

14

Every crime has a command center. Whether it's a major case or not, there has to be a place for the investigating officers to go to write their reports. Sometimes it's just a tiny cubicle at headquarters, but there's always a spot that becomes the heart of an investigation.

But rarely was it this luxurious.

Kronborg's superintendent wanted to keep Nick Dial happy, so he put him in the Royal Chambers, a series of rooms that served as the royal residence for nearly a hundred years. The suite was built for Frederick II in the 1570s and was filled with the original furnishings. A gold chandelier hung from the ceiling, dangling over the banquet table that served as his desk.

Dial rarely had any privacy when he worked a case so he viewed this as the ultimate luxury, a chance to be alone with his thoughts, if only until someone came looking for one of the files he 'borrowed' from the Danish police when they weren't looking.

Every investigator had a different technique for sorting through evidence, his or her personal way to get a grip on things. Some talked into a tape recorder. Others typed the info into their computer. But neither of those techniques worked for Dial. He was old-school when it came to evidence, eschewing the lure of technology for the simplicity of a bulletin board. To him there was no better way to organize a case. He could move things whenever he wanted until everything fit into place – like a giant jigsaw puzzle that revealed the secret identity of the killer.

The first thing he put on the Kronborg board were photographs of the crime scene. They were taken at a variety of angles and revealed all the little horrors that he would like to forget. The way two of the victim's ribs had been forced through his skin like broken chopsticks that had been plunged into a pound of raw meat. The way his jaw hung at an impossible angle. The way blood looks when it mixes with urine and feces. That's the reality of the average homicide, the type of stuff that Dial had to wade through to find the answers he was looking for.

Like finding more information about Erik Jansen. That would be the best way to determine why he was chosen to die. Learn about the victim to learn about the killer. That meant starting with the people who knew Jansen best: his friends, family, and coworkers. Of course, that was more difficult than it sounded since they were scattered all over Europe. Throw in the language barrier and the secrecy of the Vatican, and the degree of difficulty went through the roof.

It would take a team of professionals to get the information he needed.

The first person he phoned was his secretary at

Interpol. She was in charge of calling the National Central Bureaus in Oslo and Rome and telling them what Dial needed, then they would contact the local police departments and get the information for him.

Unfortunately, Vatican City wasn't one of Interpol's member countries. That meant there wasn't an NCB office at the pope's palace. No local contacts meant no insiders. And no insiders meant no information. Agent Nielson had tried to circumvent the problem by calling the Vatican directly, but as Dial had anticipated, no one returned her message.

So Dial decided to call the Vatican himself, hoping his fancy title would get someone on the line. He'd received a long list of phone numbers from Nielson and asked her to break things down according to nationality, figuring Danes and Norwegians would be most willing to help because of their connection to the crime.

After giving it some thought, though, he decided to scrap that idea and go in the opposite direction. Instead of looking at it from the victim's point of view, he decided to look at it from his own. Who'd be willing to help *him*? He needed to find someone he could talk to, someone he could bond with. That was the angle he needed to play, the way to get his foot in the door.

It was far too late to help Erik Jansen. But it wasn't too late to help Nick Dial.

*

Cardinal Joseph Rose grew up in Texas. He loved guns, red meat, and ice-cold beer. But more than anything else, he loved God, and that was the reason he was willing to move halfway around the world to work for the Vatican. This was his calling, and he was very content.

But that didn't mean he wasn't homesick.

When the call came to his office, his assistant told him that Nick Dial was on the phone. The name didn't ring a bell, so Cardinal Rose asked his assistant what it was about. His assistant shrugged and said Dial wouldn't tell him. Then he added that Dial had an American accent. Two seconds later, Rose was on the phone. 'How can I help you, Mr Dial?'

Dial smiled at the Texas twang in the cardinal's voice. It was music to his ears. 'Thanks for taking my call, Your Eminence. Please call me Nick.'

'Thanks, Nick. But only if you call me Joe.'

'You got it.'

'So, what part of America are you from?'

'All over, really. My dad coached college football, so I grew up on campuses from Oregon to Pennsylvania to Florida. Plus I spent a whole lot of time in Texas.'

They spent the next few minutes talking about the Lone Star State before Rose asked, 'So, what can I do for you? I have to admit I'm curious, since you wouldn't tell my assistant.'

'Sorry about that. I thought it would be best if I told you myself.'

'Told me yourself? That doesn't sound good.'

'I'm afraid it's not. I run the Homicide Division at Interpol, and last night one of your priests was found murdered.'

Rose tried to remain calm. 'One of *my* priests? You mean one of my assistants?'

'Maybe,' Dial admitted. 'That's the reason for my call. We know the victim's name and that he worked for the Vatican, but I'm having trouble finding out additional —'

'His name?' Rose demanded. 'Please tell me his name.'

'Jansen. Father Erik Jansen.'

The sound of relief escaped Rose's lips, a whisper that told Dial that the Cardinal didn't know the victim. 'How did it happen?'

'He was crucified.'

'Dear God!' Rose made the sign of the cross. 'Did you say crucified?'

'Yes, sir. Someone kidnapped him, knocked him out, then nailed him to a cross.'

'When? Where? Why didn't I hear about this?'

Dial grimaced, not sure what to answer first. 'As far as we can tell, he was kidnapped in Rome last night. From there he was taken to Denmark, where he was killed.'

'Denmark? Why Denmark?'

'We don't know, sir. That's what I was hoping to find out. You see, I'm in charge of gathering as much evidence as possible, but I've run into some resistance. I've tried calling several people at the Vatican, but –'

'Say no more.' Rose paused, trying to think of the best way to explain things. 'I know how we can be about information. That's probably why I haven't heard anything about this tragedy. People are reluctant to open up in our community.'

'Which is understandable, but –'

'Not acceptable. I couldn't agree with you more.' Rose shook his head, half embarrassed by the situation. 'Nick, I'll tell you what I'm going to do. I'm going to look into things myself, even if it means ruffling a few feathers. And the moment I have anything, and I do mean *anything*, I will give you a call, day or night.'

'Do you promise? Because several people have –'

'Yes, Nick, I promise. I will get to the bottom of this. You have my word as a Texan.'

And to Dial, that meant more than Rose's word as a church official.

15

Jones was obsessed with mysteries, which was the reason he wanted to become a detective. Some people see the glass as half-empty, while others see it as half-full. But Jones stares at it and tries to figure out who drank the damn water.

Anyway, Payne wasn't surprised when Jones snatched the CIA folder before he had a chance to grab it. Jones said, 'Dr Charles Boyd majored in archaeology and linguistics at Oxford and was eventually given a teaching position at Dover University in 1968. According to this, they even made him head of his department in 1991 ... Wow! How shocking!'

Manzak wasn't amused. 'Keep reading, Mr Jones. I assure you it gets worse.'

'Damn, Jon! He wasn't kidding. Take a look at this.'

Payne fought the urge to smile when Jones handed him a head shot of Dr Boyd that was taken during the Nixon administration. The type of photo that gets attached to someone's personnel file and stays there no matter what anyone does to get rid of it. Boyd wore a tweed jacket and a silk bow tie, plus the worst comb-over hairstyle Payne had ever seen. It looked like one of the *before* photos in that infomercial for spray-on hair.

'Let me guess,' Jones cracked. 'He's wanted by the fashion police.'

'No,' Manzak said in a harsh tone. 'He's the key suspect in an Interpol investigation that's been going on for two decades. Everything from forgeries to smuggling to the theft of antiquities. This guy does it all and does it at a very high level. Right now he's wanted in several countries, most notably France, Italy, Germany, Austria, and Spain.'

'Then why don't they pick him up?' Payne wondered.

'Because Boyd's a genius. Every time they get close to him, he finds a way to cover his tracks. Every single time. I'm telling you, it's like the guy has ESP.'

'Or inside information,' Jones suggested.

Payne was thinking the same thing. 'OK, let's pretend everything you've told us about Boyd is accurate. What does this have to do with the CIA?'

Manzak pointed to the file. 'Let me start with Spain. Dr Boyd stole a number of heirlooms from the Spanish government, one-of-a-kind items that have no price tag. Needless to say, they're willing to do anything within reason to have them returned. Unfortunately, the only way to retrieve their items is to find Dr Boyd and get him to talk. Sounds easy, right? Well, up until now he's managed to hide hundreds of objects under Interpol's nose, and no one has any idea where. Spain is worried if Boyd gets killed in a manhunt, then their artifacts will never resurface. And the same can be said for the rest of Europe. Everyone is panicked about this. *Everyone.* And panic is a wonderful thing, especially if you're able to take advantage of it.'

'See, that's where you're losing me. How can the CIA benefit from this?'

Manzak leaned forward and smiled, the type of smile that was usually seen next to a bubbling cauldron. 'Tell me, Mr Payne, what do you know about the CIA?'

'I know how to spell it. Other than that, I'm clueless.' Payne pointed toward Jones. 'There's the guy you want to talk to. He was tempted to join your organization at one point in time.'

Manzak looked surprised. 'Is that so?'

Jones nodded. 'Simply put, you guys collect foreign intelligence, evaluate it, then send your theories to D.C. in one of these snazzy manila folders.'

Manzak ignored the last part. 'Of course, it's not as easy as it sounds. Sometimes it takes years to get a task done. For instance, we might smuggle an agent into a country, let him become a part of the system, then go back to him much later to find out what he's learned. Sometimes months, sometimes years. That's why in certain situations we're forced to use more efficient techniques, ones with a quicker rate of return.'

Jones grinned. 'Torture?'

'You've heard the saying, *If I scratch your back, you*

scratch mine. Well, that's how we get some of our best intel. We provide a favor – weapons, cash, whatever – and get data in return.'

Payne groaned in understanding. 'And let me guess, D.J. and I are the favor.'

'Not just a favor, a *big* favor. If you catch Boyd, you're helping more than just Spain. You're helping us as well because we'll hold Boyd over Europe like mistletoe, then see which country kisses our ass first. And the best part is we don't have to risk any operatives to complete this mission. You gentlemen can do all the dirty work for us.'

'That is, if we agree to do this. You see, there's still one thing that bothers me. I take it there's no way the Spanish government is willing to put our agreement on paper.'

'That's correct, Mr Payne. No paperwork on this one. It's safer that way.'

'Safer for whom? What's to stop them from arresting us again the moment we find Boyd?'

Manzak shrugged. 'And what's to prevent you from going home the moment you leave this facility? The answer is nothing. But I'll tell you this: I think Spain is showing a lot more faith in you than you are in them. With your military backgrounds, you guys could disappear if you wanted to, and there's no way they could come to the U.S. to get you back. So what have you got to lose? If you take their deal, they'll let you walk . . . And if you don't, they'll let you rot.'

16

The police in Orvieto could not be trusted. The city crest on the side of the helicopter was proof of that. But how far did the conspiracy run? Could Boyd and Maria trust the cops in the next town? There was no way of knowing, so they decided to take a two-hour bus ride to Perugia, a city of over 150,000 people, and seek the protection of a much larger police force.

After settling into the backseat, the duo glanced out the window and searched for flashing lights, men with guns, or anything that seemed suspicious. Yet nothing disrupted the quiet serenity of Orvieto except the loud exhaust of the bus.

Once they cleared the confines of Orvieto and headed toward the Italian countryside, Boyd was finally able to relax. His breathing returned to normal. The color reemerged in his cheeks. The knot in his stomach began to loosen, and his racing heart slowly slid from his throat.

Suddenly reenergized, Boyd removed the cylinder that he'd rescued from the Catacombs and stared at it. To him, the unearthing of the Catacombs was an event that would rock the archaeological community for decades to come. But the discovery of Orvieto paled in comparison to the item in his hand. If the

Roman cylinder actually contained what he thought it did, the entire world would sit up and notice, not just a bunch of professors from the world of academia.

Front-page news all over the globe. Boyd's picture on every magazine cover.

Before he got too excited, he realized he had to make sure that the promised treasure was actually inside. While Maria took a nap next to him, he held the cylinder next to the window to see if he'd missed anything in the gloom of the Catacombs. With the exception of the engraver's inscription, the object was completely smooth, containing no ridges or flaws of any kind. Both ends appeared solid, as if the metal had no seams. But Boyd knew that wasn't the case.

The artifact from Bath had looked solid as well, yet after running it through a series of tests, he discovered that one of the ends was covered with enough metal to keep air and moisture out but not enough to make it impenetrable. All he needed was a screwdriver, and he'd be able to pierce the metal top, then peel the surface back like the top of a can of nuts.

Desperate, Boyd glanced under his seat, searching for something to break the seal. Next, he checked the video camera bag, but all of the fasteners were made of plastic, which was way too flimsy to penetrate the top.

Bloody hell, he thought to himself. *This cylinder is the key to everything. There has to be —*

And then it dawned on him. He had just muttered the answer to his problem.

Boyd removed the key to his rent-a-truck and pushed its tip against the edge of the bronze cylinder. The container hissed as the seal was broken, allowing air that had been sealed for two thousand years to escape from the tube. With trembling hands, he pushed the key in harder, then peeled the thin layer of metal toward the edge. Not the entire way, though. He had no intentions of removing the document on the bus. All he wanted to do was to see if the scroll was inside.

To get a good look, Boyd raised the cylinder skyward, hoping to use the sun as a spotlight. But as he brought the opening to his eye, his concentration was broken. The scenery that had been rushing past at a steady pace had slowed to a crawl. The roar of the bus engine, the sound of the surging wind, and the chatter of his fellow passengers had disappeared as well.

'Maria!' Boyd shook her fiercely. 'Wake up! We're stopping.'

Her eyes popped wide open. 'What do you mean we're stopping? Where are we?'

'In the middle of nowhere.'

She blinked a few times, then glanced out the side window, trying to place the terrain. Unfortunately, the sunflower fields and lush patches of green grass were commonplace for the area. There was no way she could tell anything from farmland.

Moving into the center aisle, she walked toward the driver, hoping to see a road sign or a mileage marker that would pinpoint their exact location. Regrettably, the only thing she saw was the bright hue of flashing lights. She rushed back to Boyd. 'There's a roadblock ahead!'

The color disappeared from his face. 'They're looking for us! I knew it!'

Maria realized the odds were pretty good that Boyd was right. 'The way I see it, we've got two choices. We can try to talk our way out of this, or . . .' She put her hand on the emergency door and opened it. 'Or we can get the hell out of here.'

Not waiting for his response, Maria grabbed the video camera and slid out the back of the bus. Boyd followed her lead and climbed out as well.

'Now what?' he demanded. 'Where to now?'

Maria crept to the back corner of the bus and looked around. 'Damn! Where's the rest of the traffic? There should be other cars!' She glanced back at Boyd. 'Did we go through a detour while I was sleeping? We aren't on the highway anymore.'

'I don't know. I wasn't paying attention. I was studying the cylinder.'

She growled softly. 'Damn! We'll have to run for it. That's our only alternative.' She eyed the terrain on both sides of the road and realized the field of sunflowers would be perfect. 'If we can get into the flowers, we should be able to hide until they search the bus and leave.'

Boyd nodded, then wrapped his hand around the cylinder like a sprinter in a relay race. 'All right, my dear. You lead. I'll follow.'

After taking a deep breath, Maria burst from their hiding place and leapt into the belly of the golden field where flowers sprouted to seven feet tall. Boyd followed her through the labyrinth of stalks, catching faint glimpses of her as she scurried through the sun-colored field.

The bus driver knew something was wrong the instant he heard the call. In his twenty-plus years with the company, this was the first time that the police had ever radioed him with a new set of directions. At first he figured there was an accident up ahead or maybe a traffic jam, but when he saw the flashing lights on the rural road, he knew it was something worse.

They were looking for one of his passengers.

'Ladies and gentlemen,' he announced in Italian, 'please don't be alarmed. This is just a routine stop by the local authorities. I'm sure we'll be under way shortly.'

'Are you sure?' someone shouted. 'Because two people just jumped out the back.'

'Jumped out?' he demanded. 'What are you talking about?'

Before the passenger could answer, one of the cops at the roadblock hoisted an M72 Light Anti-tank Weapon onto his shoulder and fired. The rocket launched with a mighty *whoosh*, propelled by gases that burned at over 1400°F, and slammed into the metallic grill of the bus.

Fire roared down the center aisle like a flood, burning everything in its wake: the seats, the luggage, and the people, literally melting the skin off their bodies in a horrific ball of flames. The unlucky few who survived the impact of the rocket scrambled blindly in the black smoke, searching for a way out. They flailed wildly at the broken windows, trying to squeeze through the holes that lined the frame even though the razorlike shards punctured their faces and torsos.

Finally, one of the men came to his senses and opened the emergency exit in the back.

'If you can hear me,' he screamed into the smoke, 'come this way!'

Seconds later, he saw a petite woman fighting her way through the inferno, dragging a badly burnt man whose face looked like it had been removed with a blowtorch. The first man didn't know where she'd found the strength, yet she'd somehow managed to drag him to the rear exit.

'You're almost out,' he assured her as he helped them to the ground. 'We're almost free.'

She tried to thank him but could only manage a hacking cough. At least she was still breathing, he thought. At least she had made it through the flames and had managed to save one of the passengers in the process. Somehow, miraculously, they had survived this tragedy.

At least for the moment.

While staggering from the bus, he spotted the policemen in the distance and screamed to them for aid, not realizing that they had started the fire to begin with. The smallest of the cops rushed forward like he was going to help, like he was going to put out the fire with the long nozzle that he held in his hands. But instead of giving them assistance, he did just the opposite.

Stopping fifteen feet in front of them, the cop lowered the visor on his flame-retardant helmet and hit the switch on his flamethrower, sending a deadly stream of jellied fuel into the air. The chemicals ignited in a wicked flash, covering the victims like napalm and scorching them like marshmallows that had fallen into a campfire, their white skin bubbling and turning black as they slowly became a part of the burnt asphalt.

Smiling, the cop spoke into his headset. 'The leak has been sealed.'

17

Tuesday, July 11
Dover, England
(eighty miles southeast of London)

Payne and Jones weren't born yesterday. They had been involved in too many missions to ignore the obvious: there was something fishy about Manzak's offer.

The CIA was a global organization, one that had agents and hidden connections all over the world. If they *legitimately* wanted to find Dr Charles Boyd, there was no way they would've turned to two outsiders for help. Yet for some reason Manzak came to Pamplona anyway. For some reason he wanted to go *out of house* (i.e., use non-CIA personnel) to track down Boyd and ultimately settled on two former MANIACs to do the job. Payne wasn't sure why that was, but he had some theories. Perhaps Manzak was bucking for a promotion and felt the best way to get one was by catching a wanted man on his own? Or maybe Boyd had done something to Manzak long ago, and this was Manzak's way of getting some personal revenge? Or maybe, just maybe, it was something more obvious. Maybe Manzak wanted to get his hands on Boyd so he could sell his stolen treasures and pocket the money for himself?

In the end Payne and Jones weren't sure what Manzak's motivation was. All they knew was he had the power to get them out of jail ASAP, and that's all they wanted. Besides, they figured once they got back into circulation they'd have plenty of time to investigate Manzak, Boyd, and everything else that seemed shady to them. Which was just about everything.

After accepting Manzak's offer, Payne and Jones collected their things before being herded into a helicopter and whisked away. During their flight Manzak briefed them on the mission and how to contact him once they had located Boyd. Instead of using a phone, they were to activate a high-tech beacon that looked similar to a garage door opener. Then they were to sit patiently and wait for the cavalry to arrive. Well, not the *real* cavalry. Their mission was supposed to be top secret, so the last thing they needed was for a bunch of horses to come galloping into town, shitting all over the place, while being led by a bugle-playing cowboy. Something like that might work during a gay pride parade but not on a CIA operation.

Anyway, their chopper touched down late Monday night in Bordeaux, France, where they were told to spend the night. Manzak gave them their travel itineraries for an early morning flight, then left with Buckner to save the world or something. Once alone,

Payne and Jones started working the phones – first calling the Pentagon to check on Manzak and Buckner's credentials, then calling Dover University to set up an appointment with Dr Boyd's assistant.

England is smaller than the state of Alabama yet has three of the finest universities in Europe: Oxford, Cambridge, and Dover. The first two are the most well-known and for good reason. Oxford is the oldest English-speaking university in the world and boasts a roster of alumni that includes John Donne, William Penn, J. R. R. Tolkien, and Bill Clinton. Cambridge came into existence more than one hundred years later and was the school of choice for John Milton, Prince Albert, Isaac Newton, John Harvard, and Charles Darwin.

Yet in recent years many of the top students have shied away from the big two, partially because their admission policies seem to place more emphasis on a candidate's lineage than his academic achievements. That, however, is not the case at Dover. Founded in 1569 by Elizabeth I, it had the guts to reject one of her ancestors because he failed to meet their scholastic standards. That episode, more than anything else, catapulted Dover's status to the top of the academic heap, making it the school of choice among the elite families in Great Britain.

At least that's what Jones read on the Internet while collecting intel for their trip.

The next morning they flew to London, took the express train to Victoria Station, then picked up a local line into Dover. From there it was a short walk to campus, where they had a late afternoon meeting with Dr Boyd's assistant, Rupert Pencester, a chipper young bloke who was bound to offer them a cup of tea even though it was seventy-five degrees and sunny. To prepare for their meeting, Payne and Jones decided to show up early and conduct some research on their own.

The archaeology department was part of Kinsey College, one of thirty-three colleges that made up Dover University. It sat in the northwest corner of campus, fairly isolated from the sprawling lawn that connected all the schools. Boyd's office was on the second floor of a building that was designed by England's greatest architect, Sir Christopher Wren, one filled with arches, flying buttresses, and the biggest doors Payne had ever seen. Thankfully, the massive slabs of oak were outfitted with modern locks that Jones could crack in thirty seconds.

Pushing the door open, he said, 'After you.'

There was no need to turn on any lights, since sunlight streamed through a series of recessed windows that ran the length of the wall. Boyd's desk sat on the opposite side, next to three filing cabinets and a series of bookshelves. Payne hoped to find a computer filled with Boyd's records and schedules, yet Boyd seemed to be a product of a different generation, for nothing in the room was modern. Even the clock looked like it was built by Galileo.

The filing cabinets were locked, so Payne let

Jones work his magic while he dug through Boyd's desk. Payne found the usual assortment of office supplies and knickknacks but nothing that helped their search. Next he turned his attention to the bookshelves. They were filled with books on the Roman Empire, archaeological digs in Italy, and early Latin.

'The first one's done,' Jones bragged. 'Feel free to take a look when you get a chance.'

'That would be now. There's nothing over here but books on Italy. Let's see: we got Rome, Venice, Naples, and Milan.'

Jones focused his attention on the second lock. 'Not exactly a shocker. I mean, his interview on the History Channel was on the Roman Empire. I'm guessing that was his specialty.'

'It was,' said a voice from the doorway. 'That and privacy, which is the reason his chests are locked. Or should I say *were* locked.'

Payne looked at Jones, and he looked back, the color draining from both their faces. Suddenly they felt like Winona Ryder getting busted for shoplifting.

'Listen,' Payne said, 'we weren't –'

'No need,' said the gentleman in an aristocratic accent. He was in his early twenties and wearing a red soccer outfit complete with shin guards and grass stains. A Dover emblem covered his left breast. 'It's none of my business, really. I just came to ring some of my chums. Do you mind?'

'No, go ahead,' Payne said, half stunned. They

had just been busted in someone else's office, yet he was being asked permission to make a call. God, the English were polite.

'By the way,' the guy reasoned, 'I'm assuming you're the chaps who rang me last night for an appointment. If I knew what you were after, perhaps I could expedite things?'

Payne glanced at Jones and noticed his grin. The detective gods were looking out for them.

'Actually,' Payne said, 'we have some urgent business to discuss with Dr Boyd, and time is of the essence. Any idea where we might find him?'

'Well, I can assure you he's not in that chest.' Payne waited for the kid to smile, but somehow he managed to keep a straight face. 'For the last few weeks he's been in the Umbria region of Italy, specifically the town of Orvieto. I was planning on spending my summer there until Charles told me that I'd be more helpful at home. Not exactly a vote of confidence, would you say?' The bitter tone in the kid's voice told them everything they needed to know. He was pissed at Dr Boyd, so he decided to get revenge by using Boyd's phone and helping them out.

'Do you know where he's staying?' Jones wondered.

He shook his head. 'Orvieto is pretty small. You shouldn't have any trouble finding him.' He retrieved a book written by Boyd from the closest shelf. 'Do you know what he looks like?'

Payne nodded. 'We have one picture from when Winston Churchill was still alive.'

'Most likely his annual from Oxford. It amazes me that he was willing to sit still for it. He's something of a recluse when it comes to cameras.'

The kid flipped over the book and showed them the back photo. It must've been taken during one of Boyd's lectures, for he was standing in front of a chalkboard with a pointer in his hand. His face and physique looked pretty much the same, albeit thirty years older. The only thing that had changed was his comb-over hairstyle. He had finally opted to go bald instead.

Jones asked, 'Do you mind if I keep this? I'd like to read his stuff.'

'Not at all. Feel free to take whatever you'd like.' The kid wrote his number on a scrap of paper and gave it to Jones. 'Should you have any further questions, please don't hesitate to call.'

Payne said, 'We won't.'

'Now, if you don't mind, I'd like to trouble you mates for a favor.' The kid finally cracked a smile. A devious little grin. 'When you surprise Charles in Orvieto and do *whatever* you're going to do to him, please tell him that I, Rupert Pencester the Fourth, said hello.'

18

Nick Dial knew that Cardinal Rose would honor his promise to get back in touch but doubted he'd get anything of substance within twenty-four hours. Thankfully, Cardinal Rose was full of surprises.

'Here's what I can tell you,' Rose said when he called. 'Father Erik Jansen came to the Vatican eight years ago from a tiny parish in Finland. Upon his arrival he filled a number of duties, everything from clerical to spiritual, yet nothing that stands out until a year ago.'

Dial leaned forward. 'What happened then?'

'He was reassigned to a new post with the Pontifical Biblical Commission.'

'To do what?'

Rose sighed. 'I'm not quite sure. Perhaps if I had some more time.'

'I've heard of the PBC, but I'm clueless about them. What can you tell me?'

'Where to start? Well, they've been around since the turn of the century. Make that *last* century. Somewhere around 1901 or 1902. It was founded by Pope Leo XIII and used to make crucial inter-pretations about the Bible.'

'Such as?'

'A few years ago they released a study that examined the correlation between the Hebrew Scriptures and the Christian Bible in hopes of bringing the two groups closer together.'

Dial stroked his chin. 'Sounds controversial to me.'

'You're right about that. Then again, anytime the Vatican changes their interpretation of the Bible, it's bound to cause a stir.'

'So the PBC is like the American Supreme Court. They have the final say on things.'

Rose smiled at the comparison. 'In a rudimentary way, I guess you're right – only the PBC is much slower. Take the Hebrew study. It took them ten years to draft their position statement.'

'Ten *years*? That's a long time to wait for some answers.'

'When you're dealing with the Word of God, you don't want to make mistakes.'

Dial shook his head as he wrote a few notes. 'Any idea what they're working on now?'

'Sorry. That's a closely guarded secret that only a select few would know.'

'Would Jansen be one of those people?'

'Most appointees are senior members of the Vatican, men who are even older than I am. I doubt they'd include such a young member of our community.'

'Yet he still worked for them.' Dial stared at his bulletin board and focused on a crime scene photo of

Father Jansen. Even with a broken face, he appeared way too young to have a position on such a powerful committee. 'Could he have been an intern or somebody's assistant? I mean, you mentioned that he had experience with that type of stuff.'

Rose nodded. 'That'd make more sense than a spiritual role.'

'Could his nationality be a factor? Is anyone from Finland on the Commission?'

'I can check.'

'While you're at it, see if there are any Danes. We still don't know why Jansen was brought to Denmark. Maybe it was some kind of message to the PBC.'

'You think that's possible?' Rose wondered.

'The fact is Jansen worked for one of the most powerful committees at the Vatican. That's reason enough to suspect his death was job-related. Throw in the fact that he was crucified and the killer left a note that quoted the Bible, and, well, you see where I'm going.'

'Just a second! What do you *mean* the killer quoted the Bible?'

Dial smiled. Rose had taken the bait. The truth was he was trying to shield the Bible angle from all outsiders, fearing if the media reported it that every religious fanatic in the world would be asking him questions about the Bible that he didn't know how to answer. But Dial also knew if he was going to get any top secret dirt from Rose, he was going to have to reveal some of his own. Nothing major, just enough to make it seem like give-and-take instead of take, take, take.

So he said, 'Joe, I could get in big trouble for telling you this. However, if you promise to keep this quiet . . .'

'You have my word, Nick. This is between us. I promise.'

Dial nodded, satisfied. 'The killer left a note that said, "IN THE NAME OF THE FATHER." Nailed it on the cross above the victim, just like the sign above Christ.'

'But why?' he gasped. 'Why would he do that?'

'We're not sure, Joe, we're really not. But that's why I need to know everything about Father Jansen. His duties, his enemies, his secrets. It's the only way to stop the killers from doing this again. It's the only way to save lives.'

'My Lord! You think they're going to kill again!'

'Yes, and I wouldn't be shocked if they followed the same pattern.'

'You mean more priests?'

'No, Joe, I mean more crucifixions.'

19

Ratchadapisek Road,
Bangkok, Thailand

Raj Narayan had been spoiled his entire life. His father was a powerful man in Nepal, a fact that Narayan pointed out to anyone who got in his way.

Of course there were some drawbacks to his life – the major one being his inability to do anything without it becoming national news. So when Narayan felt the urge to be bad, he was forced to leave Nepal for the anonymity of a foreign country. And this was one of those times.

Ratchadapisek Road is lined with nightclubs and fancy hotels and some of the finest restaurants in all of Asia, yet none of that mattered to Narayan. He made the two-hour flight to Bangkok every month and did it for one reason only: the world-famous massage parlors. Within a span of five blocks, there were over twenty spas. Each of them catered to the needs of foreigners, men who were willing to spend more cash in a single night than the average Thai worker made in an entire year.

Narayan was a good-looking man in his early

thirties. Jet-black hair, dark eyes, and more self-confidence than Muhammad Ali. He had visited Bangkok on several occasions and spent so much cash at Kate's Club, a quiet club off the main drag, that the manager was willing to empty the lounge whenever Narayan was in town.

He sipped on a Bombay martini as the girls, wearing high heels and short negligees, took their seats in the *fishbowl*, a gallery that was tucked beyond a thick wall of glass. Most of the women were Oriental, an even mixture of Thai, Koreans, Chinese, and Japanese. Yet the most revered women in Bangkok were the Asian girls with porcelain skin, for it gave them an appearance of purity, even though that couldn't be further from the truth.

But in this world, appearance was all that mattered.

Women were broken down into four categories: normal, super, sideline, and model – guidelines that determined how much they were paid for their services.

Normal girls were the cheapest of the four and included ladies who were dark-skinned, over the age of twenty-five, or a few pounds overweight. But they were not ugly. Sometimes they possessed a flaw as small as a tiny scar that lowered their value and status.

Super girls, on the other hand, didn't have to be super models as long as they were trained in the art of the 'super massage,' a full-body soap technique done on large rubber mats that was considered an art form in Thailand, one that was taught in special classes by Thai women who were too old to work in a club. To many foreign men, the act was so erotic that they would fly to Bangkok just to be bathed.

The *sideline* girls were the wild cards of the group. They came and went as they pleased, sometimes working in several clubs per night. They usually sat at the bar, hoping to catch the eye of a stranger while trying to convince him to buy her a drink that would ultimately lead to more.

But never with Narayan. The truth was he wasn't interested in normal, super, or sideline girls. In his mind they were undeserving of his attention or his family seed. To him the models were the only group that mattered. They were the cream of the crop. The best of the best. So stunning that many of them had been featured in American magazines like *Penthouse* or *Cheri*.

When it came to these women, Narayan couldn't help himself. They were far too beautiful to ignore. The way they pranced and preened under the spotlight. The way they smiled at him through the glass and looked at him like he was the only man in the world. The way they caressed their skin with gentle touches, rubbing the contours and crevices of their bodies in a naughty fashion, silk nighties hanging off their shoulders like dew on a lotus blossom. There was something about the way they moved that affected him, something deep inside.

He took a deep drag on his cigarette, then blew the smoke through his nose like a hungry dragon. He had already ordered 'the pigs' out of the fishbowl and was concentrating on the twenty women who stood in front of him, trying to figure out who would satisfy him the best. Each of the females had a number pinned to her dress like she was being judged in a beauty pageant. But in this case, the winner wasn't given a tiara or a fancy title like Miss Thailand. She was given a stack of money and a male companion for the next few hours.

Several minutes passed before Narayan was sure. He studied each of the girls, trying to picture what they would do to him and what he would do in return. No need to rush such a critical decision. When he was ready, he nodded toward the manager who ran to his table like an overeager butler. The sudden flash of movement unnerved Narayan's guards, who had positioned themselves near the two main exits and were ready for anything. One of them unholstered his gun and aimed it at the manager, an act that embarrassed Narayan so badly that he ordered his guards out of the club and threatened to have them killed if they came back before he was done.

The manager, familiar with Narayan's temper, took his outburst in stride. In fact, it was the main reason that he waited on Narayan himself. He knew what to expect from his best customer.

'As always, your favorite suite is waiting for you. Have you decided on a companion?'

Narayan rubbed out his cigarette on the tabletop. 'I want them all. For the entire night.'

A round bed sat in the middle of the suite, not far from a hot tub. Steam covered the mirrors that lined the walls and ceiling, a fact that disappointed Narayan. He liked looking at himself when he lay among the models, their oiled-up bodies slithering over him like a pit of horny snakes, taking turns stroking him and kissing him in all the right places. It made him feel like a king.

Narayan smiled with anticipation as he took off his shirt and threw it on the couch, soon followed by his pants and shorts. It was one of the few times that he allowed himself to be vulnerable, which only made things more exciting. No bodyguards, no weapons, no clothes. Nothing to protect him but a condom.

He put on a CD, then adjusted the lights on a nearby panel, turning them down a notch until the room felt like dusk. He heard a soft knock on the door and told them to come in as he strolled toward the bathroom. Since he was a regular, the girls knew exactly what to do. They'd enter, get undressed, and lie on the bed like icing on a cake. At least as many of them as could fit. The others would stand nearby, waiting to take their turn whenever he beckoned.

Narayan heard footsteps in the suite, and his heart started to race. He put his hands in the sink and splashed cold water on his face, trying to contain his excitement. He'd been waiting for this moment since his last trip to Bangkok. It always made him feel like the most powerful man in the world. 'Are you ready?' he called in Thai. 'Because here I come!'

The woman standing in the doorway was breathtaking – and completely naked. So was the one after that, and the one after that. Narayan pawed at all the ladies as they strode past, sometimes grabbing breasts, sometimes grabbing ass, but always doing something, just to let them know that he was their boss for the rest of the night and he could do anything he wanted.

He began by throwing five of them on the bed and spraying them with jasmine-scented body oil, just enough to lubricate every nook and cranny that he might want to explore as the night developed. Once he was positive that each of his beauties was glistening like a lotus blossom, he took a running start and dove on top of them like a little kid. The girls squealed with delight – much of it faked – as they slithered up and down his body, coating him with oil and bringing him to full arousal. From there they took turns pleasing him in a multitude of ways.

An hour later, when he tired of the first five women, he ordered them to clean themselves off and change the sheets while he climbed into the hot tub with four different models who had been sitting off to the side, watching. Narayan told one of the girls to sit on his lap and wash his hair while another rubbed his neck from behind. The other two took turns rubbing his feet and legs, all the while telling him how handsome he was and how horny he made them feel.

But their horniness disappeared when four hooded men burst through the door and charged with military proficiency toward the hot tub. One of the men pointed a gun at Narayan's head, ordering him to stay still, while the others corralled the naked models and forced them into the bathroom. The task was harder than it seemed because most of the women were either coated with oil or bathwater, a mix that made the tiled floor as slick as a frozen pond. The models were screaming and crying and carrying on, all the while slipping and sliding in every direction. Eventually they got to the bathroom by crawling, a conga line of naked asses creeping toward the back of the room.

The scene would've been comic if not for the coldhearted stares of the four men and the gun pointed at Narayan. The men didn't laugh or smile or even stare at the procession of naked women that eased past them. Instead, they held their positions like they were trained to do.

The scourging wouldn't happen there. It was far too public, and Narayan's bodyguards were way too close. Instead the men took him to a remote bungalow outside the tourist traffic of Ratchadapisek Road yet close enough to get the job done quickly.

They started by binding Narayan face-first to the bed frame, his mouth sealed shut and his arms and legs spread wide, completely at their mercy.

The man with the gun tucked it into his belt and pulled out a flagellum, a short whip consisting of three leather thongs with balls of lead affixed to the ends of each. This was the type of weapon that had been used on Christ for his scourging, the one that ripped through his back like a chain saw, the one that sapped him of his strength long before he was attached to the beams of the cross. It would do the same thing to Narayan.

The first blow hit flesh with a sickening crack, followed by the horror of Narayan's muted screams, yet no one would come running. The duct tape muffled most of the sound, and the bungalow was far too isolated to be threatened by interlopers.

For the next several minutes, the man flogged Narayan repeatedly, bruising his legs, shoulders, and back until his skin could take no more and ripped apart like wrapping paper. Blood oozed from the veins and capillaries in his epidermis, then spurted when the subsequent blows sliced through the arteries in his underlying muscle.

Just like two thousand years ago. Just like the death of Christ.

In time, Narayan passed out from the pain but not before the skin hung from his back like the remnants of a tattered flag, each strand soaked in crimson dye.

Yet this was only the beginning. Things would get worse. Much worse.

And it wouldn't stop until their message was revealed to the world.

20

Wednesday, July 12
Orvieto, Italy

Payne and Jones caught an early flight out of London and landed in Rome a few hours later. While they were in the air, Payne called an executive at Ferrari headquarters who was always trying to convince him to buy one of their newest cars and asked him for a loaner. Payne figured, when in Rome . . . well, you know the rest.

Anyway, after getting their luggage, they saw a slick-looking *pisan* in an even slicker suit holding a sign with Payne's name on it. The guy hugged them like they were kin, grabbed their bags, and then bolted down the corridor. Two minutes later he unlocked a side door and led them to a VIP parking lot filled with limos and luxury automobiles. When Payne had talked to this guy's boss on the phone, he told him that he wanted something fast but nothing too conspicuous. Maybe an older model with some miles on it. Needless to say, something got lost in the translation, because Mario pulled up in the sleekest car that Payne had ever seen in his life. A brand-new, bright red, limited-edition Enzo Ferrari, right off the showroom floor. Jones let out a gasp, which might've been followed by seminal fluid, but Payne didn't have the desire to look.

'Jon,' he managed to say, 'I know what I want for Christmas.'

Mario popped open the winglike door and held out the keys. 'Who wanna drive?'

Payne glanced at the Enzo and fantasized about its V-12, 650-horsepower engine. But he realized there was no way he was going to fit his six four frame behind the steering wheel. So he turned to Jones and said, 'Merry Christmas.'

'Are you *serious*?'

'Don't get too excited. I didn't buy it for you. I'm just letting you drive.'

Jones rushed forward to admire the interior while Mario handed Payne the paperwork for the fastest rent-a-car in history.

Payne had been to every continent in the world including an ass-freezing excursion to Antarctica, the result of him losing a bet to a three-star general on the Army/Navy football game. That being said, he couldn't remember ever visiting a place like the Italian countryside. The pastoral beauty of the rolling hills coupled with the ancient architecture took his breath away. Orvieto is sixty-two miles northwest of Rome, meaning they could've made the trip in about ten minutes if Jones had floored it. But they were enjoying the drive so much that they stretched it out over an hour.

In the distance the light gray rock of a 900-foot plateau rose out of the ground like a massive stage, framing Orvieto against the periwinkle sky and suspending it above the olive trees below. Jones noted its strong defensive position on top of the plateau and the single hue that dominated the entire town. 'I bet this place used to be a citadel. See how the buildings blend in with the rock face? They're made from the same stone as the tufa, meaning the city would've been camouflaged from a distance. Just like the Greek city of Mycenae.'

They parked the Ferrari on the west edge of Orvieto, figuring their car was bound to draw attention. After that they didn't have a plan of attack, so they strolled down the first road they saw, soaking in the architecture as they passed through a series of archways. Though slightly weathered, the structures still held their form after centuries of use, contributing to the town's allure and giving a glimpse of a different era. The only splashes of color came from the window boxes outside every window – boxes filled with pink, purple, red, and yellow flowers – and the thick patches of ivy that clung to the side of several buildings.

'Where is everybody?' Jones asked. 'I haven't seen anyone since we started walking.'

No cars, no merchants, no children playing in the

afternoon sun. Their stride was the only sound they could hear. 'Do Europeans take *siestas*?'

'Some Italians might, but not an entire town. Something must be going on.'

Five minutes later they found out what it was.

After walking through a long, curved arch, they spotted hundreds of people jamming the *piazza* in front of them. Everyone was standing with their heads bowed while facing a massive cathedral that seemed completely out of place in the monotone town. Instead of blending in with the light-gray theme of Orvieto, the Gothic church opted for the exact opposite: its triple-gabled facade was filled with a rainbow of multicolored frescoes that depicted scenes from the New Testament. They were surrounded by a series of hand-carved bas-reliefs and four fluted columns.

Moving into the crowd, Payne had a hard time deciding what to examine first: the church or the people. He had never seen a building with a more striking exterior, yet he realized they were there for Dr Boyd and should be scanning the crowd to find him. Their search went on for several seconds until the sound of a handheld bell on the church's steps ended the ceremony. Strangely, with little fanfare, the citizens of Orvieto went back to their daily lives.

'What the hell was that? Everyone looks like zombies.'

'Not everyone.' Jones pointed toward an obese man who stood twenty feet away, taking pictures.

'That guy looks like a tourist. Maybe he can tell us what we missed.'

They approached him cautiously, hoping to determine his country of origin before they attempted a conversation. His body odor screamed European, but his University of Nebraska T-shirt, tattered John Deere hat, and cargo shorts said he was American. So did his stomach, which hung over his belt like a giant beanbag chair.

Jones said, 'Excuse me. Do you speak English?'

The man's face lit up. 'Hell yeah! My name's Donald Barnes.' He possessed the flat tone of a Midwesterner and the handshake of a blacksmith, something he developed by squeezing ketchup on everything he ate. 'I'm glad someone else does, too. I've been yearning for some normal conversation.'

Payne joked, 'That's the problem with foreign countries. Everyone speaks a foreign language.'

'That's just *one* of the problems. I've had the shits since I arrived.'

Talk about too much info. 'So, what did we miss? It looks like the whole town was here.'

Barnes nodded. 'They were honoring the local cop who died in Monday's accident.'

Jones asked, 'What accident? We just got into town.'

'Then you missed all the fireworks. I'm telling you, it was the damnedest thing. This big ol' helicopter crashed into a parked truck near the base of the cliff.'

Payne whistled softly. 'No shit? Did you see it?'

'Nah, but I felt the sucker. The explosion was big enough to shake the whole damn town. I thought Mount Vesuvius was eruptin' or somethin'.'

Jones considered the information. 'I know that this is going to sound weird, but who did the truck belong to? I mean, did someone claim it?'

Barnes looked at Payne, then back at Jones. 'How did you know about the missing driver? The cops have been looking for him, asking everyone in town if we seen him.'

'And have you?' Jones wondered.

He shrugged, causing rolls of fat to gather at his neck. 'They don't know what he looks like and neither do I, so how the hell am I supposed to know if I seen him?'

Barnes had a valid point, even though his grammar – and his diet – could use some work.

Then he lowered his voice to a whisper. 'Some people think the truck belonged to a grave robber, someone who didn't want to be seen. How cool is that?'

'Pretty cool,' Jones whispered, egging him on.

'You know, I was photographing the whole scene until the cops showed up and made me put my camera away. I was gonna complain and all, but we ain't in America, and I figured they might have different rules over here. But I'm telling you, it was the damnedest thing.'

And pretty suspicious, Payne thought. What were

the odds that a helicopter blew up in the same small town that Dr Boyd was visiting, a town with rumors about a *grave robber*? He had to be talking about Boyd. So he asked, 'Are the cops still controlling the site?'

Barnes shrugged. 'I ain't been back since. I've been too busy with artwork and shit.'

Jones nodded. 'We'll be hitting the artwork and shit, too. But, man, we'd love to see the crash site. Can you tell us where it is?'

He pointed to the southeast, describing a few landmarks they'd pass on the way. 'If you don't find it, you can track me down on the east side of town. I hear there's a two-hundred-foot well over there that shouldn't be missed.'

Payne and Jones thanked Barnes for his information, then followed his directions to the crash site, unaware that he'd be murdered less than an hour later.

21

Galleria Vittorio Emanuele II,
Milan, Italy

Boyd sat in a café near the center of the Galleria, a glass-domed shopping mall that housed four neo-Renaissance streets. Tourists strolled past, taking pictures of the zodiac signs that were illustrated on the tiled floor of the atrium. The symbol that got the most attention was Taurus, for local legend said it was good luck to stand on the bull's testicles. Just not for the bull.

'*Professore?*' called a voice from behind.

Boyd froze in terror. His heart pounded in his throat until he saw it was Maria. She had gone inside the café to use the bathroom and had somehow vanished from his mind.

'*Professore,* are you all right? You look pale.'

'I'm fine.' He looked around the small café to make sure no one was listening. 'I've been giving the violence a lot of thought, yet I've gotten nowhere. I simply don't understand it.'

'Me, either,' she admitted.

Boyd paused, taking a bite of his apricot biscotti. His stomach growled in appreciation. 'What about your father? Would he be willing to help?'

'Probably. But he'd hold it against me for the rest of my life.' She took a deep breath, trying to control her emotions. 'You see, he's always viewed women as the weaker sex. So I was a big disappointment from the very beginning. He already had two sons from his previous marriage, yet I guess he wanted another. That's one of the reasons that I moved away from Italy. To prove that I could survive on my own.'

'Which means we won't be calling him for help.'

She nodded. 'Not if I have a say in the matter.'

Boyd sensed that Maria wasn't telling him everything about her father. After all, this was a life-and-death matter, not a simple favor. But Boyd had some secrets of his own, so he wasn't about to push her on the matter. At least not yet.

'And you do,' he assured her. 'Although there aren't many other alternatives. At least none that I can think of without any sleep.'

'Tell me about it. The last time I was this tired I'd spent the entire night in the library.'

Maria yawned, thinking back to her days as an undergraduate when she used to pull all-nighters twice a week. She'd fill a thermos with coffee, gather all the books she needed, then dive into her research until the sun came up.

Research. The word echoed through her mind.

Research. That's what they should be doing. Not sitting on their butts, yawning and bitching. They should be in a library, doing what they were trained to do.

'*Professore*,' she said, excited. 'Let's figure out what the scroll says.'

'Shhh!' Boyd glanced around the café, praying no one heard her. 'Keep your voice down.'

'Sorry,' she whispered. 'But we have nothing better to do. Why not decipher the scroll?'

'But how? This isn't the type of thing I could translate from memory.'

She slid her chair closer. 'What would you need?'

'Privacy, for one. We'd need to find a room where I could work for several hours in peace. Second, I'd need a translation guide. A number of books have been written on early Latin. I'd need one to help me through the obscure passages.'

'Anything else?'

'Yes, the three *P*s. Pencils, paper, and patience. No translation is possible without them.'

Maria smiled as she reached for the check. 'If that's all you need, then we're in luck. There are two schools nearby with world-class libraries.'

They caught a bus to the *Università Cattolica,* hoping that it had everything Boyd needed.

Even though they lacked a college ID, Maria turned on her charms and sweet-talked the male security guard into letting them inside. Her charisma was so effective she even convinced him to unlock a private study room so they could conduct their translation in private.

Once they got settled, the two headed in different directions, searching for materials. Boyd grabbed a map and looked for the location of the library's Latin collection while Maria sat at a computer terminal and entered EARLY LATIN. Within seconds she was staring at the name of the best books in the building. Unfortunately, when she got to the section, he was already emerging from the stacks with several books in his hands.

'Computers,' he laughed, 'are a waste of time and money!'

They returned to the study room, where Boyd unveiled the bronze cylinder. He'd peeked at the scroll during their journey to Milan and realized that it was written in the same language as its brother, the language of the Roman Empire. Now he just needed time to translate it.

'What can I do to help?' she asked.

'Why don't you use your fancy-pants computer skills and research the artwork of ancient Rome? Try to locate the laughing man from Orvieto. He has to be mentioned somewhere.'

Maria went to the same terminal as before and typed ANCIENT ROMAN ART. The computer scanned the library's resources and spat out a long list. Photographs, sketches, maps, and descriptions were available by the hundreds, all of them detailing the colorful history of the Roman Empire. Maria grabbed the first five books she found, then settled into a nearby booth.

As she opened the first book, she realized that she didn't have a plan of attack. Sure, she could flip through page after page, hoping to stumble across a picture of the laughing man, but she knew there had to be a more efficient way to conduct her research.

Giving it some thought, she decided to look in the table of contents, hoping that her theory from the Catacombs – that the laughing man was actually a Roman leader – was accurate. To her surprise, the book classified its artwork by emperor, meaning she could flip through the book's pictures until she reached the last leader of the Empire.

Starting with Augustus, she studied statue after statue and carving after carving, but none of them shared any similarities to the face of the laughing man.

After Augustus was Tiberius, a man who ruled the Empire from 14 to 37 AD, a period that covered the adult life of Jesus Christ. In her mind she felt that Rome's second emperor could be the man she was looking for. Since the laughing man was prominently displayed on the crucifixion archway and Tiberius was the leader of Rome at that time, she thought they might be one in the same. That made sense, didn't it? But as soon as she saw Tiberius's face in a series of statues, she knew it wasn't him. The two men looked nothing alike.

'Damn!' she cursed. 'Who the hell are you?'

Maria searched for the laughing man for two more hours before she finally took a break. Her lack of sleep coupled with her lack of success proved to be a powerful narcotic. So she stumbled down two flights of stairs to the basement lounge and bought the largest espresso they sold. While waiting for her order, she collapsed into a nearby booth and rested her head on the table. Unfortunately, the sound of footsteps cut her nap short.

'*La Repubblica*?' offered the server who brought Maria's order.

She didn't have the energy to read the local paper but accepted it with a nod. The instant he walked away, she brought the steaming cup to her mouth, savoring the rich aroma with several deep breaths before finally taking a sip. 'Aaaaah,' she moaned. 'Much better than sex.'

Within seconds Maria felt rejuvenated, so much so that she started to skim the headlines. She had no intention of reading any articles – she wasn't *that* refreshed – but hoped to catch up on the major news: An Earthquake in India ... A Murder in Denmark ... Violence near Orvieto –

'What?' she gasped.

She skipped back to the story and forced her eyes to read the headline, hoping it was a hallucination. Shockingly, the paper claimed that there'd been a terrorist attack near Orvieto.

Maria put her espresso aside and started to read, devouring the words of the article. The paper claimed that Dr Charles Boyd blew up a bus, killing nearly forty people in the process. It stated his whereabouts were unknown but warned he should be considered armed and dangerous.

With a mixture of emotions, she gathered her things and rushed upstairs to tell Boyd the news. She burst into the conference room, expecting to find him working, his slight frame hovering over the outstretched scroll. But he wasn't there. The ancient document sat in the middle of the table next to a translation of the text, yet his chair sat vacant. It was a sight that made no sense to her. Why did he leave the document unguarded? No way he'd abandon it for a bathroom break or a trip to the card catalog. It was far too important to leave unprotected.

God, she thought, *I hope nothing happened to him.*

She walked forward, desperate for a sign that he was OK, a scrap of paper that said *I'll be back soon* or an envelope with her name on it. Instead, she saw something she wasn't expecting, a scene that confused her even more. Dr Boyd was sitting on the floor in the corner of the room. His knees were pulled to his chest and his eyes were glazed, fixated on the far wall.

'Dr Boyd? Are you all right?'

A blink. A wince. Then a shudder. His entire body trembled as he tried to answer, as if the words he was searching for required every ounce of strength that he could produce. Finally, he managed to whisper three words, 'Christ is dead.'

'What do you mean?' she asked, confused.

'Our discovery will kill Christ. It will murder the Church.'

'What are you talking about? How does one murder the Church? The Church can't be murdered. It's an institution, not a person. Tell me what's wrong. What's going on?'

'Trust me, you don't want to know what I've learned.'

'Of course I do. I risked my life for that scroll. In fact I'm *still* risking my life for that scroll.' She held up the local newspaper and showed it to him. 'We're wanted for murder. You and me. The authorities are blaming us for the deaths of three dozen people.' Actually, Maria's name wasn't mentioned, but she figured a little white lie might work to her advantage. 'Now, unless I'm mistaken, an accusation like that means I'm entitled to full disclosure.'

With trembling hands, Boyd grabbed the paper and read the headline. 'Oh my God. This can't be! They control the police. They control the media. They're not going to stop!'

'What are you talking about? Who isn't going to stop?'

'Them! They must've known about the scroll! That's the only thing that makes sense! They knew it was in there! They knew it all along.'

'Who knew? What are you talking about?'

'Don't you see? They weren't trying to take the

scroll. They were trying to protect it. That's the only thing that makes sense. They must've known it was in there!'

'*Professore,* you aren't making any sense. We found the Catacombs. If someone had known about it, they would've taken credit for it long ago.'

'That's where you're wrong! This isn't the type of discovery that anyone wants to make.'

'What are you talking about? The discovery of the Catacombs is a major find!'

'You're not listening to me. I'm not talking about the Catacombs. I'm talking about the scroll. The scroll is what's important now. The scroll is the key to everything.'

'It's more important than the Catacombs? How is that possible?'

Boyd blinked a few times, trying to come up with an analogy that she would understand. 'The Catacombs were but a chest. The scroll was the treasure within.'

'The scroll is the treasure?'

'Yes. It was the key to the entire site.'

'The frescoes, the graves, the stone chests? They aren't important?'

Boyd shook his head. 'Not compared to the scroll.'

Confused, Maria tried to absorb what she'd been told. Unfortunately, her lack of sleep made the information impossible to comprehend.

We killed Christ. We killed the Church. The Catacombs

aren't important. The scroll is the real treasure. What did any of that mean?

When she'd left Boyd a few hours before, he claimed he'd be able to translate the document without any difficulty. Now he was like this. What could've turned him from a cocky professional to a whimpering zombie in such a short amount of time? Oh dear, she worried, maybe Boyd was having a mental breakdown. Maybe the helicopter, the avalanche, and the bus had finally gotten to him. Maybe he finally realized that their lives were in danger, unless . . .

It dawned on her that she didn't know what the scroll said. She'd left Boyd with the scroll, and when she returned he was wailing about its importance, claiming it was the key to everything. *Everything.* Could it be the key to his outburst as well? Was that possible?

'What did it say?' she demanded. 'If it's that important, I have to know what it says.'

Boyd lowered his eyes. 'I can't tell you, my dear. I just can't. It wouldn't be right.'

'*What?* After all we've been through, you owe me that and more.'

'Don't put me in this position,' he pleaded. 'I'm not trying to be the bad guy. I'm trying to save you. I really am. I'm trying to distance you from further danger –'

'Something more dangerous than snipers and exploding buses? If you haven't noticed, people are

146

trying to kill us, and I have a strange feeling that they're not going to stop until we do something about it. So stop stalling and let me know what we're up against.'

Boyd paused, unsure of what to do. He'd spent his entire career trying to establish historical truths, yet he'd never had the chance to prove anything important until now. But this would be different. This discovery had the potential to shatter an entire belief system, to change the world. It was the type of artifact that archaeologists dream of. One that had modern significance.

'Maria, I know this will sound melodramatic, but what I'm about to tell you is so shocking, so cancerous, it has the potential to destroy Christianity.'

'You're right,' she scoffed. 'That sounds ridiculous. How in the world is that possible?'

Boyd breathed deeply, trying to think of appropriate words of warning. 'If knowledge is the enemy of faith, then the Orvieto scroll is poison.'

22

Arch of Marcus Aurelius,
Tripoli, Libya

Nick Dial knew there was going to be another crucifixion. His theory was confirmed with an early morning phone call. Another victim had been found. This time in Africa.

When Dial arrived in Tripoli, he didn't know what kind of reception he was going to get. Libya was a member country with an active NCB office, yet one thing kept gnawing at him. He was an American walking into Mu'ammar al-Qaddafi's backyard. And he was unarmed.

Not exactly a dream getaway.

Of course, this wasn't a vacation. It was a business trip. He was greeted at the airport by a polite NCB agent named Ahmad, who showed no anti-American bias.

During their drive to the crime scene, Dial steered the conversation away from the case, choosing to talk about the city instead. The most interesting fact he learned was about the streets, which were laid out in a narrow, crisscross pattern and filled with dozens of blind alleyways that were built to confuse would-be attackers. A trick that was taught to them by the Romans.

Most remnants of ancient Rome were destroyed long ago, but not the *Arco di Marco Aurelio a Tripoli*. Chiseled out of white marble in 163 AD, the four-way arch soared to fifteen feet in height and was surmounted by an octagonal dome used to conceal the arch's crown. Time had eroded the outer stones, slowly chipping away at the corners, yet somehow the deterioration only added to its presence. So did the palm trees that surrounded it like centurions on guard duty. They made the monument seem like a mirage, rising out of the marketplace like an oasis. A bloody oasis.

The victim was found just before dawn. An Asian male, early thirties. Very athletic. Very naked. He was strung beneath the monument like a sacrifice to the gods, stretched out on two wooden beams and held in place with three wrought-iron spikes. Two through his wrists and one through his feet. Blood had been smeared across the monument – which arched over his body like a red rainbow – and dripped onto the ground where it collected in puddles of crimson mud.

Ahmad drove his car into the marketplace, honking in hopes of clearing the road ahead. But people continued to haggle for vegetables and handbags and fish, ignoring his horn blasts like he wasn't there. Dial sat fascinated, soaking in the local color from the passenger seat, listening to the Arabic chatter as they bickered back and forth for a better price.

'We will get not further,' Ahmad declared, pointing straight ahead. 'Crowd too many.'

Dial nodded, slowly realizing that the people in front of them weren't bartering for baked goods or a straw basket. They were there as spectators, hoping to see something at the far end of the plaza. Dial looked closer and noticed a slew of satellite trucks on the other side of the monument. Big trucks. The type that could beam TV broadcasts to the four corners of the world.

Dial tried to open his car door but couldn't, due to all the people that engulfed them. A moving, swaying wave that surrounded his car like the ocean surrounds a boat. Undeterred, he stood on his seat and thrust himself through the sunroof, squeezing his body through the opening. Ahmad followed, and before long the two of them were forcing their way through the crowd, literally throwing people out of the way so they could get to the monument. An arch that had been there for nearly two thousand years. An ancient relic that was now a crime scene.

With a single glance, Dial could tell that the Libyan police were better prepared than their Danish counterparts. Armed soldiers carrying Russian assault rifles stood on the sandstone walls that separated the Roman plaza from the curious throng, each soldier ready to pull his trigger at the first sign of trouble. Ahmad got the attention of one of the guards, who let Dial climb over the four-foot barrier where his ID was scrutinized and he was patted down for weapons.

Yet none of this surprised Dial. He was an American in a hostile land. An outsider with a badge. No reason for them to welcome him. He was surprised, though, when he realized that Ahmad wasn't allowed inside. That meant Dial would have to face the cops without a translator.

'You will be good,' Ahmad assured him.

Dial nodded but didn't say a thing, quickly turning his focus to the interior of the garden. It was thirty feet by seventy-five feet and filled with a variety of flowers that added color to an otherwise bleak landscape. But in Dial's mind, that was the reason that the arch was so striking. Its pure white surface looked like it had come from another world. Like an iceberg sitting in the middle of hell.

'Pardon me, Mr Dial?'

Dial turned and saw an elderly man resting against one of the walls, just leaning there in the hot sun like a lizard on a rock. He wore an olive suit and vest, even though the temperature was in the mid-nineties. Oddly, he seemed to be recharging in the sunlight, for his eyes were closed, and his head was tilted back at a forty-five-degree angle. 'I understand there was a similar scene in Denmark.'

Intrigued, Dial took a few steps forward. 'That's correct. And you are?'

'Pardon my manners.' The man opened his eyes and shook Dial's hand. 'My name is Omar Tamher, and I am in charge of this investigation. Normally I would've been reluctant to contact Interpol for a single murder, but due to the circumstances I felt it would be wise for both of us.'

'Thank you for thinking of me.'

Tamher nodded, sizing up Dial before he revealed any details. Dial returned the favor by doing the same with Tamher. Both men were impressed by what they saw.

'At five thirty this morning, a vendor noticed the stains and stopped for a closer look. He was expecting to find paint. He found blood instead.' Tamher took out his pen and pointed to the bottom left-hand corner of the monument. 'The killers started their painting here and finished over there. You can actually see the brush marks on the marble.'

Dial leaned in for a closer look. 'What kind of brush?'

Tamher shrugged. 'It had a wide tip. Wider than the one they used on the sign.'

'Let's talk about the sign later. If I get sidetracked, I tend to get confused.'

Tamher smiled. 'As you wish.'

'Were the stains made with the victim's blood? Or someone else's?'

'No, that's his blood. He had a deep gash in his side, caused by the tip of a sword or a very thin spear. I could be wrong, but I think they used the wound as their paint source, dipping their brush inside his rib cage on more than one occasion.'

Dial didn't blink. 'Why do you think that?'

Tamher crouched, pointing at the dirt. 'We found a thin trail of blood that started under the victim's chest. The path fanned out in several different directions. I'm assuming they kept going back for more, dripping blood as they walked.'

Dial nodded, pleased with Tamher's conclusion. 'Time of death?'

'Approximately five a.m., give or take thirty minutes.'

'Really? That's kind of ballsy, don't you think? Leaving someone to die right before sunrise. Why take a chance like that? Why not slit his throat?'

'I have no idea. Then again, I am not a killer.'

'And why paint the monument? How tall is it, anyway? Fourteen, fifteen feet? That means the killer climbed on someone's shoulders to finish the job. Either that, or this guy's a giant.'

'No ladder marks or signs of giants.'

'What about handprints? Maybe the killer leaned against the arch for balance.'

'No such luck. The monument was clean. The cross was clean. Everything came back clean.'

Dial nodded, expecting as much. The killers had been efficient in Denmark, too. 'Where's the cross now? I can't help but notice that it's missing.'

'Very observant of you, Mr Dial. We wanted to protect it so we moved the entire cross, body and all, to the coroner's office. Forensic specialists are examining it now.'

'What about pictures? Please tell me you took pictures.'

He nodded. 'We documented the entire scene. If you'd like, we can go to my office and look at them. They should be developed by now.'

'In a minute,' Dial said. 'First tell me about the sign.'

Tamher smiled. 'Are you certain you're ready? I don't want to confuse you.'

Dial laughed, glad to see the old guy had a personality. 'I'll try to keep up.'

'It was written in red paint in very neat Arabic script. Four simple words. Very distinct. If you'd like, I'd be happy to translate it for you.'

Dial shook his head. 'Let me take a wild guess. Did it say, AND OF THE SON?'

Tamher nodded, half impressed. 'How did you know?'

'Because I dealt with his father up in Denmark.'

'His father?'

'Never mind . . . So, what can you tell me about the victim? Do we have a name yet? I can run his prints through our database if you think it would help.'

'No, that won't be necessary. We're all very aware of his identity.'

'Good. That'll save me some legwork.'

Tamher paused, trying to decide if Dial was joking. He quickly decided that he wasn't. 'You have no idea who he was, do you? I can't believe no one told you. I just assumed that –'

'Assumed what? What are you talking about? No one told me anything about the victim.'

'Not even your assistant?'

'You mean Ahmad? He wanted to discuss the case on the drive in, but I wouldn't let him. I like forming my own opinions based on what I see, not what someone else has seen.'

'And the crowd? What about the crowd?' He made a wide sweeping motion, indicating the thousands of people that surrounded them. 'You have no idea why they're here?'

Dial shrugged. 'I just figured they were rubber-necking. Same with the media. I deal with crowds all the time. They aren't always this large, but they're crowds nonetheless.'

'Rubbernecking? What is this rubbernecking?'

'Sorry. It's an American term. It means to stare at the scene of an accident.'

'Interesting. We have a similar phenomenon in Libya. We call it *khibbesh*.'

'*Khibbesh*? What in the world does that mean?'

'Rubbernecking.'

Dial smiled. He rarely came across a foreign cop that shared his sense of humor. 'So, tell me, what's the deal? I'm dying to know why everyone's here. I mean, if they aren't *khibbeshing*.'

'Some people are, while others are paying their respects.'

'Their respects? To who, the dead guy?'

Tamher nodded but remained silent.

'Come on! Why would they pay their respects? Who the hell died? The king of England?'

He shook his head, suddenly serious. 'Close. Raj Narayan was the prince of Nepal.'

23

Payne gazed over the edge of the 900-foot precipice, trying to find the site that Barnes had described. No helicopter, no truck, no physical evidence of any kind. Only the fertile farmland of the southern Orvieto valley. 'Where's the damage? There should be some *serious* damage down there. Scattered debris, scorched earth, loss of vegetation, the works.'

They spotted a path about one hundred feet to the left, which took them to the valley floor in a steep, zigzagging pattern. At the bottom they noticed several sets of tire tracks in the grass that were too shallow to be spotted from the high cliffs above.

Jones sank to his knees and studied the wheel prints, an art he'd learned in the military police. 'I'd say there were three trucks heading east at a slow rate of speed, probably within the last twelve hours. Large, industrial trucks. Fully loaded. Possibly salvage equipment. Not your typical four by four pickup. The treads are too large.'

'So we're in the right area.'

Jones nodded. 'It would seem so, yeah.'

They proceeded east, following the tracks like

bloodhounds. They ran parallel to the plateau, bisecting the open space between the olive groves to the right and the rock face to the left and swerved for nothing. The trucks had plowed through a vegetable garden, a small wooden fence, and a patch of white oleander before stopping near a massive pile of rocks. Payne stared at them and realized the front edge of the stones surpassed knee level. There was no way a loaded truck could've cleared this obstacle without gutting its underbelly. There had to be a different solution, something they were overlooking. 'Could these have been dump trucks?'

'Maybe.'

'What if these trucks arrived with stones? Couldn't they have dumped their payload right here? That would account for the abrupt end to the trail. The rocks would've covered it up.'

Jones considered this as he walked several meters to the far side of the pile. 'You might be right. There are dozens of tracks here, fanning out in a wide variety of angles. And unless I'm mistaken, the depth of the tread keeps changing. That means they lessened their weight significantly in a short period of time.'

'So the trucks came speeding along in the middle of the night and dropped several tons of rocks right here in the middle of nowhere . . . Is that what we're saying?'

Jones shook his head. 'This was more than just dumping rocks. This was about picking up, too. Not only did someone beat us to the crash site, they decided to take it with them.'

Tourists were usually the only people to visit *Il Pozzo di San Patrizio* (aka Saint Patrick's Well), the artesian well built in 1527. But due to a rumor that swept through Orvieto, locals were drawn to the beige brick building like freshmen to a keg party.

Payne and Jones spotted them on the other side of the *Piazza Cahen,* a large square in the center of town, and assumed it was the line to see the well. They passed the bus station and approached the back of the throng. Hundreds of people, young and old, clogged the courtyard ahead of them, surrounding the circular building with a silent intensity quite similar to the tone of the earlier funeral. For a better view, Jones climbed on a nearby wall and searched for Donald Barnes. He wanted to see his photos of the Orvieto crash site, hoping they would reveal something important, possibly the reason that the wreckage was hauled out by trucks in the dead of night. 'I don't think they're even letting people inside the well. The door looks barricaded.'

'Maybe tourists go in as a group? Hopefully, Barnes is inside and will come out shortly.'

The comment attracted the attention of a dark-haired man standing nearby. 'I mean not to bother you,' he mumbled in broken English. 'But visits are no more today due to death. No one is inside *Il Pozzo* but the *polizia.*'

'Really? They stopped the tours because of Monday's accident?'

'No, you no understand. Not Monday, *today*. Another person is dead today.'

Jones leapt off the wall. 'What do you mean?'

The man frowned, as if he had trouble understanding the question. 'Ah, like you friend say: two persons on Monday and one person today. We no have violence in Orvieto for long time, now three dead real quick.' He snapped his fingers for effect. 'It's a funny world, no?'

Funny wasn't the *f* word that came to mind. They had come to Orvieto looking for a nonviolent criminal, at least according to Manzak's intel. Now there were three casualties in the small town where Boyd was last seen.

Payne said, 'I thought the pilot was the only person who died on Monday?'

'No, no, no, no,' the man stressed, waving his index finger for emphasis. 'The pilot is from Orvieto. Very good man. Worked with *polizia* for many years. I know him long time. The other man, he no from here. He visit *polizia,* they go for ride, they no come back.'

A theory entered Payne's mind. 'Out of curiosity, was the stranger bald?'

'Bald? What is this *bald*?'

Payne pointed to his head. 'Hair? Did the guy have hair?'

'*Si!* He have hair, just like you. Short, brown hair.'

Payne glanced at Jones. 'Who do you think it was?'

'Could've been anyone. We don't even know if Boyd is involved in this. We could be jumping the gun.'

'Speaking of guns,' Payne said. 'What can you tell us about today's murder?'

The man frowned, then paused to kiss a silver crucifix that dangled around his neck. 'Shhh,' he pleaded. '*Silenzio* is very important tradition in Italy from long time ago. We show respect for the dead with no words. Let the dead sleep in peace, no?'

But Jones wasn't buying it. 'You're not allowed to talk, yet everyone in town is already here. How in the world did that happen? ESP?'

The man eyed the hundreds of people around him, then grinned. 'Sometimes my people not very good at tradition. Word of this crime spread quick.'

Payne smiled. 'What do you know about today's victim?'

The man lowered his voice. 'I hear he found at bottom of well on donkey bridge. He was, how do you say?' He slammed his two hands together in a violent clap. 'Splat!'

'Was it an accident?'

'No, I never say that.' He slid his thumb across his neck in a slow, slashing motion. 'It be tough for him to slip without help. The windows of the well are very small, and American was very fat. He would need much help –'

'American?' Payne blurted. 'The victim was an American?'

'Yes, that is what I heard. A big, fat cowboy.'

Payne looked at Jones, irritated, realizing that Donald Barnes fit the description.

The Italian picked up on their tension. 'What is wrong? I have insulted you?'

'No, not at all. It's just, we think you're describing a friend of ours. We were supposed to meet him here, but we haven't been able to find him.'

The man turned pale, stunned at the revelation. '*Mamma mia!* I so sorry for my manners.' He grabbed them by their arms and pulled them into the crowd. 'Please! I lead you to your friend. I talk to police and let you pay your respects! Come with me! I get you inside the well!'

24

When the Vatican hired Benito Pelati, they knew they were getting one of the top academic minds in Italy. A man of passion. Someone who had dedicated his life to the art of antiquities and had risen to the top of his field. Remarkably, what they didn't know was what fueled his desire. For if they had, they would've done everything in their power to have Benito terminated.

Not just fired but killed. Before he could do any damage.

And the reason was simple: Benito's secret. One passed down from father to son for centuries. Started in Vindobona, Illyria, many generations before, spoken by a guilt-stricken man on his deathbed. Miraculously the secret had survived wars and plagues and tragedies of all kinds. Two thousand years of whispering, concealing, and protecting. And only one family – *Benito's* family – knew the truth about what had happened so long ago.

Still, in all that time, no one had the guts to do anything about it.

No one until Benito's father told him the secret so many years ago.

From that moment on he did everything in his

power to take advantage of the information. He studied longer, worked harder, and kissed every ass he needed to kiss in order get into the inner circle of the Church. And he did it with one goal in mind: to prove that the secret was real. In his heart he knew it was. Yet he realized he needed tangible evidence from the Vatican to back up his family's claim. Otherwise, his ancestors had wasted their breath for the past two millennia because no one in their right mind was going to believe it. And there was no way he was going to let that happen. He'd find evidence in the Archives or die trying.

Benito worked at the Vatican for more than a decade when he came across the first shred of proof. Twelve years of cleaning statues and logging paintings when he found a small stone chest filled with several untranslated scrolls. No one knew where they had come from or what they said due to their archaic language. Yet Benito sensed something special about them, a kind of cosmic connection that made him shove everything else aside and focus exclusively on the scrolls and the carvings on the stone box. There was just something about the main figure that gave him chills. The way the face looked at him. Laughed at him. Like he had a secret he wanted to reveal but was waiting for the right moment. Benito identified with him at once.

He couldn't explain why, but somehow he knew this was the discovery he was looking for.

Word by word, line by line, Benito translated the

scrolls. Each one giving him another clue to a giant puzzle that spanned two thousand years and affected billions of people. A puzzle that started in Rome, spread to the Britains and Judea, then ended up buried in the mythical Catacombs of Orvieto and forgotten by time. A plan hatched by a desperate emperor and carried out by his distant relative. A laughing man immortalized in stone for a secret he possessed.

Finally, Benito had the evidence he was looking for. The proof his family needed.

Now all he had to do was figure out what to do with it. How to take advantage of it.

That proved harder than he thought.

Benito left his office with his bodyguards in tow. One of them carried an umbrella, shading Benito's face from the hot sun as he made his way down Via del Corso. Streams of tourists strolled by at a casual pace, most of them heading toward the Pantheon, the Palazzo Venezia, and the rest of the sites in the center city. The sound of music could be heard above the growl of nearby traffic. The faint scent of garlic wafted from the corner pizzeria.

An hour earlier the Supreme Council had summoned him to give an update on Father Jansen's death. They wanted to know what he had learned since they asked him to look into things on Monday and what the murder meant to the Vatican. But Benito declined their invitation. He told them he wasn't ready. He needed more time to investigate.

This infuriated Cardinal Vercelli, the head of the Council, who was used to kowtowing and ass-kissing from everyone but the pope. Benito stood his ground, though, and told Vercelli that his day was filled with urgent meetings related to the investigation. Benito said he could meet with them on Thursday, if they were interested, but no sooner. This angered Vercelli to no end. Yet he had no leverage when it came to an institution like Benito Pelati, so he eventually relented.

Their meeting was set for Thursday. He would fill them in at that time. When *he* was ready.

Victorious, and with nothing better to do, Benito decided to go for a walk.

25

Dr Boyd knew that Maria would have her doubts about the document, so he started from the beginning. 'When I came to Italy, I was on a specific quest. I was looking for an artifact inside the Catacombs of Orvieto. A scroll that was more important than the vaults themselves.'

Maria pointed to the document. 'You mean our scroll? You came here looking for this and didn't bother to tell me? *Santa Maria!* I don't believe this! What's so special about it?'

'Instead of telling you, let me show you.' He removed a single sheet of paper from his fanny pack. 'This is a photocopy of the Bath document. Notice how the script matches the handwriting on the Orvieto scroll.' He pointed to the similarities in flow and spacing. 'The first scroll was written by *Tiberievm,* better known as Tiberius Caesar. Penned by his own hand in 32 AD.'

Maria's eyes widened. She'd been reading about the second emperor of Rome only a few hours before. 'Tiberius? Are you positive?'

'As sure as a historian can be. Not only was the document signed and dated, but I ran the papyrus and ink through a number of tests. The results came back remarkably clear: the Bath document is approximately two thousand years old.'

'But couldn't it have been written by someone else, a scribe or an assistant of some kind? How do you know it was Tiberius?'

'Good question,' he admitted. 'But I do have an answer. Take a look at the canister we found in Orvieto. Remember the engraving I showed you? I chose not to tell you at the time, but that's a very specific symbol assigned to Tiberius by order of the Roman senate.'

'For what purpose?'

'In his later years, Tiberius became something of a recluse, opting to live on the Isle of Capri, which was a terrible inconvenience for the senate. All decisions had to be delivered over land and sea, and that was a risky proposition. Therefore, the senate devised a way to seal their documents in metal, then added an extra safeguard by assigning a specific symbol to Tiberius. When it appeared on a chambered document, such as the one we found, it meant the information was written by Tiberius's own hand and too critical to be read by a messenger.'

Maria considered the information and accepted it. Two scrolls written by Tiberius, found over a thousand miles apart. Unfortunately, that still didn't explain Boyd's outburst and failed to clarify the connection to Christ. '*Professore,* not to be rude, but what did the document say?'

'The Bath scroll was addressed to Paccius, the top

general in Tiberius's army. You see, the general and his troops had been sent to the Britains to survey the land explored by Julius Caesar several decades before. It was a critical mission, one that would spark further expansion of the Empire. Alas, while Paccius was there, something happened back in Rome, for Tiberius sent a fleet of his fastest ships to locate him and request his immediate return.'

'What had happened?'

'The document didn't say, simply hinting at "a swelling among the slave ranks of Galilee that needs to be profited from."' Boyd paused, letting that information sink in. 'But if you think about it, history gives us a pretty solid clue as to what was taking place. What significant event occurred in that territory less than a year later?'

The color faded in Maria's tanned face. 'The crucifixion of Christ.'

'Exactly! Now maybe you're beginning to understand the importance of this.'

She nodded, trying to retain her focus. 'What else did it say?'

'Tiberius said if he died before Paccius's return, then Paccius should complete the plot by using the records that would be stored in the newly built haven at Orvieto. He said the plans would be "locked in bronze and sealed with the Emperor's kiss." Obviously a reference to the engraved canister that we found.'

'But since the scroll was still sealed, we can assume

that Paccius returned before Tiberius's death, right? They had a chance to talk in person?'

Boyd shrugged. 'That's an assumption at best. You must remember that both canisters were found sealed. Not only the one in Orvieto but the one in Bath as well.'

'So what are you saying? Paccius never got the message?'

'That's one possibility. Another is a duplicate set of messages. I figure, why dispatch a single canister when you're sending an entire fleet to locate someone? What if the message ship sank? The scroll would've been lost forever. So for safety's sake, why not send two scrolls or more?'

Maria nodded her acceptance. It seemed like a reasonable theory. 'What does history say about Paccius? What happened to him?'

'For some reason, his death was never chronicled. One minute he was the second most powerful cog in the Roman Empire, the next minute he was gone. Vanished, without a trace. Of course, his disappearance could mean many things. He might've died in the Britains or drowned at sea on his journey home. Or he might've sailed directly to Judea in order to carry out the emperor's wishes.' Boyd shook his head in confusion. 'Whichever it is, I do know this: Tiberius was a tactical genius, known for his brilliant mind and precise planning. And according to this scroll, he figured out a way to use Christ as a pawn in the most ruthless plot of all time.'

'How in the world did he do that?'

Boyd took a deep breath, struggling to find the appropriate words. How do you challenge someone's belief system without upsetting her?

'Maria,' he stuttered, 'why do you believe Christ is the Son of God?'

'Why? It's what I was taught as a child. It's what I was raised to believe.'

'But you're no longer a child. You reached the age of independent thought long ago. At some point you started challenging your parents. Whether it was Santa Claus or politics, you eventually questioned what you were taught.'

'Yes, but –'

'But what? You should draw the line at religion? If anything, religion should be the first concept that you challenge because it's the most personal thing that a person can have. Religion is what you believe, not what you're told. It's what you feel, not what others expect.'

'But I believe in Christ! I've studied the Bible, gone to Mass, and spoken to several priests. And guess what? I believe in God and Jesus Christ. It just feels right to me.'

His tone softened. 'If I challenged your faith, would it bend under the weight of my words?'

'Not a chance. I believe what I believe. Your comments aren't going to change that.'

'And what about evidence? Would your faith crumble in the face of new evidence?'

She pondered the word *evidence*. 'Does this have something to do with the scroll? You have new evidence about my religion?'

'*Our* religion. I'm a Christian as well.'

'So this isn't about the Church? This is about Christ?'

Boyd nodded, unwilling to look her in the eye. 'And the news isn't good.'

Maria didn't know what he meant, yet the claws of doubt started ripping at her faith. If the scroll's message was as devastating as Boyd insinuated, there was a chance that her entire belief system was about to be shattered. 'What does it say? I need to know what it says.'

Boyd took a deep breath. 'You realize, once I tell you, there's no turning back.'

'We reached that point *long* ago. Please, tell me what the scroll says.'

'I will, but first you must realize their writing style was different than ours. Run-on sentences were common. They just rambled on incessantly, rarely stopping for changes in subject.'

Maria knew all about it because Boyd was doing it at the moment. 'Just read it, sir. Please.'

'OK, OK. This is what Emperor Tiberius wrote.'

Tiberius Caesar Augustus to my heirs and successors.

The matters of wealth, whether trivial or colossal, rest on our shoulders, the task of all rulers, past and present, for all eternity. By doing my duty, I have filled the coffers of this great land, seizing a share from all citizens that is rightfully Rome's, recording their riches while eliminating the Empire's burden, alas their gifts are not sufficient, for Mercury thirsts for more. Upon conquering the Britains, the vastness of our domain will be detrimental, the management of snow and sun, lands more varied than Cupid and Mars, will further divide the lives of our people, the rich shall welcome the gifts from abroad as the poor suffer from the onus of our foreseeable debt. To avoid the impending poverty of our citizens, I have concluded that drastic measures must be taken, the scarcity of —

'Hold up! What does any of that have to do with Jesus?'

Boyd sighed at her impatience. 'Nothing directly, but indirectly it has everything to do with him. The scarcity of wealth in the Empire forces Tiberius to hatch this drastic scheme. According to the text, it is the central reason for his plot against Christ.'

Maria half nodded, still unsure of the scroll's opening section. 'That part about seizing a share from all citizens — was he talking about taxes?'

'He was indeed. Tiberius was known as a top-notch fiscal administrator. Most historians feel that economic policy was the strength of his reign, at least until his mental demise. At the end of his emperorship, he was something of a loon.'

'And when he wrote about the Empire's burden, he was talking about balancing the budget?'

'Exactly.'

Maria impressed herself. She understood more than she'd originally thought. 'What was that thing about the Britains? You read something about winter and summer, and I got lost.'

'Not winter and summer,' he corrected. 'Tiberius mentioned snow and sun. He said, "the management of snow and sun ... will further divide the lives of our people." Meaning once they conquered the Britains, the Empire would be too large for its own good. Rome would stretch from the land of snow, Britain, to the land of sun, Egypt. And in Tiberius's opinion, that was too much for their economy to handle.'

'But if Tiberius knew Britain was going to hurt the Empire in the long run, why go after it?'

'He claims it was for Mercury, the Roman God of Commerce. Tiberius said that Mercury thirsted for more. I guess that's his way of saying he didn't have a choice in the matter. He felt the gods would grow unhappy if Rome became content with what they had.'

'Even if acquiring more was a bad thing?'

Boyd nodded. 'But the greed doesn't stop there. You haven't heard anything yet.'

To avoid the impending poverty of our citizens, I have concluded that drastic measures must be taken, the scarcity of public wealth must be avoided at all cost, as a failure to maintain the excellence of the Empire would be attributed to a delinquency of leadership, a claim that would insult the accomplishments of Augustus before.

Word has arrived from the east that the latest Messiah has surfaced, a man, unlike the dozens that have come before him, he who reeks of piety and selflessness, a charmer blessed with throngs of disciples, power of persuasion, the gift of miracles. Tales of healing and resurrection emerge from the desert with the regularity of scorpions, but twice as deadly, for insects are easily squashed. Herod Antipas, ruler of Galilee, speaks of pride swelling among the slaves, rebellions against Roman authority, gathering of masses near Capernaum. Some feel that this threat should be extinguished, eliminated through force of will and power of sword, disposed of in its infancy like the sons of Bethlehem. But I am not one to concur, why kill a cow that has been presented by the gods? Milk it, and its sweet nectar can nourish for a lifetime.

Boyd paused, allowing Maria to absorb the message of the scroll's middle section.

She said, 'There's no doubt that this is about Jesus. The reference to healings and resurrections, the gathering of masses in Capernaum. That's where his ministry was located, right next to the Sea of Galilee.'

He nodded. 'The Old Testament referred to it as the Sea of Chinnereth, but you are right. Jesus used Capernaum as a gathering place for his flock.'

'I can't believe this. We're holding a document

that refers to Christ in the present tense. This is so wrong! I mean, it compares him to a cow that should be milked!'

'But to Tiberius, Jesus wasn't God. He was a dangerous con man. Like he mentioned, dozens of men had already come forth and claimed to be the Messiah, and most of them had throngs of followers as well. So to Tiberius, Jesus was just another in a long list of frauds.'

'I guess so, but ... I don't know. I don't know how to feel about this.'

'Don't feel, my dear. That's not your job. Your duty is to examine. Try to distance yourself from the message, especially from the part I'm about to read. If you don't, you'll be completely consumed by its message, because it's worse than you can possibly imagine.'

If the hungry are promised bread, they'll fight until their bellies are full; this much is assured by history, written by the action of men and the nature of their spirit, but a question plagues my slumber: does it matter where the feast comes from? Would a starving man turn down a meal if it is offered by his enemy? Perhaps, for fear of poison, but what if the food is presented in a manner that he'd welcome? Would the bread not be accepted with outstretched hands? I proclaim it would. Yea, the people of Judea are famished, clinging to hope and the promise of salvation, completely ignorant of Roman gods and the rightful way to live, they look for the promised one to emerge from their flock, the one who is truly their Messiah. This cannot be prevented; no war, no punishment shall remove the coming of the one from their scripture; they search for him, they pray for him, they wait for him and shall anticipate him until his arrival has been trumpeted by the masses. Why not give him to them? Let us feed their hunger with our choice of food, allowing them to feast on the coming of their savior, they can drink in their Christ and revel in his teachings, words that shall threaten us not, for we know he is merely a pawn that we have lifted to the level of Jupiter.

For such a ruse to succeed, there must be no doubt among the Jews; they must witness an act of God with their own eyes, a feat so magical, so mystifying, that future generations will sing of its splendor for eternity, ending their search for the coming Messiah once and for all, for they will think he has already come. Belief in his presence must be widespread, not birthed on the fringes of their sun-drenched land, passed from traveler to traveler in rumor alone, it shall begin in their greatest populace, spread from the heart of Jerusalem like an unstoppable plague, devouring everyone in Judea like a hungry beast. Once this occurs, once no doubt of the Christ remains, Rome shall be in a position to profit, using the Jews' unyielding faith against them and their riches to our advantage. We will mock their beliefs in public while collecting their donations in private; we will order them to worship Roman gods, knowing they will cling to their Messiah like children to a teat, but this is what we want, for the more they worship a fake God, the weaker they shall become, and from this weakness, we shall profit, yea, we shall control their bodies and their spirits as well. For the good of all things Roman, we shall begin at once, using the Nazarene as our tool, the one I have chosen as the Jewish Messiah.

Farewell, 29th August

Boyd pushed his notebook aside after reading the passage, and braced for her response. In truth, he half expected a dozen questions about the text or a volatile shouting match where she challenged everything that he had said. But what he got was the exact opposite. Maria remained quiet, distant, the color in her cheeks completely vacant, her bloodshot eyes filled with moisture.

There was no need to clarify anything. Maria grasped the scroll's significance on her own.

Amazingly, if the message on the scroll was accurate, then the miracle of Jesus Christ and the foundation of Christianity were based on the biggest scam of all time.

26

The office was bare except for some furniture and a few filing cabinets. No personal touches of any kind. It was the type of room that would make Nick Dial quit his job if he had to call it his own. Yet it was exactly what he expected in a Tripoli police station.

Omar Tamher walked in with photos of the autopsy and spread them across the desk. Sheepishly, Dial took out his bifocals and hooked them over his ears, somehow embarrassed that he couldn't see well enough on his own.

'Nick, what do you think? Any similarities to Denmark?'

Dial nodded, even though this was his first time with the pictures. 'Jansen had the same body type as Narayan. Roughly the same height and age. Both men were in good physical condition, which tells me they weren't chosen at random. They were picked for a reason.'

'Why do you say that?'

'If you were looking for an easy target, would you choose these guys? No, you'd go after someone who was older or injured. Someone you could overpower. Maybe even a female. But a young guy in good shape? Not likely. Too many things could go wrong.'

'Anything else?'

'These wounds are consistent with Jansen's. Spikes were driven through the wrists and feet while he was unconscious. Too much screaming otherwise.' He pointed to one of the autopsy photos, a close-up of Narayan's left wrist. 'See how the wound spreads away from the spike? The same thing happened in Denmark. The body weight is too heavy for the rods to handle. Something had to give, and it wasn't going to be the spikes. In time the surrounding tissue starts to tear, same with the veins, tendons, etc. A very messy way to die.'

Tamher nodded. 'The coroner said the chest wound was the fatal blow.'

Dial sorted through the pile until he found a close-up of Narayan's rib cage. 'Looks identical to Jansen's. Probably done with a spear. At least that's what the Bible tells us.'

'And the vandalism? Any theories?'

He shrugged. 'They didn't paint anything in Denmark, even though there were plenty of walls nearby. That suggests that the arch was an impulse act, not a premeditated one.'

Tamher frowned. 'They used a brush, Nick. That seems planned to me.'

'Maybe, maybe not. The brush could've been in the back of their van or in the toolbox where they kept their spikes. I mean, you didn't find any ladder marks, did you? That means they weren't completely prepared for the painting.'

'True, but . . .'

'Listen, I'm not ruling out the possibility. It might be an important clue or nothing more than a killer marking his territory. I can't tell you how many bodies I've found that were soaked in somebody else's piss.'

'Really?'

Dial was surprised that Tamher had never seen that in Libya. Then again, maybe it was a European thing. 'We'll know more once we find the next vic. Patterns will start to emerge.'

'The next one?'

'You don't think they're done, do you? Not with the Holy Ghost waiting in the wings.'

'The Holy Ghost?'

'You know, the Father, Son, and Holy Ghost? There's bound to be a victim for him. And after that, who knows? They might start on the Hail Mary.'

Tamher frowned as he took a seat behind the desk. Dial could tell that something was bothering him so he put the crime photos down, waiting for Tamher to fill the silence. It was a tactic that worked on cops and criminals alike.

'Why did they come here? We're a Muslim nation not a Christian one. Where do we fit?'

'Beats me,' Dial admitted. 'Then again, maybe the killers were looking for some R & R after they dumped the body. I've traveled all over the world to every continent on the globe, but I've never seen a country like this. Libya is simply gorgeous.'

Tamher beamed with pride, which was what Dial was hoping for. He knew how crucial it was to stay on Tamher's good side. Without him, his access to the crime scene would disappear.

'Unfortunately, it's way too early to label these as Christian murders. I wish that wasn't the case, but what choice do we have? The fact is that Narayan wasn't a Christian – he was a Hindu – so this might not be about religion.'

'You don't really believe that, do you?'

'Not really. Then again I don't know what to believe.'

In Dial's mind the only common thread between the murders was the way that they killed. These men were kidnapped, shipped to a specific location, and then crucified like Jesus Christ. But why? What were the killers trying to say? What did these guys have in common?

Not much, according to Interpol.

Jansen was a devout Catholic who grew up in Finland as the middle child in a middle-class family. He lived a clean life – no drugs, no sexcapades, no legal problems – and knew at a very early age that he wanted to join the priesthood. Dial was still waiting for additional information from Cardinal Rose, but according to preliminary reports, everyone thought very highly of him.

The same could not be said about Narayan, who spent half his time in bars and the other half in bed. He was one of several princes in Nepal, a country that had seen its share of royal tragedies in recent years, the most famous occurring in July 2001, when Crown Prince Dipendra pulled out an M16 and an Uzi at a family party and killed the king, queen, and princess.

Dial shook his head as he pondered the two victims. What did these guys have in common? Different religions. Different homelands. Different lifestyles. Their only connection was their gender and the way they died. Tortured, then nailed to a cross.

Crucified like Jesus Christ.

27

By claiming to be friends of the victim, Payne and Jones were granted immediate access to *Il Pozzo di San Patrizio*. To guarantee their cooperation a young deputy was assigned to lead them down the 248 steps to the bottom of Saint Patrick's Well, a sixteenth-century landmark named for its supposed similarities to the Irish cave where Saint Patrick used to pray.

As they began their descent, Payne lagged behind, trying to figure out how they had built it. Two diametrically opposed doors led to separate staircases, each superimposed over the other, which prevented descenders from colliding with ascenders. The original concept was conceived by Leonardo da Vinci, who devised the stairs for an Italian brothel so its patrons could sneak in and out of the whore-house with their anonymity intact. The customers were so pleased that word spread about the stairs, and the design was implemented in a number of new structures, including the pope's well. Another stroke of genius was the way the architect took advantage of natural light. The stairs were illuminated by a spiraling series of seventy hand-carved windows that allowed sunlight to flow through the gaps in the roof and filter to the outer circumference of the well, providing travelers with more than enough light to fetch water.

'Jon?' Jones called from below. 'Are you coming?'

Payne picked up his pace until he encountered Jones around the next turn in the stairs.

'Our escort was worried about you. Barnes died in here an hour ago, and the cops don't want a repeat performance.'

'I don't blame them. This place would be a bitch to clean.'

'Plus it's a historic landmark. The cop told me while Pope Clement VII was hiding in Orvieto, he was afraid his enemies would cut off his water supply. To prevent that from happening, he ordered this well to be dug. All told, it's 43 feet wide and 203 feet deep.'

'Damn! The pope must've been thirsty.'

'It wasn't just for him. See how wide the steps are? That's so pack animals could make it down the slope without falling. They were actually allowed to drink right from the source.'

Payne winced. 'That's pretty disgusting. No wonder Barnes had the runs.'

'Thankfully, the town doesn't rely on the well anymore. Otherwise I'm sure their water would taste funny for the next few weeks.'

'Oh yeah, why's that?'

Instead of speaking, Jones pointed to the violent image that gleamed in the natural spotlight. Donald Barnes lay facedown in the center of the well, his ample body bisecting the wooden bridge that connected the two staircases. Members of the local police poked and prodded him for clues as blood oozed from his ruptured gut, dripping into the water and turning it dark crimson.

The cop in charge of the investigation saw their approach and tried to prevent them from seeing Barnes sprawled in a puddle of his own blood. Unfortunately, he wasn't quick enough. 'Sorry about that,' he said in clear English. 'I know this must be difficult for you.'

Payne and Jones nodded, not knowing what to say.

The detective pulled out a notebook and pen. 'We heard his name was Donald.'

'Yes,' Payne said, 'Donald Barnes. He was an American.'

'As are you,' the cop said, never lifting his eyes from his pad. He took their names and addresses, then asked, 'Were you friends with the deceased for long?'

'Not really. We just met him today at the funeral.' Payne studied the cop, waiting for some kind of reaction. 'He willingly gave us assistance when we needed it. Directions, a list of sites to see, and so on. He also described the helicopter crash that killed your colleague on Monday.'

The cop nodded, still not reacting. 'Any idea where he was from, or where he was staying?'

Payne shrugged. 'Midwestern U.S., maybe

Nebraska. At least that's what his T-shirt says. And as far as his hotel goes, we're not sure. We didn't know him long enough to find out.'

As Payne finished speaking, the young officer who'd led them down the steps approached the detective. He whispered a number of Italian phrases, then held up a single key adorned with the monogram GHR. The detective smiled at the discovery. 'Gentlemen, are we through here?'

Jones shook his head, then lied. 'Actually, there's one more thing. We took a few pictures with Donald in front of the cathedral. Could we possibly have the film as a remembrance?'

The detective glanced at the body and frowned. 'Camera? We didn't find any camera. No wallet, film, or anything of value ... In my opinion this was just a robbery that went bad.'

Payne and Jones knew *that* was bullshit. But the last people they were going to tell were the cops. If they did that, all the cops were going to do was get in their way.

Regrettably, that ended up happening anyway.

As they emerged from the well, Jones growled, 'This wasn't a robbery. It was an assassination.'

Payne pushed through the crowd of onlookers. 'An assassination? How do you figure?'

'Because it's too coincidental to be anything else. This town hasn't seen violence in years, now there are three deaths in two days. Plus the latest victim just happens to be someone with proof of the crash site. C'mon! What else could it be?'

'So let me get this straight. We started with one case, and now we're up to three: Dr Boyd, the stolen crash site, and Donald Barnes.'

'Yep, that about sums it up.'

'Damn! We aren't very good at this.'

Jones laughed. 'Any ideas on where to start?'

Payne nodded. 'Let's stick to Boyd, since that's the reason we're here. Let's assume it was his truck at the bottom of the cliff. I mean, no one's come forward to claim it. Plus there was a police chopper hovering above it and rumors of a grave robber in the area. That means either he died in the explosion, he's still in Orvieto, or he left town some other way.'

'Makes sense to me.'

'And unless he had an accomplice, he either stole a car or bummed a ride.'

'Or used public transportation.'

'And since there aren't any airports in town, the odds are pretty good that he used a bus.'

Payne looked at Jones, then both of them looked at the row of buses parked on the far side of the *piazza*. Seconds later they approached the one-story terminal that sat on the northern end of the square. A silver bus idled near the entrance, delayed by an elderly porter who checked tickets with one hand while grabbing the butts of unsuspecting females with the other.

Jones said, 'I'll talk to the guy at the front counter and show him Boyd's picture. Why don't you look for a map so we know where we're going?'

Payne glanced around the lobby and spotted a rack of brochures leaning against the far wall. Restaurant guides, museum tours, and hotel listings – most of which were written in English. A pamphlet for La Badia, a twelfth-century ecclesiastical complex that had been converted into a local hotel, caught his eye. The blend of wooden beams and tufa walls reminded him of ancient times until he noticed a television stuffed in a tiny stone alcove. Talk about a *feng shui* killer.

Payne returned the brochure and picked up another, this one for the Grand Hotel Reale. It wasn't as well-maintained as La Badia, yet he got the feeling that it used to be something special. He marveled at the beautiful frescoes and the antique furniture in the lobby, plus the large fountain that was carved out of a shade of marble that –

'Jon? Are you ready?'

Payne turned toward Jones who was standing near the entrance. 'Yeah, I'll be there in a second. I was just –' He stopped in midsentence, thinking back to Saint Patrick's Well. Payne couldn't believe it had taken him so long to put everything together.

'You were just what?' Jones walked toward him. 'I got some good information from the front counter and . . . Are you OK? You look kind of puzzled.'

'Not at all. In fact, I'm feeling rather enlightened.' Payne handed him the brochure for the Grand Hotel Reale. 'What do you think?'

Now Jones was the one who was puzzled. 'About what?'

'The hotel. Could this be where Barnes was staying?'

He flipped through the brochure. 'I have no idea. Why?'

'Remember the young cop in the well? What did he find in Barnes's pocket?'

Jones replayed the incident in his mind. 'A key with his initials on it, right?'

'Close, but not quite. It had someone *else's* initials, not his. It had GHR, not DB.'

'Yeah, that's right: GHR. But what's that have to do with —'

And that's when he realized the same thing that Payne had. The key chain didn't have Barnes's initials on it because he didn't own the keys. And where does a tourist get keys? At a hotel. And what hotel in Orvieto had the initials GHR? The Grand Hotel Reale.

'Holy shit! Do you think the cops are there yet?'

'Probably not,' Payne guessed. 'They lost one of their officers on Monday, and the rest are probably at the well. No way they're there yet.'

'So?' The mischief in Jones's eyes told him everything he needed to know. He was going to the hotel whether Payne was joining him or not. 'What do you think?'

Payne smiled. 'I think we should see how long it takes you to pick an Italian lock.'

28

Maria Pelati was a woman torn, an archaeologist with a guilty conscience. She was possibly sitting next to the most important document ever written, yet all she wanted to do was set it on fire. But how could she? If it was real, it would bring her more fame and fortune than she'd ever dreamed possible. At the same time she knew she'd never be able to enjoy it because of all the suffering the scroll would cause.

A billion Christians suddenly doubting the existence of Christ because of her discovery.

There were so many thoughts swirling through her brain she didn't know what to focus on first. The scroll. Its ramifications. Her beliefs. The truth was, she needed to think about everything, but before she could do that, she needed to ask Dr Boyd one simple question. And his answer would help determine her plan of attack.

'Sir,' she said quietly. 'Are you sure that the scroll is real?'

The sound of her voice startled Boyd, who was lost in thought. 'I believe so, yes. I still need to run some tests to be certain. However, the grandeur of the Catacombs seemed beyond reproach, too real for this to be a ruse.'

'And your translation . . . is it accurate?'

'There's always a chance that I misinterpreted a word or two. Still, the basic message would remain the same. Tiberius handpicked Jesus as the Jewish Messiah and did so for the financial gain of the Empire.'

'But how is that possible? I mean, how does someone create a Messiah?'

'That, my dear, is a mystery that wasn't addressed in the scroll.'

She nodded, a million questions racing through her mind. 'And what about you? What do you think? Is any of this feasible?'

He paused, looking for the courage to answer. 'The possibility had crossed my mind. Although I was raised a Christian, I'm also a scholar, which means I'm forced to leave myself open to a world of possibilities. Even if the evidence goes against my beliefs.'

He paused, figuring out what to say next. 'Maria, the truth is we found Tiberius's seal on the cylinder and his handwriting on the parchment, which gives us plenty of reason to believe that he composed the note. And if he wrote it, then we'd be foolish not to examine every alternative, including the possibility that he found a way to pull this off.'

Maria swallowed hard. 'Even if that means Jesus wasn't the Son of God?'

Boyd nodded.

Silence filled the room for several seconds. The

only thing heard was the rumble of the room's air conditioner. Finally, Maria said, 'I'm sorry, *professore,* I don't think I can be a part of this anymore.'

Then, before he could say anything, Maria left the library and went on a long walk, oblivious to the fact that she would soon be making a key discovery during her journey through Milan.

Tourists marveled at the view from the roof of *Il Duomo* while Maria Pelati sat in the corner, motionless, like one of the 2,245 marble statues that decorated the cathedral. On a normal day, she would've mingled with the rest of the people, admiring the spires that soared above her or contemplating the 511 years it took to build. However, this wasn't a typical afternoon.

After pondering the scroll for over an hour, she emerged from her trance and realized she was dripping with perspiration. In an attempt to cool off, she eased down the thirty-degree slope of the slate roof toward a portal in one of the spires, yet found neither the breeze nor shade she was hoping for. *The heck with this,* she thought. *I'm probably going to hell for finding the scroll so I might as well sit in some air conditioning while I still have the chance.*

Maria passed an elaborate row of statues that depicted a medley of saints, knights, and sinners in a variety of poses. Despite their exquisite craftsmanship, none of them grabbed her attention until she approached the final one, a majestic man in a flowing toga. Strangely, there was something about his face that seemed familiar. The sweeping curve of his lips. The lighthearted twinkle in his eyes. The arrogant protrusion of his jaw. The cocky smile on . . .

'Oh my God!' she blurted. 'The laughing man!'

Stunned by her discovery, Maria considered racing back to tell Dr Boyd but realized if she didn't scour the church for information, he would insist on a return trip – a trip where he would lead the investigation. And that was something she wanted to avoid.

Thinking quickly, she decided the easiest way to get background material on the statue would be to have a conversation with one of the tour guides. There were several on the roof alone, so she infiltrated a group near the tallest spire and listened to the guide's lecture. 'The tower stands three hundred and sixty-seven feet above the plaza, an astonishing height when you consider the age of this remarkable building. To comprehend how high we are, let's walk toward the edge of the roof . . .'

When the group trudged forward, Maria approached the tour guide, a man in his early thirties. 'Excuse me,' she said in Italian. 'I was wondering if you could answer a question.'

One glance at her smoldering brown eyes was all it took. The rest of the group could fend for themselves. 'Yeah, um, sure. Whatever you need,' he replied.

'Thanks.' She placed her arm in his and pulled him away. 'There's a statue over here that looks so familiar. Do you think you could tell me about it?'

The tour guide grinned confidently. 'I'd be happy to. I've been working here for nearly five years. I know everything about this place.'

'Everything? That's amazing. Because this place is so big.'

'You're telling me,' he bragged. 'It's five hundred and twenty feet long and two hundred and eighty-four feet wide. That's bigger than a soccer field. In fact, it's the third-largest cathedral in the world.'

'And yet you know so much about it. You must be *so* smart.'

He beamed. 'Which statue did you want to know about? I've got stories about them all.'

Maria pointed to the laughing man. 'What can you tell me about him?'

The guide's cocksure smile quickly faded. 'Not very much. That's one of the few objects that's shrouded in mystery. When I was first hired, I asked the curator of the local museum about it, and he claimed it was the oldest artifact in the church, pre-dating the other statues on the edifice by hundreds of years. Plus it's made from a different type of stone than the others. Most of *Il Duomo* is made of white Carrara marble, but not this guy. He was made from marble that's foreign to Italian soil. The only place that it can be found is in a small village near Vienna.'

'Austria? That seems kind of strange.'

He agreed. 'Even stranger is this monument's

placement. Look at the other statues around us. Does he seem to belong with any of them? The others depict the struggle of the common man in their quest for God, but not him. He's *anything* but a peasant. Yet someone in the Church decided to place him here at the end of the series. Why they did we're not really sure.'

Maria closed her eyes and thought back to the Catacombs. There, just like here, the laughing man seemed completely out of place. First, in the middle of Christ's crucifixion scene, grinning his evil grin. Next, on the hand-carved box that contained Tiberius's scroll. And now, his unexplained appearance on *Il Duomo*.

This guy had a habit of popping up where he didn't fit. But why? Or better yet, who?

'One more question before I let you go. Do you have any theories on who he might be?'

The guide shrugged. 'The only clue that we've found is the letter on his ring.'

'Letter? What letter?'

The tour guide pointed at the statue's hand. 'You can't really see it from down here. The man who cleans the monuments noticed it last year. Still, we have no idea if the letter is the subject's initial or the artist's – or neither.'

'What letter is it?' she demanded. '*A, B, C*?'

'The letter *P*, as in Paul.'

Or in Paccius, she thought to herself. Excited by the possibility, she kissed the tour guide on both cheeks.

'Thank you! Thank you so much! That's the letter I was hoping you'd say.'

'It was? Why's that?'

But instead of answering, Maria ran off to tell Dr Boyd the good news, convinced she had discovered proof of the laughing man's identity.

29

Nick Dial unzipped his portfolio and carefully removed its contents. Inside, he had the portable bulletin board that he'd filled with a series of pictures, notes, and maps.

After hanging it in the Libyan police station, he tried to figure out what he needed to add. Definitely some pictures of Narayan. Maybe some close-ups of the bloody arch. He also needed to start drawing connections to the Jansen case, pointing out similarities, no matter how ridiculous they might seem. He knew the preposterous often turned out to be the most profitable.

Glancing at Jansen's side of the board, the first thing he noticed was his unblemished skin. Why savagely beat the second victim, tearing his back to shreds, but leave the first victim untouched? Did they run out of time with Jansen? Did something spook them? Or were they following the pattern that Dial had seen several times before: the more victims that someone kills, the more comfortable the killer becomes?

Or maybe, Dial thought, this had nothing to do with comfort. Maybe this had something to do with religion, something he was overlooking. Just to be safe, he decided to call Henri Toulon at Interpol headquarters to get additional background information on Christ's death.

'Henri,' Dial said, 'how are you feeling after your night of drinking?'

Toulon answered groggily, 'How did you know I was drinking? Are you back in France?'

'No, but you always have a night of drinking.'

'*Oui,* this is true.'

'Did you have a chance to research that Shakespeare stuff that we discussed?'

Toulon nodded, jiggling his ponytail like a tassel. 'Yes I did, and I decided it was bullshit. Nothing more than a red herring to lure you away from the truth.'

'I was hoping you were going to say that. My gut told me to follow the religious side of this case, so that's what I've been doing. I would've been so screwed if *Hamlet* came into play.'

Toulon smiled as he placed an unlit cigarette between his lips. 'Was there anything else?'

Dial stared at Narayan's autopsy photos. 'Just one more thing. The victim here is different than the one in Denmark. I thought you might have some theories on it.'

'What kind of differences?'

With his finger Dial traced the marks on Narayan's back. 'This one was beaten with some sort of a whip. And I mean beaten badly. We found more blood than skin.'

'The victim was scourged?'

'Scourged? Is that what the Bible calls it?'

'That's what everyone calls it. It was so common back in the day that John didn't even have to explain it in his Gospel. In John 19:1, he wrote, they "took Jesus and had him scourged." No need to go into details. Everyone knew what it meant.'

'Everyone but me,' Dial muttered. 'What did the weapon look like?'

'They used a whip called a flagellum. In Latin it means "little scourge."'

'There was nothing little about Narayan's injuries. It cut right through his muscle.'

Toulon nodded. 'That was its intent. The flagellum is a leather whip with tiny balls on the end. They were made of bone or metal barbells, some had tiny claws like barbed fishing hooks. That way when soldiers withdrew their weapons they would rip out chunks of flesh.'

'Pretty barbaric.'

'Yet common. Ultimately, it was done to weaken the criminal so he'd die quicker on the cross. In a twisted way, they did it out of mercy.'

Dial shook his head at the logic. There was nothing merciful about these wounds. He could see Narayan's rib cage through the slashes in his flesh. 'How long would the scourging last?'

'Roman law limited it to forty lashes. Most soldiers stopped at thirty-nine, one below the maximum.'

'Another way to show their mercy?'

'Exactly. After that the patibulum – the horizontal beam of the cross – was tied to the victim across both shoulders, right behind his neck.'

'Like a squat bar?'

'Yes, just like you use in the gym, only much heavier. Probably fifty-five kilos.'

Dial wrote *approximately 125 pounds* in his notebook. 'Then what?'

'He was forced to carry it to the *stipes crucis,* which was already planted in the ground.'

'And what would that weigh?'

'Twice as much as the patibulum.'

Dial noted the entire cross would've been too heavy for one man to carry. 'Out of curiosity, why do artists show Christ carrying the whole cross instead of just a beam?'

'Because it's more dramatic that way. Even Mel Gibson used a whole cross for his film, though it would've been physically impossible for Christ to carry after his scourging. As it was, he fell three times on his way to Golgotha.'

'That's right! I forgot about that. And his hands were tied, right? So he wouldn't have been able to break his fall. He would've gone face-first.'

'Undoubtedly. In fact, many people use that fact to explain the facial disfigurement that appears on the Shroud of Turin. The image shows a clean break in the nose.'

Dial shook his head at the direction that his case

was headed. Here he was in Libya, working on a twenty-first-century case, yet he was talking about the crucifixion, the Shroud of Turin, and Christ's facial scars like they were relevant to his investigation. And the most amazing thing was that they were. Not only relevant but crucial. He'd finally found significance in Jansen's broken nose. Maybe that wasn't an accident. Maybe that was done to make him more like Christ.

'Was there anything else, Nick? I'm in serious need of some nicotine.'

'Just one last thing. What do you know about the history of crucifixions?'

Toulon licked the cigarette, trying to savor the taste. 'Supposedly they were invented by the Persians, who passed them on to the Carthaginians, who passed them on to the Romans. Most people think they were invented by the Romans, but they're simply the group who perfected it. They got so proficient at it that they used to bet on the exact time that someone would die, based on the weather, the victim's age, and how much food he'd had. "Hang 'em high and stretch 'em wide," they used to say. Then they'd put money on it.'

'That seems so wrong.'

'Maybe to you. But to them it was a necessary evil in an unfair world. The quickest and most effective way to solve their problems.'

Dial thought about Toulon's comment, wondering if that's what he was dealing with in his current case. And if so, what problems did these murders actually solve?

Later, Omar Tamher knocked on the door and peeked into the tiny room. He was expecting to see Nick Dial working at the desk, not pacing back and forth like a caged puma.

'May I?' Tamher asked, not wanting to interrupt. 'I don't mean to –'

'No problem. I think better when I'm moving. Something about blood flow to my head.'

He nodded in understanding. 'I think better with no shoes . . . Airflow between my toes.'

Dial glanced downward and noticed Tamher's bare feet. 'Interesting.'

Tamher laughed as he walked over to Dial's bulletin board. 'Whatever works, you know? Take your vertical scrapbook, for example. I could never use that here. Too many prying eyes.'

'Coworkers?'

He shook his head. 'Military.'

Dial didn't know what to say, so he said nothing.

'Will you be staying another day, Nick? If so, you'd be wise to take your materials to your hotel. There's no telling what will be missing if you leave them overnight.'

Dial nodded, reading between the lines. His access was guaranteed by Interpol's agreement with Libya, but that didn't mean that he was welcome. 'I appreciate the advice.'

This time it was Tamher who was silent.

'Out of curiosity, if I were to leave tonight, would you be willing to keep me in the loop?'

He nodded. 'As long as you're willing to return the favor.'

'You got it.'

Tamher wanted to tell him it wasn't personal, that this was simply his way of protecting his new friend from the Libyan government. But Dial nodded his head in understanding. No explanation was needed. He was an American, and that made him the most loved/hated mammal in the world, depending on where he went and what day of the week it was.

That was one of the reasons that he kept his work on a portable bulletin board. It gave him flexibility and allowed him to leave on a moment's notice. Just like he would later that night.

30

Dr Boyd knew Maria would eventually come back to the library. The thing that worried him, though, was her mental status when she arrived. He remembered how he felt when he initially translated the scroll – being the murderer of one's own religion was not good for the soul – and he knew Maria had to be dealing with worse feelings since she was far more religious than he.

Yet he realized he didn't have time to help her through her spiritual crisis, not with the fate of Christianity in his hands. That meant he needed to block Maria out of his mind and focus on the only problem in the world that mattered: What should he do with the scroll?

Before he had a chance to answer that question, Maria burst into the conference room.

'*Professore*,' she blurted, 'you'll never believe what I just saw!'

Confused by her enthusiasm, Boyd motioned for her to take a seat. This wasn't the Maria he was expecting. He assumed she'd return to the library guilt-ridden, not giddy as a cheerleader. 'Are you all right? Have you had some sort of breakdown?'

'What? No, I haven't had a breakdown. Why would you ask me that?'

'It's just, you're extremely upbeat, and . . .' His voice trailed off.

'And what? That's not allowed?'

'Of course it's allowed. But when you left here, you were anything but ecstatic.'

'And for good reason. I left here without hope but came back with my faith restored. I found new evidence that might contradict what we know.'

'New evidence?' His tone was full of doubt. 'And where did you get this new evidence?'

'At *Il Duomo*,' she answered. 'I went to the cathedral to do some soul-searching. I figured, if I was going to ponder God, that was probably the best place in Milan to go. Anyway, I was up on the roof, battling the ungodly heat, when I saw him.'

'You saw Him? Just how hot was it up there?'

'Not God! I didn't see God. I saw the laughing man.'

'Once again, let me ask you how hot was it up there?'

'Not in the flesh. I saw a statue of the laughing man at *Il Duomo*!'

'Wait a moment. You're serious?'

'Yes, I'm serious. Our friend from the Catacombs is on the roof of the cathedral.'

'What? But that doesn't make any sense. The cathedral wasn't built by the Ancient Romans. In fact, if my memory is correct, it was built some time in the 1300s.'

'Hold on, there's more.' Maria smiled, enjoying her chance to teach her teacher. 'The laughing man had a letter carved into his ring. There's no guarantee that it's actually *his* initial, but I think there's a good chance that it was.'

'Which letter?' he demanded. 'Was it the letter *P*?'

She nodded, half disappointed that he was able to figure it out. '*P* as in Paccius, right?'

He held up his hand to silence her. 'Maybe, but not definitely. We mustn't jump to any conclusions. We must find conclusive proof before we move on.'

'Come on, *professore*, who else could it be? Tiberius ordered Paccius to execute his scheme in Judea, and we have the scroll to prove it. Later, during that same year, Paccius disappeared from the Roman history books altogether. That *can't* be a coincidence. I'm telling you, Paccius has to be the laughing man. *He has to be.*'

Boyd rubbed his eyes, considering her theory. Everything she said made sense, all but one thing. 'Maria, I don't mean to ruin your mood, but this news about Paccius only strengthens the case against Christ. It means Paccius received the scroll, then went to Judea to carry out the plot. It also suggests that his results were so positive that Tiberius felt obliged to honor him by building a shrine underneath Orvieto.'

'True,' she admitted. 'But I think you're the one who's missing the big picture, not me. I left here lost and depressed, filled with doubts about God, Christ, and everything else that I believe. In order to gather my thoughts, I went to the closest church I could find, looking for solace in God's house, hoping to find something, anything, that would get me through my personal crisis. And guess what? I was given a huge piece of the puzzle. Talk about working in mysterious ways! *Santa Maria!* I'll never doubt God again.'

She gazed at Boyd and noticed that his eyes were still filled with doubt.

'I know you think I'm crazy and that this was all a coincidence. But I honestly believe that this was God's way of telling me to keep looking, to keep searching, to never give up on him. And in my heart I know if I keep doing that, then everything will be all right.'

Several minutes later Maria was still riding high from her discovery at *Il Duomo*. 'You know, it's pretty obvious to me we're onto something. I mean, the historical evidence alone is mind-boggling. Throw in the assassination attempts, the lies in the newspaper, and the statue at the cathedral, and we've got the makings of a first-rate conspiracy.'

Boyd glanced at her, focusing his icy blue eyes on her face. One minute she was soul-searching, the next she was defiant. 'Yet you think that this is all a ruse.'

'Not all of it,' she stressed. 'I believe we found the Catacombs and the scroll. But I don't believe that Jesus was a fraud. I'm willing to accept that other stuff with little proof, but when it comes to my religion, I'll need a lot more evidence to convince me that I'm wrong.'

'Truthfully, I think I would've been disappointed if you'd taken any other stance.'

'Really?'

'Of course. Keep in mind that two millennia have passed since our scroll was written, and several critical events have occurred since then, things that Tiberius couldn't have foreseen. In any case, I hope you'll keep an open mind during our search for evidence. Once we've rounded up all the data, we can sit back and hypothesize as to what really happened two thousand years ago. Then we can tackle the consequences together. All right?'

'Deal!' she said, thrilled that he understood her position. 'Let's get started.'

Using the evidence they had found, Boyd and Maria drew a timeline, trying to figure out how all the pieces of their theory fit together.

32 AD

- Tiberius senses uprising among the slaves of Judea
- *Proven by Orvieto scroll*

- Tiberius plans to profit from the promised one
- *Mentioned in Orvieto scroll*

- Tiberius sends a message to Paccius in the Britains
- *Document found in Bath*

- Paccius returns to Rome and participates in plot
- *Paccius = laughing man???*

• Paccius goes to Judea to carry out plot	• *This has not been verified.*
• Paccius uses his power to manipulate Jesus	• *In what way? Proof needed.*
• Jesus becomes the Messiah in the eyes of the masses	• *How was Paccius involved?*
• Tiberius uses Jesus's power to finance the Empire	• *How is this possible???*

• Paccius disappears; never heard from again	• *Historical mystery*
• Tiberius balances the Empire's budget	• *Proven by history books*
• Tiberius becomes mentally unstable; shuns Rome for Isle of Capri; rumors of foul play involved in death	• *Dies in 37 AD (smothered by a Roman soldier?)*

Boyd said, 'If my math is correct, Tiberius wrote this scroll approximately eight months before the death of Christ. That would have given Paccius enough time to read it, return to Rome, and get to Judea to start his assignment.'

'Whatever that assignment might've been.'

'The thing that makes no sense is why Tiberius felt

Judea was so important. Egypt was Italy's most reliable source of food because of its agriculture, and Greece was a major contributor of culture. But Judea? There was nothing there but sand and an angry populace.'

Boyd considered her statement. 'Unless *that* was his reason. Maybe he chose Judea because it was so darn troublesome? He figured if he could whip the Jews into shape, so to speak, then the rest of the Empire would be a snap.'

Maria frowned. 'You mean Judea was a testing ground?'

He nodded, pleased with his theory. 'We'll still need to verify Paccius's presence in Judea and what he ultimately hoped to accomplish, but I think that sounds reasonable, don't you? Now all we have to do is fill in some of the voids on our chart.'

'Well, we know some things, don't we? Look here. "Let us feed their hunger with our choice of food, allowing them to feast on the coming of their savior . . . for we know he is merely a pawn that we have lifted to the level of Jupiter." That means Tiberius wanted to create a fake god for Jerusalem. He actually wanted them to believe that the Messiah had surfaced.'

'Yes, my dear, that's quite obvious. But how does one accomplish that? If you continue to read the text, Tiberius says, ". . . there must be no doubt among the Jews; they must witness an act of God with their own eyes, a feat so magical, so mystifying, that future

generations will sing of its splendor for eternity ..."
That means he planned to stage something in public,
something that would eliminate skepticism from
even the toughest of cynics.'

'Like a miracle?'

'Or, at the very least, an impressive magic trick.
Keep in mind, the very definition of a miracle is an
event that contradicts the laws of nature, something
that's regarded as an act of God. And I have a strange
feeling that the Romans didn't have heaven's help
on this.'

'What do the history books tell us? If Tiberius's
ruse actually worked, there must be a record of this
"miracle" somewhere in biblical folklore.'

'I already considered that, my dear, but the
accounts of Jesus's life are so varied it would be impossible to separate fact from fiction. In the Gospels
alone, there is talk of thirty-six miracles, everything
from turning water into wine at Cana to walking
on water at Lake Gennesaret. And in my opinion,
none of those events left the kind of impression
that Tiberius was hoping for.' He shook his head in
confusion. 'Furthermore, we must remember what
the New Testament is. It's a piece of propaganda that
was intended to turn people on to Christianity, not a
book of facts that was written by the hand of God ...
Even the pope would admit to that.'

Maria knew what the Bible was and wasn't, yet
there was something about Boyd's tone that made
his explanation sound harsh, no matter how accurate

it was. Take the Gospels, for example. She knew the writings of Matthew, Mark, Luke, and John detailed the life of Jesus, and most Christians believed these accounts were infallible. However, what most people failed to realize is that John's Gospel disagreed with the other gospels about *several* important events in Christ's life, meaning that large portions of the Gospels had to be wrong since they contradicted each other. Furthermore, she knew that many modern scholars claimed the Gospels of Matthew, Mark, and Luke were written by men who'd never met Christ (although some early-Christian scholars would disagree) nearly forty years after his crucifixion. That meant none of their writings were first-person accounts of Jesus's life. Instead, they were based on rumors, stories, and exaggerations that had been passed through two generations of religious turmoil.

Maria also realized the fourth Gospel, the one by John, was penned by an unknown writer with unknown credentials, although some fringe scholars have theorized that it was actually written by Lazarus, the man who Christ supposedly raised from the dead. And if that was true, his version of Christ's life would've been more than a little bit biased.

Wait a second, she thought to herself. *Could that be the miracle they were looking for?*

She asked, 'What about Lazarus? Jesus brought him back four days *after* he'd been buried.'

'Hmmm, I admit I forgot about that one. I think

that's probably the type of event that Tiberius would've had in mind, something that would have been unexplainable. Unfortunately, the Lazarus miracle didn't occur on the great stage of Jerusalem, the place where Tiberius wanted the Jews to discover their Lord. Therefore, I doubt that was the one.'

'OK, tell me this: Which of Jesus's miracles actually occurred in Jerusalem?'

'Truthfully, none of his miracles seem to match the criteria. None of them possessed the pizzazz that Tiberius was striving for.'

'Meaning?'

'We must be overlooking something. We need to keep on digging until we find a fact, no matter how large or trivial, that supports our hypothesis.'

Frustrated, Maria sank back into her chair. 'That sounds kind of tough, sir. I mean, there are so many places we could look. It would be *so* much easier if we had some idea where to begin.'

'True, but that is not the reality of things. In this business nothing is ever handed to you, and nothing is sitting out in the open, waiting for you to notice it. That's just not how it works.'

But in this case Boyd was wrong, for the answer they were looking for was within their grasp. In fact, it was lying on the table in front of them.

31

Opened in the 1930s, the Grand Hotel Reale used to be the most elegant hotel in town. Nowadays the hand-painted frescoes that once enhanced the lobby were tarnished, the result of fingerprints, tobacco stains, and years of neglect. Payne noticed the outside of the hotel was faded, too, as he and Jones scurried alongside the building to reach the back entrance. A few minutes later they were inside Barnes's room, slipping a pair of his socks over their hands to conceal their fingerprints. After that it didn't take long to find something of interest.

'Well, well, well,' Jones said. 'Look what we have here.'

Payne turned and saw him kneeling on the floor, holding a 9 mm Beretta in his sock glove. After checking the safety, Jones put the barrel under his nose and took a whiff, trying to determine if it had been recently fired. 'Found it under the bed,' he said. 'Smells clean.'

'The gun or the sock?'

Ignoring the question, Jones handed him the weapon. 'I wonder why he had it?'

Payne took it in his sock-covered hand. Suddenly he looked like a performer in a twisted puppet show who was about to kill Kermit the Frog. 'Who knows? He was traveling alone in a foreign country. He might've brought it for protection.'

Jones shrugged as he continued looking through the room.

'Speaking of protection, I'm going to borrow the Beretta. Just in case.'

'Fine with me. But I don't want to see you *borrowing* his watch or his wallet. We're here for his film and nothing else.'

Payne nodded as he dug through Barnes's suitcase. It was filled with shirts, shorts, and a wide variety of toiletries. 'And once we find his film, what are we going to do?'

'We'll leave. For some reason I got a bad feeling about this place.'

Smiling, Payne held up a Ziploc bag and jiggled it. 'If that's the case, then let's get going.'

Payne tossed the bag to Jones, who inspected the three canisters of thirty-five-millimeter film. 'If we're lucky, one of these will show yesterday's crash scene.'

'And if we're unlucky, we might see Donald sunbathing in a thong.'

'Good God, I hope not. I don't think the CIA will give us hazard pay for that. In fact, I don't think they'll . . . shit!'

Confusion filled Payne's face as he tried to determine what the CIA's bowel movements had to do with anything. 'What does *that* mean? You don't think they'll —'

Shit! When Payne heard the noise, he finally understood what Jones was talking about. It was the sound of a key going into the lock and the squeaking twist of a doorknob.

'Oh shit!' Jones repeated. 'Shit! Shit! Shit!'

Thinking quickly, Payne pushed Jones toward the door and urged him to block it. Meanwhile, Payne scoured the room for a barricade, hoping to find something that was sturdy enough to keep the visitors at bay – at least until he could figure out an alternative.

'The bed,' Payne blurted. 'Let's move the bed.'

He leapt over the mattress, then pushed the entire thing forward, a task that was harder than it looked. The bed's legs dug into the hardwood floor like talons, causing a screech that sounded like 10,000 fingernails being dragged across a chalkboard.

'*Polizia!*' shouted one of the men in the hall. He punctuated his statement by pounding on the door with such force that Jones could feel the vibrations in his chest. '*Aprire!*'

'We know you're in there!' screamed another in English. 'Open up, or we'll shoot the lock!'

Jones's eyes doubled in size when he realized his crotch was currently at lock level. In desperation, he yelled, 'If you shoot, the hostage gets it!'

'The hostage?' Payne whispered. 'Quit teasing them and give me a hand.'

Jones walked across the room and helped Payne tip the antique dresser on its side, wedging it between the foot of the bed and the closest wall. It eliminated any chance of the door being opened without a stick of dynamite. A fact that bothered Jones.

'Great!' he growled. 'Now we aren't getting out and they aren't getting in.'

'Of course we're getting out. Just relax. Have a little faith.'

But Jones wasn't the only one losing patience. The policemen were getting pissy, too. They emphasized this fact by slamming into the door with a makeshift battering ram. The sound echoed through the room like a Civil War cannon, even though it had no effect on the barricade.

Jones said, 'Now what? The door's the only way out, and they have it covered.'

Boom!

'Don't worry, we're not going through the door. We're going through there.'

He followed the path of Payne's finger and realized he was pointing at a stained glass window in the bathroom. 'No way, Jon. We're too big for that. Especially your fat ass.'

Payne stared at the window for several seconds. 'I'm pretty good with spatial relations, and I've come to the conclusion that we can fit. My ass included.'

Boom!

'No way,' he argued. 'Besides, we have company.'

Jones pointed to movement behind the window. A shadow in the shape of a human head. Someone was trying to see into their room. Someone who was about to get the shock of their life.

'No problem,' Payne bragged. Then, without warning, he launched himself toward the window, kicking his legs in front of him in a martial arts leap. The glass shattered on contact, sending multicolored shrapnel through the air like an explosion at a Skittles factory. The cop on the other side got a mouthful of glass and a taste of Payne's shoe. Unfortunately, his face stopped Payne's momentum, preventing him from making it all the way through the window. A moment later he crashed to the tiled floor as glass fell around him in a melodic song.

Jones rushed to his side. Laughing, he said, 'Damn, Jon. You need to work on your landing.'

He took a moment to catch his breath. 'I think you're right.'

'Out of curiosity, why didn't you use the desk chair to break the window?'

Payne sat up and tried to shake the glass out of his hair. 'My parents used to drag me to church every week, and I used to sit there wondering what it would feel like to jump through the stained glass window and run toward freedom. Never had a chance to try it until now.'

Boom! The sound of the battering ram brought them back to reality.

Quickly they scurried through the window and over the unconscious cop, somehow reaching the Ferrari without being seen. While waiting for Jones to unlock the car, Payne noticed he was leaking blood in about twenty places – mostly scrapes on his arms and legs. Suddenly his dream of jumping through a stained glass window didn't seem too bright.

'Do me a favor and stop at the first store you see. I need to patch up.'

'No problem. There should be plenty of stores between here and Perugia.'

'Perugia? What the hell's in Perugia?'

'Oh, didn't I tell you? When you were looking for maps at the bus station, I found out where Boyd was heading. The guy behind the counter knew exactly who I was talking about before I even showed him a picture, like he'd been asked the same question a hundred times before.'

'And?'

'And Boyd was going to Perugia, a small city about two hours from here.'

They drove fifteen miles outside of Orvieto before they found a gas station that met Payne's medical needs. He went to the bathroom to wash out his cuts while Jones went into the store and bought some bandages and whatever else he could find. Five minutes later he came into the men's room, carrying a first aid kit and a copy of the local paper.

'Hurry up,' Jones said. 'We've got somewhere to go.'

'Back to prison?'

He shook his head and held up the newspaper. 'Another crash site.'

Payne glanced in the mirror and tried to read the headline. Unfortunately, two things stopped him from reading it. The reflection was backward, making the article look like a feature story from *Dyslexia Today*. And secondly, the damn thing was written in Italian.

That being said, he was still able to make sense of things from the photos on the front page. You know the saying, *a picture is worth a thousand words*? Well, these photos were worth a million because they were graphic. Real graphic. The kind that could make a butcher puke. Mostly they focused on the burnt shell of a bus, but Payne saw some arms and legs in there, too, jutting out from the wreckage at impossible angles. He also spotted a head pinned to the ground under a massive metal panel. At least he thought it was a head. It was tough to tell since the flesh and hair had melted off the skull like a cadaver that had been dropped into a volcano.

Everything he saw – both man and man-made – was a dark shade of black.

Payne took a deep breath, rage boiling in his belly. 'Let me guess. Boyd's bus?'

But Jones didn't answer. The anger and determination on his face spoke volumes.

32

One of the major drawbacks of using espresso as an energy source was its debilitating effect on the human bladder. At least that's what Maria Pelati thought as she visited the library's restroom for the second time in an hour. After finishing her business, she headed toward the long row of sinks. Just then a heavyset intruder jumped from the far stall and grabbed her, covering her mouth while pinning her frame against the tiled wall.

'Don't make a sound,' he threatened in Italian. 'Do you understand me? Silence!'

Normally Maria would've been quick to respond. She would've bitten the man's hand, stomped on his foot, and screamed. In this case, though, she decided not to. She wasn't sure why – it might've been the man's body language or just a gut instinct – but she got the feeling that he wasn't there to hurt her. Strangely, she sensed he was there to help.

He said, 'If you promise to be quiet, I'll let you go. Otherwise, we must stay like this.' He stared at her for several unnerving seconds, waiting for her decision. 'Tell me, will you behave?'

Maria nodded her head.

'Good,' he grunted as he removed his hand.

'I hope I didn't scare you, but it was important to speak to you immediately. And in private.'

'You needed to talk to *me*? Why?'

'Why? Because you're in a tremendous amount of danger.'

Danger. The word caused the past few days to rush through her head. First, the blitzkrieg from the chopper, then the avalanche, followed by the screams of the bus victims as they fought to avoid death. Then the nauseating smell of burnt flesh as they failed.

'Who are you?' she demanded. 'Who sent you to talk to me?'

A bittersweet smile crossed his lips. 'You don't remember me, do you? I'm the guard who let you in the library, the one you flirted with.'

Her face flushed with embarrassment. 'You are? I thought you were wearing a uniform.'

The guard nodded, glad that she'd remembered something. 'My shift ended an hour ago. And you're lucky it did, because that's when I realized the danger you face.'

'Danger? What kind of danger?'

'You mean, you don't know? The lead story on every channel was about the man you came with today. Did you know that he's wanted? Every policeman in Europe is looking for him.'

Damn! she cursed to herself. Keeping her cool, she said, 'You must be mistaken. I've known him forever, and he's *not* a criminal. He's a well-known professor.'

'The TV showed several pictures of him. He's definitely the one.'

'OK,' she countered, 'let's pretend you're right. What do you think we should do about it?'

'It's not what I think we should do. It's what I've already done.'

Maria felt her heart skip a beat. 'What do you mean?'

'Once I saw his picture, I came back to make sure he was still here. Then I waited for you to leave his side – I didn't want you to be taken as a hostage – before I called the local police. If we're lucky, they're already arresting him.'

A wave of panic swept over Maria. Suddenly, before she realized what she was doing, she found herself bolting toward the door, hoping to inform Boyd before it was too late.

'It won't do you any good. You can't get out of here without a key.'

She tried the door anyway, but it wouldn't budge, just like the guard had warned.

'You have no right to lock me in here!' she shouted. 'No right at all!'

'Actually, I have every right. I'm the one who let you in without an ID, so that makes you my responsibility.' He strolled toward the door, hoping to calm her. 'Let's just wait in here until the authorities arrive, then we can sort everything out. Doesn't that sound reasonable?'

Maria sighed, then gave him the warmest smile she

possibly could. 'Maybe you're right. I mean, all of this stuff is so damn confusing. I'm so tired right now I can hardly think straight. I don't know. Maybe waiting in here is the best thing to do.'

The guard nodded at her change of heart and stepped forward to comfort her. But the instant he got close, she slammed her knee into his crotch. The strike was so unexpected and so crippling, the guard doubled over in pain, giving Maria a chance to finish him off with a vicious kick to the chin, a blow that sent him sprawling onto the bathroom floor.

'Then again,' she taunted, 'maybe not.'

Maria stole the guard's keys and ran to warn Boyd. It took them less than a minute to gather all their materials and leave the conference room. But they weren't quick enough. An Italian SWAT team had just arrived and was streaming into the building through the library's front doors. Undaunted, the duo turned in the opposite direction and scrambled toward the back exit, hoping to sneak out. As they approached the women's restroom, the injured guard stumbled out in front of them and tried to block their path.

'Stop!' he ordered.

But they were in no mood to listen. Boyd hit him first, using Tiberius's bronze canister like a club, smashing it against the guard's head. Then Maria finished him off, knocking him out with a mighty swing of the Latin dictionary that she carried.

'Lord, that felt good,' Boyd cackled.

'Didn't it? That's the second time I nailed him.'

Their mood quickly soured when they saw several policemen enter the back door.

Stopping immediately, Boyd said, 'We're trapped!'

'Not if we go up.' Maria led him to the nearest stairwell and said, 'Go ahead. I'm going to slow these guys down.'

'Don't be silly, dear –'

'Just go!' she ordered. 'They want you more than me. Get out of here! Now!'

Maria listened for Boyd's footsteps before she focused her full attention on the stairwell door. She fiddled with the guard's keys and tried inserting the first one into the lock but had no success. Cursing softly, she tried the second, then the third, and the fourth. Finally, on her fifth attempt, she found the right key and locked the door an instant before the police got there.

'Yes!' she shouted as she scrambled up the stairs to hunt for Boyd. She found him quickly, waiting for her on the second floor landing.

He said, 'There are metal bars on all the windows, and the front stairwell has been sealed for renovations. This is the only way up or down.'

'No freight lifts?'

'Nothing like that. This building is too old for elevators.'

She pondered the information. 'What's being fixed?'

Boyd pointed skyward. 'The roof. They're redoing the roof.'

'That's right! I noticed that on the way in. Come on, I have an idea!'

With a burst of energy, she charged up the stairs at a pace that Boyd was unable to maintain. By the time he reached the top, he was forced to slump against the wall in oxygen-starved agony.

'Are you all right?' she demanded.

'No,' he blurted, gasping for air. 'But I'll live.'

'Are you sure? Because –'

Her concentration was broken when she heard voices and footsteps on the stairs below. Acting quickly, she used the guard's key to open the service entrance to the roof, then helped Boyd inside just as the police lunged for his foot. Miraculously, Boyd fought them off, using the cylinder to beat on the lead cop's hand while Maria slammed the door in his face.

'That's the second time I beat you,' she teased in Italian. 'You must be quicker than that if you're going to catch a woman.'

The SWAT team replied with several curse words while trying to break down the door.

'Good Lord,' Boyd said, still gasping for breath. 'They sound terribly upset.'

'You think they're mad now? Wait until we escape. They're going to be furious.'

Boyd laughed as he watched her climb a twenty-foot ladder that extended to a trapdoor in the ceiling and work on the metal hatch. *Pssssssssss*. The water-proof seal hissed as it was being opened and was followed by a burst of daylight that temporarily blinded her. But she didn't mind. She was never happier to see the sun in her entire life.

'Is it safe?' he yelled from the bottom of the ladder. 'Is it all right?'

'Just a second.' She searched the roof for problems and found none. 'We're fine.'

'Thank goodness.' Boyd climbed to the roof at a methodical pace, trying to catch his breath as he did. Several seconds later, he asked, 'Now what? Are we just going to sit here and wait?'

'Wait? Of course we're not going to wait! For now I'm going to unscrew the bolts on the ladder so we can steal it before they have a chance to use it.'

Boyd stared at Maria for several seconds before breaking into a wheezing laugh. 'Are you sure you haven't been chased by the police before? Because you seem to be at ease.'

She shrugged. 'If you watch enough movies, you can be prepared for anything.'

'I certainly hope so because our situation is still precarious . . . Or are you keeping something from me?'

Maria laughed at the irony of his statement and gave him a confident smile. 'Everyone has *some* secrets. Right, Dr Boyd?'

It didn't take long for her to disconnect the ladder and pull it to the roof. To slow the cops even more, she jammed the hatch shut by wedging the guard's keys between the door and its sturdy metal frame, a trick she'd learned from a Bruce Willis movie.

'That ought to hold them.'

Boyd didn't answer, but his smile was a welcome sign to Maria. A few minutes earlier she was afraid that he was going to have a heart attack.

'I hope you're feeling better, because you'll need all your strength to survive our next trick.'

'And if I may ask, what do you have in mind?'

Instead of answering, she helped Boyd to his feet and led him to the edge of the hundred-foot building. 'If you're up to it, I figured we could just jump for it.'

'What?! You've got to be kidding me!'

Maria pointed to a long metal tube that ran from the rooftop at a seventy-degree angle until it flattened out near the bottom. The purpose of the chute was to aid in the disposal of unwanted materials during the construction project. Instead of carrying debris down the stairs or flinging it off the side of the building, the workers dumped their scraps down the slender tube and into a Dumpster below.

She said, 'I noticed it when I walked to *Il Duomo*. I figure if it can hold bricks and wood, it should be able to support us.'

Boyd tapped on the tube, trying to gauge how much weight it could handle. Then, after running a few calculations, he eyed the pile of rubble at the bottom and realized it wouldn't be a comfortable landing.

'All right, my dear, I'm willing to give this a shot, although I think it would be best if we attempted this one at a time. No sense putting extra strain on the chute by climbing in together.'

'I couldn't agree with you more.'

'Now all we need to do is decide who shall take the initial plunge. In most situations I would follow the rules of chivalry and insist on ladies first. However –'

'Great! Sounds good to me!'

Grabbing the top of the chute before Boyd could argue, Maria swung her body inside, giving her all the momentum she needed to get started. From there, it was all downhill as she sailed down the pipe like a bobsledder at the Winter Olympics. The ending was a little rough for her taste – she was shot feet-first into a large pile of wood and plaster – but figured that was much better than the alternative: being shot on the roof by an angry SWAT team.

After dusting herself off, she glanced toward the roof and gave Boyd a big thumbs-up. Reluctantly, he nodded his head, took one last gasp of air, and followed her lead, plunging into the escape tunnel.

In truth, their adventure was just starting. And most of the craziness was yet to come.

33

Jones could speak some Italian, so he was able to translate the article on the bus crash. Which, it turns out, wasn't a crash after all. According to the newspaper, Dr Boyd was more than just a professor/forger/thief. He was also an escape artist/munitions expert, capable of blowing up a bus in front of half the cops in Italy without getting injured or caught. Pretty good trick, huh?

The story claimed that Boyd shot down a helicopter, hijacked the first bus leaving town, and then fled down a country road that the cops were able to block. After a brief standoff, Boyd detonated a device that killed everyone except himself and managed to escape capture while the heroic police force risked their lives trying to pull injured passengers from the raging inferno.

Payne laughed when he heard that, because he knew it was total bullshit. He knew the worst thing a criminal could do was kill a cop, because it guaranteed a motivated police force, a group looking for retribution even if it meant breaking some laws along the way. Why? Because the police knew if they didn't strike quick, then every punk with a gun would think they could kill a cop and get away with it. And the next victim could be the cop's partner. Or even himself.

Therefore Payne knew there was a major problem with the story. There was no way an entire police force was going to surround a bus that had been hijacked by a cop-killer and let him get away. Not a chance. So how did Boyd survive? Furthermore, what type of explosive did he use that could blow up the bus but let him walk away? None that Payne knew, and he knew them all.

Anyway, those were just a few of the things running through Payne's mind when he listened to the details of the story. They were running through Jones's mind, too, because he insisted that they drive to the crime scene before it was too dark to see.

To get to the site, which was less than ten miles from the gas station where Payne had cleaned himself up, they pulled off the main highway and went down a country lane that wasn't built for buses, let alone a Ferrari. A wooden barricade blocked their path a few miles from the site. Plants, flowers, and a few dozen pictures surrounded the barrier, items left behind by the victims' families in a makeshift shrine. Some people were able to shrug off scenes like that without a second thought, often driving past them like they were street signs or mailboxes. But Payne wasn't one of those people. His parents were killed by a drunk driver when he was a teenager, so he got reflective every time he saw a bundle of flowers near the road. Of course, Jones knew this about Payne so he got out of the car and moved the barricade by himself.

For as long as he could remember, whenever Payne started thinking about his parents, he found that music helped ease the pain. He knew they still had a few minutes to drive to the bus site, so he decided to test the audio system in the car. Sadly, the only stations Payne could find in the middle of the Apennine Mountains were filled with the depressing sounds of Andrea Bocelli and Marcella Bella. Not exactly what he had in mind. Flipping from station to station, he hoped to find something more upbeat when Jones started yelling at him from near the barricade

'Go back!' he demanded. 'Hurry!'

Payne did as he was told, hoping there wasn't going to be opera when he returned to the previous station. Much to his surprise, there was no music at all but rather an Italian newscaster rambling in rapid Italian. It could've been the weather or a traffic report. Payne wasn't sure, because the only Italian he knew he learned from *The Sopranos*. Whatever it was, though, he knew that Jones liked it because he had a grin on his face the size of a small dog. This went on for over two minutes before Jones turned off the stereo, saving Payne from the tortuous sound of Pavarotti or whatever fat guy was about to start singing.

'You aren't going to believe this,' Jones said. 'But Boyd was just spotted in Milan.'

Payne rolled his eyes. 'Yeah, I wish.'

'I swear to God, Jon. He was just spotted in Milan. The cops tried to grab him, but he got away. Again.'

'Wait a second, you're serious? How did he get away?'

'He vanished from the roof of a library. And get this: he's running with a woman.'

'Boyd took a hostage?'

Jones shook his head. 'No, he took a *partner*. Apparently the two of them are in this together.'

34

The crucifixion in Denmark barely made a blip in the United States, and he couldn't understand why. The murder had everything that Americans usually looked for in a story — a brutal execution, a famous setting, and a Vatican priest as a victim — yet the only attention it received was a small story in the Associated Press. Nothing in *USA Today*, nothing in the *New York Times*, and nothing in the *National Enquirer*.

God, what was wrong with these people? Were they really that numb from all their horror movies and video games that they didn't care about a crucified priest? Who did he have to kill to get their undivided attention? The fucking president?

Obviously, he realized, that would be going too far. He wanted to attract as much attention as he possibly could without starting a worldwide manhunt. That was the only way that he and his partners could get this to work.

They needed attention, not intervention. A spotlight without the heat.

In his mind, the second murder was a step in the right direction. CNN sent a camera crew to Tripoli and Nepal, hoping to get a reaction from the royal family. Their footage popped up on newscasts across the U.S., which led to stories in 90 percent of the newspapers in North America, including most major cities. Not front-page coverage like they'd hoped for, but enough to make the Vatican take notice, which was the ultimate goal of the murders.

The clock was ticking, and the stakes were high. It was time to tighten the vise.

Nicknamed the Holy Hitter because of his surname, Orlando Pope was one of the best players in baseball. He hit for power, ran with speed, and did all the little things that made his team win. Simply put, he was the type of guy that every club coveted.

During the off-season, two teams – the Boston Red Sox and the New York Yankees – did everything to sign him. Not only to get Pope, which would be a coup on its own, but also to keep him off the other's roster, which was even more important in their way of thinking. Why? Because no teams in baseball hated each other more than the Red Sox and Yankees. The players hated each other. The fans hated each other. Even the cities hated each other.

This was Sparta versus Athens, only with bats instead of spears.

The bidding between the teams went back and forth for nearly a month. Ten million. Twenty million. Fifty million. One hundred million. And more. In the end, Pope signed with the Yankees. It also made Pope public enemy number one in Beantown.

Due to a scheduling quirk, the teams wouldn't play

in Boston until the upcoming weekend. They'd split an early-season series in New York and would play a dozen more times later in the year, but this was the match-up that every sports fan in New England was waiting for.

The Pope was coming to Boston, and they were going to let him have it.

Orlando Pope hated the limelight and all the attention that he got as the highest paid player in sports. He loved it on the baseball field where he had the confidence and the talent to thrive, yet hated it in his personal life. He grew up in a biracial family from Brazil – black father, white mother – which led to self-image problems. Was he black? Was he white? Was he both? In the end, he didn't feel comfortable with any group, so he spent most of his time alone, reading books and watching movies in his luxury high-rise, instead of enjoying his hero status in the Big Apple.

In his mind people led to problems, so he stayed away from everyone whenever he could.

The pizza he ordered from Andrew's was forty minutes late, and he was angry. He'd bought a brand-new DVD, *The Lesson*, and didn't want to start it until his food was there. Nothing pissed him off like interruptions when he was trying to watch a flick.

He was tempted to call and complain when he heard a knock on his door. With wallet in hand, Pope undid the lock and opened the chain without looking through the peephole.

It was the biggest mistake of his life.

Four men stood in the hall. Different men than Denmark or Libya. But a foursome with the same objective. Grab their target, take him to a predetermined location, and nail him to a cross.

The leader of the group held an M series Taser and shot Pope in his chest before he could react. The weapon sent a burst of electricity to Pope's central nervous system, causing an uncontrollable contraction of his skeletal muscles. A moment later, one of the best athletes in the world was lying on his floor in the fetal position, unable to protect himself in any way.

From there it would be easy. Carry Pope to the van, take him to a predetermined location, and then wait for the news to hit. And oh how it would hit!

This would be a home run, the biggest one yet.

Every murder was a clue. Every clue led to a secret. The secret would change the world.

In the end the Vatican would be helpless. Completely helpless.

Finally forced to honor his ancestor two thousand years after the fact.

35

Thursday, July 13
Milan, Italy

Payne and Jones's journey to northern Italy covered several hundred miles. Thanks to the liberal speed limits on the *autostrada* and the F1 power of the Ferrari, they got to Milan just after midnight. It was too late to get Barnes's film developed but was early enough to get some detective work done. With that in mind, they wasted no time and headed directly to the Catholic University campus.

Jones said, 'The first thing we need to do is find out if Boyd's been caught. Why don't I snoop around, maybe talk to a couple of reporters, while you walk around the perimeter and look for weaknesses? If all else fails, we might need to sneak inside.'

'Yeah,' Payne joked, 'and we better do it quick. If the current trend continues, Boyd's liable to blow up the library to conceal evidence.'

Laughing to himself, Payne walked past the right-hand alley and noticed several cops staring at a garbage chute and a Dumpster. He didn't want to deal with them, so he headed past the main entrance, hoping there'd be less cops on the other side of the building. That's when he noticed a security guard at the front door, deciding who got in and who didn't, like a bouncer at a local discotheque. In a heartbeat his plan of attack changed. Instead of sneaking in, he decided to be invited in, compliments of the rent-a-meathead.

Payne didn't have a badge or anything official-looking, so he knew he'd have to lay the bullshit on pretty thick. He also knew there was a damn good chance that the guard couldn't speak English any better than Payne spoke Italian, so he decided to use that to his advantage. He figured he might be able to make the guard feel so uncomfortable that he'd let Payne go inside just so he'd leave him alone. With that in mind, Payne went right up to him and started babbling in a fake accent, claiming that he was with the British embassy and was there to protect the legal rights of Dr Boyd. The fact that he sounded like Ringo Starr, had bandages all over, and carried a stolen handgun in his shorts made no difference to the guard. He looked at Payne, shrugged, and let him inside. No questions asked.

Snooping around the first floor, Payne looked for anything that might explain why Boyd was at the library. He figured it might've been something perverted, since the women's room was sealed off with yellow tape that said *Polizia*. Then again, that didn't make much sense, since Boyd was too smart to do anything that would draw attention to himself, like peeping into the ladies' room. Unless this had something to do with the mysterious female who was mentioned on the radio. Maybe she was the one who did something in the restroom? Maybe she was the reason he was running for his life after all these years toying with Interpol?

Whatever the case, Payne needed to find out what had happened in that bathroom.

Paranoid, he crept over to the door, not sure what to expect. A corpse? Some bloodstains? A battered female? At the very least he was hoping to overhear some juicy facts about Boyd and his partner, yet the only thing he saw was a technician dusting for prints. Disappointed, he turned from the door and started walking when he felt someone latch on to his arm.

'Where is you going?' demanded a man in a thick Italian accent.

Son of a bitch, Payne thought to himself. The security guard at the front door must've told some of the cops about him, and they were getting ready to haul his ass out. Payne turned around, half expecting to see a gun pointed at his chest. Instead, he found a tiny man with a smiling face and a head filled with the curliest black hair he'd ever seen in a nonpubic region.

Payne was so stunned he started babbling. 'I was, just, ah, I was –'

'Just what? Running off and no introducing yourself?'

Confused, Payne stood there trying to size up this

guy who was at least a foot shorter than he was. He wore a light-gray suit and a starched white shirt. A picture ID hung from his coat pocket, but the writing was microscopic and in Italian, so he had no idea what it said.

'Well,' he laughed, 'if you no gonna speak, I do the talking. My name is Francesco Cione. My English-speaking friends call me Frankie. I am university's media man, which, as my feet tells you, makes me busiest man in all of Milan – at least on this night no?'

And just like that, Payne knew Frankie would be a wonderful ally.

Thinking quickly, he whispered, 'Are you really the media liaison for the Boyd case?'

Intrigued by the hushed tone, Frankie looked around for eavesdroppers. 'Yes, I am media man for this school. Why do you ask?'

Payne put a finger to his lips. 'Shhhhh! Not here. Is there somewhere we can talk?'

'In private?' he asked softly. 'Yes, I can do that. I can do *anything*. Follow me.'

In all honesty, Payne didn't have anything to speak to him about – at least not at that moment. But he figured he couldn't risk standing in the hallway with a dozen cops liable to spot him. Plus, he realized he had to give Frankie some kind of explanation and figured a long walk to a secluded part of the library would give him enough time to develop a believable cover story.

Frankie led Payne to a private reading room filled

from floor to ceiling with stacks of leather-bound books. Then he asked, 'What is this? Some secret, no?'

Payne countered the question with one of his own. 'Do you have any idea who I am?'

He shook his head. 'One of guards tells me you are from British embassy, but after listening to you voice, I knows that he is wrong. You an American, no?'

'Very good.' Payne applauded. 'That means you're smarter than your guards.'

Smiling at the half compliment, Frankie said, 'So, tell me, who you are?'

'Not yet. We'll get to *that* in a second. But first I have another question for you. Do you like what you do for a living? I mean, I get the sense that you're capable of doing so much more. I picture you as someone who should be making news instead of helping others report it. And do you know what? I'm the type of guy who can make that happen. If that would appeal to you.'

Intrigued, Frankie invited Payne to sit down. 'What, are you some kind of magic wizard? You can go *poof* and fix my life?'

'How would you like to help me and my team capture Dr Boyd? Not a behind-the-scenes job, but one in which you actively participate in his capture. Would that interest you?'

Drool practically leaked from his mouth. 'Would that interest me? *Mamma mia!* I have been trying to help the *polizia* all night, but they no have been receptive. What do you need?'

'I'll get to that in a moment. But first, I need your help with something trivial.'

'You need my help before you need my help. This is very confusing, no? What is you need?'

'Actually, I just need help getting my partner inside.'

'Is that it? I can do that with my eyes tied behind my back.'

That sounded painful, but Payne didn't have the heart to correct him. Instead, he gave him all the information he needed and told him where he could find Jones. 'Before you go, though, let me officially introduce myself. My name is Jonathon Payne, and I'm working for the CIA.'

'The CIA?' he gasped. 'I heard of that in cinema, no? It is an honor to meet you *Signor* Payne. Yes, a big honor ... So, is there anything you need besides your friend?'

'Yeah, Frankie, now that you mention it, there is ...'

Dante marched into the library like he owned the place, around the crowd of onlookers, past the worthless security guard, and through a dozen cops in the lobby. He never slowed to make small talk, never gave anyone a chance to ask him what he was doing or where he was going until he reached the police tape outside the women's bathroom.

'What happened?' he growled at the lead detective.

The officer recognized him immediately and knew his connection to Benito Pelati. 'Multiple assaults followed by a well-planned escape. They eluded a SWAT team like they were statues.'

'Who was assaulted?'

'An off-duty library guard was attacked more than once. The girl hit him first. Boyd got him next, then the girl got him again. She must've been coked up or something, because he said she had the strength of ten men.'

Dante grimaced, surprised at the detective's gullibility. Didn't he know that every guy who had his ass kicked by a female was going to have an excuse? 'How'd they get off the roof?'

'A scrap tube. They slid to the alley.'

'Do we have pictures of anything?'

'Maybe. We're looking through security tapes as we speak.'

Dante frowned. The last thing he needed was for a batch of photographs to be leaked to the press. In his mind that would be more difficult to contain than the bus explosion had been. 'What about fingerprints? Are we even sure it was Boyd?'

The detective shrugged as two men – one of them short, the other one black – walked past them down the hall. 'The guard swears it was him, and so do several witnesses. We won't know for sure until later. There are a lot of prints to sort through in a building like this.'

The longer, the better, thought Dante. He needed all the time he could get to paint the appropriate picture with the media. 'Last question: Do we know what they were doing here?'

'Research, I think. They spent most of the day in a study room working on some kind of project. I can show you if you'd like.'

Dante nodded, hoping to hell that they weren't working on anything that they'd found in Orvieto. That's the one thing he couldn't contain if Boyd decided to go public.

Jones strolled into the library, bemused. He'd been standing outside, trying to find anyone who would talk to him about Boyd, when a tiny man grabbed him by the arm and pulled him toward the steps. His initial reaction was to pull away, which wouldn't have been hard, considering Frankie's size. Then Frankie said he was a friend of Agent Payne's and Jones was needed inside.

As they walked down the corridor, Jones kept his head on a swivel, memorizing the layout while trying to figure out what had taken place. A murder? A kidnapping? A rape? The only thing that stood out was the police tape sealing off the women's bathroom. Jones wanted to lean in for a closer look, but his view was blocked by an imposing man in a fancy suit who appeared to be interrogating a detective, not the other way around. That struck him as odd, so he made note of the guy, figuring he might come into play later.

Little did he know that their paths would cross again with a much more violent outcome.

36

While sipping coffee, Payne thumbed through police documents until Frankie brought Jones into the back room of the library. Payne could tell that Jones was confused because his ears had a red tint to them, and that only happened when he was scared or confused. 'D.J., glad you could make it. We've got so much to discuss.'

Jones glanced at Frankie, then back at Payne, trying to figure out the connection. Eventually, he decided it would be easier to ask. 'Jon, do you mind if I have a word with you in private?'

Payne turned toward Frankie. 'Be a champ and get D.J. a cup of coffee, would you?'

Jones waited until Frankie left the room before saying anything. 'What the hell is going on? I told you to look around, not hire an intern.'

'Calm down. Frankie's been hooking us up. He's already done more than you can imagine.'

Jones rolled his eyes. 'Like what?'

'First of all, Frankie isn't an intern. He's the media liaison for this school, which means he's privy to police documents before they go to the press.' Payne held up a stack as a visual aid. 'Secondly, he has legal access to every building on campus, which is bound to be useful. And third, he makes a great cup of coffee. You gotta try this stuff.'

The anger softened in Jones's eyes, as did the color of his ears. 'What does he know about us? I hope I didn't ruin anything by calling you *Jon*.'

'Not at all. I've been honest with the guy from the start. I told him our real names, that we're working for the CIA, and we're looking for Boyd. I also told him that we wanted to keep a low profile, so he hooked us up with this back office.'

'And he's OK with that? What's in it for him?'

'A chance to live a dream. I guess you aren't the only one who longs to be a super spy.'

Jones shrugged off the insult. 'What else did your playmate tell you?'

'It seems Boyd and the female were here for several hours doing some kind of research before a guard spotted them. When he tried to detain her, she knocked his ass out and ran to warn Boyd. Then, somehow, they got to the roof and escaped from an entire SWAT team.'

'From the roof? Was another helicopter involved?'

Frankie heard the comment as he reentered. 'What do you mean *another*?'

Payne did his best to explain. 'The police were close to nailing Boyd in Orvieto before he shot down their chopper.'

'He shoots down a helicopter? With what? Big gun?'

Payne shrugged. 'We tried to investigate the crash site, but the wreckage had been removed.'

'Is that normal?'

He shook his head. 'Not where we're from.'

Jones added, 'Our colleague took some pictures of the scene, but we haven't had a chance to develop them yet. We're kind of hoping they can clear up the mystery of the wreckage.'

Frankie raised his eyebrows. 'Do you still have film?'

'Maybe,' Jones answered. 'Why?'

'Because I have school photo lab. I can do pictures for you now, if you like.'

Pleased by the development, Payne looked at Frankie and said, 'Yes, we like.'

'Good! Just give me film, and I do my job quick!'

Reluctantly, Jones handed the film to Frankie and watched him leave. The instant he was gone, Jones said, 'I hope you're right about this guy. We just gave a big piece of evidence to a stranger. We don't even –'

'Relax! I got a good feeling about Frankie. He's going to be a big help to us.'

As if on cue, Frankie walked back into the room, holding a photocopy in his hand. 'Special delivery, *Signor* Payne. I think you want to see this.' He accented his statement by kissing his fingertips in a classic Italian gesture. 'The guard was right. This woman is *bellissima*!'

'Really?' Jones grabbed the picture before Payne

had a chance to see it. 'Wow! You weren't kidding. This woman is beautiful. Where'd you get this?'

'The *polizia* find image on security camera, and I get from them. I hope you is pleased.'

'Very pleased,' Payne said. 'Exceptionally pleased.'

Frankie grinned at the praise. 'Good! Is there anything else before I go make film?'

Payne shook his head, then waited for Jones to respond. Unfortunately, he was somewhere in la-la land, soaking up every nuance of the woman's face. The intensity of his gaze told Payne his interest was something less than professional.

So Payne said, 'D.J.? What do you think? Do we need anything else?'

Smiling, he looked at Payne. 'Just time. Give me some time, and this woman is mine.'

37

The abandoned warehouse was crawling with spiders, yet Maria Pelati didn't mind, since it gave her a safe place to rest. Dr Boyd felt the same way, even though it took him a lot longer to warm to the concept. To him, the thought of sleeping like a hobo seemed preposterous until he stretched his tired frame atop the concrete floor. Within seconds his body whispered its approval.

'*Professore,*' she said, adjusting the rag under her head. 'May I ask you a personal question? I was wondering if you've ever been married.'

'I should've guessed; the age-old query that has plagued me for years. No, my dear, I've never been married. Between teaching and traveling, I never found the right person ... And what of you? Why is there no man in your life?'

'In some ways I guess I'm following your lead. I've been working too long and too hard to screw things up now, especially with my doctorate close at hand. But I'll promise you this: Once I obtain my degree, my life is going to change drastically.'

'Just like that?'

'Yes, just like that,' she assured him. 'I've always wanted a family. So there'll come a point in the near future when my personal life becomes my number-one priority. And when it does, look out. No guy on the planet will be safe.'

'A beautiful girl like yourself shouldn't have difficulty finding a suitor. Or hundreds of them, for that matter.'

Maria blushed at the compliment.

'And what does your family think about all of this? I've heard you grumble about your father on more than one occasion. Does he really look down on your choices as much as you claim?'

The color in her cheeks grew even brighter. 'I don't think he looks down on my choices as much as he looks down on me. My father has an old-world mentality, one in which women are considered the weaker, dumber sex. He truly believes that we were put on earth to serve men.'

'Old-world, indeed! And how does your mother feel about his barbaric views?'

She paused before answering. 'I wish I knew, sir . . . My mother passed away before I ever had the chance to ask her.'

'Oh, Maria, I had no idea. I'm so sorry for bringing it up.'

'That's all right. I think it actually does me some good to get this stuff off of my chest.'

Boyd offered her a smile, then laid back to listen.

'When I was growing up, my mother and I were best of friends. We played together, went to the park together, read books together. My father didn't allow her to do any work – we had a staff of servants to take care of the house – so she had plenty of time to spend with me. And let me tell you, she was the greatest mother in the world. So loving, so thoughtful. Always encouraging me to pursue my dreams. Just the way you'd want a parent to be . . .'

Her voice trailed off as she searched for the words to continue.

'Unfortunately, my dad was just the opposite, at least toward me. I have two half brothers, and my father treated them like gold. Especially Roberto. Always showering him with attention. Always bragging about his potential. Always taking him to work and on business trips. But I wasn't jealous. I had my mom and my brothers had my dad. I just figured that was the way things were supposed to be.' She paused, her eyes focusing on the moonlight that streamed through the warehouse's dirty windows. 'At least I thought that way until I was nine.'

Maria took a deep breath. 'I'd never heard my parents fight until that year. And I mean really *fight*. Screaming, crying, threats of all kinds. It was a nightmare. The two people in the world that meant the most to me were going head-to-head in a heated battle. God, when you're a child, there are never any winners in a situation like that. And if that wasn't bad enough, it got even worse when I figured out what they were fighting about.'

'And what was that?'

'They were fighting about me.'

She nodded her head, slowly, like she was still coming to grips with the memory. 'They were in the kitchen, and my dad was screaming right into her face. The veins bulging in his neck. I still find this next part hard to believe, but my father ordered her to stay away from me. He told her that I was a girl and nothing could change the fact that I was worthless. Then he insisted that she start paying more attention to my brothers because they still had a chance to be something. Can you believe that? I'm nine years old, and my dad was already giving up on me.'

Boyd didn't know what to say.

'My mother argued that I could be just as good as a man, but he laughed at that. Literally laughed in her face. Then, when he was done laughing, he informed her that he was sending me away to boarding school so they wouldn't have to deal with me anymore.'

'You have to be joking.'

A tear rolled down Maria's cheek. 'I didn't even know what boarding school was, yet I could tell from my mother's reaction that it wasn't a good thing. She immediately burst into tears and ran from the kitchen.'

'My God! You were sent away?'

Maria nodded. 'Nine years old and I was shipped off to the Cheltenham School for Girls.'

'The one in Gloucestershire? That's a top-notch academy, my dear.'

'Maybe so, but it couldn't make up for the things that were taken from me.'

Boyd flinched at her tone. 'Maria, I didn't mean to suggest that –'

The anger in her eyes softened slowly. 'I know. At least they had the decency to get me a good education, right? Well, that was my mother's doing, not his. She figured, if she couldn't stop him from sending me away, the least she could do was find me a school where women were treated with respect. And do you know what? For the most part, things turned out well. Once I adjusted, I started to thrive in my new environment. I was introduced to girls from several countries and backgrounds. I learned half a dozen languages. In fact, I got to the point where I started to look down on all things Italian. The language, the culture, the food. I figured if I wasn't good enough for Italy, then Italy wasn't good enough for me. It wasn't until much later that I even set foot in this country again.'

'Not even for the holidays?'

'Why would I want to ruin my holidays? There was nothing in Rome but my father, and he didn't want anything to do with me, remember?'

'And what of your mom?' he asked delicately. 'I take it she passed on shortly thereafter?'

Maria took another deep breath. 'My mother rang me a few weeks after I arrived in England. The call was against the rules, but she managed to get through by claiming a family emergency. I was expecting dreadful news – I mean, the headmistress was ashen when she came to get me, so what else could it be? –

but I couldn't have been more wrong. My mother was ecstatic. She told me she'd been looking for a way to get me home and finally stumbled upon a way to do it. She wouldn't tell me what it was but assured me that I would be by her side very soon.

'Well, as you can imagine, I was thrilled. I ran down the hall and started to pack, expecting her to be at the front gate that very night. Of course, she wasn't. Nor the next night. Nor the night after that. This went on for weeks and not a single word from her. Finally, after two months, my headmistress retrieved me again, her face even worse than the first time. I picked up the phone, dying to hear the sound of my mother's voice, but it wasn't her. It was my brother, Roberto. Without so much as a hello, he informed me that my mother had died a few months back, although the official inquiry had only been wrapped up that day. The Italian courts ruled that she became depressed over my departure and had taken her own life.'

Boyd winced at the news. It wasn't what he was expecting.

'It was bad enough that my mother was gone, but to be told that *I* was the cause . . .' She paused to catch her breath. 'To be called several weeks after her death by one of the people who forced my departure, well, that somehow made it worse.'

Boyd had always assumed that Maria was a pampered rich kid who was biding her time until she inherited her father's throne as the minister of antiquities. Now he knew different. This trip had revealed a side of Maria that he never knew existed. She was a fighter.

'And out of curiosity, how is your current relationship with your father?'

Maria wiped her eyes while she thought of the appropriate words. 'I wouldn't call it cordial, but he's definitely an important part of my life.'

'Are you serious? That's awfully surprising, considering the story you just told.'

'Don't get me wrong, *Professore*. I hate the man for what he put me and my mother through. But after giving it some thought, I decided it would be foolish to exclude him from my life.'

'And why is that, my dear?'

'Why? Because I want him to see that my mother was right, that his worthless little girl was able to make something of herself. I want that bastard to have a front row seat in my life so I can rub his nose in everything that I achieve.'

38

All of the police files were written in Italian, so Payne wasn't very useful as Jones translated them and took notes. After ten minutes or so, Payne couldn't take it anymore. He needed to do something productive while waiting for Frankie to develop the film, or he was going to start bouncing off the walls. Jones sensed it, too. 'Did you forget to take your Ritalin?'

'You know how I get. I'm not wired for this office crap.'

Jones laughed while pulling a phone number from his wallet. 'Do you remember Randy Raskin? I introduced you two a few years ago.'

'Computer guy at the Pentagon, right?'

'Yep, that's him.' He handed Payne a card. 'That's his direct line. Tell him I need to cash in a favor – he'll know what I mean. Have him search his system for any background info on Boyd. See if he's dating anyone or has ever been married. Maybe this woman is his long-lost daughter.'

'What about Donald Barnes? Maybe there's something there that we don't know about.'

'Same with Manzak and Buckner. He might be able to find some dirt on them. I didn't have enough time to dig into their files.'

Thankfully, Randy Raskin was more helpful than any computer-tech guy Payne had ever talked to. At first Payne figured Jones was just humoring him, giving him some busy-work so he'd leave him alone. Turns out that wasn't the case at all, because Raskin hooked Payne up with some serious information. Payne scribbled furiously as Raskin told him everything that he needed to know about Dr Boyd and their friends at the CIA, Manzak and Buckner. He was so forthcoming Payne was tempted to ask him if the U.S. government still kept aliens in Area 51.

Anyhow, after thanking Raskin, Payne hustled back to Jones to brief him on his conversation. 'Let's start with Boyd. He's been a member of the Dover faculty for over a decade. During that time he's taken several leaves of absence to go on archaeological digs around the world, including the privately funded excavation he was on in Orvieto.'

'No shocker there.'

'Hang on, I'm getting to the good part. In addition to funds he received from private donors, he also received a yearly stipend from American Cargo International.' He glanced at Jones and waited for a reaction. 'Does that name ring any bells?'

'Not really.'

'Well, it should. We've done business with them on more than one occasion.'

And that's when the name clicked in Jones's head. American Cargo International wasn't a business. It was a front, a company in name alone that enabled groups like the MANIACs to carry out their missions. The money for their operations had to come from somewhere, and it obviously couldn't be a public source – that would be too difficult to explain to the taxpayers. So dummy companies were established to help foot the bills. The FBI had Red River Mining, the Navy had Pacific Salvage, and the Pentagon had too many companies for Payne to remember.

Yet that wasn't the case with ACI, because the men who ran that particular fund were so egotistical, so sure that they'd never get caught, that they barely bothered to hide what they were doing. Scramble the initials of American Cargo International, and the identity of its parent organization could quickly be discovered: ACI stood for the CIA.

'So what does that mean?' Jones asked, still trying to connect the dots.

'It means that Boyd was onto something big, and the CIA wanted to be a part of it. By financing his dig, they had a rightful claim to anything he discovered.'

'So *that's* why Manzak has such a hard-on for him. He thinks Boyd found what they were looking for, then decided to skip town.' Jones chuckled to himself, half-embarrassed. 'Man, I feel so used! We're nothing more than Manzak's bill collectors.'

'Not exactly . . . The news gets worse from here.'

He looked at Payne, concerned. 'What did we do now?'

'Nothing. It's what Manzak and Buckner did that scares me.'

'Oh God, what did those schmucks do?'

'It seems that they got themselves killed.'

'As in dead? Manzak and Buckner are *dead*? Who the hell killed 'em?'

'Strangely, a team of Serbian rebels outside of Kosovo.'

'Kosovo? What the hell were they doing there? We just talked to them . . .' Click. His mental lightbulb went on. 'Ah, son of a bitch! I can't believe this shit. What *year* did they die?'

'According to the Pentagon computer, 1993. Of course, the CIA still lists them on their active roster because they're unwilling to admit that Manzak and Bucker were even in Kosovo. I mean, that might cause a *scandal*.'

Jones sighed, ignoring the sarcasm. Payne could tell he was pissed that he hadn't discovered the Kosovo information two days ago. If he had, it would've radically altered their plan of attack. Instead of searching for Dr Boyd, they would've spent all of their time trying to uncover Manzak's true identity and what he wanted from them.

'That's why they were clean when I searched their backgrounds,' Jones explained. 'I only have partial access to the database, but my intel listed them as active agents in good standing.'

'Of course they were in good standing. It's tough to break the rules when you're dead.'

'Good point.'

'Speaking of which, why do I get the feeling that *we're* going to end up dead if we don't figure out what we're involved in?'

Jones nodded, sensing the same thing. They weren't dealing with petty criminals who'd let them walk away without completing their agreement. These men had enough power to swing a deal with the Spanish government, forge impeccable CIA credentials, and uncover their top secret backgrounds without any problems at all. There was no way in hell that they would let Payne and Jones turn their backs on them without finding Boyd.

They were loose ends that they'd have to deal with whether they finished their task or not.

That's why Payne and Jones decided to push on. They figured the more cards they had, the safer they'd be.

Manzak and Buckner had died in 1993, yet Payne had talked to them a few days ago without a séance. Dr Boyd could be linked to the CIA through a series of payments, although the dead spooks failed to mention anything about that. Plus, more than forty people had been killed near Orvieto in the last week, yet Payne didn't know why. Or by whom. Or where all the evidence was. These were just a few of the things Payne discussed with Jones as they walked to the university's photo lab to see the photos that Frankie had developed for them.

'You know,' Payne grumbled, 'the more I learn about this case, the more I get confused.'

'Really? I think things are coming together nicely. Let's assume that Boyd was paid to steal some antiques from some key European countries. That way, when the CIA needed some top secret information, they could trade the artifacts for whatever they needed. But let's assume that Boyd got greedy and decided to keep the relics for himself. In that case, what were Manzak and Buckner – or whatever their *real* names are – supposed to do? Chase Boyd all over Europe and risk getting caught? Why do that when they could get two ex-MANIACs to track him for free?'

Not too shabby, Payne thought to himself. His theory didn't explain everything – like the exploding bus, the identity of the brunette, or the true identity of Manzak and Buckner – but it utilized everything else. Of course, Payne didn't have anything to support Jones's hypothesis, things like proof or evidence. But he wasn't a cop, so he didn't give a damn about that crap. All he cared about was finding Dr Boyd. Payne figured by getting ahold of him he'd have enough leverage with Manzak and Buckner to break away cleanly.

Anyhow, they reached the darkroom a few minutes later and were pleased to find Frankie waiting with the film. He said, 'I not sure what you learn from these. There is hotel, and the church, and the helicopter . . . Orvieto is quite beautiful, no?'

'Very,' Payne said as he flipped through the prints. 'How'd you recognize the town?'

'Orvieto is known to my people. Just like Egyptians know the pyramids of Giza or Chinamen know Xi'an, we know about Orvieto – and the stories of its treasure.'

'Treasure?' Jones asked. 'What treasure?'

'*Mamma mia!* You been there and not know its treasures? How can this be?'

'We weren't exactly on a sightseeing tour.'

'Ah, yes, I forget! You there on official business. Please, since this is so, let me explain Orvieto to you. It will make you – how you say? – understand photos good.'

Jones shook his head. 'Maybe some other time. We're in a hurry right now.'

'Please! This may explain why *Dottore* Boyd was in Orvieto and what he is wanting.'

They somehow doubted that, but they humored Frankie anyway.

'For years there are stories about Orvieto. When pope looked for shelter during holy war, people say he no live on top of rock. They say he live under rock, deep inside land. No one knows how this be since no one dig for him, but too many stories for me not to believe.'

'What are you saying?' Payne asked. 'He lived underground?'

'Yes! He so scared for his life he do what he can. He make tunnels to escape. He grow crops to eat. He

266

make well to have water. All of this to hide from enemies.'

'We saw the well,' Payne admitted. 'Regrettably, so did our friend with the camera.'

'But what of tunnels? Did you see the tunnels? They are – how you say? – very cool crap. They go beneath the street like sewer. I feel like Indian Jones when I crawl through them!'

Payne smiled at the reference. 'Didn't you say something about a treasure?'

'*Si!* A magnificent treasure, one that no one has found.'

Jones shook his head. 'Sorry, but I find that hard to believe. I'm a huge history buff, and I've never heard anything about Orvieto's treasure. How famous could it be if I've never heard of it?'

Frankie shrugged. 'Maybe your country no make it famous? I do not know. In my country Orvieto be famous. Catacombs be famous. Everyone in my country know Catacombs.'

'Fine,' Jones relented. 'If that's the case, how come no one has found the treasure? Orvieto isn't a big place. I mean, if there was gold in them there hills, someone would've found it.'

'No! The land beneath town is illegal for shovels. No digging allowed. Not for treasure seekers. Not for anyone. If you caught, you go to jail. You see, big hill is like old mine, filled with many caves. People is worried if someone dig in wrong place, then all of Orvieto go splat!' He slammed his tiny hands together. 'And that would suck big one, no?'

Payne laughed until he realized Jones wasn't. 'You OK?'

Jones blinked a few times. 'You know how there's been a hole in this case, something out of our grasp? What if this turns out to be a treasure hunt? It would explain Boyd's presence in Orvieto and the CIA's interest. If the Feds were able to get data with a few trinkets, imagine what they could get for an entire site.' He paused, thinking things through. 'Furthermore, a jackpot of this size would explain the Italian authorities. I mean, there's no way a local bureau could've pulled the cover-ups that we've witnessed. To hide a helicopter crash and manipulate a bus wreck, you have to have the backing of some very serious people.'

'True, but where do we fit in?'

'Our friends at the CIA must've known Boyd was onto something. That's why they panicked when he disappeared. They knew if the Italians found him first, they'd be screwed out of everything they'd been financing for years. That's why they came to us. They needed to find him ASAP and thought we could do the job.'

In Payne's mind the theory made sense. Of course, he realized it might make even more sense if he knew more about the Catacombs. 'Hey Frankie, tell us about the treasure.'

'My people say that Clement VII feared for Church's wealth. Even when pope return to Vatican, he still be scared for it. That is why people say he leave the best things in Orvieto.'

Jones whistled softly, thinking of the Vatican's treasure. 'Frankie, if we wanted to dig in Orvieto, who would we have to talk to? Is there a local bureau that could give us permission?'

'No, there is nothing like that in all of Umbria . . . But in Rome, yes, there is an office. It is called Department of Antiques, and it be very high power in government.'

Payne assumed he meant the Department of *Antiquities*. 'How so?'

'The minister of antiques is named Benito Pelati, and he very important man. He is very old, very well-respected throughout Italy. He is done so much to save our treasures, our culture, that people line up to kiss his feet.'

'This Pelati guy, would he have the authority to let someone dig in Orvieto?'

'*Si,* but this is something that *Signor* Pelati no gonna do. We Italians is very proud. And because of pride, sometimes we is very stubborn. For long time, *Signor* Pelati has said to my people that *Cata-comba di Orvieto* is made-up. He even go on TV and say it no real, that people should forget tales be-cause they not true. But some scholars want proof. They no even want to dig. They just want pictures of ground with giant X-ray to see if anything is there, and he no even allow that. Too much at stake for him.'

Payne nodded in understanding. 'Out of curiosity, how does Mr Pelati prevent illegal digs?'

'He has special team who live in Orvieto and watch everything. Many people sneaked into town to find the Catacombs and many people not come back. In time, people no longer look for treasure . . . Myth not worth dead.'

'Hypothetically,' Jones said, 'if someone wanted to dig there, what would it take?'

Frankie shrugged. 'Permission from *Signor* Pelati. But, like me say, that no gonna happen. *Signor* Pelati is no gonna let someone find treasure in Orvieto. *In nessun momento!* In Italy, an important man like Benito Pelati would rather be dead than look foolish.'

Payne and Jones continued talking with Frankie until he was called back to the library on business. They stayed in the photo lab, though, using a work-table to examine the photos of the crash site. Each of the pictures had been taken atop the plateau. The initial shot revealed a panoramic view of the landscape, followed by several of the wreckage itself, concentrating on Boyd's truck and the left side of the helicopter. Most of the chopper's rear section was scorched, but not enough to obscure the last three digits of its serial number.

'That's about all I found, unless you count these,' Payne said.

Oddly, the final two pictures of the roll were taken from the opposite end of the ridge, which meant

Barnes walked several hundred feet to film the reverse angle of the crash. To Payne's eye it seemed like a huge waste of time, because they didn't reveal anything of value – mostly scorched grass, huge rocks, and chunks of burnt metal. 'So, what did we learn?'

'We learned that Barnes was telling the truth. The helicopter crashed on top of the truck, even though the truck wasn't mentioned in the newspaper. That seems strange to me.'

'Maybe it has something to do with the truck's location,' Payne suggested. 'There isn't a road at the bottom of the plateau, which tells me that Boyd went way out of his way to get down there. Why would he do that? If he was a thief like the CIA claims, why would he risk driving down there unless it was necessary? If he wanted to blend in, he would've parked in the lot where we parked then walked into Orvieto like a tourist.'

Jones nodded. 'Furthermore, if Boyd was there for an illegal dig, there's no way he would've parked at the bottom, not with Pelati's men running around. They would've spotted him for sure. Unless, of course, he wasn't worried about Pelati's men ... Wait, maybe that's the thing we've been missing. Maybe he wasn't hiding from Pelati because he was working for him?'

'Doing what? Searching for buried treasure?'

'Maybe. That would explain why Boyd's truck was in the valley. He wasn't worried about being spotted and wanted his equipment as close to the site as possible.'

'And the helicopter?'

Jones shrugged. 'Who knows? Maybe it was there to protect Boyd and some interlopers shot it down. Or maybe it belonged to treasure hunters and Pelati's crew took them out?'

'Or maybe it belonged to the CIA. Ever think of that?'

'The thought had crossed my mind.' He studied the chopper's rear section. 'If I had to guess, I'd say this bird was made by Bell. Perhaps part of their 206 series. Possibly an L-1.'

'You can tell all that from one picture?'

'Trust me, this was a Bell. Just like the chopper that Manzak and Buckner used. Same color, too. As black as my uncle Jerome.'

Payne took the picture out of Jones's hand. 'Probably not a coincidence, huh?'

'Probably not.'

'Which means one chopper was in Pamplona while a second was in Orvieto.'

Jones nodded. 'But that's where things get tricky. No one knows what the chopper was doing there. Furthermore, we don't know who we talked to in Pamplona, because Manzak and Buckner are dead. Speaking of which, why kill Donald Barnes and all the people on the bus?'

'Yeah, that doesn't make sen –'

The sound of ringing stopped Payne midword. He

probably shouldn't have answered it, but it was after midnight, and he was curious. Thankfully, it turned out to be a good choice because Frankie was on the line, and he sounded very excited. 'I leaving library right now. Bring pictures and meet me in my office. I promise, you will like! This will be good!'

39

The thought of asking her father for help was enough to keep Maria awake. No matter how she rationalized it, she just couldn't get past his basic ideology of life. Women were weak, and men were strong. God, it infuriated her. How could someone living in the twenty-first century think in such an old-fashioned way? To make matters worse, she knew if she went to him for assistance, he'd use it as proof that when the going got tough, all women turned to men for help.

Then again, what choice did she have? She realized if she wanted to go public with the Catacombs, she needed to get everything documented by her father's office. Otherwise she and Boyd would be labeled grave robbers, not archaeologists, and they would lose the rights to everything they found. The fact that he was a blatant sexist and an asshole of a father shouldn't factor into it. He was the minister of antiquities, and he needed to be notified immediately.

Both she and Boyd knew it. Yet it was a call she was unwilling to make.

The thought of him saying that *he* would rescue *her* was one she couldn't bear. The bastard had abandoned her as a little girl and turned his back on her when she needed him the most. So she refused to turn to him now. Not if she could help it. No way in hell.

'*Professore*,' she whispered. 'It's time to wake up. The sun will be up shortly.'

Boyd opened one eye, then the other, desperately searching for clues to his location. The first thing he noticed was the intricate design of the spiderwebs that hung from the ceiling. Next he felt the coldness of the concrete floor against his back. Breathing deeply, he noticed the distinct stench of urine in the air. Ah, yes! The memories came flooding back. He was in a warehouse.

'Come on,' she snapped. 'We need to get out of town before breakfast.'

'Why's that, my dear?'

'Because we're bound to be on the front page of the local paper. Once people see that, the odds of us being spotted go up significantly.'

The moment Payne and Jones got to Frankie's office they could tell he was bubbling with enthusiasm. 'One of my jobs is making monthly bulletin for our school. Lotsa pictures, lotsa stories, lotsa nothing.' Frankie rummaged through his desk and found an old newsletter. It was the type of thing sent to graduates and big-money donors. 'I do whole thing myself from here.'

'That's great,' Payne said. 'But what's that have to do with us?'

Frankie walked over to his computer and opened his scanner. 'We scan pictures. We make pictures big on screen. We see why pictures is so important. Good idea, no?'

Payne agreed and handed him the pictures. Frankie put the first photo in and hit start.

The basic purpose of a scanner is to convert a document into a digital format (i.e., a computer file) so it can be stored on disk or manipulated on-screen. They were interested in option two, hoping to magnify Barnes's pictures to several times their original size. Ten seconds passed before the first signs of color started to appear. The three of them stared at the image as it slowly filled the screen. A rainbow of dots here, a massive shape there. After a while it was obvious that the photo was coming in upside down. Jones had the most experience in the computer field, so he offered to man the keyboard.

'Not to worry,' he bragged. With a touch of his mouse, the image flipped 180 degrees and continued to grow. 'OK, what do you want to look at first?'

Payne pointed to a section of wreckage. 'Zoom in on the helicopter. I want to see if we can make out more of the serial number besides the last three digits.'

Jones clicked a few of buttons on the toolbar and waited for the image to be redrawn. Charred metal filled the screen, but no additional numbers could be seen. 'Now what?'

'I don't know. I was hoping the chopper would

show us something useful. Maybe if we –' That's when Payne thought of a different approach. 'Hey Frankie, give me the photos.' He glanced through the pile until he found the one he wanted. 'Try this instead.'

Frankie put it in the scanner, and soon they were looking at the picture on-screen.

'Zoom in on the truck,' Payne said. 'Maybe we can see a make or model.'

Jones moved his mouse across the desk. 'And what good will that do?'

'I bet Boyd's truck was a rental. And if we figure out where he rented it, we might be able to get some additional information, right?'

The moment the close-up of the truck filled the screen, they realized they were on the verge of a major discovery. Jones attacked the keyboard with zeal, hoping to magnify the picture. Soon they were able to see the make and model of Boyd's truck and his license plate as well.

'*Mamma mia!*' Frankie blurted. 'You guys is good!'

'Thanks,' Jones said as he sent the image to the printer. 'But we ain't done yet.'

Seconds later, Jones logged on to the Internet and went to his personal website, where he punched in his secret code. Even though he rarely used his system outside the office, he'd set it up so he could access it from any terminal in the world. Once his password was accepted, he typed the truck's license plate number into a military search engine where he was given the name of the vehicle's title holder. The truck belonged to Golden Chariots, a rental agency on the outskirts of Rome. Next, with a quick click of the mouse, he went to the company's website, looking for anything that might help their search.

'What you looking for?' Frankie wondered. 'Name? Address? Money-saving coupon?'

Jones shook his head. 'I need a twenty-four-hour hotline that I can call this late at night.'

Frankie pointed to the screen. 'Look! Right there. That is number, no?'

Jones nodded. 'And since you found it, I'm going to let you make the call.'

'Me? Why me? Why do I make call?'

'Frankie, relax. I'll do the hard part. All I want you to do is call this number and pretend you're the manager of a local hotel. I don't care which hotel, just pick one, OK? Then I want you to find out if the rental agent speaks English. If he does, tell him one of your guests needs to talk to him about a car problem. Got it?'

'*Si*, I got it. And if he no speak English?'

'If that's the case, I'll talk to him in Italian. But our charade will work better in English.'

Frankie nodded and dialed the number, although he had no idea what Jones was planning. Neither did Payne, for that matter, yet he patted Frankie on the shoulder and assured him he'd be fine. A woman answered on the fourth ring, and Frankie spoke to her in rapid Italian, explaining who he was and what he needed. Thankfully, she said she could speak English and would be willing to talk to Jones. Frankie handed him the phone and whispered, 'Her name is Gia.'

Jones thanked him with a wink. 'Gia, I'm so sorry to call you at such a late hour, but there's been an accident.'

'Are you all right?' she asked in near-perfect English.

'I'm fine. A little banged up but fine. Although I can't say the same about your truck.'

'The vehicle is in bad shape?'

'Yeah, the whole side's caved in. I plowed into it something good.'

'Pardon me?' she said, confused. 'I don't understand. You hit your own truck?'

'What? No!' Jones sighed loud enough for her to hear. 'I'm sorry. I guess I'm doing a pretty bad job of explaining this. You'll have to forgive me. I'm still a little shaken up from things.'

'Not a problem, sir. Just take a deep breath and tell me what happened.'

He sucked in a gulp of air for her benefit. 'Boy, let me try this again. I rented my car from a different agency, not yours, and as I was backing out of my parking space, I slammed into one of your trucks. I should've seen it because it was just sitting there. But, man, I hit it pretty good.'

The sound of typing preceded her next comment. 'And the vehicle is heavily damaged?'

'Yes, ma'am. I caved in the whole side and shattered its window.'

More typing. 'And why are you calling us instead of the actual renter?'

'Well, that's just the thing. I don't know who it belongs to. I assume it's someone at the hotel, since it was parked in their lot, but I don't know who. I came inside and asked the manager if he knew, but he didn't. That's when he suggested that we call you to find out.'

The clicking of keys continued. 'And you're sure it's one of our vehicles?'

'I think so. When I checked to see if anyone was inside, I noticed a pamphlet on the front seat with your company's name on it. That's how I got this phone number to begin with.'

Silence engulfed the line for the next few seconds. 'Do you have any other information, sir? The make of the truck, the registration number, the –'

'I wrote down the license plate. Will that help?'

'Yes, sir, that would be great.'

Jones read off the digits and waited for her reply.

'Sorry, sir, there seems to be a discrepancy here. The license you gave me belongs to one of our vehicles, but its itinerary says nothing about Milan. That's where you are, right?'

'Yes, ma'am.'

'Then I don't see how you could have hit this

truck. The vehicle with this particular license should be in Orvieto, *not* Milan.'

'Orvieto?' he said, feigning confusion. 'Is that near here?'

'Not at all. That's why I'm guessing you've made a mistake.'

'But I'm not. There's no doubt in my mind I hit this truck. If you don't believe me, I can put the hotel manager back on the phone. This truck is sitting twenty feet from us.'

The sound of clicking started up again. 'Hold on, sir. I'll double-check my records if you'd like. Can you give me that license plate again?'

Jones repeated the numbers, even though he started to doubt his plan. He figured, if she was reluctant to believe that the truck was even in Milan, then there was little chance that she'd answer any of his questions about Boyd.

'Sir,' she finally said, 'while I was rerunning the license plate, something caught my eye. The customer you're looking for is obviously in Milan, just like you suggested.'

'Really? Why's that?'

'I noticed on my computer that she just rented a second vehicle.'

'Excuse me?' It took a few seconds for things to sink in. 'Wait a second! Did you say *she*?'

'Yes, sir. The driver of the truck just rented a Fiat from our Linate Airport office.'

Jones mouthed *holy shit* to Payne before he talked to Gia. 'And how long ago was that?'

'About a minute, sir. The order just came up on my screen.'

40

Nick Dial had always wanted to see Fenway Park. There was something about the Green Monster, the thirty-seven-foot left-field wall, that captivated his imagination. His obsession started when he was a boy, during the summer he lived in New England. He and his father used to listen to games on the radio, then they'd go in their backyard and imitate their favorite Red Sox players.

Dial smiled as he thought about the ballpark on his flight to Boston. He imagined what the grass was going to smell like, the dirt was going to feel like, and the Monster was going to look like. He'd been waiting for this moment his entire life and couldn't wait to get there.

All that changed, though, when he walked out of the tunnel and saw the crime scene spread before him. The playground of his dreams had been stained by the reality of his job.

Dial wasn't there for a baseball game. He was there to catch a killer.

The cross had been planted on the pitcher's

mound with the victim facing home plate. His muscular arms stretched toward first and third, while his feet were angled toward the pitching rubber. A garbage bag had been slipped over the victim's head to protect his identity from the news choppers that hovered over the field. Meanwhile, several officers searched around the cross for physical evidence.

Strangely, Dial saw a second team of cops standing in front of the Green Monster. He tried to figure out what they were doing, but the fence was over 300 feet away, and his already shitty vision was being obscured by the spotlights. Throw in the wattage of the stadium lights, and Dial felt like he was standing in the harsh glare of the afternoon sun, even though it was midnight in Boston.

'Hey you,' a cop yelled in an accent thicker than chowder. 'Get outta here. This field is off-limits.'

Dial whipped out his credentials. 'Where can I find the man in charge?'

'Probably takin' a leak in the dugout. Captain's got a wicked large prostate. Can't last ten minutes without hittin' the crapper.'

Dial nodded, pulling out his notebook. 'What can you tell me about the vic?'

'He was an asshole. Wicked bat, wicked arm, but nothin' more than a cock tease. Can you imagine him in our lineup? No way the Yanks beat us.'

'Hold up. The vic was a ballplayer?'

The cop stared at Dial with a mixture of amusement and disgust. 'That's right, Frenchie. He was a ballplayer. You guys have baseball over there in Paris? Or are you too busy eatin' cheese and watchin' Jerry Lewis movies to play sports?'

Ouch! Dial wondered, *Where did* that *come from?*

The truth was, he'd been told very little about the case from Henri Toulon, only that a third victim had been found. Dial knew if he wanted to see the crime scene, he needed to take the quickest route to Boston, even if it meant not being fully briefed on the case.

Unfortunately, now he was paying for his haste.

At least until he decided to do something about it.

Dial took a step toward the cop. 'First of all, you Beantown piece of shit, if you were half the cop that I am, you would've noticed that I can speak English better than you. So your theory that I'm French is as misplaced as my assumption that you're drunk just because you're a Boston cop. Secondly, I grew up in New England, so I know more about the Sox's history than half the players on the team, which isn't saying much, since most of them aren't American. Finally, if you would've taken the time to read my badge, you would've noticed that I *run* the Homicide Division at Interpol, which means if someone dies on planet Earth, the odds are pretty good that I'm in charge. You got that? Now why don't you run off like a good little batboy and tell your captain that *his* boss is here.'

The cop blinked a few times, then did what he was

told. Five minutes later Captain Michael Cavanaugh was introducing himself with a firm handshake. 'Sorry about our lack of hospitality. We're spread a little thin right now. Hell, if we had known a bigwig was coming to town, I'm sure the mayor would've greeted you himself.'

'I'm glad he didn't. I'm here to find a killer, not get my ass kissed.'

Cavanaugh laughed and patted Dial on his shoulder. 'Then you'll fit right in with me. Just tell me what you want to know, and I'll be happy to help.'

'We can start with the vic's name. I understand he's an athlete.'

'Yes, sir, a helluva athlete. Truth be told, we were kind of looking forward to booing the bum all weekend. I guess the good Lord decided to protect him from the abuse.'

This was *protection*? Holy shit! That meant the victim could only be one person. The most hated man in Boston: Orlando Pope. Stunned, Dial tried to figure out how a Yankee fit in with the others. First a priest, then a prince, now a Pope. Maybe the killers had something against the letter P? If so, the plumbers of the world should be very afraid. 'Mind if I take a look?'

'I don't mind if he don't mind.'

Dial nodded, his eyes searching for anything that seemed out of place. He dealt with copycat crimes on a regular basis, so his first order of business was figuring out if Pope was victim number three or just a copycat corpse, someone's sick way of stealing the spotlight from the real killer.

Most investigators would've started with the body, but not Dial. He knew most copycats got the body right – at least until the forensic experts got involved with all their high-tech toys and found fifty things that didn't belong. But the place they normally screwed up was in the minutiae, the small facts that were never released to the press, all the things that couldn't be known by simply looking at a picture that had been published on the Internet.

In his world, the trivial was sometimes more important than the significant.

Dial started with the construction of the cross, making sure that the wood was similar in color and age to the African oak. Then he examined the three spikes, eyeing their length and making sure that the victim was positioned in the same way as the others.

When that checked out, he turned his attention to the body, first looking at the wounds on his back, the way his skin had been sliced open with repetitive blows of a metal-tipped whip during the scourging process, then examining his rib cage, probing his puncture wound with a gloved finger, hoping that the tip of the blade had fractured and remained imbedded in his chest.

'Whatcha lookin' for?' Cavanaugh wondered. 'The wound's clean.'

'Just doing my job. I tend to double-check every-thing.'

'Yeah, I noticed.'

Dial smiled, then glanced at the choppers still hovering overhead. 'Can't you do anything about them? I need to remove the bag to see the handwriting on the sign.'

Cavanaugh stared at him like he was crazy. 'There ain't no sign under there. Just Pope's ugly mug, which we're trying to keep out of the papers.' He chuckled to himself. 'He's been crucified enough in our sports pages.'

Dial ignored the joke. It was typical police humor. 'I'll be damned. The most famous vic yet, and they eliminate the sign. Why would they do that?'

Cavanaugh shrugged. 'Then again, I don't know what you're talking about. What type of sign were you expecting? I didn't hear anything about a sign.'

'That's because we've been keeping it quiet.' Dial took a step toward Cavanaugh, making sure no one else was listening. 'The first two bodies had signs that referred to the cross. "IN THE NAME OF THE FATHER" was on the first. "AND OF THE SON" was with the second. I was kind of expecting the third one tonight. Makes me wonder if this is a copycat.'

Cavanaugh nodded, like something finally started to make sense in his mind. 'No, this isn't a copycat. I can promise you that.'

'Really? How can you be so sure?'

'Because of the sign.'

Dial winced. 'What sign? I thought you said there wasn't a sign.'

'Not under the bag, at least.' Cavanaugh searched Dial's face, trying to figure out if he was kidding. 'I guess you haven't made it to the outfield yet.'

'The outfield?' Just then it hit Dial. 'Ah, son of a bitch. Not the Monster.'

Dial took a deep breath and shifted his gaze to the left-field wall, which was blurry to him. Several cops were still out there, and Dial finally knew why. They were taking pictures of the message, debating if they should hose the blood off the wall or rip it down as evidence.

Plus they were trying to figure out what the killer meant when he wrote, 'AND OF THE HOLY.'

Disgusted, Cavanaugh sighed, 'After tonight, it's gonna be called the Red Monster.'

41

The Linate Airport was about four miles from the *Università Cattolica* campus. Frankie told Payne and Jones the fastest way to get there, which they hoped would be fast enough to grab Boyd, if he even appeared. Since a female had rented both vehicles, they knew there was a good chance that Boyd wouldn't show his face. If he did, great. They'd take him down quickly before he knew what hit him. But if he didn't, they'd follow his accomplice, hoping she led them to his hideout. Payne asked, 'Do we know what color the car is?'

Jones shook his head. 'The lady said it was a '98 Fiat. And since Fiat stands for *Fabbrica Italiana Automobili Torino*, there's bound to be plenty of 'em floating around Italy.'

Due to the early morning hour, they got to the rental office in less than five minutes. They parked across the street and spotted the female instantly. She was wearing a silk scarf over her dark brown hair, but the rest of her clothes were the same as they were in the surveillance photo.

This would be easier than they thought.

*

Paranoid, Maria glanced in her rearview mirror and saw nothing that concerned her. Traffic near the airport was virtually nonexistent, and the only visible light was from the iron lampposts that lined the roads of the desolate textile district. If all went well, she figured she'd be out of the city before the streets filled with the prying eyes of the Milanese workforce.

At least that was her plan.

The return trip to the abandoned warehouse was an uneventful one. As an extra precaution, she drove around the block two extra times, making sure that no one was following her. Once she was certain, she pulled her yellow Fiat down the cobblestone alley near the warehouse and parked behind a Dumpster, where she left the headlights on in order to find her way back inside.

'*Professore,*' she called as she entered the building. 'I'm back.'

Boyd emerged from the shadows and greeted her with a warm smile. 'Thank goodness, my dear. I've been worried sick. I kept having these dreadful thoughts that you were apprehended.'

She shook her head as she removed her silk scarf and replaced it with a ball cap. 'Are you ready? We need to take advantage of the darkness while we can.'

'Yes, by all means. Let me gather our things, and we can depart. Just give me a moment.'

Earlier that morning she'd wanted to take Boyd with her to the rental agency, although after much discussion, they decided it would be best if she went alone. It would've been faster if he'd tagged along, but he assumed the *polizia* would be staking out the airports and figured the farther he stayed away from the place, the better. And it was a good thing, too, for she noticed a number of officers near the terminal, and most of them were carrying Boyd's picture.

'*Professore!*' she urged. 'We have to get going. Please hurry.'

But unlike before, he didn't respond. In fact, the only noise she heard was the beating of her own heart, a sound that suddenly increased in volume and rapidity.

Curious and slightly concerned, Maria crept past several wooden crates and headed toward the area where they'd slept. Unfortunately, the deeper she ventured into the building, the darker it got, and before long she found herself struggling to see even a foot in front of her.

'*Professore?* Where are you? What's wrong?'

When she heard no response, her curiosity was replaced with fear. What if someone had found him? What if he'd tripped in the darkness and hurt himself? What if someone . . . ?

Just then Maria heard movement behind her. She ducked under several cobwebs and sidestepped a stack of boxes while heading toward the car's headlights. To her surprise she saw Boyd sitting on the hood of the Fiat the moment she reached the alleyway.

'*Professore!* I've been looking all over for you. How'd you get out here?'

'With a little help, my dear.'

She smiled, glad that he was safe. 'The lights *were* helpful, weren't they?'

He sighed, 'Regrettably, that's not what I meant.'

'It wasn't? Then what are you talking about?'

At which point Payne introduced himself. 'He's trying to tell you I dragged him out.'

She whirled and saw his Beretta, his eyes completely hidden behind dark shades.

'Who the hell are you?' she demanded in Italian. 'What do you want from us?'

But Payne refused to answer. Instead, he grabbed her by her hair and threw her against the car. She briefly resisted until he let her know that he was in charge, shoving her face against the warm metal of the Fiat. Then he strengthened his hold by ramming his knee between her thighs and pinning her in place with his body weight. From there he was able to frisk her and tie her hands behind her back with a piece of cord that he'd found inside the warehouse. Finally, once she was secured, he spoke. 'Now, what were you asking?'

She looked at him, confused. She had assumed that Payne was with the *polizia* because of his dark hair and his Beretta. But the more she heard his voice, the more certain she was that he was an American. 'Who are you?' she demanded in English. 'What the hell do you want?'

Payne grinned at her profanity. 'Hey, Doc! Where'd you find her? She's feisty.'

'You're damn right I'm feisty. Now answer my damn question before I start screaming.'

'Excuse me?' Payne took a step forward and placed his gun under her chin. 'Listen up, lady, I'm not sure you understand the situation, so I'm going to break it down for you. First of all, what's your name? I don't think it's appropriate to call you "lady" when you don't act like one.'

'Mmrria.'

He eased up slightly so he could understand her.

'My name's Maria.'

'OK, Maria, here's the deal: I currently have a gun buried in your throat. Do you feel it?'

She nodded carefully.

'Good. I thought you would. It's kind of hard to miss, huh?'

She nodded again.

'Wow! You're getting pretty good at this. I ask a question and you answer it. Very softly. OK? There's no shouting, no anger, and no feistiness. Men with guns don't like feistiness. Do you understand me?' She nodded one more time. 'Now then, my partner and I have a few questions that we've been dying to ask you guys.'

'Your partner?'

Jones announced his presence by opening the Fiat's door.

'Oh,' she grunted.

'*Oh?*' Jones mocked. 'I make a cool-ass entrance, and all you have to say is, "*Oh*"?'

She looked at him and sneered. 'What would you like me to say?'

'I don't know. I figured a good lookin' lady like yourself would at least try to butter me up. You know, turn on the sexual charm to sweet-talk your way out of this. And if that didn't work, I figured you'd club me like the security guard at the library.'

Maria turned a bright shade of red. 'I swear to God I didn't mean to hurt that guy. I just wanted him to let go of me. That's all! I had to warn –'

Payne waited for her to finish, but she never did. 'You had to warn who? Your boyfriend?'

'Good heavens!' Boyd snapped. 'I'm not her boyfriend. What kind of man do you think I am? Maria is simply a student of mine! Nothing more!'

Payne said, 'A student? A student in crime, maybe. I mean, you guys have been on quite a roll. The helicopter in Orvieto, the exploding bus, the library guard with the swollen nuts. Tsk, tsk, tsk. You should be ashamed of yourselves.'

'Ashamed?' she cried. 'We haven't done anything wrong! The helicopter and the guard were self-defense. And the bus was an attempt on *our* lives.'

'On *your* lives? Please! Why would anyone murder so many people just to kill you?'

She was ready to answer until she noticed Boyd shaking his head.

'Come on,' Payne goaded. 'We know all about the

treasure in the Catacombs. Or is there some other secret that you're trying to keep from us?'

Boyd's mouth fell open. 'But how? Who? . . . Who are you two?'

'Now, Doc, why should we answer that? You guys won't answer our questions, so why should we answer yours?'

Jones chuckled. 'I don't know, maybe we should introduce ourselves? It would be the polite thing to do.'

'Yeah, you're probably right.' Payne turned toward Boyd and grinned. 'Hi! I'm Jon and this is my buddy, D.J. We work for the CIA.'

'The CIA?' Boyd echoed.

Payne replied in a thick German accent. 'Yes, *Herr* Doctor! And ve know you are a spy!'

'A spy? What in the world are you talking about?'

Jones laughed. 'Quit the games, Doc. We know all about your past.'

'My past?'

'You know,' Payne said, 'where you steal antiquities from half the countries in Europe, then figure out how to hide the stuff. Not a bad scheme, but why in the world would a smart guy like you double-cross men like Manzak and Buckner? Those guys are kind of scary.'

Suddenly Maria's eyes filled with doubt. *'Professore?'*

'Good Lord, you mustn't believe these chaps! I've never heard anything so outrageous in all my life! Double-crossing the CIA? That's bloody pre-posterous!'

Payne pushed the issue. 'What about American Cargo International? Does *that* name ring a bell?'

Cracks started to surface in Boyd's veneer. 'Yes, but . . .'

'But what? They've been financing you for years, haven't they?'

'Yes, but, that doesn't mean –'

'Doesn't mean what? Doesn't mean you're connected to the CIA? Come on! I got the information straight from the Pentagon. I know you're on the CIA's payroll.'

Boyd blinked a few times, trying to hold his facade. 'Maybe so, but that doesn't mean I've double-crossed them. I mean . . .' His voice trailed off.

'Go on,' Payne insisted. 'What *do* you mean? You obviously did something to piss them off. They wouldn't have brought us into this if you weren't a priority.'

Suddenly, horror filled his eyes. 'They what?'

'You heard me. They brought us in to track you down. We're what you call specialists.'

'Wait a bloody second! You mean you're not *in* the Agency?'

'Hell, no!' Payne said. 'We're world-class bounty hunters, hired to find your ass.' He reached into his pocket and pulled out Manzak's tracking device. 'One touch of this button, and our obligations are done. They'll come running, and we'll get to go home.'

Boyd stared at the device for several seconds. 'Yes,' he finally said, 'you'll get to go home all right . . . in a fucking body bag.'

Maria gaped at the comment. It was the first time she'd ever heard him swear.

'Jesus!' Boyd continued. 'Open your fucking eyes! The CIA doesn't go out of house for help. They've got agents planted in every country in the world, ready to handle anything that could come up. There's no way they'd turn to someone outside their network to hunt me down. That's not how they work!'

'Oh yeah,' Jones challenged. 'And what makes you such an expert?'

Boyd glared, locking his eyes on Jones's. 'Because I'm one of those agents.'

'Excuse me?' Payne said.

'What?' Maria shrieked.

'You heard me. I've been with them for years, using my professorship to travel abroad.'

Jones rolled his eyes. 'Oh really? What kind of secret agent comes right out and says he's an operative? Not a real one, I know that.'

'You know what? You're right. In most situations that would be unheard of. Treasonous, even. But I'm afraid this isn't an ordinary situation. Due to the false press I've been getting, my career as a spy is over. Plus, I get the feeling if you push that button, my life will be finished, too. So what do I have to lose?'

'Wait a second!' Payne demanded. 'You're trying to tell us you're a CIA *agent*? Get serious! Can't you come up with something better than that?'

'Well I certainly could if I was trying to come up with something, but the fact is, I'm telling you the truth. Sure, I know I don't look like an agent. But the truth is, most company men don't. If we did, we would all stand out.'

Jones smiled at the logic. 'He's got a point there.'

'What? Don't tell me you believe him! He's been working at Dover for thirty years!'

'Yeah, but I've heard some crazy shit about the CIA. They've got NOCs everywhere, just waiting to help their cause.'

Payne knew NOC meant *nonofficial cover*, a government officer working behind foreign lines without diplomatic immunity, but wasn't sure what Jones was insinuating. So Payne grabbed him by his arm and pulled him off to the side, never taking his eyes off Boyd and Maria. 'What are you saying? We should believe this wacko?'

'No, I'm not saying that at all. There's a chance he's bullshitting us to save his ass. Then again, he could be telling us the truth. The point is, I don't really know.'

'Then let's push the button and talk to Manzak. Personally, I don't give a damn what happens to these two as long as we're out of the mix. We gotta deal with him at some point, so let's just get it over with. I mean, what's the worst that can happen?'

'Don't do it!' Boyd begged from a distance. 'I'm telling you, if you push that button, we'll all be killed.

Just like the people on the bus. Don't you understand that? These guys can't afford to leave any witnesses. An entire religion rides on this.'

Payne laughed at his claim. 'Rides on what? A buried treasure? What religion are you talking about, Greedism?'

'Greed? You think this is about greed? Dammit, man, you don't know anything! The scroll we found in the Catacombs isn't about money. It's about the truth! It will cast doubt over everything that you've been taught to believe. Even Christ himself.'

'*Professore!*'

He turned toward Maria to explain. 'They *have* to hear this, my dear. If he pushes that button, we're going to die, and so is this secret. It's as simple as that. The Church cannot allow this to get out. It will shake the foundation of Christianity.'

Payne looked at Jones and whistled. 'Well, that settles it. I'm pushing the button. I mean, first he claims to be in the CIA, now he says the Church is trying to kill him. This guy's a loon.'

Jones stared at Boyd. 'Personally, I've always had my doubts about the pope. Anyone who wears a hat like that is up to no good.'

'Good Lord!' Boyd shouted. 'I'm not saying the pope! But someone in the Church is linked to this. They have to be. I mean, they're the only ones that –' Boyd stopped his speech in midsentence and inexplicably turned his head upwards. 'Oh, no!'

'What?' Payne asked. 'Is God talking to you now?'

'Shhh!' he ordered. 'That sound. Don't you hear it? I heard the same thing in Orvieto.'

Payne and Jones had no idea what Boyd was talking about, but when they stopped to humor him, they actually heard a rumble above the Fiat's engine. They weren't sure where it was coming from due to the echo in the alley. The sound was getting louder, though.

Jones turned off the Fiat and whispered, 'Did you push the button by mistake?'

Payne shook his head as he walked down the alley, away from the others. He traveled nearly fifty feet before he tilted his ear toward the sky.

'Choppers,' he announced. 'More than one. And they're coming this way.'

'How did they find us?' Jones asked.

'I don't know. Maybe this unit's been tracking us the whole time.' He slammed the device to the ground and smashed it. 'Doesn't matter. They won't find us if we don't want them to.'

Payne hustled toward Boyd and rammed his gun under his chin. 'Where were you born?'

Boyd breathed deep, then said, 'Do you want the truth, or what I've been taught to recite?'

Payne wasn't in the mood for games so he pushed the Beretta even deeper into his throat.

'Fine,' he grunted. 'Seattle, Washington.'

'Where'd you go to school?'

'The U.S. Naval Academy. Then Oxford.'

Payne eased up slightly, just in case he was a fellow midshipman. 'Bad answer, Doc. It just so happens I know a thing or two about the Academy.'

'Great! Ask me anything! Just do it quick, or we're going to die.'

Payne paused for a second, trying to think of a good one. 'Name a road on the Academy grounds.'

'What? There are quite a few –'

'Name one, or I shoot.'

'Fine, er, King George Street.' Which, no matter how inappropriate it seemed, was actually the main road at the Academy. 'I can continue if you'd like. Wood Street, Dock Street, Blake Road, Decatur Road, College Ave –'

Payne nodded, half surprised by his response. 'Where were classes held during the war?'

'Which war?'

'You tell me.'

'I imagine you're referring to the Civil War, since that's the only time sessions were held elsewhere. And the answer is Newport, Rhode Island – moved there for safety reasons.'

'Not bad,' Payne admitted. 'But this last one is the clincher. Any red-blooded Academy man would know the answer to this in a heartbeat. Are you ready? Because this is going to determine if you live or die. Got it? When you were in school, what was the name of the women's dorm?'

Boyd smiled, quickly realizing it was a trick question. 'Alas, there wasn't one. Much to my disappointment, females weren't admitted until *after* I'd departed. Around 1976, I believe.'

Begrudgingly, Payne lowered his gun. He still wasn't certain about Boyd, but his gut told him that he was telling the truth. 'So, you went to the Academy?'

Boyd nodded. 'I take it you're an Academy man, too?'

'Yes, sir. Jonathon Payne, at your service.'

'Well, Mr Payne, if you're interested in survival, I recommend we get moving. Otherwise, we will be killed before we leave this alley.'

42

It happened years ago, right after finding the scrolls in the secret vaults. Documents that the Vatican didn't even know it had. Following their intricate instructions, Benito Pelati journeyed to Orvieto and took pictures of the ground using geological prototypes that he had borrowed from Germany. High-tech stuff that no one else had access to. Equipment that allowed him to chart every inch of the town from the topsoil to more than a hundred feet below. Studies no one had conducted before and hadn't been allowed to run since.

Needless to say, there was a very good reason.

More than fifty tunnels were detected near the surface, all of them starting in private property and branching through the tufa like a tangle of arteries. Most of them stopped abruptly – either because the locals hit a section of stone they couldn't penetrate or they ran out of patience and quit looking – while others interconnected with their neighbors' tunnels. The deepest anyone got was twenty-three feet underground. Impressive, considering their rudimentary digging techniques, yet not deep enough to reach what they were hoping to find: the Catacombs of Orvieto.

Benito knew the Catacombs existed. Or *had* at one time. The scrolls he found were proof of that. So were all the other documents he'd read in the Secret Archives. But prior to his geological testing, he had no idea if the Catacombs would still be there. Or what condition they might be in. One record at the Vatican mentioned a massive cave-in shortly after the Great Schism. If so, it could have wiped out everything he was hoping to find. All the proof he needed.

But thankfully, that wasn't the case. One look at the geological report confirmed it. The Catacombs were still there and in great shape. Furthermore, they were more substantial than the Vatican had ever realized. Papal records from the time of the Schism indicated one floor of chambers and tunnels. Nothing else. But Pelati saw more than that on this report. He saw multiple levels. And stairs. And areas so far under the soil that he doubted the Vatican had ever reached them. He wouldn't know for sure until he explored the tunnels himself, but from the look of their design, Pelati sensed the ancient Romans had built a lower tomb, then immediately sealed it off from the upper chambers. Why the Romans did this, he wasn't sure. But if his family's secret was to be believed, that was probably where he'd find the evidence he was looking for.

Of course, he had other things to worry about before he could investigate.

His first order of business was to stop all digging

in Orvieto. Another cave-in was the last thing he wanted, so he went to the local police chief and told him that Orvieto was in danger of collapsing. To bolster his case, he showed the chief the seismic studies that he'd conducted – conveniently omitting the information about the Catacombs – then walked from house to house pointing out all the tunnels that had been constructed.

Locals still refer to it as the Shovel Act of 1982, because digging became a criminal offense.

Next Benito bought the land above the twenty-three-foot tunnel, claiming the government needed to stabilize the property, or Orvieto might implode. The owner was so embarrassed by his handi-work and mortified by what could've happened that he sold everything to Benito to ensure the safety of his hometown. Except Benito had no intention of filling the hole. Instead, he planned to lengthen it to the depth of thirty-six feet, for that was where the Catacombs began.

All told the process took several weeks. Benito eschewed attention, so he used unobtrusive equip-ment and a skeleton crew made up of miners from eastern Europe who couldn't speak or read Italian. He knew if he used local workers they'd be familiar with the legend of the Catacombs and would figure out what Benito was doing. But the foreigners were clueless. He could keep them quiet without doing any of the digging himself. That is until his miners reached a depth of thirty-five feet. One foot short of history. From there he couldn't risk their further involvement. So he thanked them for their effort with a big celebration. He put a bullet in each of their brains, then buried them with their own shovels. Just like the great explorers of yesteryear. Men who cared more about fame and fortune than the hired hands who helped them achieve it.

Ruthless. That's what he slowly became when he found the scrolls at the Vatican. Until that point he was a passionate academician, nothing more, someone who wasn't afraid to take chances and fight for what he believed in. But when he found the scrolls, his persona started to change. He slowly became wicked. Malicious. Immoral. All of it fueled by what the scrolls stood for: power and un-imaginable wealth.

From that point on, Benito didn't care about his workers. Or the town of Orvieto. Or the sanctity of the Catholic Church. All he cared about was himself and his family's secret.

It had been dormant for several centuries. He planned to release it like a plague.

Benito had set things in motion once before, a few years ago. He had determined the best way to use the Catacombs and had scheduled a meeting with the Vatican to discuss his discovery.

But a potential windfall appeared. One that forced him to shift his timeline.

A translator working for Benito found a reference

in an ancient manuscript that described the home of a Roman hero who lived in the foothills of Vindobona, Illyria. Inside a tomb of marble, he had placed a relic and a first-person account of the crucifixion. It threatened to contain everything that the world and the Church should know about the events in Jerusalem.

Details from before, during, and after the death of Christ.

Benito's oldest son, Roberto, felt they should meet with the Vatican as planned. He reasoned their organization was ready to strike, and it would hurt their cause if there was a delay. But Benito disagreed. He canceled their meeting, reassuring his son that this discovery would actually increase their bargaining power with the Catholics. Roberto eventually relented.

From that point on, finding the Roman vault became the number-one priority in Benito's life.

Everything else would be put on hold until the tomb was discovered in the hills of Illyria.

Recently, his goal had been accomplished.

43

Same agenda, different crew. That's what Dial decided as he studied the haphazard way the blood had been splashed across the Green Monster, the way the message was scrawled as an afterthought instead of a fancy signature claiming responsibility. No way these were the same men who'd killed the priest in Denmark. The original sign had been painted with the skill and precision of a calligrapher, while the latest sign looked more like a kid's finger painting. Like it was done by someone who didn't understand what they were being asked to do but did it anyway. Someone who was going through the motions.

Alas, that made the middle case an enigma. The sign in Libya was painted with painstaking precision, yet blood was spread all over the Roman Arch in a spontaneous display of rage.

Dial wondered, why be precise and sloppy at the same crime scene? Could it have been done by a third crew? Or a mixture of the other two? Furthermore, did it even matter? Maybe he should be concentrating more on the message instead of the killers themselves. It was an interesting notion that he wanted to pursue. That is until he was interrupted by a tap on his shoulder. He turned and saw an Asian man standing behind him, just looking at him as though he wasn't sure what to do next. Dial said, 'Can I help you?'

Mark Chang nodded and fumbled for his ID. He was a first-year agent at the NCB office in Boston, which meant he was Dial's main contact while he was in town. The man in charge of the man in charge. 'I'm sorry I didn't meet you earlier. I would've, had I known.'

Dial looked at the kid and figured he was no more than twenty-two. His hair was a mess, and so were his clothes. They looked like he had found them at the bottom of his hamper. 'Known what?'

'Known you were in town. No one told me, I swear. I rushed down here as soon as I heard.'

And he looked like it, too. Like he jumped out of bed and caught the first bus he could find.

'Don't worry, Chang. I didn't know I was coming until the last minute. I grabbed the last flight out of Paris and –'

'Wait. Paris, *France*?'

'Yeah. Big country on the other side of the Atlantic. It's listed on most maps.'

'Yes, sir, I know where it is. It's just, um, how did you beat me here? I thought maybe you were in town already, but to beat me from France? I mean, they found Pope's body less than two hours ago, which means your plane had to –'

'Whoa, whoa, whoa! Slow down, son. Say that again.'

Chang double-checked his notepad. 'According to

911, the groundskeeper reported Pope's murder just after ten. From there, Boston PD notified Interpol, who then notified me an hour ago.' He checked his watch to be sure. 'I don't understand, sir. How'd you get here so fast?'

But Dial ignored the question, turning his back on Chang to replay the past twenty-four hours. He'd started the day in Libya, where he caught a plane to France. That's when Henri Toulon notified him that another victim had been found, this time in Boston. From there he hopped on another plane and flew to America.

That meant he knew about the victim several hours before his body was actually found.

'Holy shit! We've got ourselves a taunter.' Dial grabbed Chang's notepad to be sure of the timeline. 'I knew about the murder before it happened. The bastards called us ten hours ago.'

'They what? Why would they do that?'

'To taunt us, Chang. To taunt us. Hence the name.'

'Yeah, but –'

'They're letting us know that we can't stop 'em, not even with a head start. They're saying we can investigate them all we want, and it won't make a damn bit of difference. They won't stop until they're ready to stop.'

'And when will that be?'

'Soon. They're running out of words.'

'*Words?*'

'Yeah, Chang, words. You know, the things in a dictionary? I can't believe you don't know what words are. What, is English your second language?'

'No, sir. I was born right here in —'

Dial rolled his eyes. Rookies could be so dumb. 'It was a joke, son. Just a joke.'

'Oh, but —'

'Listen, Chang, I like you, so let me give you a piece of advice that my captain once gave to me. Just shut the fuck up and listen, OK?'

'OK, sir, I'm listening.'

'No, Chang. That *was* the advice. *Just shut the fuck up and listen.* Understand? There's no need to repeat everything I say, and there's no need to question everything I do. Your main job as a rookie is to observe. Learn the basic techniques, do the simple tasks that I give to you, and remember everything I say. Don't question what I say, just remember it, write it down if you have to. Got that? There's a big difference between listening and speaking.'

Chang nodded, not saying a word.

'See? You're learning already ... Now, are you ready to go to work?'

Chang nodded again, this time smiling.

'Good. Then this is what we need to do.'

44

Payne and Jones knew little about the streets of Milan, so there was no way they could outmaneuver a helicopter. Especially in a Fiat. The truth was, they probably could have in the Ferrari, except it was too small for four people, and they didn't want to split up. That left only two options: hide in the warehouse or turn themselves in.

And guess what? All of them voted for number two.

Of course, that's misleading. The truth was, they weren't actually going to surrender. Payne felt if he offered Boyd as a sacrificial lamb, then he could buy Jones enough time to pull off a miracle. At least Payne hoped he could. If not, he knew he'd regret the decision for the rest of his very short life.

After finalizing their plans, Payne dragged Boyd into the middle of the darkened street where they stood, looking skyward, as two Bell helicopters settled in a neighboring lot. The insurgence of rotors kicked up enough wind and dust to rival a cyclone. But it didn't stop Payne from seeing, thanks to his custom-fit sunglasses. Not only did they shield his eyes from the elements, but they concealed his true emotions, which would be even more important if his ruse was going to work.

'It's time to begin,' Payne shouted over the tumult. 'Don't take this personally.'

He put his hand on Boyd's back and shoved him to the ground, knowing that they were being watched by Manzak and his friends. He continued his charade, dropping to one knee and double-checking the cord around Boyd's wrists. Boyd played along by squirming and making girly noises that sounded like they belonged at a sorority pillow fight. Payne let him know he was overdoing it by slapping him in the back of the head. 'Knock it off, Suzie, and start acting like a criminal.'

The hatch on the front chopper swung open, and Manzak climbed out. Not smiling. Not waving. Not giving Payne a thumbs-up or any signs of approval. In other words, he was the same stoic bastard that had shown up in Pamplona. Part killer. Part robot. All asshole. Unfortunately, the biggest problem for Payne was he didn't know if Manzak was going to honor their original deal. Sure, Payne knew he wasn't the real Manzak, but the truth was, he still could've been with the CIA since he had enough clout to pull Payne out of prison. For all he knew, maybe Manzak was a name the CIA gave out to several undercover operatives just to confuse people.

If that was the case, it was definitely working because Payne was confused. He didn't know if Manzak was going to take Boyd back to CIA headquarters and milk him for information, or if he was going to shoot him in the back of the head the moment they left Payne's side. The truth was, he didn't know who or what to believe, and neither did Jones. They didn't know if Boyd had done any of the things that they had been told – the forgeries, the smuggling, the exploding bus – or if he was the victim of an elaborate setup. Simply put, Payne and Jones didn't know shit.

Anyway, Manzak shouted, 'Nice work, Payne! I'm impressed by your efficiency.'

'And I'm impressed by your clairvoyance. How'd you know we had him?'

'We have our ways. And they're rarely wrong.'

'I'm glad you're on my side,' Payne said without smiling. 'So what's the next step?'

Manzak moved closer. 'I need to debrief you before you're officially done.'

Payne wondered if he meant that literally. 'Then what are we waiting for? Which one of those choppers is mine?'

'You'll be in the first one with me.' He took another step forward. 'But first I'll need to check you for weapons.'

'Excuse me?'

'Listen, Jon, I know how you must feel. But I can't let a nonagent on board without searching him. It's departmental policy.'

Payne stared at Manzak for several seconds, tempted to make a nasty scene, even though he realized it would hurt his plan in the long run. So instead of doing anything foolish, he placed his hands on top of his head and reluctantly agreed to the search. 'Try not to touch my ass, OK? I don't want to make Buckner jealous . . . Speaking of which, where is the big lug? I miss our conversations. He's quite the intellectual.'

'He's shutting down the chopper. He'll be out to greet you shortly.'

'Oh, I thought maybe he was at home, making you dinner.'

Manzak forced a laugh. 'You know, I find your humor ironic, especially since *you're* the one with a boyfriend. Where is Jones, anyway? Getting his nails done?'

'Well, I'll be damned! You made a joke! Not a funny one, but still a joke. Wait until I tell D.J. He won't believe me.'

'You still haven't answered my question. Where's your partner?'

'He's around the corner in our Ferrari. One signal from me, and he'll pull forward with the girl. That is, if you even know about her.'

'Of course we know about Maria – and your Ferrari. Although for safety's sake, it might be best if they stayed where they are.'

'Oh yeah? Why's that?'

Instead of answering, Manzak pulled a Hantek detonator from his coat pocket and pushed the button. A second later, the Ferrari erupted in a massive explosion, one that shot flames and debris high above the warehouse roof, literally propelling the frame of the car more than twenty feet in the air. But that was just the beginning. The fallout pelted the surrounding terrain like meteors, igniting the adjacent buildings and shaking the ground beneath their feet like a California quake.

Normally, Payne would've flinched. Or grabbed Boyd and made a mad dash for cover.

But not tonight. Not when the flames in the sky paled next to the fire in his eyes.

He'd been set up, and he finally had the proof that he was looking for.

Without saying a word, he took a step toward Manzak, looking forward to the popping sound his neck would make when he twisted it 360 degrees like that bitch from *The Exorcist*. Unfortunately, Payne's assault was interrupted by the swarm of bullets that buzzed over his head. Warning shots that had come from Buckner's gun as he emerged from the chopper.

'You vill stay still,' he growled in a thick European accent. 'I be seein' to zat.'

Manzak grinned at his arrival. 'Now you know why he didn't talk in Pamplona. Otto's still working on his English, but you can't beat him as a bodyguard.'

His bodyguard? Who the hell were these guys? Payne knew they weren't CIA the moment they blew up the Ferrari. Instead, he assumed they were part of the Italian crew that had covered up the two accidents. But now that he'd heard Otto's accent, that didn't seem likely. Otto/Buckner *wasn't* Italian. German maybe, but definitely not Italian.

Shit, Payne thought, how many countries were involved in this mess?

'Pick up ze doctor an' bring him to me!'

Payne was tempted to flip him off, but one look at the Russian assault rifle in Otto's hands changed his mind. If he'd felt like it, he could've ravaged Payne with multiple 5.56 mm rounds with the touch of a finger. Which put a whole new spin on the term *Otto*-matic weapon.

No, he decided, it would probably be best if he picked up ze doctor an' kept his mouth shut.

At least for the time being.

Less than twelve hours before, Jones had been staring at Maria's picture and dreaming of the romantic possibilities. Now he was lying next to her in the darkness, unsure if either of them were going to survive.

Jones said, 'Since we're risking our lives together, I figure we might as well introduce ourselves. My name's David Jones. D.J. for short.'

She shook his hand. 'Maria Magdalena Pelati. Kind of rolls off the tongue, doesn't it?'

'Pelati?' He considered her name for a few seconds but figured it had to be some kind of a coincidence – especially since she spoke with a faint English accent. 'Is that Italian?'

She nodded. 'I've lived in England for most of

my life, so I don't really consider myself Italian. Or English for that matter. Hell, I don't know *what* to consider myself.'

'How about exotic temptress?'

Blushing, she smiled at his comment. 'Works for me.'

'Good! Now that your identity crisis is over, let's get down to business. See those two helicopters over there? I need to take one of them out.'

'And how are you going to do that?'

'Sorry. You're going to have to wait and watch. I don't want to ruin the surprise.'

She sighed, disappointed. 'Fine, but can you at least tell me *when* you're going to —'

Just then the Ferrari erupted, lighting the sky with a burst of flames that rattled their chests like a jolt from a defibrillator. Jones instinctively threw himself on top of Maria to protect her, and as he did, he found the composure to say, 'I think *now* would be a good time, don't you?'

Following orders, Payne walked over to Dr Boyd and picked him up off the ground, giving him a chance to whisper in his ear. 'Stay very still . . . Things are about to get interesting.'

'Silence!' Otto screamed from several feet away. 'No talkin' to ze doctor.'

Payne nodded and placed his hand in the small of Boyd's back. 'Damn! I was just making sure he was all right. Show some compassion.'

'Compassion?' Manzak growled. 'There was no compassion during the Crusades, so there's no place for it now. Don't you get that? This is a holy war, and to guarantee our triumph there must be *no* compassion.'

Payne lifted Boyd's shirttail and grabbed the Beretta he had stashed in his belt. 'But doesn't that go against everything you're trying to protect?'

'You have no idea what I'm trying to protect! You probably think I'm fighting for Christ or some other fallacy. But I'm not. Those things have no meaning in *my* world, because I know the truth. I know what happened two thousand years ago. I know who the *real* hero is.'

Payne had no idea what Manzak was talking about but figured if he was in a talkative mood, the least he could do was listen. So he said, 'Are you referring to the scroll? Hell, I know all about it. Boyd's been so excited he's been blabbing to everybody that he's come in contact with. Hell, how do you think we found him so fast?'

Manzak's face went pale. 'Let's hope that isn't the case – for *their* sakes. I'd hate to see the death toll in this country continue to rise.'

'Come on! What's another exploding bus or two when you're in the middle of a holy war? Just keep laying the blame on Dr Boyd, and you can keep your hands clean.'

'Actually,' Manzak said, 'we've ridden that gelding long enough. Just to be safe, I think it's time to put two new horses into the mix, a couple of Thorough-breds with a history of violence. Personally, I think the press will find you and D.J. a lot more believable as cold-blooded killers.'

OK, now things were starting to make sense to Payne. They weren't just recruited for their ability to track Boyd. They were handpicked because of their violent pasts, making them the perfect scape-goats for any bloodshed that happened during this case. A dead body here, an exploding car there. All of it could be blamed on them.

Of course, Manzak — or whatever his real name was — needed the backing of a *powerful* entity to make that happen. Someone with the resources to acquire classified data from the U.S. Defense Depart-ment, forge picture-perfect CIA credentials, and manipulate the world media. Someone who would never be suspected, no matter how violent things became or how deeply they were involved in this mess. Someone who was willing to take some awfully big chances because they were desperate and had everything to lose.

At that moment Payne decided there was only one organization in the world that had the power and the incentive to pull something like this off.

And they got their mail at the Vatican.

45

The metal squealed as Jones shoved his switchblade into the seam, a sound Payne couldn't hear over the roar of the chopper's engine. Once his knife was in deep enough, he wiggled it back and forth until the fuel tank popped open. The insulated cap came off next. And he was greeted by the overwhelming scent of aviation fuel until he took off his shirt and stuffed it in the mouth of the fuel tank. Not only would that seal the vapors inside, but he could use the cloth as the wick for his Molotov *cockpit* – Jones's version of the original Russian cocktail. From there, all it would take was a single spark to do a hell of a lot of damage. With extra emphasis on the word *hell*.

Payne could see all of Jones's actions in the background, although his adversaries couldn't. He made sure of it by positioning Boyd and himself at a very precise angle.

'So,' Manzak taunted, 'where's your quick wit now? A minute ago you were teasing me about my clothes; now Otto shows up, and you're completely silent. How disappointing.'

'Don't you worry. I'll be taking some shots at you any minute now.'

'Oh really? And what is it you're waiting for?'

Several wisecracks ran through his mind. But instead of saying anything, he simply smiled and let the helicopter provide the punch line for him. The instant flame touched fuel, the chopper erupted, sending fire and metal in every direction. Payne used the tumult to his advantage, whipping out the Beretta from behind Dr Boyd and firing it at the biggest target he could find. His first shot ripped through Buckner's collarbone about six inches lower than he'd been aiming. He adapted to the conditions and put his next shot through the bridge of his nose, shattering the back of his skull and spraying gray matter everywhere, including on Manzak's face.

The sight and taste of Otto's brain caused Manzak to panic. Instead of shooting back or fighting Payne like a man, he scrambled to his feet and tried to run away, an attempt Payne thwarted by putting a bullet into the back of his left knee. Just like that he crashed to the ground like a bat with a broken wing, an image that seemed kind of fitting.

In truth Payne was tempted to finish him off right there. Hell, it would've been easy, maybe even pleasurable. A quick shot to the dome and he would've been done. The only problem was all the questions that still danced through Payne's mind. They needed to be answered before Manzak could be eliminated. That's why Payne jumped on his back and frisked him for weapons, finding a knife and a SIG Sauer P226 service auto.

'Hey, Dick! How ya doing? Not too good, huh?'

Manzak responded with a shriek that rose above the roar of the nearby flames.

'That's it, let it all out. You got a boo-boo on your knee, didn't you? Well, you should've thought of that before you tried to blow up my friends. You see, that made me *very* angry.'

He screamed again, this time directing several vulgarities at Payne.

'Yeah, yeah, yeah. Curse it up. That's always a good idea when someone's pointing a gun at you. Oh, speaking of guns.' Payne glanced at Boyd and noticed that he was sitting on the ground, half-shaken. 'Hey Doc? Don't even think about going for Otto's rifle. I've got the peripheral vision of a housefly and two handguns to work with.'

'Fear not. My hands are bound behind me in some kind of elaborate knot.'

'That's a Payne special. You aren't getting out of that without a knife.' Payne glanced at Jones and noticed him giving a thumbs-up. 'You're able to walk, aren't you? Why don't you stumble over to D.J. and ask him to cut you free? I don't want to dull this blade before surgery.'

'Surgery?'

Payne gave him a hard look, one that told him he should know better. 'Sorry. Doctor/patient confidentiality. It's between Manzak and me.'

'Ah, yes. How silly of me. Perhaps it would be best if I left the operating room.'

Payne kept his eyes on Boyd until he reached

Jones. At that point he was able to relax and focus on Agent Manzak, who was still writhing in agony underneath Payne.

'You know, Dick, I almost hate to admit this, but I've wanted to hurt you from the moment we met. I don't know what it is about you – maybe it was the way you blackmailed me into helping you or maybe it's because you just blew up an exquisite automobile. Whatever the reason, I thought you should know I'm gonna enjoy every minute of this.'

Grinning sadistically, Payne showed him a stick that he'd found on the ground. It was no more than six inches long, yet it was the perfect size for what he was about to do.

'I once talked to a POW who said the most pain he'd ever experienced in his entire life was from a simple piece of wood. Hard to believe, huh? But if you think about it, I'm sure you can imagine some *vicious* and *barbaric* possibilities for a stick like this. Can't you, Dick?'

Manzak didn't want to, but his mind naturally focused on the most horrendous things he could think of. His eyes being gouged out. His eardrums being punctured. His anus being violated by the world's largest splinter. Crippling acts that would scar him for the rest of his life.

And that was the reaction Payne was hoping for.

Back when he was training for the MANIACs, he learned one of the most effective ways to get information from a prisoner wasn't through torture but rather the *foreshadowing* of torture – the act of planting a psychological seed in someone's head, then waiting for panic to set in. If done right, some people would literally piss their pants long before they were touched. Of course mere threats wouldn't work on everyone. But Payne figured anyone who traveled with a bodyguard would crack quicker than Humpty Dumpty in a mosh pit.

'Hey, Dick,' he said, 'you've read my personnel file, right? So I'm sure you realize I'm fully capable of making a Dick-kabob. You know that, don't you?'

Manzak grimaced and nodded his head.

'Very good! Now all you have to do is keep answering my questions, and there's a chance I'll let you live. However, if I get the sense that you're lying to me *or* you choose to remain silent, I'm going to show you the Vietnam stick trick. Understood?'

He nodded again.

'OK, let's start with some easy ones. You know, just to help you get into the flow of the game … How'd you know that we had Boyd?'

'Your car. We put a sensor under the Ferrari. We were able to follow that.'

'Bullshit!' Payne threw a savage punch into his kidney. 'Remember what I said about lying? Now tell me how you found us.'

Manzak gasped for air, yet somehow managed to answer. 'I just did.'

'No way! Even if you tracked the car, there's no way you could've known we had Boyd. How'd you know we had him?'

'The airport ... we had a man at the airport ... When we saw your beacon there, we had him investigate ... just to make sure you weren't leaving the country ... He went outside and saw the girl ... That's when he notified us ... from the airport ... I swear!'

Payne was tempted to smile – Manzak had broken easier than an antique teacup – but he knew it would ruin the mood. For this to work, he had to maintain the austere glare of an executioner.

So he said, 'Where else did you have men? Were you following us the entire time?'

'There wasn't a need. The beacon did it for us. We just followed you from afar.'

'Dick, Dick, Dick. I find that *so* hard to believe.' He took the chunk of wood and pressed it against Manzak's neck. 'You didn't, for instance, have someone in Orvieto?'

'No,' he cried, 'I didn't have anyone in Orvieto. That's the last place Boyd would be!'

'Man, I'm *so* disappointed in you. I wanted to christen this stick on an important question. But if you keep lying, I'm gonna have to use it now.'

'I'm not lying!' he shrieked. 'I swear to God I'm not!'

'So your men weren't in Orvieto?'

'No!'

'And you had nothing to do with Barnes's death?'

'Who the hell is Barnes?'

'Donald Barnes, the American who was killed yesterday in Saint Patrick's Well. Ring a bell?'

'Yesterday? I swear I had nothing to do with that. That wouldn't make sense. The police presence in Orvieto was already too high. Why would I want to bring more?'

It was an interesting question, one that Payne wanted to examine at length. However, he knew the Milanese police were probably on their way, meaning if he didn't hustle, he wouldn't have a chance to get to the information he really cared about.

'So, who do you work for? And don't say the CIA, because I *know* that's bullshit!'

Manzak remained silent, so Payne slammed his elbow into the back of his head. It was his way of helping him reconsider. 'Don't make me ask you again! Who do you work for?'

'I'll never tell,' he screamed in Italian. 'Ever!'

Payne grinned in victory, even though he had no idea what he'd shouted. The truth was, his choice of language revealed a lot. 'So, is that your native tongue? It sure sounded natural to me.'

Manzak realized his mistake and tried to wriggle free. Payne stifled his movement by slamming his face into the ground with another blow from his elbow.

'I'm getting bored with this, Dick. I think it's time for you to make a decision that's gonna affect our session. Is it time for the truth or the twig? You decide.'

Once again Manzak refused to speak, and in Payne's mind, *that* was the wrong answer. Grabbing the back of his head, he slammed it into the ground repeatedly, accenting every word with violence. 'The . . . truth . . . or . . . the . . . twig?'

Blood gushed from Manzak's forehead, yet Payne felt no pity for him. He'd tried to kill Jones and Maria with a car bomb and would've murdered Payne as well. So in his mind, he wasn't doing anything immoral. 'What's it gonna be, Dick? Tell me now! Who are you working for?'

'I don't care what you do. I won't tell!'

Payne shook his head. 'You dumb bastard. This could've been *so* easy. All you had to do was answer my questions, and I would've let you go. But not now. Now you have to suffer.'

'No!' he shouted back. 'It is *you* that will suffer when you ultimately discover the truth! I promise you, my pain will be temporary. But *yours* will last forever.'

Payne considered his words for a moment. Then showed him what he could do with a stick.

When Payne climbed into the chopper, he looked like a butcher at the end of a long shift. Blood covered his hands and face and leaked from the bulge in his shirt pocket. Jones said nothing, focusing his attention on the nearby power lines and the flashing lights that filled the ground below. Eventually, once they were out of danger, Jones turned toward Payne. 'Stick trick?'

'Yeah,' he answered into the chopper's headset. 'Molotov Cockpit?'

Jones laughed. 'How could you tell?'

'You're missing a shirt.'

'Very observant of you ... Speaking of shirts, what's in your pocket?'

Payne shrugged. 'Souvenirs.'

'Of what?'

'Their identities. Manzak wouldn't tell me his name, so I borrowed some fingers.'

'You mean the stick trick didn't work?'

'Actually, it worked *too* well. The bastard kept passing out on me.'

'That's been known to happen ... So, how'd you leave him?'

'Just like Otto.'

'Otto? Who's Otto?'

'Oh, that was Buckner's *real* name. He was Manzak's bodyguard.'

'Buckner was his bodyguard?'

Payne nodded. 'And get this, he spoke with a German accent.'

'Otto *spoke*? I didn't know he could.'

'Well, he can't anymore.'

Jones smiled. 'OK, funny man, any suggestions on where to go next?'

'What are our choices?'

He checked the fuel gauge. 'I'd say Switzerland or possibly Austria. We can't risk farther.'

Payne clicked the button on his headset and talked to Boyd in the chopper's backseat. 'Hey Doc, any suggestions on where we should land?'

Boyd discussed things with Maria for several seconds before answering. 'There's a lovely research facility in Küsendorf that might be able to aid our cause.'

Payne glanced at Jones. 'What do you think?'

'What do I think? I think we'd be crazy to fly right there. The odds are pretty good we're being tracked by radar, and I can't risk flying underneath it.'

'So what do you suggest?'

A smile crossed Jones's lips. 'Don't worry. As long as we have some money and a few credit cards, I'm confident they'll never find us.'

The squadron of black helicopters hovered over the Bern-Belpmoos Airport (six miles southeast of Bern, Switzerland's capital city), searching for their sister chopper. When one of the pilots spotted it at the far end of the airfield, he ordered the tower to redirect all current air traffic to other Swiss facilities. Planes, he informed them, shouldn't be landing in a crime scene.

A dozen men, each dressed in military fatigues and carrying automatic weapons, circled the craft, then stormed the chopper, searching the cockpit, backseat, and rear hatch for any available clues. Nothing turned up except a cold engine, which meant it had been on the ground for at least twenty minutes. Maybe more.

The team leader spoke into his headset. 'The bird is clear. Starting ground surveillance.'

'Be careful,' the command post warned. 'These men are clever and quite dangerous. Double-check all leads, then radio back to me. Is that understood?'

'Don't worry, sir. We'll find them or die trying.'

After figuring out a way to get to Switzerland, Payne and Jones realized they had a decision to make, one that was more important than where they were going to spend the night. The sole reason they were in this mess was their agreement with Manzak and Buckner. Now that they were dead, Payne and Jones had to decide if they wanted to stay involved.

'What do you think?' Payne asked. 'Have we completed our end of the deal?'

'Technically, I'd say yes. We found Boyd and delivered him to Manzak, just like we agreed. Of course, you did kill Manzak during the exchange.'

'Hey! Don't pin this all on me. You blew up their chopper. Then stole another.'

'Yeah, but only *after* they trashed our Ferrari. Come on, someone had to pay for that.'

Payne didn't want to think about the car because his gut told him *he* was going to pay for it. 'So what do you think?' Payne asked again. 'Should we stay involved with this mess?'

'I think we better. At least until we know who's running things and why they wanted us involved. I mean, if we don't, we're gonna have to watch our backs for a very long time.'

46

Küsendorf, Switzerland
(eighty-two miles southeast of Bern)

Clinging to the southern slopes of the Lepontine Alps, Küsendorf is a village of nearly 2,000 people in Ticino, the southernmost canton (or state) in Switzerland. Known primarily for its scenic views and local brand of Swiss cheese, Küsendorf is also the home of the Ulster Archives, one of the finest private collections of rare documents in the world.

The manuscripts themselves are housed in a well-guarded chalet. Built as a temporary haven for Austrian philanthropist Conrad Ulster, it eventually became his permanent home. During the early 1930s, Ulster, an avid collector of rare artifacts, sensed the political instability in his country and realized there was a good chance that his prized library would be seized by the Nazis. To protect himself and his books, he smuggled his collection across the Swiss border in railcars, hidden under thin layers of lignite, a low-quality brown coal, and dropped from public view until after World War II. He eventually died in 1964 but expressed his utmost thanks to the people of Switzerland by donating his estate to his adopted hometown of Küsendorf – provided that they keep his collection intact and accessible to the world's finest academic minds.

Payne wasn't sure if his ragtag group of fugitives would qualify under those high standards, but they were planning to find out the instant the facility opened in the morning. While they waited, he booked a large suite at a local lodge and bribed the night manager to open the lobby store so they could get a fresh set of clothes and something to eat. They took an hour to get cleaned up, then met in the main room of their suite to discuss Boyd's affiliation with the CIA.

Boyd said, 'I realize I don't possess the suave looks of a spy. But there's no need to. The fact is I've spent the better part of three decades working at Dover as a professor. The only time I do otherwise is when I'm asked to complete a task. Sometimes it's something simple like smuggling documents out of a country. Other times it's more complicated like convincing a diplomat to defect. The truth is, I never know what it's going to be until I'm notified.'

Payne asked, 'And what were you told in this case?'

'That's the amazing thing – this *isn't* a case. This was strictly an academic dig. Or at least it was supposed to be. This had nothing to do with a CIA agenda. Absolutely nothing.'

Payne grimaced. 'See, that's where I'm having a problem. Unless I'm mistaken, most academic digs don't involve helicopters, guns, and exploding buses. Right?'

Boyd was about to explain the legend of the Catacombs when he realized he could do better. Instead of dealing in myths and theories, he could use Maria's video as the ultimate visual aid. Payne and Jones watched, speechless, as the tape documented the grandeur of the Catacombs and the bronze casing of the Tiberius scroll. Boyd chirped in whenever he felt it was necessary, but the truth was they barely listened to him, for the details on the screen were more than enough to convince them that Boyd and Maria weren't a modern-day Bonnie and Clyde.

When the video ended, Jones focused his attention on Boyd. 'Back in Milan you said something about your discovery *killing a religion*. What were you talking about? I didn't see anything on this tape that would have a negative effect on the Church.'

Boyd shook his head. 'The last object you saw – the bronze cylinder we found – contained a papyrus scroll with a very significant message. A message that casts doubt over the entire world of Christianity. If made public, people would simply stop believing. Churches would crumble. Coffers would turn to dust. In a word, *ruin* – both spiritual and financial.'

Jones glanced at Maria, then back at Boyd. 'That seems a bit dramatic, doesn't it? I mean, I'm not the most religious guy in the world, but even if I was, I certainly don't think an ancient piece of paper would have that much effect on my beliefs. If any at all.'

'Well,' Boyd sneered, 'we'll have to see about that. You wait right there, and I shall fetch the document that will make you feel the fool.'

Maria kept quiet until Boyd left the room. Then she apologized for Boyd's tone. 'Don't take that personally. I just think it's his way to blow off steam ... Besides, the fact is you *should* have some doubts about this. I know I did – even about the Catacombs themselves. Of course, there's nothing like some visual proof to contradict a childhood of lectures.'

Jones smiled. 'A childhood? Just how long have you known Dr Boyd?'

'Oh, not *his* lectures. My father's. He's always been a disbeliever when it came to the Catacombs. And trust me, his words carry more weight than most. He's something of an expert.'

There was something about the way she said 'expert' that made Jones flash back to their conversation in Milan. Maria Magdalena Pelati. Her name was Pelati, and her father was an expert on Orvieto. Suddenly, Jones realized that wasn't a coincidence.

'Maria,' he stuttered, 'is your father's name Benito?'

'Yes,' she said, confused. 'How did you know?'

Jones rubbed his eyes. 'Holy shit! You're *his* daughter. Benito Pelati's daughter!'

Payne winced. 'What? Why didn't you tell us you were *his* daughter?'

'I didn't know you knew who *he* was. Besides, what does he have to do with anything?'

Payne looked at her in disbelief. 'You can't be that

naive. He has everything to do with this. He's the goddamned godfather of Orvieto! He runs the whole town.'

Boyd heard the commotion and emerged from the other room. 'People, what is it?'

Payne answered. 'We just found out who she is. She's Benito Pelati's daughter.'

'And that upsets you? Why would that upset you?'

Payne gaped at his response. 'You gotta be kidding me! Her father *runs* Orvieto. He *controls* its security. You don't think that's relevant?' He took a deep breath, trying to calm himself. 'Did it ever occur to you that the soldiers who shot at you in Orvieto might've been working for Benito? That maybe they shot at you because they didn't want you digging there?'

'Nonsense,' Boyd scoffed. 'His office gave us permission to dig there in the first place. You can't start digging without the appropriate paperwork. If you did, you'd be arrested on the spot.'

Permission? They had permission? That didn't make sense to Payne. If Benito Pelati was trying to protect his reputation like Frankie claimed, then why would he allow anyone to dig in Orvieto? And of all the archaeologists in the world, why his daughter? Wouldn't he look even more foolish if his own child – his own *female* child – showed him up in the public eye?

Then again, maybe she was selected because she

was a relative. Maybe Benito knew the Catacombs were there all along and figured if Maria made the discovery then he could bask in her spotlight. Benito could tell the media that he had discovered new evidence about the Catacombs and sent his own child into Orvieto to uncover the truth once and for all.

Payne and Jones discussed the possibilities until Boyd changed the subject, assuring them that there was something more important to discuss. The message on the scroll.

'Jonathon,' he said, 'I was wondering if you could assist me for a moment. I'm afraid I've forgotten the exact terms that your friend Manzak shouted at us in Milan, something about fighting a war. Do you recall with any clarity what he said?'

Payne nodded. 'There was no compassion during the Crusades, nor during this holy war.'

'Holy war, yes!' Boyd jotted the phrase. 'And Christ? What did he say of Christ?'

'Something about how I thought he was fighting for Christ. Then he said he didn't care about Christ because he knew what actually happened back then and realized who the real hero was.'

'Real hero! Yes, those were his words! Splendid job, just splendid!'

'And that means something to you?'

'It might. It just might.' He flipped to a clean sheet of paper. 'And once I left, did he say anything else? Anything about God, or scrolls, or this holy war?'

Payne looked back on his conversation with Manzak and tried to recall what he'd said. Ultimately the tough part of being an interrogator is sorting through all the nonsense in order to expose value. 'He said something about *the truth* at one point that kind of confused me.'

'The truth?' Boyd glanced at Maria for help. The term didn't make any sense to her, either.

So Payne continued. 'He said his pain would be temporary because he knew the truth and assured me that my pain would be eternal because I didn't.'

'Is that what he told you, that he already knew the truth?'

'Or words to that effect.'

'How bloody confusing! If he already knows what the scroll says, then there must be more than one. But how?'

Maria spoke up. 'If Tiberius sent multiple scrolls to Paccius in England, couldn't Paccius have sent several scrolls back to Rome describing his success?'

'Paccius?' Jones mumbled. 'Tiberius?'

'Of course!' Boyd exclaimed. 'How foolish of me! Paccius would certainly feel the need to update the emperor on everything that he accomplished in Jerusalem, and anyone reading those messages would become fully aware of their plot – even if they had no knowledge of our scroll!'

'But wouldn't –'

'Hold up!' Payne demanded. 'You two are getting *way* ahead of us. You're starting to talk about other scrolls before you've even explained this one.'

Jones nodded. 'Jon's right. If you want our help, you have to fill us in. And the only way to do that is to start at the beginning.'

'That might take a while.'

'Don't worry,' Payne assured Boyd. 'We bought ourselves some extra time at the airport.'

Lars knew his commander was expecting an update, but the truth was, he didn't want to deal with him. At least not yet, not with such disappointing news.

At first he thought their mission was going to be simple, especially when they learned that Payne had used his credit card to buy four tickets to Geneva at the local train station. Unfortunately, while they were busy flagging down the angry conductor near Fribourg, they received a report that Jones and Boyd had both rented cars from an agency back in Bern. Confused, he ordered half his men back and told the others to continue their search of the train.

But that was only the beginning.

Before his men returned, Lars was informed that Maria Pelati had rented a limo to Zürich, and any attempts to contact her driver would be pointless, because of cellular interference in the Alps. Then he was told an American named Otto Buckner, a gentleman matching Payne's description, had purchased eight pairs of tickets on eight different buses, and all of them were currently on the road and heading in opposite directions around Switzerland.

Of course what Lars didn't know was that all of those purchases were false leads. The truth was that Payne and Jones had found their transportation in the long-term parking area at the Bern airport. They simply waited for a businessman to pull into the lot, then had Maria flirt with him to obtain his travel information. Once she discovered he was flying to Paris and would be gone for an entire week, Payne and Jones knew they could take his BMW to Küsendorf and wouldn't have to worry about the car being reported stolen for days.

Dr Boyd managed to explain everything they needed to know: his discovery in Bath, his theories on Emperor Tiberius, and his translation of the scroll. Then, once he had answered all of their questions, Maria pointed out the mystery of the laughing man, described the statue on the roof of *Il Duomo,* and gave them some facts about Tiberius's right-hand man, General Paccius.

Needless to say, their heads were swimming at the end of the session.

Just to be fair, though, they returned the favor by briefing them on their backgrounds, their deal with Manzak and Buckner, the cover-ups at the crime scenes, and everything else they could remember. By the time they finished, there were only two things that everyone was able to agree on. One, all of them were baffled. And two, if they had any hope of learning anything at the Ulster Archives, they needed to get some sleep.

Because tomorrow would be filled with even more excitement than today.

47

Nick Dial rented a hotel room a few blocks from the crime scene so he could walk to Fenway in the middle of the night if he felt the urge to reexamine the evidence. And the truth was, he probably would, since his body was still on European time. Or was it African time? Honestly, he didn't know, since he'd passed through eight different time zones in the last day alone.

Dial checked his watch and decided he might be able to catch Cardinal Rose at the Vatican. They hadn't spoken since Tuesday, and he was hoping Rose had found some additional information on Father Jansen. He already knew that Jansen was affiliated with the Pontifical Biblical Commission (PBC), though he didn't know his exact role. Dial needed to know if Jansen was interning with a cardinal from Denmark or Finland, or if his position was more substantial.

The phone rang eight times before someone answered. 'This is Cardinal Rose.'

'Joe? This is Nick Dial at Interpol.'

'Nick! I was wondering when you were going to get ahold of me. I left several messages.'

'Sorry about that. It's been a busy couple of days.'

'CNN just reported that another body was found in Boston. Is that true?'

'Very true. I just left Fenway Park.'

'Was the victim another priest?'

'Nope. This time it was a Pope.'

'Excuse me?'

Dial clarified his statement. 'The victim was Orlando Pope, a ballplayer for the Yankees.'

Rose took a few seconds to absorb the news. 'That can't be a coincidence.'

'Probably not.'

'Was there another note?'

Dial grinned. 'Are you sure that you're a cardinal? You sound more like a cop.'

'Sorry, I don't mean to pry. It's just that I'm trying to get a clear picture. I figure, with my knowledge of the Vatican and your knowledge of the case, we might be able to help each other.'

'Speaking of which, what did you learn about Father Jansen?'

'Nothing useful, I'm afraid. I talked to all my friends on the PBC, and they were saddened by the loss. It seems Erik was one of the good ones, one of those people that everyone knew and liked. In fact, the more I learned about him, the more I regretted not knowing him.'

'What about his job? Did you find out what he did?'

'A little bit of everything. Part clerical, part researcher, part messenger. He was a jack-of-all-trades, just trying to learn the ropes.'

'What about funny business? Sex, drugs, anything?'

Rose took a deep breath. 'The kid was clean.'

Dial made a note to himself. 'So this wasn't about him. That's what you're telling me, right? Father Jansen was the victim, but it wasn't about him.'

Rose nodded. 'That would be my guess.'

'What about the Vatican? Anything going on that I should know about?'

'What are you implying? That *we* had something to do with it?'

Dial shook his head. 'I'm not saying that at all. I'm just wondering if there's anything going on that I should be aware of. Any scandals? Controversies? Bitter feuds? Give me some help, Joe. People are dying, and I don't know why.'

Rose stayed quiet for a moment, gathering his thoughts. When he finally spoke, he did so in a much softer voice. 'All organizations – even the innocuous ones – have enemies. No matter what you do, whether it's good or bad, someone's bound to be offended. I shouldn't be telling you this, but the truth is, the Catholic Church gets more threats than any organization in the world. It's so bad we have a special staff whose sole job is to sort through our mail and separate the real threats from the fake ones.'

'Is that so? What do they do with the real ones?'

'I guess that depends on the threat. We have a first-rate security staff that would handle things on our grounds. Anything else would be turned over to the police.'

'What type of threats are we talking about?'

'Bombs, fires, assassinations. Everything that you'd expect. Then, of course, there are the white-collar threats. Lawsuits seem to be popular these days. So does blackmail. You know, "Give me a million dollars, or I'll tell the press that a priest molested my son."'

'You've got to be kidding me.'

'I wish I was, Nick. Unfortunately, that's the world we live in today. What's that expression? Money is the root of all evil . . . Whoever said that was a very wise man.'

Benito Pelati spent the night in his office, waiting for an update. Twenty years ago he would've been in Milan himself, doing the things that had earned him his reputation as one of the most feared men in Italy. Now he was relegated to the sidelines, stuck with Dante running things. Not that Dante wasn't capable, for he was. Still, Benito would've preferred his presence in Vienna, working on the excavation that was so important to their cause.

When the call finally came, Benito was angry. He wasn't one to tolerate inefficiency.

'What took you so long? You were supposed to call me hours ago.'

Dante replied, 'I would've if it wasn't for *her*. Her involvement has complicated things.'

The comment stunned Benito. He wasn't used to backtalk from anyone. 'What are you talking about? Who's involved?'

'I'm staring at surveillance photos from the library, and *Maria* was there with Boyd. You know, I wondered why your guards in Orvieto waited so long to take him out.'

'*Maria?* But why? Why would she risk everything that we hoped to achieve?'

'*We?* She hasn't been a part of *we* since you shipped her off to school. I don't know when that's going to sink in, but the sooner it does, the better we'll be. Trust me, if we don't get to her soon, she's going to ruin everything you have planned. And she'll love every minute of it.'

Benito stayed silent for several seconds. He was scheduled to meet with the Supreme Council later that day, and the last thing he needed was a distraction. He had worked too hard and waited too long to have his moment in the spotlight ruined by his insolent daughter. He was getting ready to drop the bomb of all bombs on the Vatican, and he needed to be focused.

He said, 'Then you know what you need to do.'

Dante nodded, smiling. He'd been waiting for this day since Benito had sent her away.

48

The Ulster Archives sat nestled against an out-cropping of rock, one that shielded the wooden fortress from the Alpine winds that roared through the region during the winter. Nut-brown timber, the color of surrounding trees, made up the bulk of the chalet's framework and blended perfectly with the broad gables and deep overhangs of the reinforced roof. Square windows were cut into the front facade at regular intervals and were com-plemented by a triangular pane that had been carved under the structure's crown. A large picture window ran vertically through the middle of the frame, giving people on the main staircase a spectacular view of the Alps.

'That's a library?' Jones asked as they approached the gate. 'It doesn't look like one.'

'That's because it isn't,' Boyd said. 'The goal of this facility is *not* to provide books but rather to bridge the ever-growing schism that exists between scholars and connoisseurs. As I'm sure you're aware, several of the world's finest treasures are hidden from public view, selfishly hoarded away by a prestigious minor-ity. Did you know that the typical big-city museum displays only 15 percent of its accumulated artifacts?

Which means most of the world's historical wealth is currently sitting somewhere in crates.'

Payne whistled softly. 'Eighty-five percent.'

'Alas, that's just the museums. If you factor in the billionaire collectors who have Monets hanging in their bathrooms, then I'm sure the overall percentage would be well over ninety. Thankfully, this institution is doing something about it. Since this building opened, the Ulster Foundation has promoted the radical concept of sharing. I know *sharing* doesn't sound radical, but when you're talking about priceless artifacts, it actually is.'

'I'm not sure I follow,' Payne admitted.

'Let's say you teach at Al Azhar University in Cairo. While authoring a book, you realize you're lacking some critical information on the Nubian sites in Sudan – data that can be found in the Archives. So what do you do? Do you fly here empty-handed and use their books? Of course not. That would be selfish in the eyes of the Foundation. Instead, you loan them an artifact that other scholars might be interested in – perhaps a discovery that you made in Giza – and in return this institute will provide you access to the documents you requested.'

Jones nodded his approval. 'Sharing . . . I like it.'

'Well,' Boyd argued, 'you might not like it nearly as much in about ten minutes, because we have nothing to offer these people. Sure, we have the scroll, but I'm afraid this isn't an appropriate time for its debut. There are still too many riddles to solve before we go public.'

'What about your video?' Payne suggested. 'Would there be any harm in showing that?'

'The video of the Catacombs?' Boyd pondered the notion for several seconds. 'Alas, I must admit that film is not my handiwork. Therefore, I must defer to young Miss Pelati. My dear, how does a premiere strike your fancy?'

A broad smile crossed her lips. 'Since I haven't had my fancy struck in quite some time, I confess the concept sounds exhilarating ... Wouldn't you agree, David?'

Jones glanced at her and winked. 'Yes, Maria, I'm with you on that one.'

'Outstanding!' Boyd cheered, failing to pick up on the flirting. 'Then let's get to it. I can't wait to see what we uncover.'

'Me, neither,' Jones mumbled to himself. 'Me, neither.'

A team of armed security guards led the foursome across the wooded grounds and into the lobby of the chalet, where the director of the Archives was waiting to greet them. Petr Ulster, grandson to the institute's patriarch, was a round man in his early forties with a thick brown beard that covered his multiple chins. Yet somehow he came across as boylike, mostly due to the twinkle in his eye and his enthusiasm for knowledge.

'Hello,' he said with a faint Swiss accent. 'My name is Petr, and it is an honor to make your acquaintance. How is it I may help you?'

Under normal conditions, Dr Boyd would've taken charge, explaining who he was and what they were hoping to find. But his current standing as an international fugitive made that pretty impractical, so Payne took it upon himself to be the group leader.

'It's nice to meet you, Petr. My name is Jonathon Payne, and these are the members of my traveling party: D.J., Chuck, and Maria.'

Ulster shook hands with each. 'And what type of excursion are you on?'

'A confidential one.' Payne nodded toward the guards. 'Is there somewhere we can talk?'

'Of course. Follow me.'

Ulster practically skipped down the hallway, leading them to his private office. Bookshelves filled with leather-bound first editions dominated the suite. The rest of the wooden walls were covered in framed photographs depicting colorful scenes from Switzerland and abroad.

'I must admit,' he said, 'I'm particularly intrigued by your appearance. Most academics call ahead before visiting Küsendorf. Very rarely do they show up at the front door.'

Payne took a seat next to Ulster. 'Sorry about that, but the truth is, I'm not a scholar.'

'Oh? Then I'm doubly fascinated by your appearance. What in the world are you then?'

'Me? I'm the CEO of an American company named Payne Industries.'

Ulster beamed. 'A businessman! How wonderfully wonderful! It *has* been a while since we've been visited by an American collector. Tell me, what's your area of interest?'

'Actually, Petr, I'm not a collector. I'd say I'm more like a financier.'

'Marvelous! Simply marvelous!' He put his hand on Payne's knee and patted it a few times. 'My grandfather would applaud your philanthropy. He really, truly would!'

Payne wasn't sure how to handle Ulster's enthusiasm or abundant use of adverbs, but he was tempted to recommend decaf. 'It's funny you should mention your grandfather, because from what I understand he came to Switzerland looking for the same thing that my team requires.'

'Really? And what is that?'

'Sanctuary.' Payne leaned closer and whispered, 'We're at a critical point in our journey, and I'm afraid if word leaked out, a rival faction might be able to use it against us.'

'A rival faction?' Ulster rubbed his hands in anticipation. He wasn't used to dealing with such excitement. 'This information you seek, what is it?'

Payne nodded toward Boyd. 'Chuck? Would you mind handling this one?'

'We're looking for any information you might have on Tiberius and his right-hand man, Paccius. Preferably data about their later years.'

'Ah, the mysterious General Paccius. We're blessed with several documents from the Empire that might help your cause. As luck should have it, my grandfather had a particular passion for the ancient Romans, since they once occupied his native Austria.'

'Brilliant! Bloody brilliant!'

'Regrettably your research might be difficult, for several pieces in his Roman collection have never been translated, and many others have never been logged.'

'Not to worry,' Payne assured him. 'When we're done, we'll be more than happy to leave our translations behind. That is, the ones that won't put us in harm's way.'

Ulster chortled loudly. 'Oh, Jonathon, you *are* mysterious. And I'm certainly glad I've made your acquaintance. Nevertheless, before I can let you upstairs, I'm afraid I must ask the one question that we pose to all visitors.'

'And that is?'

'What can you offer this institution as repayment for our services?'

'I don't know. We're traveling kind of light, being in the field and all. What type of donation would be acceptable?'

'I'd love to offer you a suggestion. Sadly, since

I know very little about your journey, it's tough for me to say. Perhaps if you threw me a hint or two, I could assist your selection.'

'A hint or two?'

He nodded, sliding closer to Payne on the couch. 'Or even a crumb. I can assure you whatever you tell me will remain in the strictest of confidence. The documents in this chalet would never have survived the war if it wasn't for secrecy. My grandfather relied on it, and he taught me how precious it can be. So rest assured I would never dishonor his memory by breaking my word.'

Payne glanced around the room and noticed a large TV sitting in the corner. It would do nicely when the moment was right. 'Petr, as I mentioned, I'm a businessman, not a scholar. And as a business-man, I *always* try to negotiate the best deal for myself before I agree to anything.'

Ulster leaned forward. 'I'm listening.'

'You see, my team requires more than just admittance to the Archives. While we're in town we'd like round-the-clock access, a private room to conduct our studies, *plus* your services as an extra researcher. I figure no one knows your documents better than you.'

'My services? Oh, Jonathon! You slay me, you really do! But I'm afraid it would take something staggering to consider such an agreement. Abso-lutely, completely staggering. But let's be honest, what could you possibly be involved in that would make it worth my time?'

Petr Ulster started canceling his appointments before the video was half finished. He'd always believed in the existence of the Catacombs, and now that he'd seen visual proof, he could think of nothing he'd rather be working on. Payne didn't even mention the scroll or the religious overtones of their mission, yet Ulster was bouncing around the room like a goat in heat.

'Tell me,' he begged. 'What are you're looking for? It must be something unbelievably important, or you wouldn't be squelching this discovery.'

Boyd nodded. 'There is some doubt in our minds why the Catacombs were built. We believe it was to celebrate a clandestine deal between Tiberius and Paccius, but we're lacking proof.'

Ulster rose from his chair. 'Then what are we waiting for? Let's see what we can discover!'

The Roman Collection was stored in the largest room in the chalet, even though its basic design was similar to all the other document vaults. The floors were made out of fireproof wood – boards that had been coated with an aqueous-based resin – while the white walls and ceilings had been treated with a fire-retardant spray. The texts themselves were kept in massive fireproof safes, which were well-guarded behind bulletproof security doors.

Ulster invited them to find a seat before he

accessed the control panel. Beeps filled the air as he entered his ten-digit security code, a sound replaced by the low rumble of the partitions as they inched across the floor in their motorized tracks. Once the glass had disappeared into the walls, the knobs on the individual vaults started to spin in unison, then popped open.

Ulster asked, 'Have you figured out how you want to conduct this search? Like I mentioned before, much of this collection has not been logged or translated.'

'And those that have been logged?'

'Sorted by approximate date and/or subject matter, depending on my mood that day.'

Boyd took a deep breath. This was going to be far tougher than he had originally hoped.

Although far from home, Jones accessed the databank in his Pittsburgh-based office to retrieve background information on Boyd and Maria – specifically Boyd's involvement with the CIA and Maria's family history. If Payne and Jones were going to work side-by-side with them, they needed to know everything they could about their backgrounds.

Boyd's real name was Charles Ian Holloway, and he graduated from Annapolis in the early sixties. After that, things got murky. He was loaned to the Pentagon for an 'alternative tour of duty,' at which time he dropped off the Academy radar. No more records. No forwarding address. Nothing. He was effectively wiped from their system, which, Jones assumed, was the moment that Charles Boyd was born and began his new career in the CIA.

To verify this fact, Jones downloaded a picture of Boyd from a local news agency and sent it to Randy Raskin at the Pentagon with a message that said: 'Is Chuck safe to drink with?'

This was a coded way to find out if Boyd was viewed as a threat by the U.S. government. If Jones had wanted to know about Boyd's access to top secret information, he would've asked if Boyd was 'safe to dine with.' If Raskin's response mentioned a 'one-course meal,' then Boyd was cleared to discuss first-level documents. A 'two-course meal' meant second level, and so on. But Jones didn't care about that. He wasn't looking to share secrets with the guy. He simply wanted to know if Boyd was in good standing with the Agency.

Jones also wanted to know why Raskin didn't warn them about Boyd's duties with the CIA when Payne called him from Milan. That just didn't make sense.

While he waited for Raskin's response, Jones switched his focus to Maria Pelati and found everything he was looking for. She grew up in Rome, moved to an exclusive prep school in England before she reached her teens, and then enrolled in Dover, where she'd been studying for the past ten years. Interpol documents proved that she rarely left the U.K., even for the holidays, which suggested that her relationship with her father was, in fact, strained.

Her only extended visit to Italy in the past decade was the one she took recently, flying from London to Rome on the same flight as Dr Boyd two weeks ago. From there, Jones was able to track their whereabouts around Orvieto by following a string of credit card transactions. A hotel bill here, a store purchase there – always within their means – and absolutely nothing to suggest that they were treasure hunters on the verge of a big payday.

As Jones continued his research, his computer let him know that Raskin had replied to his e-mail. He opened the message with a click of his mouse. It said:

Drink away, my friend, but *not* in public. Foreign bouncers will be checking IDs.

49

At first Payne thought Dr Boyd was joking when he asked him to leave the Roman Collection room to give them more space. That is until he started talking about claustrophobia and claiming there wasn't enough air to breathe with so many people around the table.

Needless to say, Payne was stunned. After giving it some thought, though, he realized Boyd was right: Payne was pretty useless in the research department. He couldn't read Latin or log ancient scrolls. And he certainly didn't have the computer skills that Jones possessed. In fact, when it came right down to it, there wasn't anything that he could do except guard the door and fetch prosciutto sandwiches when they got hungry.

That's right, he was their rent-a-cop sandwich bitch.

Anyway, Payne decided not to make a scene and asked Ulster if he could use his office to work on a project of his own. Ulster laughed and told him to help himself, which was probably a mistake on his part, because Payne was about to fingerprint two suspects who weren't even there, using the specimens that he collected in Milan.

The process itself was rather straightforward. Press the specimen in ink, then roll it on paper. Just like finger painting in kindergarten. Only this time, Payne used someone else's fingers.

When Payne was done, he put them in a brown paper bag that said DON'T EAT ME and returned them to Ulster's freezer. Then he faxed the prints to Randy Raskin, figuring if anyone could determine who Manzak and Buckner were, it would be him. Payne included a short note that told him to send the results to Jones's computer as soon as possible.

After that, Payne had time to kill, so he decided to explore the Archives. He walked up and down the halls looking at everything: the paintings, the statues, and all the display cases. The thing he liked the most was a series of black-and-white photos that Ulster's grandfather had shot in Vienna in the 1930s. Most of them featured landmarks Payne didn't recognize, but the final one, a photograph of the Lipizzaner stallions, instantly warmed his heart.

When he was a boy, his parents tricked him into watching a TV performance of the majestic white horses by telling him that they were unicorns that had lost their horns. Payne believed them, too, because he had never witnessed a more magical display of showmanship in his entire life. The horses entered the Imperial Riding Hall of the Hofburg to the violins of Bizet's 'Arlésienne Suite,' then proceeded to glide through a gravity-defying series of pirouettes, courbettes, and caprioles. Payne never knew animals could dance or spin until that moment.

He took the picture off the wall and ran his fingers over the faded image. All the horses in the photo had died decades before Payne was born, but because of their careful breeding – each Lipizzaner was branded with specific marks to signify their historic bloodlines – they looked eerily similar to the ones he'd seen as a boy. The same high necks and powerful limbs, muscular backs and well-formed joints, thick manes and remarkably limpid eyes.

'Didja know you saved their lives?' someone growled down the hall. '*Ja, ja,* it's true!'

Bemused, Payne glanced at the old man trudging his way. His name was Franz, and he was Ulster's most trusted employee. 'What was that?' Payne asked.

'You American, no? *Ja,* you rescued those horses.'

'I did? How the hell did I do that?'

A smile exploded on Franz's wrinkled face. 'Not you! But men from your country. *Ja, ja!* They risked their lives to save them.'

Payne had no idea what he was talking about, so he asked him to explain.

'Back in 1945, Vienna was under heavy attack by Allied bombers. Colonel Podhajsky, the leader of the riding school, was afraid for his horses – not only from bombs, but from hungry refugees who were scouring the city for meat.'

'Did you say *meat?*'

'*Ja,*' he answered, the smile no longer on his face.

'With Vienna unsafe, the colonel smuggled the horses many miles north to Saint Martin's. Now, as fate would dictate, he came across an old friend who could help protect the horses. Do you know who he was?'

Payne had never heard of Podhajsky, so he was clueless. 'I give up. Who?'

'American General George S. Patton.'

'Really? How'd he know Patton?'

Franz chuckled with delight. 'Would you believe they met at the 1912 Olympics? *Ja, ja,* it's true! Both men competed in pentathlon in the Stockholm Games.'

'Patton was an Olympian? I never knew that.'

'That is nothing. Wait till I tell you what happened next. To convince Patton that the horses were worth saving, the colonel staged a Lipizzaner performance right there on the battlefield. Can you imagine the spectacle? Horses dancing in the middle of a war!' Franz laughed so loud it hurt Payne's ears. 'The general was so impressed that he made the horses official wards of the U.S. Army until Vienna was safe enough for their return.'

Payne smiled at the photograph. 'I guess my parents were right. They are magical.'

'Hmm? What was that?'

'Nothing,' he fibbed, half embarrassed. 'Out of curiosity, could I borrow this picture for a few minutes? I have a buddy upstairs who always tries to impress me with facts about everything, and I doubt he knows that story. Would it bother Petr if I carried this upstairs?'

'Petr!' Franz groaned. 'I'm glad you said his name, because I almost forget to tell you. Petr sent me to find you. He wants you to go upstairs at once. Your friends would like to talk to you.'

Excited by the possibilities, Payne thanked Franz for the news, then hustled upstairs with the photo. But when he entered the room he quickly realized he'd have to save his story for later, because the look on everyone's face told Payne something bad had happened.

Dr Boyd's complexion was paler than usual, which made the bags under his eyes stand out like layers of football eye black. Maria sat to his left, her face buried on the table under her tightly clenched arms. And Ulster, whose lips had been frozen in a perpetual grin since Payne had met him, seemed to be frowning, even though it was tough to tell through the thicket that he called a beard. Jones was the last person Payne noticed, since he was sitting in the far corner of the room, but it was the look on his face that told Payne everything he needed to know.

Somehow, some way, their mission had suffered a major setback. He just didn't know how.

Since Ulster had sent for Payne, he decided to start with him. 'Franz said you wanted to see me. Is everything all right?'

'Metaphorically speaking, I'd say we hit an iceberg.' He pointed to a scroll that sat on the table before him. 'This was one of the documents in my grandfather's collection. It was sent to Tiberius by an injured centurion right after a war in the Britains. If you look closely, you can see where the soldier gripped it, for his blood stained the papyrus as he wrote his message.'

Payne saw the stain yet had little interest in two-thousand-year-old plasma. 'What did it say?'

'He apologized for writing, which was an unspeakable breach of protocol for a centurion, then informed Tiberius that a hostile Silurian tribe had attacked his unit while they slept, slaughtering hundreds of Romans in the dead of night.'

'And that's important?'

'Not by itself, but the next part is. You see, the soldier mentioned that General Paccius was one of the earliest victims of the raid, stabbed in his heart as he slept.'

'And that's bad, right?'

'Bad?' Boyd growled from across the room. 'It's bloody *horrible*! Since Paccius was slain, he obviously didn't pilot the conspiracy against Christ, now did he?'

'I guess not, although I don't understand why that's so horrible. Didn't you just clear the name of Christ? As a Christian, I figured you'd be happy about that. You, too, Maria.'

She flinched at the mention of her name, surprised that a man was actually asking for her opinion. 'I wish that were the case. The only thing we cleared up was Paccius's disappearance. After all of these years, we finally know why he was never glorified in Roman history books. He died without dignity, slain while sleeping on the battlefield.'

'But isn't that good for you? I mean, shouldn't that end your speculation about Jesus?'

Maria shook her head. 'Now that Paccius is no longer a suspect, we have no idea who Tiberius would've turned to next.'

'But that's kind of what I'm getting at. How do you know he turned to *anyone*? Why are you positive he went through with his plan against Christ?'

She said, 'Because the artwork in the Catacombs tells us as much. Remember the carvings that illustrated the crucifixion of Christ? The keystone figure is laughing at Christ, actually mocking his death. Why would it be there – in a vault that Tiberius built – if the plot hadn't succeeded? The carvings were historically accurate, so they were obviously created *after* Christ's crucifixion. That's the only way they could've gotten the details right.'

The light finally clicked in Payne's head. 'Oh, I get it. See, I interpreted the artwork differently than you. You're saying Tiberius was so thrilled with the outcome he decided to honor his accomplice in stone, chiseling his face up there as appreciation for a job well done.'

'Exactly. Only we don't know who helped Tiberius or what he did to convince everybody that Jesus was the Messiah. According to the scroll, Tiberius wanted to stage something so amazing that people would talk about it for years. But we don't know what that was.'

'You don't?'

'No,' she assured Payne. 'If we did, we'd have something to pursue. But as it stands now, we don't know where to look next. Paccius's death has knocked the wind from our sails.'

Payne leaned back, astonished. How could four of the smartest people he'd ever met be so blind to the obvious? 'I don't want to step on any toes, but I think I might be able to help.'

'Oh?' she said in a less-than-confident tone. 'How is that?'

'By telling you how the Romans amazed Jerusalem.'

'Jon,' Jones whispered, 'this isn't the time to be joking around.'

'Who's joking? The truth is, I have a theory about Tiberius. In fact, I'm surprised you guys haven't figured it out by now. It's actually kind of obvious.'

'Obvious?' Boyd snarled. 'We've been thinking about this for two days now, researching day and night, trying to grasp this bloody thing, and you mock us by calling it obvious?'

'Just a second. I wasn't trying to insult you. The truth is, sometimes a person can become so immersed in things that he loses sight of the obvious. And I think that's what's happening here, because I'm pretty sure I know what the Romans did to fool the masses. Remember when I said I'd interpreted the archway differently than you? Well, if you don't mind, I'd like to fill you in on my theory. I think it could be the key to everything.'

'Your theory is the key?' Boyd laughed. 'Oh, this ought to be rich.'

'*Professore!* You're being rude! If it wasn't for Jonathon, we'd probably be dead right now.'

Payne looked at Maria and thanked her, glad to see at least one person was taking him seriously. 'Now, I admit I don't know a whole lot about first-century Jerusalem, but if I remember correctly, you're searching for an event in Christ's life that would've amazed everyone.'

'Let me cut you off right there,' Boyd snapped. 'We examined each of Christ's miracles – turning water into wine at Cana, feeding the hungry of Bethsaida, and so on – but didn't feel any of them were miraculous enough to influence the masses. Furthermore, Tiberius claimed that his event needed to be staged in Jerusalem, and Christ's miracles were performed elsewhere.'

'Doc, if I'm not mistaken, Tiberius talked about staging a single event, an act so magical that people couldn't possibly ignore it, no matter how hard they tried?'

'Or words to that effect, yes.'

'But only one event, not two or three?'

Boyd nodded. 'That's correct. The scroll refers to a *single* act that future generations would sing about

368

for eternity. Something magical and mystifying in the heart of Jerusalem.'

Suddenly, Payne was more confident than ever. 'If that's the case, then there's only one event in Jesus's life that can fit your criteria . . . And trust me, people are still talking about it.'

50

Henri Toulon had a history of showing up late and going home early. So Nick Dial was far from surprised when he called Interpol and Toulon was nowhere to be found. It wouldn't be the first time that they butted heads – partially because Dial got the position that Toulon had coveted and partially because Toulon was an agitator who loved picking fights with everyone. Yet Dial put up with all the bullshit because Toulon did his job better than anyone he'd ever worked with.

After leaving a message, Dial focused on the bulletin board in his Boston hotel room. He looked at the crime photos from all three cases and tried to figure out a connection. A priest from Finland who was kidnapped in Italy yet was killed in Denmark. A prince from Nepal who was kidnapped in Thailand but murdered in Libya. A ballplayer from Brazil who was kidnapped in New York, then crucified in Boston. What was the thread?

Jansen, Narayan, and Pope were healthy men under the age of forty. None of them were married, had children, or had significant others of any kind. In fact, all of them went out of their way to avoid relationships. Jansen had taken a vow of celibacy,

Narayan preferred prostitutes, and Pope was a borderline recluse. On the other hand, their list of differences was twice as long. They practiced different religions, had different ethnic backgrounds, and came from opposite ends of the globe. They spoke different languages, had different jobs, and had no connections other than the way they died.

To Dial it was clear this case wasn't about the victims. It was about the message.

While sipping coffee, he shifted his focus to the crime scenes themselves. Normally he would've worked with a single map because his cases were usually contained in a limited area. In this case, though, he had to look at the entire world because his victims and their locations were so scattered.

To keep track of things, he used a series of push-pins, each color representing something different. He marked the hometowns of all three men with white pins, placing one in Lokka, Finland, one in Katmandu, Nepal, and one in São Paulo, Brazil. Next he located their abduction points with blue pins: Rome, Bangkok, and New York. Finally he tracked the murder sites with red ones, a fitting color, considering how much blood was found at each scene.

Nine pins in total, scattered all around the map. Three in Europe, two in Asia, two in North America, one in South America, and one in Africa. The only continents not covered were Australia and Antarctica, which was fine with Dial. He didn't feel like fighting dingoes in the Outback or frostbite at the South Pole.

A ringing phone snapped him back to reality. He hustled over to his desk. 'This is Dial.'

'This is not,' teased Henri Toulon.

Dial wasn't in the mood for games, so he got right to the point. 'Last night when I arrived in Boston, I found an interesting fact about the latest victim . . . He wasn't dead yet.'

'What? You mean he's still alive? I heard on the –'

'No, Henri, he's dead now, although that wasn't the case when I was landing at Logan. In fact, according to 911 logs, the cops didn't know about it until I was in America.'

Toulon paused for a moment, letting the information sink in. 'But how can that be? We were faxed about the murder last night.'

'That's my point. We knew about the case before there was a case. Looks like we've got another taunter.'

Toulon mumbled a bunch of curse words in French, then shouted to one of his assistants in German, which illustrated why Toulon was so valuable to the department. He could speak a dozen languages, which enabled him to talk to nearly every employee at Interpol, witnesses from multiple nations, plus NCB officers from around the world.

'Sorry about that,' he apologized. 'I had the fax right here on my desk, but some asshole on the late shift messed with my things again. I'm telling you,

Nick, if you want me to be efficient, I need an office of my own.'

'I'm not in the mood, Henri. Just tell me about the fax.'

'It came from a police station in Boston, maybe ten minutes before I called your cell phone. It said another victim had been found at the baseball stadium in Boston, and they needed someone from our office to verify its link to our other cases.'

'Do you have a name or a number or a station location?'

'I had all of that, Nick, right on the fax. It came in on stationery.'

Dial growled softly. This was the best lead they had, and someone at his office had lost it.

'Nick?' Toulon said. 'Hans is checking the fax machine right now. It stores the last fifty documents in its memory, so there's a chance we'll be able to print another copy. I'll also check our phone records to find out where the fax came from. That way, you can investigate the suspicious fax machine before you leave Boston.'

Dial took a deep breath. Maybe this wouldn't be a total disaster after all. 'Get me that info as soon as possible. This could be the break we've been waiting for.'

Frankie Cione loved hanging out with Payne and Jones. He didn't know if it was their coolness under pressure, their good-natured teasing, or the fact that they were tall. Whatever it was, Frankie knew that they were special. Not only did they go out of their way to make him feel important – something his friends and colleagues rarely did – but he got the sense that they actually liked him for who he was, *not* what he could do for them.

After Payne and Jones left Milan, Frankie pondered ways he could continue to help them. It took him all day to figure it out, but he realized that they had left several scraps of evidence in his possession, including photographs of the helicopter crash site and data from the car rental office. Of course Frankie had no idea where any of it was going to lead, yet the thought of helping them in any capacity was enough to give him chills.

Francesco Cione, Italian private eye. No case is too big, although I'm quite small.

Laughing to himself, Frankie realized the pictures of Orvieto were the best place to start, since Payne and Jones had left his office before they had a chance to enlarge them all.

The initial picture he examined was one that Jones had scanned into the computer. Frankie took his time searching every centimeter of the film, blowing up the image to eight times its normal size and viewing it from four different angles, before he decided it was time to move on. After clearing the file from his screen, he thumbed through the rest of the photographs and settled on the last two pictures in the roll.

At first glance there was no visible reason for his selection, though Frankie figured if Donald Barnes was as obese as Payne and Jones had claimed, then *something* had to motivate him to walk halfway across the plateau and take additional photographs of the wreck. And since that something didn't jump out at him, he hoped he might find it under magnification.

By moving his mouse, Frankie was able to slide the image in any direction. That allowed him to focus on several areas of the crash site that Payne and Jones had never seen.

The first section of the photograph proved to be nothing more than a shadow created by a wisp of smoke and the rays of the summer sun. The second was a rock, partially covered in green moss, while the third turned out to be part of the rotor blade that Boyd had fractured with his toolbox. The fourth section, though, proved to be much harder for Frankie to define. So much so that he was forced to magnify it to five times its normal size, then brighten the pixels of the image before he could even hazard a guess as to its identity. After doing all that, there was little doubt in his mind as to what he was looking at, for the scene was quite horrific.

Buried in rubble at the base of the cliff was the flattened corpse of an Italian soldier. His head had been crushed by the initial impact of the avalanche, while the rest of him was mangled by the 400-foot drop that followed. Limbs pointed backward. Entrails oozed from his midsection like uncooked sausage links. Blood covered everything nearby.

'*Mamma mia!*' Frankie said to himself. 'This be why fat man is killed! Not because he speak to my friends. He dead because he film this body!'

And he was right, too. Of course, that was nothing compared to the evidence that Frankie was about to uncover next. Evidence that would help Payne and Jones put everything together.

51

The hush that filled the room reminded Payne of his days with the MANIACs. Everyone was staring at him, waiting to be briefed. Eventually, Maria couldn't handle it any longer.

She said, 'Tell us what you're talking about. We're dying to know.'

Payne grimaced at her choice of words. 'It's ironic that you mentioned *dying* because that has a lot to do with my theory.'

And just like that they realized Payne was talking about the crucifixion. *The* crucifixion. That was the event that Tiberius had used to trick the masses. It had to be. Nothing else made sense. Especially if you consider the artwork in the Catacombs.

In Payne's mind the hand-carved images of the archway weren't there to mock the death of Christ. They were there to honor a special moment in Roman history. And the only thing that would make Christ's death an important event to the Romans was if it wasn't a *real* crucifixion. It had to be a ploy, an event staged by Tiberius to help the Empire get a stranglehold on the new religion and the flood of donations that was bound to follow.

'*For the good of all things Roman, we shall begin at once,* using the *Nazarene as our tool, the one we have chosen as the Jewish Messiah.*'

Boyd considered the theory. 'Why are you so certain that Tiberius faked the crucifixion?'

'Why? Because if Jesus wasn't the Son of God, how can you explain his resurrection? Either they faked his crucifixion to make it look like he came back from the dead, or they didn't, and Jesus is *actually* the Messiah. I mean, those are the two possibilities, right?'

Payne figured, without assistance from Rome, there was no way a mortal could've cheated death and made a triumphant return to society. Not after what they put him through – or *seemed* to put him through. If Jesus wasn't the savior, the only thing that could've saved his life was the mercy of the Empire. However, mercy was the one thing they *weren't* known for.

Maria said, 'Not to play devil's advocate, but wouldn't it be impossible to fake a crucifixion in first-century Jerusalem? They'd be lacking the special effects that modern magicians have. Plus they'd be dealing with an unwilling subject.'

Jones motioned toward Payne. 'Hey, you're talking to an expert in that field. Jon's been studying magic tricks for as long as I've known him.'

And he was right, too. Payne had been intrigued by magic since his grandfather pulled a quarter out of his ear back when Payne was still wearing pajamas with feet. The tricks. The secrets. The performers.

The history. He'd been a connoisseur for as long as he could remember.

So he said, 'The first documented magic tricks were performed in Egypt about 3,000 years before the Roman Empire. Their tricks ranged from the simplistic – the ball and cup tricks that are still prevalent today – to the complex. Around 2700 BC, an Egyptian magician named Dedi gave a performance where he decapitated two birds and an ox and then restored their heads.'

'Really? How'd he do that?' Ulster wondered.

Payne ignored his question. 'With enough preparation the Romans could've figured out a way to make it work. In fact, it probably would've been easier than Dedi's performance because everybody in his audience would've been expecting a trick, whereas the people in Jerusalem were expecting a crucifixion. I mean, nobody would've been looking for a sleight of hand or a last-minute substitution since they weren't expecting a show.'

Maria grimaced. 'That being said, how would *you* have done it?'

Payne gave it some thought. 'Hypothetically, you could fake a crucifixion by drugging the victim. I mean, the victim would look like he died on the cross, right? And a large crowd would've witnessed it. From there you hide the victim until he wakes up. Just like that, the illusion of resurrection.'

The room grew silent as they considered Payne's theory.

'Of course, the toughest part would've been figuring out what drug and dosage to use. In addition, you'd have to administer the drug in front of an audience, which might've been tricky.'

'Actually,' Ulster stated, 'the Romans had a great understanding of pharmaceuticals and had mastered the art of capital punishment. The guards sometimes killed up to 500 prisoners a day, so they would know the best way to accomplish this. All they'd have to do is slip the prisoner a drug while he was on the cross, and he'd fall into a comalike sleep within minutes.'

Jones asked, 'But how would they do that? Wasn't Jesus surrounded by his followers at the time? Surely they would've objected if the Romans had tried to drug him.'

Maria shook her head. 'According to the Bible, Jesus sipped wine vinegar from the end of a long stalk while he was hanging on the cross. It was such a common practice during crucifixions that no one would've given it much thought.'

Boyd added, 'I recall several historical references to *mandrake,* a plant that still grows in Israel today. The Romans used the ground-up root as a primitive anesthetic.'

'Furthermore,' Ulster added, 'mandrake would explain the speed of Christ's death.'

'How so?' Payne wondered.

'To put it simply, crucifixion was a lengthy process, one that typically lasted more than thirty-six hours and sometimes as long as nine or ten days. In the end the victim usually died from hunger or traumatic exposure, not because he bled to death.' Ulster paused for a moment, searching for the right words. 'On occasion, when the Romans wanted to accelerate the process, they would smash the victim's legs with a hammer or a war club to steal his ability to breathe. After that the victim was no longer able to prop himself up on the nail through his feet, and that put too much strain on his arms and chest to take in any air. Suffocation quickly followed.'

Payne asked, 'But they didn't do that with Christ, right?'

'No, they didn't,' Boyd assured him. 'Which is an issue that has bothered historians for centuries. Most victims lasted at least thirty-six hours, like Petr mentioned, whereas Christ died very quickly, spending no more than a few hours on the cross. Remember, Christ was crucified alongside two other criminals, men who had their legs broken to hasten their deaths. Yet when the Romans moved into position to shatter Christ's legs, they realized he was already dead.'

'"Not one bone of his will be broken,"' Maria whispered, quoting the scripture. 'The way Christ died fulfilled a prophecy. A prophecy that the Romans would've known about.'

Boyd nodded. 'So did the actions of Longinus, the centurion who stabbed Christ in the side after his death. John 19:31–37 stated, "They will look to the one whom they have pierced." And in time, the Romans looked to Jesus as their God. Just like Tiberius and his accomplice wanted.'

Jones asked, 'Out of curiosity, what proof do we have that a drugging took place?'

Boyd frowned. 'One panel in the archway *does* show Jesus drinking from the hyssop stalk. I failed to give it much thought at the time since it's a fairly obscure moment to memorialize. Come to think of it, I can't remember seeing that event honored in stone before.'

'Nor I,' Ulster said. 'What about you, Maria?'

'Not really.' Then after a moment of silence, she surprised everyone by blurting, 'Wait! The archway! I just remembered something about the archway.' She leapt to her feet and bolted toward the door. 'Nobody move. I have to check on something. I'll be right back.'

The four of them nodded in unison, half afraid to disobey her order. At least for the first few seconds. After that, Payne's curiosity got the best of him. He had a feeling that she was on the verge of a major breakthrough and wanted to be there when she had it.

'Damn, D.J., will you look at the time? We're missing my favorite show!' He grabbed the photo of the Lipizzaner stallions and rushed toward the hallway. 'Wait, Oprah! I'm coming!'

To keep from laughing, Jones nearly bit through

his bottom lip. 'Sorry you had to see that. Jon's in a delicate place in his life right now and my ebony sister is teaching him how to cope.'

Payne and Jones hustled down the wooden stairs and found Maria sitting in Ulster's office, scouring her videotape for new evidence about the crucifixion.

She said to them, 'You must think I'm crazy, running out of the room. It's just all that talk about the archway made me realize something. I think there's a clue on one of the carvings.'

Jones raised an eyebrow. 'What kind of clue?'

'I barely gave it any thought until now, but when Petr started talking about the use of mandrake as an ancient Roman drug, it opened my eyes to a possibility.'

'Just a second,' Payne grumbled. 'What's this mandrake stuff you keep talking about? Some kind of exotic poison?'

'Not exactly,' answered Boyd as he burst into the office. Ulster arrived a few seconds later, his cheeks bright red from exercise. 'Mandrake is a plant with a forked root that closely resembles the human body. Because of this resemblance, many early cultures believed the plant possessed magical powers. That's how it got its name. Mandrake is an abbreviated version of the original Latin term, *mandragora*, which means the plant is part man and part dragon.'

Maria continued, 'As I was saying, I think I found

some evidence that might shed some light on the crucifixion. I'm pretty sure there's an anomaly in one of the carvings.'

Boyd said, 'An anomaly? What kind of anomaly?'

Instead of answering, she hit play on the VCR, then moved aside so everyone could witness the tragedy that was about to unfold. Images from the Catacombs rolled past like tanks toward a defenseless village. In her heart she knew the closer the camera got to the archway, the sooner Christianity was going to take a serious blow.

'To be honest, I'm surprised that one of us didn't notice this earlier. Focus on the archway. Look at the different scenes of the crucifixion. Do you notice anything that looks out of place?'

The two lowest blocks showed Jesus getting nailed to the cross and being hoisted into the air by a team of Roman soldiers. The next pair depicted Christ as he hung from the cross, blood pouring from his hands and feet onto the rocky ground below, a sign over his head that read, *"Iesus Nazarenus Rex Iudaeorum."* The crowns, the two stones that sat near the top of the arch, revealed the events right before his death: the moment he drank wine vinegar from the end of a hyssop stalk and the instant his head fell to his chest in acceptance of death.

'I'm sorry, my dear, this is pointless. I just don't see anything anomalous.'

'Then look closer!' she ordered. 'Ignore what you think you know about the crucifixion and view these carvings as a brand-new story. What's the artist telling us about this moment?'

With a prolonged sigh, Boyd inspected the scenes even closer. In his mind it was hardly necessary, since the images were burned into his brain like a cattle brand. But in his heart he somehow hoped the videotape would reveal something his eyes had missed in the Catacombs. Possibly a name or a face that he'd somehow overlooked. Or even the location of another scroll.

Ulster gasped. 'Oh my Lord, look at the ground in the fifth carving!' To make his point clearer, he ambled to the TV and pointed to the block directly to the left of the laughing man. 'Look beneath my finger, near the base of the cross.'

Payne studied the image. 'Looks like a flower.'

'Not just any flower,' he corrected. 'That's a very *specific* flower.'

'Specific? In what way?' Payne studied the rest of the archway and slowly realized the image appeared in only one carving: the scene where Christ was drinking from the hyssop stalk. Oddly it was the only panel that had *any* background scenery at all – a fact that spoke volumes to Payne and the rest of the group. 'Wait a second! Are you telling me that . . . ?'

Payne glanced at Maria, and she nodded, letting everyone know that Ulster had found the clue that she was referring to. The flower in the picture was unmistakable to her and anyone who was familiar with the odd-looking species. It was *Mandragora officinarum*, better known as mandrake, the plant that fueled the most popular narcotic of the Roman Empire.

One that was on the verge of changing the course of religious history.

For the *second* time in the past two thousand years.

52

The Roman Catholic Church is one of the wealthiest organizations in the world, with an estimated worth in excess of one trillion dollars. In addition to their priceless art collection, they own more stock, real estate, and gold than 95 percent of all countries on earth. Yet, amazingly, the Church swears they're broke, claiming they're the caregivers for more than a billion people around the world, which has prevented them from stockpiling the assets that most experts insist they have. In fact, some Vatican officials have stated that the Church is *losing* money every year and has been operating in the red for nearly a decade.

Benito Pelati laughed the first time he heard that rumor because he knew the truth about the Vatican's finances. He knew about their diverse accounts with the British Rothschilds, Credit Suisse in Zurich, and the Chase Manhattan Corporation. He knew about the gold ingots they kept at the U.S. Federal Reserve Bank and the various depositories in Switzerland. Knew this for a fact.

Hell, he had seen the books himself, compliments of his best friend Cardinal Bandolfo.

Until a few months ago, the Supreme Council was run by Bandolfo, a charismatic public speaker who could've convinced the Keebler Elves to buy Girl Scout cookies. Neither slick nor grating, he had a way of expressing his views in such an eloquent fashion that the rest of the Council rarely contradicted him. It was the only reason that the Vatican turned to Benito when they needed things done outside of legal channels. Half the Council admired Benito for his tactics and his results; the other half despised him. In the end it was Bandolfo who always convinced the Council to call on Benito again and again.

But that was about to change. It had to. Three months ago Bandolfo passed away.

As Benito walked into the room, the look on their faces told him everything. The Supreme Council was upset. Upset with the situation. Upset with the negative publicity. And most importantly upset with his results. What had started off as a single death had turned into a major crisis. Now the onus was on him to explain. In person. And the fact that Benito had refused to meet with them Wednesday had made things worse. Especially with Cardinal Vercelli.

Vercelli, a native of Rome who was now in charge of the Council, preached that rules had to be followed in order to preserve the sanctity of the Church. Even so, he knew that Benito was so well-respected in the Italian community – mostly because people didn't care about his criminal ways as long as he got the job done – that it would be foolish to take him on without provocation. So he opted to wait, all the while praying that Benito did something so reprehensible, so unforgivable, that the Council had no choice but to dismiss him.

Simply put, Vercelli was waiting for a day like today. A day when he could pounce.

What he didn't know was that Benito was waiting, too. Waiting to launch a surprise attack on Christianity.

It would make for an interesting meeting.

'As all of you know,' Benito told the Supreme Council, 'the first note arrived at Cardinal Vercelli's office on Friday, July seventh. The demands were quite simple: one billion dollars or confidential information about the Church would be leaked to the media. We get nonspecific threats like this every day, so His Eminence did nothing wrong by putting it into the system.'

Vercelli spoke from the head of the table. 'I did everything by the book.'

That included contacting the Congregation for the Doctrine of the Faith, an intelligence agency that operates out of the Vatican and has been compared to the Russian KGB. Five hundred years ago it was known as the Holy Inquisition. Now it was simply called the CDF.

Benito added, 'In addition to the CDF, His Eminence felt it would be appropriate to bring in an outside handler, someone with the Council's best interest in mind.'

All the cardinals in the room nodded. They knew

why Benito was there and what he could do for them. The CDF was required to report directly to the pope, whereas Benito had the freedom to do what the cardinals wanted. It was a luxury that the Council had used many times before.

Benito continued, 'The second letter arrived on Saturday, and it was much more specific than the first. It said an offshore bank account had been set up for a wire transfer. If their demands weren't met in forty-eight hours, they would go public with the first clue.'

'What kind of clue?' asked the Spanish cardinal who was taking notes.

'They didn't say. But they hinted that their price would escalate as the clues advanced. They also threatened to harm a Council member so we would take them seriously.'

He glanced around the room, letting his words sink in. Everyone knew what had happened to Father Jansen, the priest who used to take the minutes at every meeting. Still, this was the first time that his death was put in the appropriate context. Jansen had been killed as a warning.

'If they had chosen one of you,' Benito said, referring to the cardinals on the Council, 'there would have been a full investigation by the CDF, Vatican security, and the Italian police. Financial accounts would've been locked, and we would've been forced to issue a statement. By choosing Father Jansen, they got their point across without making a major scene.'

Vercelli cleared his throat. 'If you think crucifying Father Jansen isn't a major scene –'

'Not compared to a cardinal. Believe me, it could've been much worse. What if they had chosen you instead? Don't you think that would've received more publicity than Father Jansen? His murder, as brazen as it was, let us know that we were dealing with professionals. These weren't street hoodlums looking to make a quick buck. These were men who knew the inner workings of the Vatican. Men who knew our system. Men who we should fear.'

Vercelli stated, 'Which is why I called you on Monday. With your intimate knowledge of the criminal mind, I figured you'd be the man to stop the bleeding. At least that was my hope.'

Benito ignored the insult. He'd deal with Vercelli later. 'We received our third note on Monday, twelve hours after Father Jansen was discovered. Their asking price went up to 1.1 billion dollars. The message stated that four people would be crucified in the four corners of the world, each one bringing more attention to the sins of the Church – sins that we buried in Orvieto.'

'Orvieto?' asked the Austrian cardinal, the young-est member of the Council. He'd been brought in when Bandolfo passed away. 'What did we bury in Orvieto?'

'The past,' the Spaniard grumbled. 'We buried the past.'

While the cardinals whispered among themselves,

Vercelli sensed the opportunity to make a speech. He was well-versed in Church history and liked to show off his knowledge.

'When the papacy split in two, the holy father found shelter in the hills of Orvieto. He stayed there, secretly, for many years and was often joined by the wealthiest families in Europe, Catholics who feared for their lives due to their alignment with us. As you might imagine, the demand for those spots was very high, exceeding the space available. In time, the Church brokered a compromise: entrance to the city was sold to the highest bidder.

'Later, once the factions settled and the papacy returned to Rome, there was plenty of rancor between the sides, enough to pressure the Church into making some questionable decisions. You see, while these wealthy patrons were hiding in Orvieto, dozens of them passed away. Something needed to be done with the bodies, so the Church stored them in a series of ancient tunnels that we'd found hidden in the plateau.'

The Austrian gasped. 'The Catacombs of Orvieto?'

Vercelli nodded. 'Over the years, the legend picked up a wave of momentum. What was nothing more than an underground mausoleum grew into a tomb of mythical proportions.'

'Come, come,' the Brazilian teased. 'That isn't true, and you know it. You have been telling the same story for so many years that you're starting to confuse our fiction with the real facts.' He turned toward the

Austrian. 'We have no one to blame but ourselves. If we had come clean in the very beginning, we would have ended the myth once and for all. The Italian cardinals wanted to protect the secrecy of Orvieto, just in case another schism occurred and we were forced back into hiding. The only way to do that was to pretend that they were never there. And it was that denial that got them into trouble.'

'In what way?' the Austrian asked.

'In every way! We are the Catholic Church, not the U.S. Senate. We simply don't know how to lie. I'm telling you, it will be our downfall.'

Everyone laughed, thankful for some humor in an otherwise tense meeting.

But Vercelli ended the levity. 'The problem occurred when the families left Orvieto. They hoped to bury their ancestors in their family plots, just like they'd done for centuries. However, the decision makers at the Vatican felt it would be in everyone's best interest if the bodies remained in the Catacombs, at least until the Church was sure that the schism was settled.'

The Brazilian chirped in. 'Simply put, we kept the bodies as ransom. The families promised to stay quiet about Orvieto, and we promised to guard their loved ones for eternity. At least that's what we told them. Two months later the main entrance collapsed, and we didn't have the manpower to rebuild it. That's when we decided to wash our hands of everything. From that point on, the Catacombs no longer existed to the Roman Catholic Church. We eliminated them from our records and denied that they had ever existed in the first place.'

'Just like that?' the Austrian asked.

The Brazilian nodded. 'You must remember, all of this took place several hundred years ago, well before any of us were born. I'm sure the holy father had a good reason for his decision, one that undoubtedly helped us get through the greatest period of turmoil in our history.'

Vercelli glanced around the room, making sure no one had anything else to say. 'The question we must ask ourselves is whether we need to keep this secret for any longer. I, for one, don't understand why anyone would think that this story was worth a billion dollars. Furthermore, I don't understand why Benito was unable to handle this problem on his own.'

He stared down the table at Benito. 'As far as I can tell, you're the only person who stands to lose anything here, since you put your reputation on the line years ago when you swore to the media that the Catacombs never existed . . . Isn't that right?'

The temperature in the room seemed to rise several degrees as the cardinals waited for Benito's retort. They knew he would say something – probably loud and persuasive – but none of them could've anticipated his response. Never in a million years did they expect Benito to turn on them and attack every-thing that they stood for. Never in their wildest dreams did they expect to hear something so scandalous that it made a billion dollars seem like the bargain of the century. Then again, none of them knew the secret that he possessed.

Or how long he had been waiting to use it.

53

Dr Boyd paced around Ulster's office, trying to comprehend the mandrake carving on the archway. If Maria's discovery was legitimate, then they were close to proving the biggest fraud of all time. Close to shattering an entire belief system. Close to killing the most popular religion on the planet. And the anxiety was starting to get to him.

'Don't you see what this means?' he barked at no one in particular. 'The *Romans* were the ones who started Christianity. Not the apostles or the Jews or even Jesus himself, but the bloody Romans! Can you believe that? Tiberius actually pulled this off.'

Payne said, 'But why? Why would Tiberius do this? That *still* doesn't make sense to me.'

Boyd stopped moving. 'Tell me, my boy, what do you know about organized religion?'

'Religion? It's a set of beliefs that a person has about God.'

Boyd nodded. 'And what do you know about the origin of religion?'

'Not much. I know the basics about Christ from Sunday school but nothing more.'

'Actually, my boy, I didn't mean Christianity. I was referring to the origin of religion, *not* the genesis of a particular faith ... Do you know why religion was started? To put it simply, religion was created for control. At the rudimentary level, religion is simply an organized system of control used by the upper hierarchy to keep the masses in line. Consequently, he who possesses the ear of God is a *very* powerful man.'

'Makes sense,' Payne conceded.

'Yes, it does. So much so that men of intelligence have been using this for centuries, wielding the wrath of God as a weapon and using it to achieve supremacy over the masses. Of course this method of control isn't permanent, for the world has a way of changing everything over time. Evolution, war, and technology have played their parts during history, eroding the fabric of society just enough to make sure that nothing human is permanent.

'Hundreds of years passed before ancient Egypt crumbled and with it its widespread belief that Ra was the creator of the universe. Then came the Greeks and their notion of Zeus. The Incas had Viracocha. The Mayans had Hunab Ku. The Vikings had Odin and the great hall of Valhalla. Each of these deities was revered for centuries by legions of devoted followers, yet today they're viewed by society as antiquated notions from our uncivilized forefathers.'

'Out of curiosity,' Payne wondered, 'what does any of that have to do with Tiberius?'

'Everything, my boy, everything! You see, the religious structure of ancient Rome came directly from Greece, stolen from the heights of Mount Olympus. In fact, there's a term, *interpretatio Romana*, meaning the Roman understanding of things. Its roots can be traced to the third century BC, when the Romans pilfered the Greeks' religion and made it their own. One minute Zeus was the ruler of the cosmos, the next it was Jupiter – same god with a new Roman name. Poseidon became Neptune, Hades became Pluto, Eros became Cupid, and so on.'

Boyd looked around the room to make sure that everyone understood.

'Of course this type of transition has an incubation period. Just because a government wants its people to follow its official religion doesn't mean they're going to do it – especially since most Roman citizens weren't even born in Rome. You see, ancient Rome was the original melting pot, a merging of several different cultures under one imperial flag. Alas, unlike the United States where its people longed to come to America, most families in the Empire had no choice. The Greeks, Gauls, Britons, and Jews were all conquered and assimilated into the Roman culture, as were the Egyptians, Illyrians, and Armenians. My Lord, by the time Tiberius came into rule in 14 AD, the Empire stretched from the North Atlantic Ocean to the Red Sea.'

'The lands of snow and sun,' Maria stated. 'That's what Tiberius wrote in the scroll. He said Rome needed to do something drastic because the Empire had gotten too large for its own good.'

Payne asked, 'And the something drastic was to fake the crucifixion of Christ?'

Boyd nodded, glad that Payne was starting to grasp the big picture. 'As I mentioned earlier, men of intelligence have used the power of religion for centuries. It's one thing to threaten the masses with punishments of the flesh; it's quite another to threaten eternal damnation. Tiberius was never able to wield this ultimate power since most Roman peasants – especially those who lived on the fringes of the Empire – never believed in the same gods as he. Therefore, he never fully had control over them. Or their wealth.'

'OK,' Payne said, 'now I'm beginning to understand. The only way he could unite everyone was to get them to support the same thing. And since they'd never unite for the sake of Rome, he knew he had to give them an alternative. Something they could believe in.'

Boyd nodded. 'Tiberius started Christianity for one reason only: to gain control. He knew all about the unrest in Judea and figured the best way to placate the Jews was to give them the Messiah that had been prophesied. Then, once the Jews started to believe in Christ, he was going to take their Messiah away, which would allow him to grab control of this new religion.'

'But how?' Ulster asked. 'Wouldn't Jesus have to be in on things?'

Boyd shook his head. 'Not if they drugged him

like Jonathon suggested. Think about it. Jesus would have awoken in the tomb of Joseph of Arimathea, and his disciples would've told him that he had died on the cross and the Lord brought him back. Furthermore, if skeptics needed evidence of Jesus's identity, they could've done what was described in the Bible – because that part of the crucifixion probably wasn't faked.'

According to John 20:25–27, Thomas told the disciples that he wouldn't believe in Christ's resurrection until he could place his finger in the holes of Jesus's palms and his hand in the wound in Jesus's side. Eight days later Jesus reappeared, giving doubting Thomas the opportunity.

'OK,' Payne said. 'Let's pretend you're accurate. Tiberius faked Christ's death for the good of the Empire. What would he have done next?'

Maria answered for Boyd. 'After giving them their new God, Tiberius planned to strengthen their unity by giving them a common enemy to fight against.'

'A common enemy? What enemy?'

'Rome,' she answered. 'Tiberius actually wanted them to unite against the Empire.'

Boyd smiled at the irony. 'Don't you see? For this to work, Rome couldn't roll over and play dead. They had to fight back with everything – or in this case what Tiberius allowed them to fight with – or else people would've caught on. That's one of the main reasons that he wanted Paccius to run things in Jerusalem. Not only could he trust him, but he knew his general had the experience to throw a battle or two to Christianity, which in turn would be a victory for Rome.'

Payne shook his head in disgust, staring at the photo of the stallions. He couldn't imagine riding into battle on such a magnificent beast, fighting side by side with his armor-clad men, knowing full well he wasn't supposed to win.

'Of course,' Boyd theorized, 'Tiberius would've required a long-term plan if he wanted the Empire to profit from any of this, for the switch to Christianity wouldn't have happened overnight. In fact, it took three centuries before Rome actually made it their official religion.'

'Did you say centuries?'

He nodded, letting that fact sink into Payne's head. 'That meant Tiberius couldn't have pulled this off alone. He had to have a partner in this, someone who was in Judea at the time of Christ's death. Moreover, Tiberius knew if the Empire was ever going to profit from this scam, he had to notify his line of successors of the entire plot and pray that they kept the ruse up long enough for it to take hold. Otherwise, everything would've been for naught.'

'Perhaps,' Jones suggested, 'that's the reason Tiberius built the Catacombs in the first place? Maybe he built them to protect his secret. That would explain why he made them so damn grand. It would've convinced future emperors that Rome had invested quite a bit in this plan, no matter how outrageous it seemed. And if they stayed the course, they had even more to gain.'

Maria looked at him, impressed. 'That's not half bad.'

'No, it's not,' Boyd concurred. 'Of course that doesn't mean that his successors followed his wishes. Recorded documents prove that Tiberius feared for his safety during the last few years of his life. Consequently, he left Rome and lived on Capri, a tiny island off the western coast of Italy, until his death. During that time he only talked to his most trusted advisors, and later they admitted that he went a little crazy toward the end. Who knows? Maybe his bout of insanity prevented future emperors from taking Tiberius's plot seriously?'

'Which means what?' Payne asked.

'Which means we've hit another roadblock. Right now there are three distinct possibilities in my mind. And as far as I can tell, we're lacking evidence to prove any of them.'

'Three?'

'Yes, three,' Boyd assured Payne. 'Number one, everything went as Tiberius had hoped, and the Empire milked Christianity for three centuries before adopting it as its official religion. Number two, the crucifixion of Christ was faked, but future emperors went against Tiberius's plot, thereby preventing the Empire from taking full advantage of the anticipated windfall.'

'And number three?'

'The death of Paccius — or another unforeseen obstacle — ended Tiberius's plan before it could be carried out, meaning Christ was actually crucified, died, and was buried, then came back to earth to prove that he was, in fact, the Son of God.'

All of them sat, silent, pondering the final scenario.

Eventually, Jones cleared his throat and spoke. 'So what are you saying? We're stuck?'

Boyd nodded. 'It's starting to look that way. Unless you're keeping something from us.'

'I wish. But the truth is, my mind is spinning from all of this new information.' Jones turned toward Payne. 'What about you, Jon? Are you holding something back?'

Payne looked up from the photo of the stallions, half stunned by what he had just seen. So he rubbed his eyes and looked at the picture again. 'Holy crap. I might be holding something back.'

'You are?'

Nodding, Payne handed him the framed picture. 'Look at this. What do you see?'

Jones glanced at the photo. 'If I'm not mistaken, those are the Lipizzaners . . . Hey, did I ever tell you the story about General Patton and those horses?'

Payne rolled his eyes, thankful that he hadn't brought it up earlier. 'Come on, D.J., focus! Do you really think this is an appropriate time to talk about Patton and those albino ponies?'

'No,' he said, embarrassed.

'Tell me, what do you see *behind* the horses?'

'Behind them?' He studied the building in the background. 'I'm not sure. Is that the Hofburg Palace in Vienna?'

'Yes it is. Now look at the artwork on the building.'

'The artwork? Why in the world –'

'Dammit, D.J.! Just look at the picture!'

The black-and-white photograph showed the horses on their home turf, parading gracefully in the stone courtyard of the Hofburg grounds. Yet Jones had to ignore their magnificence. He had to force his eyes to look beyond the focus of the lens, to search the shadows and crevices of the building itself while ignoring the heart of the picture. Of course, when he came across the image in question, a look of revelation filled his face. 'Oh my God! Where did you find this?'

But Payne chose not to answer. Instead, he simply leaned back and laughed as Maria, Ulster, and Boyd tried to attach meaning to Payne's lucky discovery.

54

Frankie was the official spokesman for *Università Cattolica*, so he was well-known at the campus police building. He nodded at the man behind the front desk, a sergeant who had more important things to worry about than the midget from the PR office. It was the reaction that Frankie had hoped for. If his plan was going to work, he needed to be left alone for the next few minutes.

After checking the roll-call sheet, Frankie knew which officers were gone for the day and went to one of their offices. Acting quickly, he turned on the computer and accessed the police database, which allowed him to search for the identity of the men who died in Orvieto.

Shortly after spotting the first victim, Frankie found visual proof of a second soldier twenty feet away. That meant four people had died in the accident, not two, a fact that struck Frankie as suspicious. What were the two soldiers doing at the time of the crash? And why in the world were they *outside* the helicopter? That didn't make sense. Neither did the cover-up in the middle of the night. Why remove the wreckage before anyone had a chance to examine it?

From his perspective, it reeked of conspiracy, even though he didn't have much to go on.

He scanned the photo of the first corpse into the police computer, then narrowed the parameters of his search by eliminating men over forty-five years old. It was tough to determine the climber's exact age because of his bruised and bloodied features, yet Frankie assumed that he had to be young. An officer with any seniority wouldn't have been climbing the cliff face.

Pictures started flashing across the screen. Sometimes they lingered for an instant as the program examined distinguishing marks on each person – the slope of the man's brow, the curve of his jaw, the length of his nose – only to be discounted a half second later. This went on for several minutes. Face after face whizzed by like passengers on a speeding train until the computer beeped, a sound that told him it had found a name.

Jean Keller, thirty-three, was born and educated in Switzerland, then moved to Rome in his early twenties to join the *Guardia Svizzera*, an elite fighting unit known as the Swiss Guard. According to tradition, the Guard had only one mission – to protect the pope – although Frankie couldn't understand what that had to do with modern-day Orvieto. In fact, he was so confused by the guard's dossier he double-checked Keller's address and read the details of his career before he was finally convinced that Keller was a member of the Guard.

Which left Frankie with even more questions than he had started out with.

But instead of jumping to conclusions, he scanned the next picture into the computer and started a second search. The details of this photo weren't as clear as the first one – Keller was in the sunlight, whereas this victim was in the shadows – but he still hoped to find something.

Ten minutes later Frankie found the type of data he was looking for, evidence so shocking it made him run to the phone.

The picture of the Lipizzaners had been hanging on Ulster's wall for decades. He had passed it thousands of times and had never noticed anything other than the stallions themselves. At least not until Payne pointed out the statue of the laughing man behind the horses. A statue that decorated a famous Viennese building known as the Hofburg.

As Boyd, Maria, and Jones argued its significance, Ulster went downstairs to dig up information on the photograph. He knew his grandfather had taken the picture in the 1930s. What he didn't know was if the statue was still in Vienna or if it had been a casualty of World War II. But even if that was the case, they still had visual evidence of the laughing man and could always contact historians at the Hofburg for additional information.

Strangely, while excitement erupted around Payne, he found himself sitting in the corner, trying to decide if he wanted to stay involved. Two weeks ago he and Jones were eating lunch in Pittsburgh. Now they were in one of Europe's premiere research facilities looking for evidence that would obliterate the world's most popular religion.

Did he really want to be a part of this?

And if so, which side should he be fighting for? For the Christians or the Romans?

On the surface, it seemed like a no-brainer. He should be fighting for Christ, right? Yet this issue wasn't as black-and-white as it seemed. What if they found indisputable evidence that Tiberius had pulled this off, that he handpicked Jesus as the Messiah and managed to trick the masses of Judea? If so, what was the morally responsible thing to do? Should he allow Boyd and Maria to announce their findings? Or should he do everything in his power to suppress it? Should he call the Pentagon and ask for their advice? Or should he call a priest and ask for his?

Anyway, he was about to ask Jones for his thoughts on the topic when his cell phone started to ring. Payne checked the caller ID and saw an unfamiliar number. An international number. He showed it to Jones, and he didn't recognize it, either.

Payne asked, 'Are you sure your encryption program will work?'

Jones nodded. Several weeks ago he placed a microchip in Payne's phone that prevented it from being traced – something to do with tricking the relay stations into misinterpreting his signal location.

Ultimately it prevented his cell phone from being used like a homing beacon. 'The chip should buy you a minute. Maybe more. It all depends on who's looking for you. To be safe, hang up within forty-five seconds.'

Payne hit the timer on his watch then answered the phone. 'Hello?'

'*Signor* Payne? Is that you?'

He recognized the sound of Frankie's voice. 'Yes, it's me.'

'Oh, I so glad. I no sure you gonna answer the phone.'

'No time for small talk, Frankie. This call can be traced.'

'But this be important. Life or death.'

Payne glanced at his watch. 'If I hang up, wait an hour before calling back. Got it?'

'*Si*, no problem. One hour.'

'So, are you all right?'

'*Si, signor*, I be fine. It's you and D.J. that I be worried about.'

'Us? Why are you worried about us?'

'I just learn something you not know.'

Twenty-five seconds left.

'What's that?'

'I know why they kill your American friend.'

Payne raised an eyebrow. 'Friend? You mean Barnes?'

'Yes, the red-necked fat man. Is that how you say?'

Twenty seconds.

'Frankie, I thought I told you to stay out of this. It's not safe.'

'Yes, and not for you either. I learn why they hide bodies.'

'Bodies? What bodies? What are you talking about?'

'When I look closer at film, I see them. There be two bodies at crash. One, two!'

'Yeah, the pilot and the shooter.'

'No, *signor*, not inside. Outside.'

Ten seconds.

'Outside? What do you mean? Outside the chopper?'

'*Si!* Like they fell from cliff.'

'There were four corpses? Two inside and two outside?'

Five seconds.

'*Si!* And you no believe who one of them be!'

'Who? Tell me who!'

'I go to police station and I –'

'The names!' Payne demanded. 'Tell me the names!'

Unfortunately, the second hand on his watch hit zero before Frankie could reply.

'Shit!' Payne cursed as he hung up the phone. He didn't want to hang up, but he had to. It was either that or risk being found. 'Why didn't he say the damn –' Payne stopped his rant midstream and took a deep breath. It didn't help that everyone was staring at him.

Jones asked, 'What did Frankie say?'

Payne focused on Boyd and Maria, hoping to catch their reaction. 'It turns out Dr Boyd's toolbox was more deadly than we thought. Frankie put Barnes's photographs under the microscope and discovered four people had died. Two in the chopper and two on the rock face.'

Maria said, 'But that doesn't make sense. Why were they there if they had a helicopter?'

'They were coming to kill you, up close and personal.'

'But the guy in the chopper had the gun.'

'Don't kid yourself, Maria. They all had guns.' Payne grabbed a sheet of paper and made a simple diagram. 'Classic two-by-two formation. The men on the cliff were the assault team. The watchdogs in the chopper were backups.' He drew a few more lines. 'They planned to enter the Catacombs, making sure that they silenced you. It's a good thing that Dr Boyd heard the chopper, otherwise they would've picked you off and left you to rot with all the others.'

'But how did they –'

'Yeah,' Payne said. 'If your discovery was such a secret, who told them you were there?'

Boyd looked at Payne, speechless. So did Maria.

Jones said, 'Back in Milan, you told us that you had permission to dig in Orvieto. Yet our friend said it was common knowledge that Benito Pelati –' He looked at Maria. 'Your *dad* wouldn't grant access to anyone . . . I take it you sweet-talked your old man.'

Maria blushed. 'I did no such thing. I'd *never* ask him for a favor. Ask Dr Boyd. He wanted me to call him the moment we got to Milan, but I refused. I'd rather die than go to him for help.'

'That's a definite possibility if we don't find out who's after you.' Payne stared at Boyd, who looked frazzled. 'Doc, how'd you get the digging permit? Or was that just a big ol' lie? You didn't you have one, did you?'

Sheepishly, Boyd glanced at Maria. 'I swear to you, if I had known about the acrimony with your father, I never would've used your name to . . .'

'What?' Her eyes filled with anger. 'You used my name for *what?*'

'To secure the permit.'

She jumped out of her seat. '*Santa Maria!* I don't believe this!'

'Maria, listen to me. I never talked to your father. I swear I didn't. I tried to get the paperwork through the proper channels, but –'

'But what? You got turned down so you decided to use me!'

'No, it wasn't like that –'

'You *swore* that you invited me because I was your best student, not because of my name. Now I find out *that* was the only qualification you were looking for!'

'Maria, I swear that wasn't the –'

Payne grabbed Boyd before he could say another word and eased him into the far corner. Meanwhile,

Jones put his arm around Maria and tried to comfort her. It was a good move on his part because the last thing they needed was for her to start hating Boyd.

'Doc,' Payne said, 'you can talk to her later, after she calms down. But right now I need you to focus on one thing. Who gave you permission to dig in Orvieto?'

'What?' he asked, distracted.

'You said you never talked to Maria's father about Orvieto. So who gave you the permit?'

Boyd blinked a few times. 'Some chap named Dante who works for her father. I told him that Maria and I were looking to dig in Orvieto, and he said he'd take care of it. A week later he rang me and told me that he'd made all the necessary arrangements.'

'So you never talked to Benito?'

'No, I swear, Dante handled *everything*. The permits, the signatures, the guards. He cut through all the red tape for me in less than a week.'

'And you're sure the permit was authentic?'

'Of course it was authentic. We were required to present the bloody thing the moment we arrived in Orvieto. Moreover, the guards double-checked it before we were allowed to dig. I'm telling you, we had permission to be there!'

Payne studied Boyd's eyes and could tell that he was telling the truth. Up until now Payne kind of assumed that Benito Pelati was behind all the violence in Orvieto. He figured they were trying to keep the Catacombs a secret and had done everything in their power to stop Boyd and Maria from telling the world about their discovery. But since they had permission to dig, Payne no longer knew what to think. So he said, 'What does your gut tell you about this?'

'About what?'

'About the violence. Who tried to kill you in Orvieto? Who blew up the bus?'

'I have no idea.'

'Come on, Doc. I don't believe that for a second. You're in the CIA, for God's sake. You have to have a theory. The CIA *always* has a theory.'

Boyd shook his head. 'Not this time. I've been too wrapped up in the mystery of the Catacombs to consider my personal safety. My sole focus has been on the scroll.'

'The scroll? Someone's trying to kill you, and your focus is on the scroll? Give me a break! I don't buy that at all. At some point self-survival has to enter your mind. It has to. That's just human nature.'

'Really?' he argued. 'If self-survival is so important, then why are you here?'

It was the question that Payne had been struggling with for the past few days. And the truth was, he didn't have a solid answer until Boyd forced him to respond. 'As crazy as this sounds, I think I'm here to figure out why I'm here.'

'A bit of a paradox, wouldn't you say?'

Payne nodded at Boyd's assessment. 'But if you

think about it, it makes sense. Manzak wanted me involved in this mess for some crazy reason. Now I feel obligated to figure out why.'

55

Once everyone calmed down, Payne told Jones about Manzak and Buckner's fingerprints. Jones's computer was still in the Roman Collection Room, so they headed upstairs to see if Randy Raskin had sent the results from the Pentagon. Thankfully, there was an e-mail waiting for them.

hey guys,

i checked our records. neither dude is cia. definitely not the real manzak and buckner. you guys should've been more thorough ... i ran their prints through some european databases and got 2 hits. the results are interesting. what are you guys involved in now?

r.r.

p.s. did i mention you guys should've been more *thorough*?

Payne read the message over Jones's shoulder and sensed his stress over the *thorough* line. If there's one thing that Jones prided himself in, it was his thoroughness. Then again, that's probably the reason that Raskin mentioned it twice. Why have friends if you can't bust their balls? Still, Payne didn't want

Jones to get upset, so he said, 'Someone at the Pentagon needs to show Raskin how to use the shift key. Seriously, how hard is it to capitalize?'

Jones laughed as he clicked on the first attachment. 'OK, who do we have first?'

Sam Buckner's ugly mug filled the screen. Or in reality Otto Granz, because that was his real name. Born near Vienna, he entered the Austrian army at the age of eighteen for his mandatory six-month stint and decided to stay on for an additional ten years. From there he bounced around Europe, doing all kinds of mercenary work, before he took permanent residence in Rome.

Last employer: unknown. Last whereabouts: unknown.

'We should tell Raskin he can update the second category. Otto's on a slab in Milan.'

Jones nodded. 'We probably should, just to be *thorough*.'

Payne laughed, while Jones opened the second attachment. They knew Manzak was running the show, so in their minds the organization he worked for would be the key to everything. 'Richard Manzak, come on down. You're the next contestant on the –'

And that's when they saw the name. A name that ended their joking.

'No way,' Jones groaned. 'You gotta be shitting me.'

Payne looked at Manzak's face. It was definitely him. Payne never forgot a guy he had recently killed.

Jones knew it was him, too. But it took him longer to accept it. Mostly because he had the hots for Maria and realized he had to confront her with the new information. He had to march right up to her and ask her which side she was on. And her reaction would be the key. It would tell them everything they needed to know. Whose side was she really on?

Jones skimmed through Manzak's personnel file as he printed a copy as evidence. When he was done, he said, 'Let's get her. We need to talk to her now.'

Payne nodded. 'Lead the way. I got your back.'

Little did Payne know how prophetic his words would be.

As they hit the front stairs, Payne glanced out the window at a distant peak, half expecting to see snow, even though it was the middle of July. Instead, what he saw was a blur in the corner of the property grounds. Something human. Someone scrambling for cover.

'Hold up,' he said, grabbing Jones's shoulder. 'Check three o'clock.'

That was all it took. One simple phrase, and he entered war mode. From researcher to soldier in half a second, like Payne had flipped a switch in the back of his head. No debating or questioning. He trusted him enough to know if Payne was worried, then he should be, too.

They were halfway down the stairs, so Jones hustled to the bottom while Payne ran back to the top, figuring two perspectives were better than one. There was a vertical notch in the wood paneling of the left-hand wall. Payne squeezed his body into the crevice, hoping to get a clean view while still being protected. The sun was fading in the western sky, which meant the overhead lights were bound to give their position away on the stairs. Payne searched for a light switch but saw none. 'What do you see? Anything?'

Jones was blessed with eyes that allowed him to see things that other people couldn't. That was one of the reasons he was such an effective sniper. While most soldiers were busy adjusting their scopes, Jones was pulling his trigger. 'Not yet . . . Wait! We have a man down. Eleven o'clock, near the boulder.'

The notch in the wall obstructed everything to Payne's left. He dropped to the floor and scurried to the opposite side, where he verified what Jones had spotted. There was a guard lying facedown. The back of his shirt was stained red. 'Get Boyd and Maria. I'll get Petr.'

Jones flung the bottom door open while Payne bolted in the opposite direction. Neither of them had any weapons, since they weren't allowed to bring them into the Archives. Somehow they doubted the enemy would follow the same rules.

At this time of day, most of Ulster's employees had gone home for the night, making Payne's job a lot easier. Protecting twenty is a lot harder than protecting one. Payne shouted Ulster's name several times, hoping to get his attention. But the only person he spotted was Franz, the gentleman who'd told him about the Lipizzaner stallions. 'What's wrong?' he demanded.

'We're under attack. One guard's dead. We need to get everybody out of here.'

Payne shouted for Ulster again. 'We need weapons. Do you have any?'

'*Ja*, in the basement. There is armory. Many weapons.'

Thank God, Payne thought to himself. 'Do you have the key?'

'*Ja*, I have the keys.'

'Then you're coming with me.'

'What about Petr? We need to find Petr.'

'We will once we're armed. We can't save Petr without guns.'

Franz moved fast for an old guy. Two minutes later they were standing outside the basement armory. Its door was made of German steel and was built to withstand an atom bomb. No way Payne could've kicked it in. Thankfully, Franz knew his keys, so they got inside without delay. The concrete room was smaller than he'd expected yet had enough weapons to overthrow a Central American country. Rifles lined the far wall while a variety of handguns hung on wooden pegs. To Payne's right there was a series of wooden shelves jam-packed with ammo and gear bags, plus several military helmets and a wide variety of . . . Oh shit. Payne forced his eyes back to the helmets. They weren't *normal* helmets. They were Nazi helmets. From World War II.

And that's when it hit him. He wasn't standing in a twenty-first-century armory. He was in a museum. A fuckin' war museum. And everything around Payne was older than he was.

Franz sensed Payne's concern. He said, 'I assure you, they will kill just the same. I have seen it with my own eyes.'

That was good enough for Payne. He grabbed one of the gear bags and jammed it with three rifles, five handguns, and all the ammo he could carry. Franz did the same with a second bag and flung it over his shoulder. Payne wasn't leaving the room unarmed so he loaded three Luger P-08 9 mm pistols and handed one of them to Franz. The look on his face told Payne he knew what to do with it, like he had been here before. The look on Payne's face said the same.

Franz smiled. 'Let's go save some horses.'

An old guy talking smack. You had to love it.

Payne had two objectives as he left the basement: locate the members of his team, then find a way out. Küsendorf is in the middle of nowhere, nestled on top of a mountain, which meant there was no way in hell they were going to get police help. And even if they did, how helpful would it be? The Swiss weren't exactly known for war. For all Payne knew, they might show up and say, 'We will watch your fight, then serve cocoa to the winners.' The pansies. In Payne's mind they were worse than the French.

Anyway, they reached the ground floor with no resistance, though they had a surprise waiting for them when they opened the basement door: the distinct smell of smoke. The Ulster Archives was a wood-framed chalet that was jam-packed with thousands of books and manuscripts. The last thing anyone wanted to smell in this place was smoke. It was a library's worst nightmare.

Payne whispered, 'How good is your fire system?'

'The best. All the rooms will be sealed behind fire-proof doors. The rooms will be filled with carbon dioxide, protecting the safes where the documents are stored.'

As Franz finished speaking, Payne heard a loud rumble in the ceiling above. It sounded like someone pushing a grand piano down the hallway. First on his left, then on his right, then a sudden symphony of sound being repeated all over the building. The noise was so intense he could see the framed pictures rattling on the walls and felt it under his feet. He looked at Franz for reassurance, and he simply nodded. It was the fireproof doors moving into place. Soon it would be followed by the light spray of water from all the sprinklers. 'Will people be trapped inside?'

Franz shook his head. 'There is button by every door. People can get out but can't get back in. Not until system is deactivated.'

Payne glanced down the corridor looking for movement. Water was falling from the ceiling, and all the doors were closing. Rooms that couldn't offer them sanctuary as they moved down the hallway. For the next fifty feet or so, they were fighting naked. No turning back. No protection of any kind. A blind man could rip them to shreds with a slingshot. He didn't even want to consider what a well-trained soldier could do. 'How's the heart, Franz?'

'It is fine . . . How's your bladder?'

More smack talk. Payne was still lovin' it.

'I'll go first. Do not, I repeat, do *not* follow me until I reach the end of the hall. If anything happens, lock yourself in the armory. You'll have better odds against a fire than multiple guns.'

He put his hand on Payne's shoulder. 'Be safe.'

Payne dashed down the hallway at half speed, trying to get there as quietly as possible. The gear hung over his right shoulder, occasionally clanging against the back of his legs as he moved. He clenched two Lugers in his hands. He'd never used one in combat, although he'd fired several on the range. He hoped like hell they would hold up in the downpour.

Halfway down the hall, he heard footsteps coming behind him. He dropped to one knee and spun, ready to take out his target. But it was a false alarm — just Franz disobeying orders. Payne waved for him to go back, but he continued to charge forward like a Brahma bull.

'What are you doing?' Payne demanded.

He knelt beside Payne. 'I thought you reached the end of the hall.'

Payne looked him in the eye. He was dead serious. 'You're nearsighted, aren't you?'

'*Ja.* Nearsighted, farsighted, middlesighted. I'm an old man, what didja expect?'

Things just got harder. 'Don't shoot at *anything* unless I shoot first. You got that?'

'*Ja, ja.*' He gave Payne a mock salute while mumbling a few vulgar words in German.

Payne started down the hallway again, followed by his geriatric shadow. As they reached the end, they heard footsteps up ahead and the sound of Maria whispering. Ten minutes ago it would've been a welcome sound. Now Payne didn't know what to think in light of the Pentagon information. Was she whispering to Jones or the enemy? Was she the one who called the soldiers, or had someone else from the Archives tipped them off? In Payne's mind the next few seconds would tell them everything.

Payne signaled for Franz to get behind him, then positioned himself on the floor along the right-hand wall. It gave Payne a chance to fire without giving his adversary much of a target. He sat like that for thirty seconds, struggling to hear what she said. But the sound of whispering had stopped. Either they had turned and were headed in the opposite direction, or they were doing the same thing that Payne was: sitting and waiting. His guess was the latter. The smoke was getting thicker, so there was no reason to head deeper inside the building. The risks were too severe.

In truth Payne would've sat like that all night or until he felt flames, because he knew patience was a soldier's best friend. However, their standoff ended quickly when he saw the tip of a knife slip out into the hallway near the base of the archway. The blade tilted back and forth like it was being pushed into a grapefruit, and he immediately knew what was happening. Jones was trying to see who was in the hallway by using the reflection of the stainless steel.

Payne growled, 'Drop that blade, soldier!'

Jones paused before answering. 'Come and make me.'

Payne grinned, then looked back at Franz. 'He's on our side. *Don't* shoot.'

Once again, Franz mumbled in German. The same words as before.

The first person in the corridor was Jones, followed by Ulster, Maria, and Boyd, who had a back-pack strapped over his shoulders. Payne was relieved that everyone was together, because he didn't feel like heading upstairs on a rescue mission. Somewhere above them fire-resistant boards were burning. Same with the carpets, the pictures, and all the knickknacks. He hoped like hell that the sprinklers were working on every floor, or the Archives were about to become a pyre.

Payne handed his bag to Boyd and told him to

start loading the weapons with ammo. Meanwhile Maria just stood there, watching, not really sure what to do. At the time Payne didn't know if it was because she didn't know how to help or didn't want to, but her lack of action caused Payne to pull Jones aside. 'Did you confront her yet?'

He shook his head. 'Been kind of busy.'

'Should we give her a gun?'

Jones looked over his shoulder and stared at Maria. She gave him a sweet smile. He didn't smile back. 'Maybe a rifle. That'll be tougher for her to use against us.'

'Fine, but I'm keeping an eye on her. One false move, and I'm taking her out.'

He nodded. 'Shoot to maim, not kill. She might have helpful intel.'

His answer didn't surprise Payne. Over the years they'd heard too many horror stories of soldiers getting killed because they were thinking with the wrong gun. That's why Payne positioned himself as her executioner, not Jones, just to be safe. No sense letting Jones's hormones cloud his judgment. Changing subjects, Payne asked, 'What are we facing?'

'Four-man team out front, wearing camo. No guards in sight. The peak to our rear has us pinned. So does the perimeter fence . . . You and I could clear it. Not them.'

Payne looked at his crew. A rusty CIA agent, a possible turncoat, an Austrian with an attitude, and a fat guy with a beard. Not to mention weapons built for World War II.

All things considered, he liked their chances.

56

The pushpins were pissing Nick Dial off. They were supposed to be helping his focus – marking the kidnappings, crucifixions, and homelands of the victims – but they were having the opposite effect. One dot here, another there. No rhyme or reason. Just random spots on the map.

Yet Dial knew it shouldn't be that way. There should be a pattern, a logical pattern. But as far as he could tell, the only connection between the victims was their age and gender – two traits that they shared with Christ who also died in his early thirties. Dial wasn't sure if that was a coincidence or not, but at this point he wasn't going to rule anything out.

Find the pattern to find the killer. That's how it was supposed to work. But three different victims killed by three different crews in an identical way? That was unique.

Frustrated, Dial removed the white pushpins – they represented the victim's hometowns – and tossed them aside. He figured Erik Jansen hadn't lived in Finland for years, and Orlando Pope had moved from Brazil when he was a child, so the odds were pretty slim that their hometowns had anything to do with this.

Next he examined the blue pins – they represented the victim's abduction points. One was an apartment in Rome, one was a sex club in Thailand, and one was a luxury high-rise in New York. Two of the three were the victims' homes, although that wasn't enough to establish a pattern. To do that he needed something consistent, something that didn't change. He needed to find a rule. A steady rule. He could study it, crack it, and follow it right to the killer.

But 66 percent? What could he do with that?

In his mind it wasn't even worth the space on his board, so he pulled the blue pins, too.

That left only the red pins, which represented the murder scenes. One in Denmark, one in Libya, and one in America. Three victims scattered around the globe. None of the murders occurred on the same continent, let alone the same country, so how could there be a link? Then again, how couldn't there be? There had to be a connection, maybe something so small that he'd overlooked it a hundred times. He just had to have the patience to find it.

'Give it time,' he mumbled to himself. 'Just give it time.'

Dial took a deep breath and glanced out the window. People wearing shorts and tennis shoes strolled by at a leisurely pace. It had been so long since Dial had taken a vacation that he almost forgot what it was like. To wake up feeling refreshed, to eat breakfast while reading a newspaper instead of a forensic report, to spend the day at the beach or the museum or a –

Tourist attraction. Somewhere like Disneyland. Or the Grand Canyon. Or the Eiffel Tower.

Or a famous castle. Or a historic arch. Or a storied ballpark.

A place where people go. Lots of people go. Where hundreds and thousands and millions of people go. Every day, every year. Guaranteed . . .

Holy shit! That was it. *Crowds* could be the thread. The killers wanted crowds. Big crowds. Massive crowds. But why? Why did they need crowds?

People. The killers needed people. Attention from the people. Of all races. And religions.

Good Lord! That's why the victims were so different. They represented all types of people.

Dial rushed to his bulletin board, theories flying through his mind. Jansen. A priest. Crucified. In Denmark. IN THE NAME OF THE FATHER. The beginning of a prayer. But what did it mean?

Next case. Narayan. A famous prince. The son of a king. Crucified. In Libya. AND OF THE SON. The second part of the prayer. The same damn prayer.

A priest then a prince. The Father then the Son.

Keep going. Keep thinking. Put them together. String them together.

Third case. Pope. The Holy Hitter. Crucified. In Boston. AND OF THE HOLY. The third part of the prayer. Add 'em up. Add 'em all up.

A priest, a prince, and a Pope. In the name of the Father and of the Son and of the Holy.

What did it mean? What did the message mean? What were they saying?

A priest = a father.

A prince = a son.

Orlando Pope = the Holy Hitter. No, just Holy. The Pope = Holy.

The Father, Son, and Holy . . . shit! What's missing? The Spirit was freakin' missing!

Where's the Spirit? Where's the damn Spirit?

Wait! It hasn't happened yet. The fourth murder hasn't happened. Where will it happen? At a tourist spot. It's gotta be a tourist spot. But where? Think, Nick, think!

The pattern. Follow the pattern. Find the pattern to find the killer. What's the pattern?

The Spirit. Find the Spirit to find the killer. Wait, who the hell was the Spirit? He didn't know any goddamn Spirit. How could he find the Spirit? That was ridiculous! He needed to find the spot. Beat the killers to the spot. Don't worry about the Spirit. Just find the spot.

Dial glanced at the map, frantically searching for the spot. 'People,' he mumbled. 'Millions of people. Where will people be this weekend?' He ran dozens of events through his mind. 'Think! Where are the most people? What's the pattern? What's the goddamn pattern?'

Denmark. He placed his finger on the red pushpin at Helsingør.

Libya. He drew his finger to the south to the pushpin at Tripoli.

America. He ran his finger across the Atlantic and stopped at Boston.

He held the fourth pushpin in his hand, not sure where to put it.

'Dammit!' Dial cursed as he punched the wall in frustration. He knew he was close. He knew he was on the verge of cracking this case wide open. All he had to do was finish the pattern, and the game was over. 'Think, Nick, think. Where will they strike next?'

Getting agitated, Dial rubbed his eyes, trying to massage away the stress that was building. It was a simple act, one that he did all the time, yet there was something about his hand moving toward his face that made him realize what he was missing. It was the hand movement, the simple gesture that all Christians did.

'IN THE NAME OF THE FATHER.' *The hand goes up to the forehead.*

'AND OF THE SON.' *The hand goes down to the heart.*

'AND OF THE HOLY.' *The hand goes to left.*

'SPIRIT.' *The hand goes to the right.*

Dial looked at the map and suddenly realized that

Denmark was near the top. Way up at the top. Just like the Father. Just like his forehead. It was the beginning of the sequence.

The next case was in Libya. Down near the bottom. Just like the prayer. That was the Son.

The third was in Boston. Way over to the left. Following the pattern. It was the Holy.

Which left the Spirit. Way over to the right. Somewhere on the right. But where on the right?

With a burst of energy, he fumbled for a pencil and ruler. Three seconds later he was putting them next to the pin in Denmark and lining them up with the pin in Libya. He was about to draw a line between the two when he realized one existed. A freaking line already existed.

Faintly, very faintly, he saw a thin blue line that stretched from the top of his map to the bottom, a line that arced ever so slightly along its path but went just to the right of Helsingør and Tripoli. Looking closer, he realized it was the longitude mark for 15° E, which meant the first two cities on his list were directly lined up at 12° E.

Thousands of miles apart but in a straight line.

Next he turned his attention to Boston, trying to remain calm, trying to stay focused even though he knew that he had cracked the riddle. He placed his ruler below the pushpin and ran the pencil from left to right, 5° below the 45° N line, near 40°.

He traversed the Atlantic, continued through France and Italy and Bosnia and extended through

China and Japan before ending in the Pacific. Then he traced his finger from left to right, searching for major cities on the line, looking for anything that jumped out at him.

Nothing in France. Or Italy. Or the war-torn lands of eastern Europe. But there, just beyond the Gobi Desert, just before he reached the Sea of Japan and the warm waters of the Pacific, he found the spot that he was looking for. The perfect spot. The one that followed the pattern. A city that was directly east of Boston. Far east of Boston yet in a straight line. Right near 40°.

Located in China, the most populous country in the world. A nation where billions of people were suddenly looking to the West for organized religions. A place where the killers could get more bang for their buck than anywhere on earth.

The Spirit would die in Beijing.

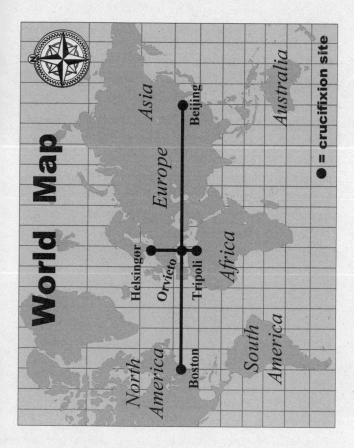

World Map

North America

South America

Europe

Africa

Asia

Australia

Helsingør
Orvieto
Tripoli
Beijing
Boston

● = crucifixion site

57

The Forbidden City,
Beijing, China

This one was going to be special. Not only because it was taking place so far away but because it was the final clue in a massive puzzle that would rewrite the history of religion. This would be the pièce de résistance that revealed their secret to the world.

It would complete the sign of the cross.

The Forbidden City, called *Gu Gong* in Chinese, served as the imperial palace for several centuries, and ordinary citizens were prohibited from entering its grounds until 1911. Protected by a moat twenty feet deep and a wall that soared to over hundred feet high, the rectangular city is composed of 9,999 buildings on 183 acres of land. All told, it took over one million workers to finish the project. Most of the large stones were quarried from Fangshan, a local suburb, then moved into place during the winter months on giant sheets of ice. To make the process go smoothly, the Chinese built a well every fifty meters to have a steady supply of water to repair the frozen road.

Nowadays *Gu Gong* is one of the most popular

tourist destinations in Asia, attracting millions of visitors a year, people of all ages, races, and backgrounds. People with cameras and sketch pads. People like Tank Harper. Except, unlike most tourists, the photos he'd taken over the past few days weren't of paintings or shrines, but rather to illustrate the position of the armed guards and the weaknesses in the massive gates. Because unlike the tour groups who helped him blend in, Harper didn't give a damn about China or their fucked-up Commie culture.

Why? Because Harper wasn't a tourist. He was an executioner.

He'd been contacted a month earlier by a man named Manzak who'd heard of Harper's exploits as a mercenary in Asia. One conversation led to another, and before long, Manzak was offering him a job. A big job. The one that would allow him to retire.

After hearing the terms, Harper was asked to choose three men he'd worked with before, three men he'd go to war with. Manzak took their names and ran a background check on each. They were natural-born killers, the scum of the universe, the type of men who would scare Satan.

Simply put, they were perfect.

Manzak insisted that he meet the four of them at once. Somewhere distant, somewhere private. It didn't matter where, he'd said, just pick a spot and I'll be there. Anywhere.

Harper wanted to see if Manzak was as good as he'd claimed, so he decided to test him. He picked a bar in Shanghai near the Huangpu River, a place that only the locals knew about. No way Manzak would find it. Not in forty-eight hours. It was next to impossible.

When Harper arrived, Manzak was waiting at the bar. He wasn't smiling or gloating. He wasn't even drinking. He was just sitting there, quiet, as if to say, *Never doubt me again.* Not surprisingly, Harper and the others agreed to his terms later that night.

Manzak's rules were simple. Sixteen men had been chosen to commit four crucifixions. Four men were assigned to each location. 'Do not discuss your mission in public. Do not split up at any time. If a member of your crew is caught or killed, your team is disqualified. Same thing if someone talks or walks. The murders must be done as outlined. Bodies must be left as planned. Do not improvise at the crime scene. There is a reason for everything, even if you don't understand it.'

At the end of the week, everyone was to meet near Rome where the survivors would split up sixteen million dollars. In other words, if his crew didn't choke, the least Harper would make was a cool million. And if the other teams fucked up, he could possibly take home four.

Not a bad payday for something he was going to enjoy.

Paul Adams was born in Sydney, Australia, the only child of two missionaries who spent their lives trying to make the world a better place. Whether it was bringing food to India or vaccinations to Africa, their only goal was to help those that were less blessed than they were.

Remarkably, even as a child, Paul Adams enjoyed the missionary lifestyle even more than his parents. Where most children would've crumbled under the severe conditions, Adams managed to thrive. He shrugged off the heat and the bugs and the lack of creature comforts because it was the only life he'd ever known. Why would he waste his time watching TV when he could be helping his fellow man instead? That's what was really important.

When he reached his twenties, he knew it was time to leave his parents' side and start his own ministry. Not because he didn't love them or the life that he was living, but because he knew that he could do more on his own. And everyone around him sensed it. There was an energy about Adams, a glorious mixture of compassion and charisma that drew people to his side, a force that made people want to follow him and work for him no matter where he went.

In his native Australia, the Aborigines called it 'the golden spirit.' They claimed it was a gift that was bestowed by the gods every hundred years or so. In their culture it was the greatest quality that a person could possess, a quality that only the eldest Aborigines could recognize because they were the wisest members of their tribe, therefore closest to

God. And according to the elders, Paul Adams was the man who had the spirit.

He was someone who would change the world. The chosen one for this century.

The media seemed to agree. *Time* magazine referred to him as the 'Mother Teresa of the New Millennium' while *Newsweek* dubbed him 'Saint Sydney.' He was young, charismatic, and loved throughout the world. Which was the main reason he was chosen to die.

The sun wouldn't be up for hours, giving Tank Harper and his men plenty of time to work. They had grabbed Paul Adams two days before, nabbed him in Morayfield, Australia, while he was on his way to Brisbane. They'd done it so cleanly that it looked like Adams had been plucked off the face of the earth by the right hand of God.

No witnesses. No evidence. No problems.

A day later they were in Beijing going over their plans one last time. Advance surveillance told them that they couldn't get inside the Forbidden City without being seen. It was surrounded by a moat and steeply angled walls that would've been doable with some light gear but not while carrying a 500-pound cross and a 175-pound victim. That meant his team had to figure out a different way to get inside. Something that the Chinese would never expect.

Harper considered many concepts, everything from a winch system that would hoist the cross over the wall to a giant Trojan horse. Nothing excited him, though, until he heard an ancient Chinese proverb about treasures falling from the sky. At that moment Harper realized that he was looking at the problem all wrong.

Why go up when it was much easier to come down?

58

As smoke filled the hall and sprinklers drenched them, Payne realized something was missing: the sound of a fire alarm. Most of the time the order went: fire, smoke, alarm, then sprinkler. But not today. He wondered why that was and if it was important.

'The alarm should be on,' Ulster assured him. 'Both here and at the firehouse in Biasca ... It must've malfunctioned.'

Somehow Payne doubted that. 'Is there a manual turnoff?'

He nodded. 'It can be deactivated with the proper key.'

'Who has the keys?'

'Me, Franz, and all the guards.'

Kill a guard, take his key, and turn off the system before it could warn the fire department. That's what Payne would've done to stop help from coming. 'Where's the switch?'

He pointed to the eastern section of the house. 'There's an electrical panel in a back hallway. Everything can be run from there.'

'Then that's where we're going.'

Ulster looked at Payne like he was crazy. So did

Boyd, Maria, and Franz. The heat was starting to build and so was the smoke, yet Payne wanted to head deeper inside. The only one who understood was Jones, because they'd been stuck between a rock and an even bigger rock several times before. They knew in situations like this they weren't going to outgun anyone. That meant they had to outthink them. They had to do something unexpected, or they were going to be slaughtered. 'Trust me on this one. I know what I'm doing.'

Everyone nodded tentatively.

'Petr, lead the way with D.J. Doc and Franz, you're in the middle. Maria, you're fifth, followed by me.' Payne gave her a rifle. 'This will be easier to aim than a Luger.'

The fear in her eyes told Payne that she was worried. Whether it was from the soldiers, the fire, or Payne, he didn't know. In truth, he was tempted to tell her that they'd discovered her connection to Manzak just to clear the air. That way, he could stay focused on everything around them instead of keeping an eye on her. Unfortunately, if he told her he knew, he ran the risk of dealing with an emotional mess, which might be tougher to control than what he was facing. That's why he decided to wait. He would hit her with it later. If both of them survived.

Sprinklers sprayed water through the billowing smoke, causing black rain to fall. It clouded their vision and affected their breathing. They tried to compensate by staying as low to the floor as possible, but that slowed their pace as they moved deeper inside the building.

As they approached the final hallway, Jones signaled for them to stop, then waved Payne forward. Refusing to take his eyes off Maria, he walked backward until he reached the front. At that point he turned to Ulster and said, 'Maria's getting a little jumpy from the stress. See if you can calm her down.' He grabbed his arm for emphasis. 'And if she does *anything* irrational, ask to inspect her gun, then refuse to give it back. I don't want her hurting herself or anybody else.'

Ulster nodded and headed toward Maria. Payne watched them interact for a few seconds before he turned his attention to Jones. 'How do you want to play this?'

'You lead, I'll follow.'

'Works for me.' Payne stepped forward and peered around the corner.

According to Ulster, the security panel was down the hallway to the left, so he stayed as close to the left wall as possible, hoping to hide his approach until he was on top of them. That is, if anyone was even back there. The truth was, all of this was an educated guess on Payne's part. For all he knew, the fire alarm could've malfunctioned, and he was risking death for nothing. Then again, it wasn't like they had a better alternative, because Payne knew if they ran out the front door they were going to be gunned down before they made it halfway to the fence.

At least this way they had a chance to get out alive.

Three steps from the bend, Payne heard two muffled voices. He pointed to his ear then raised both Lugers in the air to let Jones know that he had heard two men. Jones slid beside Payne and waved his gun near the floor. That let Payne know he was shooting low. Payne nodded while taking another step. One of the men was speaking in Italian, while the other answered in Schwyzertütsch, the German dialect that most people used in Switzerland. They were teamed together yet communicating in two different languages. Payne hoped Jones was listening, because he knew he'd have some theories on what that meant and what they were saying.

Of course, they'd have to worry about that later, because it was time to take them out.

Payne pointed to his watch, then mouthed, 'Three . . . two . . . one . . . go!'

Jones stepped low and wide, while Payne stayed high and tight. Their movement was so quick the soldiers didn't have time to react. Both of them wore military fatigues and gas masks, which accounted for their muffled voices. AK-47s hung off their shoulders on straps.

In a normal assault, Payne would've ordered them to surrender before he did anything violent. But not here. There was a language barrier to consider, so Payne decided to be aggressive. His first bullet went through the Italian's biceps about the same time Jones put one through his calf, a shot that tore through his muscle and imbedded itself in his other leg. He dropped to the floor in a writhing pile of agony as blood oozed from him in several different directions. Meanwhile, the Swiss soldier stood there with a deer-in-the-headlights look, not really sure what was going on, even though he saw Payne and Jones at the end of the hall.

Payne knew they had to use one of the enemies to get them to safety, so Payne opted not to shoot him. Instead he rushed forward, disarmed both men, took off their masks, then put his Luger under the Swiss soldier's chin, even though he knew the barrel would be hotter than a curling iron. 'Do you speak English?' Payne demanded as he heard the sizzle of burning flesh.

'Yes,' the Swiss soldier groaned. 'Yes.'

'Cooperate or die. How large is your squad?'

'Six . . . Us plus four.'

The Italian continued to writhe in pain, so Jones kicked him and told him to shut up.

Payne continued. 'Where are the others?'

'Outside. All outside.'

'How do you communicate?'

'A radio . . . in my pocket.'

Jones grabbed it, making sure it wasn't transmitting their interrogation.

'Why are you inside?' Payne demanded. 'What's your job?'

'To prevent your retreat.'

That meant the moment Payne had stepped

outside, they would've snuck behind him and stopped his crew from reentering. It was their way to guarantee a slaughter in the yard.

Payne pushed harder on his Luger. 'What were you waiting for? What was your signal?'

'Their call. We'd wait until their call.'

Payne shook his head. 'Change of plans. You're the one who's going to call or you two are going to die. Got me?'

He tried to nod, but the barrel of Payne's Luger prevented it.

Jones handed him the radio and told him exactly what to say. Then, just to be safe, Payne assured the soldier that Jones spoke several languages and if he heard anything that resembled a warning, Jones would tell Payne to pull the trigger. Payne knew the soldier didn't believe him, so Jones said a few words to him in German and Italian and several other languages. The guy's jaw would've dropped if Payne wasn't holding it in place with his gun.

Payne growled, 'Make the call. Now.'

The soldier turned on the mic and spoke in his native tongue. 'Max, they're getting away! We missed an escape tunnel! They're running near the base of the mountain! Hurry!'

Jones grabbed the radio from the Swiss soldier and complimented him on his theatrics. Payne had no idea what the guy had said, but he could tell that he'd put his all into it. It was a performance that saved the soldier's life. And Payne's crew as well.

All of them stood there, patiently, waiting to hear Max's reaction. Ten seconds later, they heard a stream of chatter going over the air. First Max. Then someone else. Then Max again. Payne looked to Jones for a translation, but he signaled him to wait. Another voice. Then Max. Then Max again, only this time much angrier. Payne could tell that from his tone.

Finally, Jones heard what he had hoped for. 'They bought it. They're heading for the back.'

Payne smiled at the news. 'Call me crazy, but what do you say we head for the front?'

Everyone laughed except for the two guards. They knew it was just a matter of time before they were dragged outside and knocked unconscious.

59

The lodge in Küsendorf was two blocks away and probably under surveillance. That meant they needed to find an alternate means of transportation. Franz suggested one of the Archives' delivery trucks. They were parked outside the compound in a separate lot.

There was room for two people up front and about twenty in back. Franz offered to drive, since he was familiar with the roads, and Ulster offered to keep him company. The rest of the crew made themselves comfortable among the boxes and crates. An overhead light let them see, or Payne would've opted for different arrangements. He was about to have a critical conversation with Maria, and her reaction would tell him more than her words, so visibility was a requirement.

Once they got settled, Payne retrieved everyone's weapons. He made an excuse about old guns needing maintenance if they got wet, and everyone handed them over without suspicion. Next he asked Boyd what he was carrying in his backpack, and he told Payne it contained the videotape, the scroll, and as many books as he could grab.

'OK,' Jones said as he unfolded Raskin's e-mail. 'There's something we need to discuss.'

Payne sat to Jones's right, pretending to dry a fully loaded Luger that he kept aimed at Maria. With her legs tucked under her, she sat across from Payne, while Boyd sat beside her on the floor.

Jones said, 'Right before we were attacked, we received some information from the Pentagon. Data that I was able to print out. It seems that one of you has been keeping some secrets from us. Secrets about your involvement with the men from Milan.'

Boyd looked at Maria, and she looked at him, neither sure who he was talking about. It was a tactic that sometimes revealed secrets from both parties. Maria asked, 'Can you give us a –'

'Just come clean,' Jones demanded, glancing back and forth. 'We need to know everything, right here, right now, or we're turning you over to the authorities. Consequences be damned.'

Boyd and Maria stared at each other. Neither of them talking. Both of them paranoid.

Finally, Boyd said, 'Enough with the games. I've been through enough training to recognize your tactics. It's obvious that you want one of us to break and provide you with something substantial. However, I can assure you that neither of us has a hidden agenda.' He pointed to the paper in Jones's hand. 'Tell us what's on the sheet. I'm sure it can be logically explained.'

Jones glanced at Payne, and Payne nodded. It was time to reveal their cards.

'Back in Milan,' Jones said, 'when Maria picked up the rent-a-car, what were you doing?'

Boyd answered, 'I was waiting at the warehouse.'

'Maria, did you call anyone at the airport?'

She seemed startled by the question. 'Who would I call? It was the middle of the night, and I was trying to sneak out of town. Why would I use the phone?'

Jones nodded, still hoping she was innocent. 'Did either of you recognize the men from the choppers?'

Boyd shook his head. 'Not I.'

'And Maria? What about you?'

She looked at Jones, confused. 'You were with me the entire time. You know damn well that we couldn't see anyone. It was too dark, and we were too far away.'

'True,' he admitted. 'Very true.' He paused for a moment, letting them soak in the tension. It was more than enough to frazzle Boyd.

'That does it. We demand to know what's going on and demand to know now. We're on *your* side, for heaven's sake. Not theirs.'

'Is that so?' Payne asked, entering the conversation. 'We'd like to believe you, but this information causes us to have doubts. Especially since we know the enemy is Maria's brother.'

Both Maria and Boyd went pale. Slowly, they looked at each other, searching each other's eyes for the slightest hint of guilt. Then they turned toward Payne and Jones, speechless.

Jones asked. 'What's the deal?'

'There is no deal. I don't even know which brother you're talking about.'

'Roberto,' Payne said. 'We're talking about Roberto. He was the guy who came to Pamplona and claimed to be Richard Manzak. The same one who showed up in Milan and pulled a gun on us.'

'The one you killed?' she gasped.

'And tortured. And maimed.' Payne was trying to get her to lose her cool, so he poured it on thick. 'Did I tell you what I did to him while you were on the chopper? I needed to get his name, but he wouldn't tell me, so I was forced to improvise.'

Without warning Payne leapt to his feet and grabbed her hand, slamming it down with such force that she gasped in terror. Then he spread her fingers on the dirty floor and used the barrel of his Luger to tap the main knuckle of her index finger. Tapping it over and over, again and again, letting her feel the cold metal, letting her imagine what her brother went through in Milan. And he did this in hopes of getting her to talk. He hated to be so rough with her – especially since she could be on his side – but he was doing it for the safety of others.

He had to know where her allegiance was. It was imperative.

'The blade went in here. Right through his skin and veins and bone. I sawed his finger in two, then put its tip in my pocket so I could fingerprint it. That's right, while we were in the chopper, I was carrying your brother's finger, dripping with your family's blood.'

Maria's olive skin turned pale, which Payne assumed was because of his monologue. But when he pushed her further, she pointed out something that they had overlooked, a simple fact that told Payne and Jones a lot about her family and whose side she was fighting for.

'You're forgetting something,' she said. 'That night in Milan, when you made contact with Roberto, you told him that I was in the Ferrari, right? Hiding with D.J.?'

Payne nodded. That's what had happened.

'And how did he respond?'

Oh, shit! Payne thought to himself. How could he have been so dumb? How could he have overlooked *that*? Roberto had pushed the button on his detonator like he was stepping on an ant. No guilt. No remorse. No indecision. In fact, he seemed to enjoy it. For some reason the thought of killing his baby sister had brought him immense pleasure.

Suddenly Payne had all the proof he needed. Maria and Roberto were not on the same side.

60

Benito Pelati didn't shout. Or scream. Or lose his cool. He simply leaned back in his chair and smiled. It was a reaction that Cardinal Vercelli and the rest of the Council hadn't expected.

'Am I missing something?' Vercelli asked. 'Your reputation will be *ruined* if we allow the blackmailers to tell the world about the Catacombs. You understand that, don't you?'

For years he had kept the secret of the Catacombs to himself. Partially out of respect for his best friend, Cardinal Bandolfo, who would've been devastated by the betrayal; partially because he was waiting to uncover the first-person account of the crucifixion from the tomb in Vienna. But now that Bandolfo was gone, the Viennese vault was being unearthed, and his son Roberto had been killed, Benito realized it was time to act.

'Why are you smiling?' Vercelli demanded. 'You have no reason to be smiling.'

'Actually, it's *you* who has no reason to be smiling.'

Vercelli remained quiet. There was something about Benito's tone that was disconcerting. It was cold and assured. Like an assassin who was ready to strike. And everyone in the room sensed it. All eyes followed Benito as he stood from his chair and moved toward Vercelli.

'The Council asked me to find the person responsible for Father Jansen's death and for the blackmail scheme, and I have done so. Why shouldn't I be happy?'

'You know who's responsible?' asked the Brazilian. 'Then tell us. Who?'

Benito stared him in the eyes. 'It was me.'

'You?' shouted Vercelli. 'What do you mean, *you*?'

'Just as I stated, I'm the man behind his death. In fact, I'm behind all the crucifixions.'

It took a moment for his words to penetrate the fog that clouded the Council's thoughts. Once it happened, though, outrage filled the room. Unadulterated venom. And Benito reveled in it. He soaked it up like applause, enjoying every last insult that was fired in his direction. Somehow it made him feel better about what he was about to do. Then, when he reached the end of the table, the seat reserved for the Council leader, he leaned toward Vercelli's ear and whispered softly, 'You're sitting in my chair.'

To punctuate his point, Benito put his hand on the cardinal's head and slammed his face into the hard table. Blood gushed from Vercelli's nose and mouth, dousing the bright red of his clerical robe with even more red – a color meant to signify that he was willing to die for his faith, if necessary. Yet Benito didn't get that vibe from Vercelli. His point was proven when Vercelli abandoned the chair without further provocation. Meanwhile, none of the other cardinals dared to move, secretly wondering if Benito was armed and planning to kill them.

But that wasn't the case at all. He simply planned on killing their religion.

He'd been recruited by the Council to catch a criminal, yet Benito was the mastermind behind everything. His men were killing innocents on the world's stage to draw global attention. People from every continent. People of different religions. Letting the media debate the crucifixions in order to put more pressure on the Council. Benito needed them to know that he was ruthless and would stop at nothing to get what he wanted.

But that would come later. For now all he longed to see was the expression on Vercelli's face when he explained the true meaning of the Catacombs. When he told him that underneath the Church's burial plots there was a hidden chamber, accessed by a staircase that the Vatican never knew existed. And in that room, there was a deadly secret. One that would kill the Church.

Finally, after all these years, Benito and his family would get everything that they deserved.

61

Friday, July 14
Daxing, China
(twenty miles south of Beijing)

The cargo plane took off from a small airfield that few people knew about. Grass covered the only runway, which was more like a field than anything else. The only air traffic controller was the farmer who moved his livestock whenever he heard the rumble of a distant engine.

The plan came to Tank Harper while he was figuring how to hoist their massive cross over the walls of the Forbidden City. After giving it some thought, he decided it would be much easier to drop the cross from above instead of lifting it from below. Not only would it increase the ease of their escape, but the scene would generate the media attention that they were looking for.

Except Harper knew he'd have to break a number of Manzak's rules in order to make it work and didn't want to risk his share of the money. So he called him early in the week, looking for clearance. Manzak was so thrilled with the idea that he told Harper if his crew could pull it off that they would be awarded a bonus of $100,000 on top of their normal share. From that moment on, there was no turning back. They would use the air.

Or as Harper referred to it: Operation Jesus Drop.

Before they took off, Harper and his men were forced to do the same things that the other crews had done to their victims. Scourging him with a leather whip until the skin hung off his back. Nailing him to the cross one spike at a time. Hanging a sign above him. Then, on top of everything else, they made sure the modified cross – a reinforced base, steel hooks on top, etc. – was going to hold. Otherwise, things would get messy when it hit the ground.

'Two minutes,' said the pilot as he scanned the horizon. 'We can go lower if you want.'

'Just stick to the plan,' Harper growled. In his mind this wasn't the time to improvise. He'd made all the necessary calculations earlier in the week, double-checked his figures after some test runs, and scouted the interior of the Forbidden City for the best place to aim. All they had to do was follow his numbers, and everything would be fine. 'Move into position.'

The other two crewmen jumped to their feet and slid Adams and the cross to the special hatch that allowed large crates to be dropped behind enemy lines. Above the door was a series of clasps that connected to the cross's parachute, guaranteeing that the forty-foot canopy would open the moment it hit the air.

'Thirty seconds,' the pilot shouted.

Harper looked at his watch. They were right on schedule. All that was left was to administer the final blow before he pushed Adams from the plane. 'Any final words?'

Adams tried to speak but wasn't able to because of the gag in his mouth. The entire crew laughed as Harper put his hand behind his ear and leaned forward, pretending to listen.

'Twenty seconds,' the pilot warned.

Harper smiled as he positioned the iron-tipped spear. He'd been waiting for this moment all week. 'Since you have nothing to say, I guess you're ready to die.'

'Fifteen seconds.'

The cargo door fell open as Harper rammed the spear into Adams's side. The roar of the outside wind covered the snapping sound of Adams's ribs and the wet sucking of his punctured lung. Blood poured from the wound like a cracked bottle of Chianti, its contents gushing down the victim's skin. Harper wouldn't risk being identified, so he pushed the spear in deeper until the metal tip actually burst through the other side. Only then was he willing to pull the spear out.

'Five seconds.'

Harper cut the gag off Adams's mouth while his crewmen cut the safety cords near the base of the wood. Suddenly the giant canopy sprang to life, pulling the cross from the plane with a mighty whoosh and sending Adams toward the grounds of the Forbidden City.

Catrina Collins had honed her skills at the *Washington Post* and the *New York Times* before taking a job at CNN. She was used to living out of her suitcase, flying wherever the news took her. In the past it had always been a week here or there, never three months in one place. Yet that's what she had to look forward to: a summer in Beijing.

A summer of unbelievable boredom.

Her assignment was to monitor a series of economic summits that were scheduled in the Far East. Ambassadors from all over the world were in China to discuss capitalism and its long-term benefits for Asia. Not exactly earth-shattering news but important enough to cover.

Collins woke up early Friday, dreading the thought of going to work. If she had to listen to one more lecture on free trade, she was going to vomit. Thankfully, a phone call from CNN headquarters gave her a reprieve. Someone had called in an anonymous tip about a demonstration near the Forbidden City. The caller didn't give many specifics, only that it was going to be violent. And *violent* was a magic word in the world of television.

Collins was disheartened when she realized several networks had beaten her to the scene. ABC, CBS, NBC, and Fox were already there; so were dozens of reporters from around the world. Yet no one really knew why, only that they had received the same tip as CNN.

'Cat,' called Holly Adamson, a reporter for the *Chicago Sun-Times* who used to cover the same beat as Collins. 'What are you doing here?'

Collins smiled as she gave Adamson a hug. 'Economic summit. What about you?'

'Human interest stuff.' In the world of journalism, that was a polite way to say, *I'm not allowed to tell you.* 'What have you heard about this?'

She shrugged. 'Not much. What about you?'

'Even less.'

Collins laughed. 'You know how most tips turn out. It's probably just BS.'

'If this falls through, we should grab a beer or something. It is Friday, after all.'

'You know what? That doesn't sound like a bad idea –'

The sudden clicking of cameras caught the women's attention. Both of them turned toward the photographers and noticed them pointing their lenses toward the sky. Collins shielded her eyes and tilted her head back, trying to figure out what was falling from the clouds.

'What the *hell* is that?' Adamson asked.

Collins shrugged and turned toward her camera crew. 'Shawn, you getting this?'

Shawn Farley adjusted his focus. 'Not sure what it is, but I'm getting it.'

Collins dug through their gear and found a pair of

binoculars. The sound of clicking continued up and down press row. 'What is that? Is that a parachute?'

'Definitely a parachute. A red one. Not sure what it's attached to.'

'I hope it's not a bomb. That would ruin my day.'

'Cat,' he said, serious. 'I might be seeing things, but I think that's a guy up there.'

'Wow. A Chinese skydiver. Stop the press.'

'And it looks like he's attached to, um . . .' Farley zoomed in closer. He couldn't believe what he was seeing. 'A *cross* . . . I think he's attached to a *cross*.'

Collins had followed the crucifixion cases while killing time in her committee meetings, often scouring the Internet for the latest developments. She had gotten her start with the D.C. crime beat, so she was a sucker for a good serial killer. Without delay she called her boss.

'You aren't going to believe what I'm looking at.'

'Let me guess. A naked poster of Yao Ming.'

She ignored the wisecrack. 'The fourth crucifixion.'

'Excuse me?'

'And you *won't* believe where the victim came from. I swear to God you won't.'

'Where?' he demanded.

She watched the parachute drop slowly from the sky. 'Heaven.'

62

Austrian Expressway,
Swiss/Austrian Border

Border crossings could be tricky, especially if the guards had your photo and were promised a large bonus if they spotted your ass. Therefore, Payne felt it would be best if Ulster and Franz dropped everyone off about a mile from the border, allowing them to hike into Austria on their own. Payne figured the sky was dark, the trees were thick, and he and Jones had the survival skills to help Maria and Boyd avoid detection. But Ulster laughed at the suggestion. He promised he knew everyone at the border and said they wouldn't search his truck due to a prior agreement.

And Ulster was right. Ten minutes later they were on the open road to the capital city of the *Republik Österreich*. Vienna (or *Wien*) is located in the northeastern corner of Austria and has over two million citizens. Known for its contribution to classical music (Mozart, Beethoven, and Brahms) and psychotherapy (Sigmund Freud), the city's most amazing spectacle is the Hofburg, a sprawling hodge-podge of a palace that covers 2.7 million square feet and holds over a million pieces of art. The Hofburg became the official royal residence in 1533 when Ferdinand I of the Hapsburg dynasty moved into the imperial apartments. Since then, the Hofburg has housed five centuries of dignitaries including the rulers of the Holy Roman Empire (1533–1806), the Emperors of Austria (1806–1918), and the current Austrian federal president.

The most interesting aspect of the building wasn't a list of its former residents but rather what they did to the place while they were there. From 1278 until 1913, every monarch contributed his own addition in the prevailing taste of the day. The resulting mix was a time capsule of interior design, spread throughout eighteen wings and nineteen courtyards in a wild assortment of styles that included Baroque, French and Italian Renaissance, Gothic, and nineteenth-century German.

Yet the only decoration that mattered to them was the laughing man statue that Payne spotted in Ulster's picture. A statue that was inside the front gates of the Austrian White House. Somehow they needed to find a way to examine the piece without being shot or arrested.

While running scenarios in his head, Payne gazed across the cargo hold and listened to Boyd and Maria discussing the significance of the statue. The rumble of the truck's engine drowned out half their words, but their passion for the topic made up for the missing syllables. Boyd argued that the laughing man's presence in Vienna was proof that the Romans succeeded in their plot to fake the crucifixion. Why else would he be honored in such an important building?

But Maria wasn't as confident. She reminded Boyd that she saw the laughing man on the roof of *Il Duomo* in Milan, even though no one knew who he was or why he was there. Furthermore, since that statue was made out of Viennese marble, she argued it was probably the work of a local artisan. That meant the Hofburg piece might be nothing more than a replica of the Milanese design. Or vice versa.

Jones was sitting next to Payne, researching the Hofburg in a travel guide that he found in a box. He said, 'Ever hear of the Vienna Boys' Choir? They sing Mass at the Hofburg every Sunday. If we wait until then, we could sneak in with the rest of the churchgoers.'

The mention of a weekly Mass in a government building intrigued Payne. Not only because it was a security hiccup that could be exploited but because it highlighted an interesting difference between Austria and the United States. By hosting a Catholic service in the Hofburg, the Austrian government was openly endorsing Catholicism as its official religion.

Payne asked, 'Haven't they heard of the separation of church and state?'

Jones pointed to the guidebook. Inside it referred to the relationship between Austria and the Roman Catholic Church as the throne and the altar, two entities that worked hand in hand for the betterment of Catholicism. 'It says the Vatican has an agreement that guarantees financial support from the Austrian government. Citizens can follow any religion they want. However, one percent of their income goes straight to the Roman Catholic Church.'

'Really? I've never heard anything like that.'

'Me, neither. Then again, I guess their union makes *some* sense. Their connection with Rome goes back two thousand years when Vienna was a Roman military post. In fact, you'll never believe who one of the founding fathers of Vienna was. None other than Tiberius himself. It seems he was the leader of a Roman garrison that occupied the foothills of the Alps. While there, he grasped the importance of the region and ordered his men to take over the Celtic city of Vindobona. Once they did, it became a military stronghold for the next five hundred years.'

Until that moment Payne wasn't sure if the laughing man statue was worth a ten-hour drive. He figured they might find a clue or two but wasn't convinced it was worth their exposure time – especially since the Hofburg was a federal facility. Too many things could go wrong, he told them. Too many well-trained guards would be nearby. Yet Boyd and Maria persisted, practically demanding that they go to Vienna.

This latest bit of information helped Payne understand why.

Strangely, the link between Tiberius and the

466

laughing man was irrefutable, yet for some reason their partnership had never been acknowledged in history books. That meant some group went out of its way to hide the alliance between these men. And the instant their secret was threatened, they panicked, sending in a hit squad to take out Boyd and Maria at the Catacombs, then blowing up a bus to silence anyone who might've overheard them talking.

But why? And more importantly, who? No one would go through that much trouble unless there was a modern-day consequence to the secret. And if so, then this had to be about Christ and the people who believed in him. There was no other explanation for such desperate behavior.

Payne whispered, 'What's your take on the Catholic Church? I mean, do you think they could be behind this?'

'That's a difficult question. Most people like to view their church as infallible. But any time you throw humans into the mix, anything is possible.'

Jones pondered his next statement for several seconds. 'Are you familiar with Pope John VIII? Legend has it that he was an English scribe who signed up for work as a papal notary. Years later, after dedicating his entire life to the Church, he was named pope. Great story, right? Unfortunately, there's a tragic ending. Shortly into his reign he was overcome by excruciating pain in the middle of a public processional. Before anything could be done to help, the pope died right there on a Roman street in plain sight of everybody ... Any idea how he died?'

'Let me guess. He was poisoned by a priest.'

'Nope. He died giving birth. You see, it turns out John VIII was actually a pregnant woman.'

'A woman?'

'Amazing, isn't it? The head of the Roman Catholic Church lied to everyone for several years in order to get what *she* wanted out of life. Her vows didn't matter. Catholic law didn't matter. The only thing she cared about was becoming Pope Joan.'

'Pope Joan? That was her name?'

'Not her actual name. That's what fourteenth-century academics named her.'

The legend of Pope Joan goes beyond Christian history. Medieval tarot cards used to honor her with the papess card (*la papessa* in Italian) before the Catholic Church applied enough pressure to have the card changed to the priestess card, hoping to minimize the scandal.

'And she isn't the only one who has broken church laws. From what I've read, popes have fathered several hundred kids over the years. Plus many popes obtained the papal throne through illegal means to begin with: bribery, blackmail, extortion. And even worse, many of them committed crimes while they were the pope, everything from theft to assault to murder.'

Payne grew silent as he thought about Jones's words. Finally, he said, 'If you worked for the

Vatican and you heard rumors about an ancient scroll that threatened everything that you'd dedicated your life to, what would you do to stop it?'

'Not to be rude, but I think you just asked a flawed question. In my mind a more appropriate question would be: What *wouldn't* I do?'

Their truck stopped a quarter mile from the palace. Payne made his way to the driver's window, anxious to talk to Ulster and Franz about the Hofburg. He knew both of them had been there. What he didn't know was how knowledgeable they were about the security and the layout of the grounds. He asked, 'How many times have you been inside the palace?'

Franz answered. 'That is tough one. I lose count after all the years. Maybe thousand times?'

'Are you serious?'

'*Ja!* Didn't Petr tell you? Scholars from Vienna have been coming to Archives for years, mostly because of Petr's grandfather. The Hofburg is a national museum, several large museums all tied together. Their curators have brought many items to the Archives for us to study. Often they were too large or valuable to be moved without help. That is why we have the trucks.'

'I guess that means you know the security guards, too?'

Franz smiled. '*Ja, ja!* I know them all by name.'

Suddenly, getting inside the Hofburg wouldn't be as tough as Payne had thought.

Jones stayed in the truck with Ulster and Franz while Payne led the way across the Volksgarten, a colorful stretch of land that decorated the area near the Parliament Building. Maria followed several steps behind, her hair tucked under a ball cap, her face hidden behind a pair of movie-star sunglasses that she had bought from a street vendor.

Further back was Dr Boyd, the person Payne was most concerned for since his picture was on the front page of every newspaper in town. Thankfully, he blended in perfectly with a Scottish tour group that happened to be walking in the same direction. His pale features and bald head were buried under a red sun hat. His nose was slathered in a thick layer of zinc oxide. He objected to it at first, claiming that he'd look like an old man. Payne assured him that was the point. Everyone in Europe was looking for a ruthless killer, not a pasty-faced geezer covered in lotion.

It took several minutes to snake their way to the front edge of the Heldenplatz, the main courtyard in front of the Hofburg. Payne pretended to tie his shoe on the cobblestone sidewalk, allowing Boyd and Maria to catch up. Then, as a group, they crossed in front of a row of *Fiakers*, horse-drawn carriages that have been used in the Inner City for over three hundred years.

Boyd asked, 'How are we to do this? May I walk over and examine the statue?'

Payne answered, 'I don't see why not . . . But when

the truck arrives, we leave at once.' He pointed to an equestrian statue near the Outer Gate. 'I'm gonna hang back there and keep on an eye on you. While I do, please do me a favor and find out why that bastard is laughing.'

The laughing man statue was identical to the one in Milan. The weathering of the marble was different due to Austria's harsher climate, yet there was no doubt in Maria's mind that the two were made by the same artist, a fact that confused Boyd. Why would an artist waste his time and chisel two identical statues? Why not vary the positioning of the subject or the look on his face? And why was the laughing man grinning so broadly in every piece of art?

Maria whispered, 'Is there any way we can trace the sculptor?'

Boyd blinked a few times before her question sank in. 'It's funny you should ask, for I was thinking the same thing myself. Alas, any research we conducted would probably result in a bloody cul-de-sac. Although a great number of sculptures and paintings exist from the days of the Empire, the names of very few Roman artists were ever recorded. In their culture, art was created for viewing not for creative recognition.'

'Not even the masters?'

He shook his head. 'Tell me, my dear, who designed the Colosseum? Or the Pantheon? We're talking about two of the most famous buildings in the world, yet no one knows who designed them. That's simply the way the Romans were. They didn't value the artist.'

'Then let's ignore the artist and focus on the history of the piece instead? If the Romans cared about record keeping as much as you claim, maybe we'll determine where the statues were created or why they were placed in separate cities. Who knows? Maybe everything we're looking for is somewhere inside these walls.'

Boyd sighed. 'I hope so, my dear. Otherwise the truth about Christ may never be learned.'

63

Franz pulled their truck into the Josefsplatz, a small square on the eastern side of the Hofburg. Half a century ago, American troops risked their lives smuggling the Lipizzaner stallions out of German hands. Now he was repaying the debt by smuggling Americans into the home of the Lipizzaner stallions, past an armed guard whose father had fought for the Third Reich in World War II.

Irony, delicious irony.

From the security booth, Karl recognized the truck and hit the button that opened the security door. The massive gate, made of iron and topped with a series of decorative spikes, screeched as it inched its way across its mechanical track. Franz pulled into the narrow courtyard, making sure he didn't pass directly under the security camera.

'Hello,' the elderly guard said in German. 'I was wondering if I'd ever see you again.'

Franz climbed from the truck and greeted him with a warm hug. 'Why is that, Karl?'

'I figured one of us would be dead by now.'

Franz laughed as he pointed to the passenger seat. 'Do you remember my boss, Petr Ulster?'

'Of course!' Karl assured him. 'The Ulster family is revered in these parts.'

Ulster shook the guard's hand. 'Nice to see you again.'

The three strolled to the back of the truck, completely comfortable in each other's presence. Normally Karl was a lot more wary about deliveries, but not when it came to Franz. Their paths had crossed so many times that they had developed a casual friendship.

'You know you're lucky I opened the gate for you. I really shouldn't have.'

A number of things flashed through Franz's mind. 'Why's that?'

'They're cleaning this part of the building. It's closed to all outsiders until Sunday.'

Ulster said, 'We don't want to get you into trouble. Would you like us to come back?'

'No, Mr Ulster, that won't be necessary. We're always willing to make an exception for you.' Karl watched as Franz opened the hatch. 'Are you picking up or dropping off today?'

Smiling, Ulster answered, 'Dropping off. Definitely dropping off.'

Common sense told Payne that breaking into a facility with some of the world's greatest treasures wouldn't be as easy as Franz claimed it would. But he knew what he was talking about because Karl unloaded one of the crates without inspecting the rest of the cargo hold. So they simply waited there until Karl went inside, then slipped out the back of the truck.

The four of them entered the ground floor of the Hofburg's eighteenth-century wing, near the entrance to the Austrian National Library, home of one of the most impressive book and scroll collections in the world. The mammoth center section of the library was named the Great Hall and ran the entire length of the Josefsplatz. Measuring 250 feet long, 46 feet wide, and 65 feet high, the long gallery was lined with carved wooden bookshelves, colorful frescoes, Corinthian columns, and several marble statues. The library was closed to the public today, so it was lit only by the sunlight that streamed through the circular windows in the domed ceiling.

Payne was the first to enter the library, strolling across the patterned stone floor without a hint of sound. Head held high, eyes wide open, he traveled more than fifty feet, scanning the balconies that rose above him like an ornate opera house. The only thing that looked out of place was the large wooden crate that sat in the middle of the floor, compliments of Ulster and Franz. They said it was common procedure to place the item in its ultimate destination, where it would be opened by a scholar or facility manager. But in this case, they planned on opening it themselves. As Payne headed back to the group, he whispered, 'Where should we start?'

Boyd turned in a tight circle, gaping at the rows of shelves that stretched beyond the limits of his eyesight. More than 2.5 million books filled the library, plus 240,000 sheet maps, 280,000 geographical views, 43,000 sixth-century manuscripts, and over 24,000 autographs. 'We should search for a list of the Hofburg's sculptures or a log of Austrian artists from the time of Christ. Sadly, there's a bloody good chance that such documents won't be in English.'

'That rules me out,' Payne admitted. 'Is there anything else I can help you with?'

'Actually,' Boyd said, 'you have a keen eye for detail. Perhaps you can look for pictures of our laughing friend. Who knows? He's liable to be lurking in here.'

Payne nodded, glad he could do something that didn't involve breaking and entering or shooting bad guys. 'Where will you be?'

'Most of the older volumes are kept on the second and third floors. With any luck Maria and I shall find documents that date back to the time of Christ.'

'I'll go with 'em,' Jones added. 'Just in case the upper floors aren't clear.'

Payne watched them struggle with the crate of books but didn't offer a hand. He knew he had more important things to worry about than heavy lifting, like searching the ground floor for guards. He'd keep an eye out for the laughing man, too, but until he knew they were alone, his main concern was making sure the library was free of danger.

Safety first, success second. It's a good creed to live by.

Gun in hand, Payne crept toward the rear of the Great Hall, passing through a fresco-covered arch, supported by a series of treelike columns. Beyond it was the most spectacular feature of the National Library. Over ninety feet in height, the cupola – a dome-shaped roof that allowed natural light to flow inside – rose above him like a crowded theater gallery, yet none of the people that filled the balustrades were real. Instead they had all been painted on the oblique oval space by Daniel Gran in 1730. Payne walked to the center of the Dome Room, his eyes glued above, when he felt his cell phone buzzing on his hip. 'Hello?' he whispered.

'*Signor* Payne?' Frankie said. 'Is that you? I no sure if you gonna answer phone. I be calling every hour since yesterday. Why you no answer phone?'

Payne didn't have time to explain – they needed to wrap up their conversation in less than a minute or he risked being tracked – so he said, 'I turned it off to conserve its battery.'

'Ah! Good thinking. Use only in emergency. That be smart!'

Memories of yesterday's conversation came rushing back. Not only because Payne hung up on Frankie before he could tell him about the dead soldiers in Orvieto but because they were attacked in

Küsendorf less than an hour later. Maybe his cell phone wasn't safe after all?

So Payne said, 'Write everything that you want to tell me, and I mean everything. I'll call you later with a fax number where you can send the report. But don't send it from your personal fax. Send it from a public one that can't be traced. Got it?'

'Yes, but –'

'And stop calling this phone. It's not safe.' Payne hung up before Frankie could say another word, proud that their conversation lasted only twenty-three seconds.

Alas, it didn't make any difference. Payne and his crew were discovered shortly thereafter.

Nick Dial didn't have the time or the paperwork to fly to China. But he called the NCB office in Beijing the moment he figured out the riddle of the pushpins.

At first the cops were skeptical, at least until members of the media were notified of an upcoming demonstration that hinted at violence. That was all the proof the Chinese needed. Within minutes they were reassigning ground troops to protect all the major tourist sites in their city, doing everything in their power to look efficient in the eyes of the press.

Catrina Collins was part of the press corps. She stood there, transfixed, her deep-blue eyes following the giant cross as it floated across the sky. Shutters clicked and journalists scrambled, trying to figure out where the parachute would land. Soldiers with M14s aimed their weapons at the sky, waiting for orders, while their commanding officers figured out the threat level.

Was it a bomb? A terrorist? Or the fourth victim of the crucifix killer?

The news director at CNN shouted into Collins's earpiece. They were going live in less than a minute. Shawn Farley, her cameraman, was told to follow the action as long as possible while Collins described the scene she saw on a small monitor.

'Shit, shit, shit!' she cursed to herself. Her makeup needed to be touched up, and she had no idea what she was going to say. 'I'm not happy. Not happy at all.'

The director ignored her comments. 'You're on in three . . . two . . . one.'

The image of the falling cross popped onto television sets around the world. 'I'm standing outside the Forbidden City in Beijing, where a moment ago a parachute was spotted high above the city . . . As you can see, it appears that we are looking at the fourth victim in a bizarre string of crucifixions that has captured the world's eye.'

Graphics detailing the other cases scrolled across the bottom of the CNN broadcast.

'The victim appears to be a white male in his thirties. He's been attached to the cross with a series of spikes, similar to the crucifixion of Jesus Christ.'

The director shouted into her earpiece. 'God-dammit! Don't make this religious!'

Collins gathered her thoughts. 'Blood can be seen pouring from the victim's hands and feet, dripping down the wood like a grisly horror movie.' Farley zoomed in closer, trying to get the best shot possible. 'I can see blood pouring out of his side, gushing from his wound in little bursts like ... Oh God! Look at his face! He just opened his eyes! Jesus! He isn't dead!'

'Fuck!' shouted the director. '*Don't* use Jesus in vain! You'll piss off the Bible Belt.'

Collins tried to stay calm. 'Soldiers are filling the streets around me, unsure of what to do. I don't know if they realize the victim is alive, that there might be a chance to save him and find out information about the killer.' She glanced at her monitor, searching for something to describe. 'I'm scanning the sky for a plane, but I don't see or hear one. That only adds to the mystery. Where did it come from? Why did the killer choose China? What is he trying to say?'

The cross continued to fall, drifting slowly toward the inner courtyard of the Forbidden City.

'We're about to lose contact with the parachute due to our vantage point. Right now he's about five hundred feet above the great palace, a place where the media are not allowed to enter. We'll stay with the victim as he continues to fall. Troops are rushing toward the closest gate, each of them carrying rifles

just in case this is an attack ... Right now I don't
see any medical personnel. I'm hoping they're already
inside the City's massive walls, waiting for the
parachute to land.'

Farley followed the chute until it fell out of view,
then quickly panned back to a shot of Collins
standing on the sidewalk. Her blue eyes were staring
directly into the camera.

'I've been in the news business for many years,
but I've *never* seen anything as bizarre as this ...
And thanks to the magic of television, you got to see
it, too.'

In his Boston hotel room, Nick Dial nodded at her
comment. 'Talk about reality TV.'

He turned down the volume and walked over
to his bulletin board. Four red pushpins marked
his crime scenes. Four different continents, four
different victims. All of them connected on the world
map by two straight lines. Lines that formed a giant
cross. Lines that intersected in Italy.

But where in Italy? That was the question.

The geographical cross missed Rome and Vatican
City by over fifty miles. That surprised Dial, since
both places fit the criteria of the other cases. Famous
cities and tons of tourists meant plenty of attention.
Yet as far as Dial could tell, the center point of the
cross was somewhere in the Umbria region, smack-
dab in the middle of nowhere.

Dial leaned in for a closer view but realized he

needed a detailed map of Italy to find the precise town where the longitude and latitude lines met, because something was going to happen there. Something big. He didn't know what, but he knew the location was the key to everything.

He knew that X marked the spot.

64

Boyd and Maria fanned out on the upper floors of the library, searching for information about the laughing man. This gave Jones the perfect opportunity to spend some alone time with Maria. He found her near the manuscript collection on the second floor. 'What are you looking for?'

She whispered, 'A needle in a haystack.'

Jones did a three sixty turn, soaking in all the books and artifacts that surrounded them. 'Big haystack . . . What's your needle look like? Maybe I can help.'

She shrugged. 'I have no idea . . . Absolutely none.'

'Great! That narrows it down for us.'

Maria moved toward him, gently rubbing her fingers over the spine of the books. 'You have to admit there's some irony to being here. I mean, of all the places in the world, we're at the Hofburg looking for proof of Christ's death. That seems so fitting because of the spear.'

'Spear? What spear?'

'The Spear of Destiny. The lance that pierced Christ's side. It's here at the Hofburg.'

'Oh. *That* spear.'

She nodded. 'Did you know the first thing Hitler did when he claimed Austria in 1938 was to come here and get the spear? Historians say it was the thing that motivated him to rule the world. He saw it as a young student and had a vision that the spear would make him invincible.'

But Hitler wasn't the only one who believed in the weapon. According to legend, whoever possessed the lance was granted the power to conquer the world. But it was also said if the owner ever lost the spear, he would die a swift death – a fact that played out when Hitler took his own life a mere eighty minutes after American troops seized the bunker where he was safeguarding the relic. Some attribute this to coincidence while others ascribe it to fate.

The history of the Holy Lance (aka the Spear of Destiny) can be tracked through the centuries, even though no one knows for sure if it was actually used by Longinus, the Roman centurion who supposedly pierced the side of Christ. Some historians believe that the twenty-inch blade was forged several centuries after the death of Christ and is nothing more than a hoax.

Some biblical historians are willing to go one step further. Not only do they feel that the Lance is fictional, but they also claim that Longinus is fictional as well, since no records or texts mentioned his name until the Gospel of Nicodemus appeared in 715. Furthermore, since 'Longinus' is a Latinized version of *longche*, the Greek word for 'spear,' they feel the name was created by the Church to attach a name to an otherwise faceless man.

Maria said, 'The Gospels say the spear proved that Christ had died. Now here we are, where that mythical spear is kept, and we're looking for proof that Christ *didn't* die on the cross. The irony is staggering.'

Jones paused, considering her statement. 'What if it isn't irony? What if there's a reason that the lance and the laughing man are both here? What if Longinus *was* the laughing man?'

Maria laughed. 'You're joking, right?'

'Not at all,' he stressed. 'Longinus was involved in the crucifixion, right? Yet no one can describe what he looked like, and he never appeared in the history books until after the fall of the Empire. That seems pretty strange, considering how anal the Romans were about record keeping. Well, maybe his identity was being protected by Tiberius. Maybe he had it removed from the history books.'

'What about the *P*? The statue's ring had a *P* on it. That has to stand for something.'

'Maybe it does. What if Longinus's name *was* fictionalized by the Church like some people claim? His real name could've been Peter or Paul or whatever. I mean, Longinus was standing right next to the cross during the crucifixion, so he could've slipped Christ the mandrake. Plus he told the crowd that Jesus had died, then proved it by stabbing him in the side.'

Maria stood there, silent, comparing Jones's theory to the knowledge she possessed. Deep down inside she sensed something didn't fit, that something was missing from the big picture.

She would learn what that was a few hours later.

Nick Dial flipped through his atlas until he came across a map of Italy. He carefully drew two lines across the colorful surface while constantly glancing at the red pushpins on his bulletin board. He knew if he was off as little as a quarter inch, he could miss his target by fifty miles.

As expected, the two lines met in Umbria, a fertile region that was better known for its farmland than its tourist attractions. Intrigued, Dial adjusted his bifocals and focused on the intersection point, searching for the exact spot where the four crosses pointed.

'Orvieto,' he whispered. Something about it sounded so familiar. Something recent.

Dial checked the e-mail on his laptop computer. Several messages mentioned the recent bus explosion near Orvieto and the ongoing manhunt for Dr Charles Boyd.

Dial grabbed his cell phone, dialed the local NCB office, and was patched through to Henri Toulon's desk. He answered on the third ring. 'Nick, my friend, where are you today?'

'Boston, but that's about to change.'

'Oh? Have you decided to quit your job and leave me in charge? That is awfully sweet of –'

'Boyd,' he interrupted. 'Dr Charles Boyd. What can you tell me about him?'

'He is a very popular man right now. All of Europe is looking for him. Why do you ask?'

'I have a feeling he might be connected to my case. What can you send me?'

'Whatever you want . . . But I'm confused. How can he –'

'Just playing out a hunch. Can you send me that info ASAP? I need it before my flight.'

'A flight? But you aren't done in Boston. I got the info that you wanted on the fax.'

Shit, Dial thought. He had forgotten about the fax. The person who sent it to Interpol knew about Orlando Pope's death before it even happened. If Dial found him in Boston, he might blow the case wide open. 'OK, give it to me, quick. I still want to catch my plane.'

'But Nick, don't you think –'

'Come on, Henri! Can't you hear the sound of my voice? I'm not in the mood for your bullshit, not today. Just send me what I need. Not later, not after your next cigarette break, but *now*! Do you got me? Right fuckin' now!'

Toulon grinned. He loved pissing off his boss, especially since Dial had been promoted ahead of him for the job. 'Nick, relax! Check your in-box. The info should be waiting for you.'

*

Nick Dial knew the warning fax was important. He knew if he tracked down the sender that he'd be able to establish a direct link to the crime, possibly identifying the killer or one of his associates. Yet in this case he decided he had more important things to worry about, so he called Chang at the local NCB office and told him to look into it.

'Don't screw this up,' Dial said as he hustled through Logan Airport. 'And once you get the information, I want you to sit tight. Don't pursue any other leads. Don't tell anyone else. Just hold onto it. You got me? I'll give you a call in a few hours from the plane.'

'Not a problem. I'll go home and wait for your call . . . Anything else, sir?'

'Yeah. Find out as much about Beijing as possible. I'll want an update when we talk.'

'Yes, sir.'

Dial glanced at one of the departure monitors, trying to figure out where his gate was. 'You ever been to China?'

'No, sir.'

'What about your parents? Where are they from?'

'Noank.'

He grimaced. 'Noank? Never heard of it. Is that close to Beijing?'

'Not really, sir. It's in Connecticut.'

Dial felt like an idiot, so he did his best to change the topic. 'Get me that info, Chang. I'll give you a call before I hit the ground.'

'Sir? Out of curiosity, how long's your flight to China?'

'*China?* I'm not going to China. I'm going to Italy.'

'Wait,' Chang said, confused. 'I thought you were investigating today's murder?'

'Not at all. I'm flying to Italy to stop the next one.'

Dante Pelati walked into his father's office and saw him sitting behind his desk, cradling a family picture. His father was a private man, someone who preferred to keep most people at a distance. The biggest exception had been Dante's older brother. Roberto was Benito's firstborn son, which made him the crown prince in Benito's world. The two of them shared a bond that Dante never could. At least not while Roberto was alive.

'You got my message?' Benito asked. His eyes were bloodshot, and his cheeks were stained with tears, a scene that Dante had never seen before. It was a sight he actually enjoyed.

'I came at once,' he whispered. 'What can I do for you?'

Benito placed the picture on his desk and faced Dante. He realized he was the key to everything now, everything that the Pelati family had been hiding for centuries. And that forced Benito to do something that made him uncomfortable. He was about to have a personal conversation with his second son. 'I know I haven't always been there for you ... like a father should have been ... I realize that now, and . . . it is one of the biggest regrets of my life.'

Dante was stunned. He had waited a lifetime to hear those words, always wondering what would have to happen to hear those sentiments from his father's lips. Now he knew.

'I could sit here and make excuses . . . but that would be wrong . . . You deserve better than that . . . You deserve the truth.'

Benito sank into his chair, struggling to breathe. He had given this talk once before, a long time ago when Roberto had reached the right age. But this conversation would be different. No longer would Benito be talking about secrets hidden in Orvieto and what he hoped to do with them. Instead, he'd be outlining a plot that was already in motion. One that was near completion.

'Father,' Dante asked, 'the truth about what?'

'The truth about our family.'

65

A stack of newspapers wrapped in a bright yellow cord sat near the circulation desk. It had been a few days since Payne saw the news, and he wanted to read the latest on Orvieto. He flipped through the stack until he found one written in English. He took it upstairs and found a quiet spot where he could look out for guards and read about the most dangerous man in Europe.

Every story painted Dr Charles Boyd as a cold-blooded killer, a man who'd do anything to get what he wanted, although the paper didn't have any theories on what that might be. In their view he was a dangerous fugitive on the run, leaving a trail of blood and bodies wherever he went. No word about the Catacombs or the helicopter that apparently tried to kill him. Nothing about his thirty years of teaching or all the awards that he won at Dover. Why? Because that kind of stuff would cloud the picture and make him seem human. And as everybody knows, human doesn't sell. Violence sells. That's what people want to read. That was the thing that sold papers.

Proving Payne's point was the article that ran next to Boyd's. The headline blared 'Crucifix Killer,' right above a close-up of someone who had been murdered in Denmark. Normally Payne would've ignored the story, just to make a point. Just because the photo and the headline were so sensationalized it drew attention from all the other articles in the paper that were more important than the death of one man, no matter how brutal and violent his death was. Still, there was something about the word *crucifix* that grabbed Payne's attention. He quickly skimmed the story, which explained everything that happened in Helsingør and all the events in Libya, too. The piece concluded with an editor's note that referenced breaking news in the sports section, simply saying: 'Pope is Third Victim.'

'Holy shit,' he muttered, knowing who had died before he even turned the page.

Orlando Pope was one of the most recognizable names in sports, right up there with Tiger Woods and Shaquille O'Neal. If he was dead, his story was going to dwarf every other headline in the world, making Dr Boyd a sudden afterthought. Payne flipped to the sports section but found nothing more than a brief paragraph stating that Pope had been found crucified at Fenway Park and nothing else could be confirmed because of the late hour. No pictures, quotes, or reaction from the team. The biggest sports story of the decade, and he knew nothing about it.

Frustrated, Payne grabbed the newspaper and went to tell Jones the news. Before he could, though, Jones and Maria started talking to Boyd, who had been skimming through a modern text that detailed the history of the Hofburg and the royalty who shaped it. Boyd hoped to learn which ruler built the portion of the building where the laughing man resided.

'Find anything?' Maria asked.

Boyd kept reading for several seconds before he turned their way. 'Hmm? What was that?'

She smiled. Same old Dr Boyd. 'Did you find anything?'

'Bits and pieces, my dear. Bits and pieces. If only I had a morsel to guide me, I am *certain* I could locate the smoking gun.' He made a sweeping gesture with his hand, indicating the rest of the library. 'I am confident the answer is in here somewhere.'

'I agree,' she said, smiling. 'D.J. has a theory that I wanted you to hear.'

Boyd glanced at Maria, then back at Jones, trying to decide if they were serious. The look on their faces told him they were. 'Go on. I'm listening.'

Payne was listening, too. But before Jones could spit out a single word, Payne's attention was diverted to the commotion he heard on the far side of the library. First the opening of a door, then the muffled sound of footsteps. Multiple footsteps. Many people entering the facility at the exact same time. Maybe it was a cleaning crew or a team of armed guards, Payne couldn't tell from there. Either way, he knew they were in trouble.

'Hide them,' Payne told Jones. And just like that,

he knew what to do. They had been together long enough to know each other's tactics.

Payne pulled the Luger from his belt and dashed quietly across the second floor, slipping between pillars and statues. Thousands of books lined the shelves behind him, protecting him from a rear attack, while a thick wooden railing encircled the balcony to his front. His position was elevated, at least fifteen feet above the first floor. He curled up underneath a rail-side table and glanced between the carved balusters where he was able to see most of the Great Hall.

Two men in dress clothes stood in the shadows of the main entrance while their partner fiddled with something behind a tapestry on the right wall. Payne doubted the library had a safe in a public space, leaving only two choices in his mind: a security system or an electrical panel. He got his answer a couple of clicks later when the roof exploded with light.

Payne kept his focus on the men as they converged near the middle of the floor. They were over a hundred feet away, which prevented Payne from seeing or hearing much. There was a mumble every once in a while, followed by a quick reply, but nothing he could comprehend. Partially because of the distance, partially because of a language barrier. Whatever the case, he had no idea who these men were or why they were here.

His gut told him they weren't looking for his crew.

If they were, they wouldn't be standing in the middle of the library making so much noise. They'd be scurrying along the walls, pointing weapons in every corner and crevice until they figured out where they were hiding. Payne didn't see any of that, though, which led him to believe that they were fine, that they had no idea that they were there and they'd be safe as long as they stayed quiet.

Payne's theory changed an instant later when one of them yelled, 'Boyd, there's no sense in hiding. I know you're in here. Come out and face me like a man.'

Payne had seen a lot of messed-up things in his years of combat, but this was the first time that anyone ever dared one of his troops to show his face. Come-out-come-out-wherever-you-are doesn't factor into many military situations. Amazingly, the strangeness increased when Dr Boyd emerged from the stacks. With a look of defiance on his face, a look that said he was about to do something stupid like challenging this guy to a duel, Boyd shouted across the Great Hall. 'Come and get me, you big wanker!'

Well, Payne almost crapped himself right there. Of all the screwed-up, dim-witted things he'd ever seen in his life, why in the world would a CIA-trained operative, someone who was supposed to be a genius, be willing to give up his position and risk everything that they were trying to accomplish? The idiot! What the hell was he thinking?

Boyd was standing twenty feet away, completely unaware that Payne was under one of the tables. For an instant Payne was tempted to shut him up and protect the rest of them. A couple of slugs in his knee and he would've flipped over the railing like Damien's mom when he hit her with his tricycle in *The Omen*. That thought left his mind, though, when he saw Maria creep up behind Boyd. Just like that, Payne's whole world flipped upside down. Something was going on, but he didn't know what. Were there more guards than he could see? Were Boyd and Maria giving up? Or were he and Jones being double-crossed?

Payne received his answer the moment he saw who was down below. It was the grinning face of Petr Ulster, his red cheeks glowing in the lights of the Great Hall. He looked up at Payne and said, 'Jonathon, my boy! There you are. I hope you don't mind, but I thought we could use some reinforcements.'

Everyone met downstairs, where formal introductions were made, and Boyd was reunited with an old colleague. Dr Hermann Wanke was wearing a shirt and tie yet had slippers on his feet. He claimed it was to make less noise as he strolled through the Hofburg, but Payne could tell from the twinkle in his eye that he did it for his own amusement. Most people considered Wanke the world's top expert on Austrian history, so he figured it was his God-given right to be eccentric. Personally, Payne didn't care what he wore as long he could help their mission. He asked Wanke how he knew Dr Boyd, and he launched into a five-minute soliloquy about their days at Oxford where, according to Wanke, they got along brilliantly despite their diverse backgrounds.

The other man they met was Max Hochwälder, Wanke's soft-spoken assistant. He was closer to Boyd's age than Payne's, although it was tough to gauge since he was reluctant to speak, and his short blond hair concealed any traces of gray. He shook Payne's hand with a timid grip, then faded back into oblivion, virtually disappearing in the roomful of strong personalities.

Anyhow, after a few minutes of small talk, Payne knew it was time to get back to business. He started with the most obvious question. Why was Wanke at the Hofburg?

'Research, *Herr* Payne, research.' His English was perfect, with little or no accent, although he dropped in a German term every once in a while for his own pleasure. 'I was arranging to view one of the royal collections when I saw my old pals, Petr and Franz. I could tell they were up to no good and decided to have some fun with them.' He showed them what he meant by shouting a number of Austrian terms that sounded like they belonged in a *stalag*, not in a library. 'When they tossed their hands in the air, I knew they were doing something scandalous. Something that *I* should be involved in.'

Ulster rubbed his face in embarrassment, a reaction that told Payne his recruitment of Wanke was not so much planned as stumbled onto.

'From there it was easy,' Wanke said. 'I sent Franz outside to occupy the guard while Petr filled me in on the basics. The moment I heard Charles's name, I knew I had to help. Whether he wanted me to or not.'

'I hope that's all right,' Ulster apologized. 'I know I should've fibbed and kept Hermann out of this, but considering his background, I figured he might be useful. At least I hope so. I'd hate to think I messed this up.'

Boyd gave Payne a *what-are-you-going-to-do?* shrug that summed up his feelings perfectly. They weren't about to yell at Ulster or kick him out of the library. He simply invited one of Boyd's oldest friends, a man who knew more about Austrian history than everyone else combined, to help them with their research. If he had to blab to someone, this wasn't a bad choice. Thankfully, Ulster hadn't spilled as many secrets as they had feared — just some basics about the laughing man and nothing about the Catacombs. So Boyd filled Wanke in on some of the facts, and Wanke quickly transformed from a goofy eccentric into a world-class historian.

'Where to start, where to start?' he mumbled under his breath. Then, without saying another word, he headed into the bowels of the library, followed by Boyd, Ulster, Maria, and his mimelike assistant.

Payne grabbed Jones before he could join them, telling him that he needed a word.

'What's up?' Jones asked.

'Lately I've gotten the feeling that we're spending so much time worried about Boyd that we've lost track of the big picture. Like something bigger than the Catacombs.'

'Bigger than the Catacombs? You realize we're on the verge of proving that Christ *wasn't* crucified. That seems kind of important to me.'

'Yeah, I know but . . . I just get the feeling that something else is going on.'

Jones studied Payne's face. 'Ah, man! Don't tell me your gut is acting up again.'

'Actually, it moved beyond a gut feeling when I read this.' Payne handed him the newspaper that he'd been reading. 'This seems like too much of a coincidence not to be connected.'

'What does?'

'The fact that we're researching the crucifixion, and people are turning up crucified. First it was some priest from the Vatican. Then it was a prince from Nepal. And last night it was someone bigger. They got Orlando Pope.'

'The Holy Hitter?'

He nodded. 'They found him at Fenway.'

'No shit?' Jones paused in thought. 'And you think this has something to do with us?'

'Guess when the crucifixions started. On Monday. The same day Boyd found the Catacombs. The same day the bus exploded. The same day *we* were brought into play . . . Call me paranoid, but that *can't* be a coincidence.'

'It could be,' Jones insisted. 'Hell, this could be nothing more than –'

'What? A fluke? When was the last time you read a news story about a crucifixion? A long time, right? And when was the last time a Vatican priest was murdered? Can you think of a single example in the last twenty years?'

Payne waited for an answer that he knew wasn't coming.

'I'm telling you, D.J., this stuff has to be related. I don't know how or why, but we're caught up in something that's bigger than Dr Boyd. And my gut tells me if we don't figure it out soon, things are going to get a lot worse for everyone.'

66

Tank Harper and his crew reached the Daxing airfield before the body hit the ground. The pilot circled low and wide, meaning radar wouldn't be a problem. Not with the Chinese. By the time they got their search planes in the air, the entire landing strip would be covered with livestock, and Harper's plane would be buried in vegetation.

But that's why Manzak handpicked him for the job. He knew Harper wouldn't get caught.

What Manzak didn't know, though, was that Harper had seen through his bullshit from the very beginning. In his line of work, Harper realized the toughest part of a job wasn't the mission itself but rather collecting compensation. That was the task that had the most danger and the most fun – especially when he was working for a new employer. Someone he didn't have a track record with. Someone he couldn't trust. Someone like Richard Manzak.

Manzak had called Harper earlier in the week and told him the money would be divided on Saturday at a villa in Rome. All Harper had to do was get there in time for the payoff. Harper smiled when he heard this, then asked a point-blank question: 'Will you be there to meet us?' Manzak assured him he would, giving him his word as a gentleman.

Of course Harper knew that Manzak's word didn't mean shit. Not only had he lied about his name – Manzak's *real* name was Roberto Pelati – but for some reason his alias was the name of a missing CIA operative. Why would someone do that? Why select a name that had a history?

Harper couldn't figure that out for the life of him. Still, Pelati's deception told him all he needed to know: he had no intention of paying him. And to make matters worse, since Pelati wanted to meet Harper and his crew the moment they got to Italy, Harper knew something big was going to happen at the villa. Something bloody. Something violent.

And the truth was, he didn't have a problem with that.

Harper had been hoping for a million dollars, but he would settle for someone's scalp.

Harper's cross landed in the main courtyard of the Forbidden City, where it was swallowed by a masked team of armed soldiers. Representatives of the local NCB office were standing nearby, thanks to the phone call from Dial, who told them to protect the evidence as much as humanly possible, though that term had a different definition in China than it did in America.

Chinese HAZMAT personnel scanned the cross for threats, then radioed their reports to headquarters. Several minutes passed before a decision was made to allow army medics to examine the victim. Doctors determined that Paul Adams had a decent chance to live, but only if they rushed him to the hospital for surgery. The on-site commander thanked them for their efforts and told them he would try to get permission. Nodding, the doctors went back to work on Adams without voicing a single complaint. They knew this was the way it was done in their country, and an argument would only get them and their families into trouble.

An hour later word filtered down from the top: medical evac had been denied.

Adams was forbidden to leave the Forbidden City for any reason. Even if it meant his death.

Payne and Jones caught up with the others in a section of the library that was filled with thousands of copies of the same book. At least that's how it looked to Payne. Every copy was bound in red, blue, and gold Moroccan leather and embossed with a coat of arms that belonged to Prince Eugene, a member of one of the elite families in Europe during the Middle Ages.

Even though he was born in Paris, Eugene was revered in Austria, where he made his name fighting the Turks for the Holy Roman Empire. In later years he added to his reputation by donating his private library – tens of thousands of books, including some of the rarest manuscripts that Italy and France had to offer – to the Hofburg, where they could be enjoyed by the people of Vienna. Centuries later they were still being used.

Anyhow, Dr Boyd was sitting next to Dr Wanke as he flipped through several books. As soon as he spotted Jones, Boyd called him over to the table.

Boyd said, 'Maria told me about your theory on Longinus, and I applaud your effort. The group that had the most access to Christ during his ordeal would've been the centurions, thereby making one of them a legitimate candidate as a coconspirator ... Regrettably, as I am sure you're aware, many scholars believe that Longinus never existed, that he was simply the figment of a writer's overactive imagination.'

'Maybe not for long,' Wanke claimed. 'I think I found something.'

Boyd turned. 'What do you mean by *something*?'

'You want information on the statue, right? Well, I found him.'

Wanke held up one of Prince Eugene's books, revealing a black-and-white sketch of the laughing man that had been drawn by a local artist in 1732. Next to it was a detailed account of the statue, written in Italian and German by a member of Eugene's staff. Information that covered nearly 2,000 years.

'According to this text, a man of great importance came to Vindobona in the early years, a man with no name who was guarded by several centurions as if he were royalty. Peacefully, he was given a spot of land on the outskirts of town near a marble quarry. He paid the townsfolk to build him a home, one that was protected by massive walls and the blades of his guards. He took residence there for the next three decades until he succumbed to disease.'

Wanke continued, 'The nameless man did everything he could to be accepted in the community – giving jobs to the peasants, teaching religion to the children, donating his time and treasures to anyone he deemed worthy. In fact, he was so loved and cherished by the locals that they dubbed him the Saint of Vindobona.'

Boyd asked, 'Are you familiar with him?'

Wanke nodded, putting the book aside. 'I am, although the myths I have heard might not match the facts that you are looking for. According to history, the Saint of Vindobona was one of the first believers of Christ. He was an ardent preacher of Christianity.'

'Christianity?' everyone said in unison.

Wanke smiled. 'I warned you it might not fit.'

Stunned, everyone debated this development until Boyd brought their attention back to Wanke. He said, 'Tell us about the statue. Who built the statue?'

'Good question, Charles. One that I was just getting to.' Wanke flipped ahead in Eugene's book. 'A few years after the saint's arrival, Vindobona was visited by a team of Roman artisans sent by Emperor Caligula to honor this man in a series of marble sculptures.'

'Did you say Caligula? How bloody brilliant! That means we have a date! The sculptors arrived here within four years of Tiberius's death, some time between 37 and 41 AD.'

Gaius Caesar, better known as Caligula, had a four-year reign that started after the death of his great-uncle, Tiberius, in 37 AD. One of Caligula's first acts as emperor was to publicly honor Tiberius's bequests – including the commissioning of several works of art – in order to win favor of the Roman citizenry. However, he did all this while nullifying Tiberius's will and destroying most of his personal papers to protect the reputation of his family. He was forced to do so because Tiberius spent the last few years of his life acting like a madman.

Ironically, it was Caligula who did more damage to the family name than Tiberius. Caligula's four years as emperor were stained by tales of insanity and sexual depravity that are still shocking to this day. They included flaunting the incestuous relationship he had with his sisters, torturing and killing prisoners as dinnertime entertainment, delivering political speeches while dressed in drag, seducing the wives of officers and politicians in front of their dismayed spouses, and honoring his favorite horse by making it a Roman senator.

Wanke continued his summary. 'Following Tiberius's final wishes, Emperor Caligula ordered several statues to be constructed from local marble. The face on each was to reflect joyful triumph, as if mocking the world with knowledge of an extra-ordinary secret. Then, upon completion, one was to adorn the saint's home high atop the white hills of Vindobona. The others would be spread evenly across the lands of snow and sun.'

Maria gasped at the word choice. 'Snow and sun' had appeared in the Orvieto scroll as well.

'In time the saint grew weary of looking at his own face. Citing humility, he had the statue removed and ordered it to be destroyed. But his centurions didn't have the heart to demolish something so exquisite. Instead they placed the statue on the far edge of town, where it became a shrine for the townspeople, a place to honor the saint's kindness and charity. And it stayed there for several centuries, until construction of the Hofburg began, at which time it was moved across town and placed in a position of honor on the outer shell.'

Silence filled the library. Time to ponder what they had just learned.

Eventually, Boyd spoke. 'Is there anything else? Anything about the man's name or deeds?'

'No, nothing like that. Later there was mention of the centurions burying the saint's secrets in the ground of the white hills, but that's probably just a reference to his gravesite.'

'Yes, probably.'

Wanke stared at Boyd for several seconds before he spoke again. 'Charles, forgive me for being so bold, but what exactly are you looking for? It must be something extraordinarily important, or you wouldn't be showing your face in public.'

Boyd stared right back, refusing to acknowledge anything. Partially to protect Wanke, partially because of greed. To Boyd, this was *his* discovery and the thought of anyone stealing his glory, especially this late in the chase, made him nauseous. 'Hermann, do you trust me?'

'Believe it or not, I don't make it a habit to assist fugitives.'

'Then believe me when I tell you this: You don't want to know what we're looking for. Dozens of people have died during the past week, innocent people, and all because of this secret.' Boyd thought about all the victims on the bus and how they screamed in agony. He didn't want that to happen to one of his friends. 'Hermann, do yourself a favor and forget you even saw me today. Once this quiets down, I promise I'll get in touch and explain everything. But until then *please* keep our meeting to yourself. Your personal welfare depends on it.'

67

They stayed at the Hofburg for a few more hours, until paranoia crept in and thoughts of armed guards bursting into the library fueled their desire to leave.

Besides, at that point most of them needed to use a phone. Petr Ulster needed to call Küsendorf to check on fire damage. Jones wanted to call the Pentagon to get an update on Orlando Pope's crucifixion and anything else he could track down. And Payne promised to call Frankie with a fax number so he could send his information. The only call-free people were Boyd and Maria, who were so intrigued by the journal that they'd borrowed from Prince Eugene's collection that they were content sitting in the back of Ulster's truck discussing it.

The group settled on an Internet café in the middle of Vienna, smack-dab in the center of the Ringstrasse, a two-and-a-half-mile boulevard lined with monuments, parks, schools, and the world-famous State Opera. To the northeast they could see the top of Saint Stephen's Cathedral, its 450-foot tower thrusting out of the building like a Gothic stalagmite. The café itself was large and bustling, filled with tourists who were getting food and caffeine while checking their e-mail.

Payne got in touch with Frankie at his office and told him to send the fax with all the information that he had discovered. Payne wasn't willing to tell him the café's fax number, just in case Frankie's phone was tapped, but they figured a way around that. The only problem was, Payne had to wait until Frankie drove down the street and accessed a clean line.

Meanwhile, Jones reached Raskin at the Pentagon and learned that a fourth crucifixion had just occurred in Beijing, a case receiving serious airtime around the world. He told Payne to find a TV that was broadcasting CNN while Jones got background info on the other three murders. The television coverage was stunning. A man nailed to a crucifix was floating through the air while blood oozed, in slow motion, from wounds in his hands, feet, and side. An announcer droned on about the recent rash of tragedies, followed by an interview with an 'expert' who claimed he had no idea why any of these murders had taken place.

Payne watched for several minutes until he felt a hand on his shoulder. Not a threatening hand, just a tap. He turned and saw Ulster, his skin pale and his cheeks streaked with tears. He had just gotten off the phone with Küsendorf and was obviously shaken by the news. Payne helped him to one of the chairs and sat next to him, not pressing him for details until he was ready to talk. He had comforted enough grieving soldiers to know that was the best approach.

A few minutes passed before Ulster talked about

the damage to the Archives. They were more severe than he had anticipated. All the vaults had held, protecting his most valuable collections from fire and water damage. Still, many of the building's outer walls had been destroyed, making the Archives structurally unsafe. That meant even though his artifacts were fine for the moment, they would be destroyed if the building collapsed.

'I've got to go back,' he told Payne. 'I don't care if I'm risking my life; I have to go.'

Payne agreed with him, even though he knew that Ulster was walking into a death sentence. Soldiers were bound to be waiting there, men who were salivating at the thought of grabbing him and torturing him for information about Boyd, the Catacombs, and everything else. Normally, Payne would've offered to go back with him as his personal guard, but not today. Not with all that was going on. Payne's services were needed in Vienna or wherever they were headed next.

But that didn't mean he was going to abandon him.

'Can you wait twelve hours?' Payne asked.

Ulster blinked a few times then looked at him, confused. 'Why?'

'Twelve hours. Can you wait that long before going back?'

'Jonathon,' he said, 'both of us know you can't accompany —'

'You're right, I can't go with you. But that doesn't

mean I can't help. You give me twelve hours, and I promise I can have team of armed guards waiting to protect you. Furthermore, I'll get you the best engineers that money can buy to save your property. Trust me, they'll do a better job than any of the local salvage companies.'

Ulster was about to turn Payne down; he could see it in his eyes. He was about to thank Payne for his offer, then politely decline because of the cost, his pride, or a hundred other reasons that he could've chosen. Payne knew all this because he would've done the exact same thing. That's why Payne decided to beat him to the punch, reminding him of their earlier agreement.

Payne said, 'When we met I promised if you gave me full access to the Archives and the use of your services that I would make it worth your time. Well, it's time for me to pay up.' He told Ulster to look at his watch. 'Tell Franz to drive slowly on the way home, because twelve hours from now I'll have men waiting for you at the Swiss border. You'll know they're with me because they'll know our special password.'

'Password?' Ulster asked with tears in his eyes. 'What password?'

Payne grabbed his hand and shook it. 'The password is *friend*.'

Payne made a few calls to his colleagues back home, and they assured him that they knew what to do.

From that moment on he knew Petr Ulster and his Archives would both survive.

The vibration on Payne's cell phone forced his focus back to Vienna. Frankie was calling for the café's fax number, so Payne answered by saying, 'Did anyone follow you?'

'No,' he assured Payne. 'I be very careful.'

'Write this down.' He gave him the number, then told him to burn it and the confirmation sheet when he was done. He also told him to delete the fax's memory. 'Where can I reach you?'

'My office. I be at my office.'

Payne groaned. That's the last place he wanted him to be. Why did Frankie think he had him using a public line? 'Go somewhere else but not your house. That's too easy to trace.'

'I can get hotel.'

'Perfect,' Payne told him. 'Pay in cash and use a fake name, something you won't forget, like . . . James Bond.'

'*Sì!*' he shrieked. Obviously he liked the choice.

Frankie named the closest hotel he could think of, and Payne memorized its name. 'Go there when you're done. Your room and room service are on me, OK?'

'*Sì,*' he repeated.

'And don't use your credit card for *anything.*'

'No card. I promise.'

'Thanks, Frankie. I'll talk to you soon.'

Thirty-four seconds. Not too bad. Especially if his

fax helped Payne figure something out. But he had his doubts. What in the world could Frankie know that Payne didn't?

A few minutes later he got his answer. That little bastard was a lifesaver.

Boyd and Maria brought Prince Eugene's journal into the café and took a seat in front of one of the computers. Maria manned the keyboard while Boyd, still wearing that ridiculous suntan lotion on his nose, told her what to type. Curious, Payne wanted to know what they were searching for but couldn't leave the machines until Frankie's fax arrived.

Jones joined Payne a moment later, right after finishing a twenty-minute call to Randy Raskin. He said, 'Man, I love calling the Pentagon collect. Paid for by our tax dollars.'

'A collect call from Austria? That's like a thousand bucks.'

'But worth it.' He flipped through his notes. 'So far there's been four crucifixions, one each in Denmark, Libya, America, and China. All the killings were too similar to be copycat crimes.'

'In other words, one crew.'

He shook his head. 'Four *different* crews.'

'Four? The murders were on separate days, right?'

'True, but the abductions overlapped. Throw in the travel and the time zones and everything else, and the cops think there were multiple crews. If not four, at least two.'

Payne considered this for a moment, trying to figure out what anyone could gain by crucifying random people. 'Any connections between the victims?'

'Nothing obvious. Different homelands, different occupations, different everything – except for the fact that they were males in their early thirties. Just like Christ when he died.'

'Jesus,' Payne gasped.

'Yep, that's the guy. Anyway, I told Randy that the crucifixions might have something to do with our case, so I had him check all the phone records for Agent Manzak, i.e., Roberto Pelati. Remarkably, he made calls to Denmark, China, Thailand, America, and Nepal within the last six weeks. Either he's planning one big-ass vacation, or he's our man.'

'Our man for what?'

Jones shrugged. 'That seems to be the million dollar question.'

A million dollar question. What a joke. That term no longer had the same significance as it used to. Nowadays it seemed everybody had a million dollars. Game show contestants, dot-com geeks, reality show winners, third-string linebackers. Payne really doubted if Roberto Pelati would've gone through any of this for a mere million dollars. A billion, maybe. But certainly not a million. That was play money to the modern-day criminal.

Then again, who in the world had a billion dollars

to spare? Bill Gates, Ted Turner, and the rest of the *Forbes* list. Probably a sheik or two. Maybe some royalty. Other than that, it would take a large country to toss around that much coin without having it missed by their citizens.

Unless . . . wait a second . . . unless . . .

Holy shit! Unless it was a country without citizens.

A country that had billions of dollars hidden away that no one knew about.

A country that stood to lose everything if this scandal was ever made public.

Good lord, that was it. This was about money. The Vatican's money.

Everything that was happening – the Catacombs, the crucifixions, the search for Dr Boyd – was about cash. Pelati's group wanted it and would do anything to get it.

That had to be it. It had to be.

The beeping of the fax ripped Payne from his thoughts. He had no idea what Frankie was sending, but he prayed it backed his revelation. Otherwise he'd find himself confused again before he even had a chance to tell anyone his theory. Anyway, he grabbed the first page and skimmed it for information. Somehow Frankie had figured out who had died during the chopper crash from Donald Barnes's photographs, where each soldier had been positioned, and had tracked down their personal histories. Everything in his report was typed except for a handwritten note at the bottom of the page that said pictures and graphs were still to come.

Payne had to laugh at that one. He was kidding, right?

Nope, Frankie wasn't joking. He included head-shots (pre- and postmortem) of all four victims, then used a line graph to illustrate where the three soldiers had received their training and how many months they had been stationed together before their fatal mission. In a side note, he mentioned that the pilot was an Orvieto cop who didn't seem to fit with the rest of the crew because he wasn't a member of the Swiss Guard like the others had been.

The Swiss Guard. That was the smoking gun, the one piece of evidence that couldn't be denied. If the Guard were involved, then the Vatican had to be, since the Guard's only job was to protect the pope. Unless, of course, Benito was behind the attack. Maybe he hired ex-members of the Guard to do all of his dirty work?

Payne said to Jones, 'You know that missing piece of the puzzle? I think we just found it.'

He filled him in on everything: the money, the murders, and his theory on Benito. He knew most of it was conjecture, but that was the beauty of their role in this: They didn't give a damn about the law. They weren't cops, nor were they looking for a conviction. They were simply trying to get to the truth, no matter what it was.

Praying that they got the chance to punish the people who brought them into this.

Miraculously, their prayers would be answered less than an hour later.

68

Chang heard the phone and checked his caller ID. He muted the TV coverage of Beijing, then answered. From somewhere over the Atlantic, Nick Dial said, 'Tell me about the fax.'

Chang flipped open his notes. 'I went to the station where the fax came from and talked to their station chief. And, um, I think we were given some bad information.'

Dial leaned his forehead against the plane's wall. 'What do you mean?'

'The fax couldn't have originated from that number because that particular machine can't make outgoing calls. It's wired so it can only receive faxes, not send them. Something about too many cops sending personal faxes.'

Dial smirked, impressed. He realized technology was good enough nowadays for someone to alter the number on a caller ID. Maybe this was another red herring to throw off his search while the killer planned something else. 'Tell me about China.'

Chang filled him in on the latest, including an unconfirmed report that the victim was Paul Adams, a man known around the world as Saint Sydney, due to his missionary work.

'I'll be damned,' Dial mumbled. 'They got the Spirit.'

In his mind this was the news he was hoping for. It proved his theory about the sign of the cross was accurate. Plus it also meant if the killers continued with their current pattern, they were going to be arriving in Italy about the same time he did.

Ulster and Franz were on their way back to Küsendorf, leaving Payne's crew with two options: catch a cab or steal a car. They eventually settled on number two, hoping to avoid Jamie Foxx's situation in the movie *Collateral*, where a taxi driver got mixed up in a very bad scene.

They roamed the streets until they came across a vehicle that met their needs. It was a double-parked Mercedes G500, an SUV that looked like the offspring of a sedan and a Hummer. The keys were in it, so they didn't even have to hotwire the ignition to steal it. Nevertheless, Jones fiddled with the electrical system to prevent their vehicle from being tracked by the European equivalent of OnStar. Once inside, they drove down the alley past Vermählungsbrunnen, a giant fountain depicting the union of Mary and Joseph. The irony of its image made everyone slightly uncomfortable. Here they were trying to dispel the myth of the crucifixion and were forced to do so under the gaze of Christ's earthly parents.

Across from the fountain was Hoher Markt, home of a public gallows until archaeologists realized they were built on top of the original Roman settlement of Vindobona, including the barracks where Roman emperor Marcus Aurelius might've died in 180 AD. Apparently there's a longstanding rift between historians on whether or not he had actually visited. Some claim he came to this area to expand the north-eastern boundary of Rome's territory, while others say he died in Sirmium, found in modern-day Serbia, over 500 miles away. Needless to say, this discrepancy fueled a lot of speculation. And controversy. Boyd theorized the difference between these stories could've been due to the mission he was on at the time of his death. What if Aurelius, who had a reputation for persecuting Christians more than any other emperor, was in Vindobona to find out the truth about the laughing man? It would explain why two different accounts were entered into the Roman history books. The real one and the cover story about expanding the Empire.

But the thing Payne didn't understand was why Marcus Aurelius didn't know about the laughing man to begin with. If the Empire was going to benefit from Tiberius's scheme, wouldn't his secret have to be passed down from emperor to emperor? That was the only way Rome could've profited from Christianity, since Tiberius died within five years of Christ's *death*.

Boyd corrected Payne's assumption, noting that Tiberius went mad during the last few years of his reign. His successor, Caligula, destroyed most of

Tiberius's records, knowing full well if they got into the wrong hands that they would bring shame to Rome. Therefore, in Boyd's mind, there was a very good chance that no emperor after Tiberius would've known about his plot or if Christ's crucifixion had actually been faked.

As they left Vienna on a major highway, their focus shifted to a map of the surrounding area. Boyd said, 'According to Eugene's journal, the Saint of Vindobona lived north of the city near a marble quarry of some repute, a mine that gave birth to the laughing man statues and much of the raw material for the early Roman settlement.'

Boyd handed Payne the book. Inside was an artist's rendering of what this area might have looked like in the first century. But it wasn't much help now. 'So how do we find it?'

'Hermann told us to drive north until we see a white mountain near the edge of the highway. It's a private stretch of land that has been owned by the same family for generations. According to legend, it used to be a functioning mine until they had a massive cave-in several centuries ago. To this day the whole mountain is fenced off for safety reasons.'

Great, Payne thought to himself. People were trying to kill them and they were about to play Indiana Jones on an unstable mountain. 'What's our plan when we get there?'

Smiling, Boyd patted Payne and Jones on the shoulder. 'I was hoping the two of you could come up with something to get us inside. You know, something illegal.'

The sky was bruised, streaks of black and purple cutting across a sea of gray warning them that a major storm was on the way. Payne stuck his hand out the window and felt the humidity, gauging how long they had before the heavens opened. Maybe thirty minutes, if they were lucky.

Their search for the white mountain had been easier than expected. They had driven less than three miles north when they saw its peak thrusting out of the terrain like an iceberg in the middle of a green forest. Jones found a service road off the main highway that led them to the front gate. The property itself was protected by a fifteen-foot-high steel fence capped with barbed wire and a series of signs that read, *Danger: Falling Rocks*, in multiple languages.

Jones worked on the front lock while Payne strolled along the perimeter, hoping to find a flaw, just in case they needed to make a quick getaway. Unfortunately, the place was solid. For a property that was supposedly abandoned, someone had put a lot of money into keeping people out. Even the lock was tricky, taking Jones double the time that he would normally need.

Raindrops started to fall as they got in the SUV and weaved their way back and forth through a thick maze of trees. It came down even harder when they eased into a large clearing at the foot of the mountain. A wooden barricade with more danger signs stopped them at the entrance to the quarry. Payne took a moment to study the terrain before he moved the barrier aside. What looked like a mountain from afar turned out to be the shell of one. Workers had gutted the entire peak, carving several paths that zigzagged at forty-five-degree angles from the base to the apex. Chalky residue spilled over the rock face like white blood. Leaning back, Payne tried to examine the summit, hoping to see what was lurking in the fog and mist one thousand feet above the ground, but the falling rain and setting sun prevented it.

Payne slipped back into the car and started gathering supplies. 'What's our goal here?'

Boyd looked at the mountain and shrugged. Accounts from Prince Eugene's journal were over two centuries old, so there was no telling what was up there. Possibly remnants of a house. Or maybe the laughing man's grave. The sobering part was they were about to risk their lives climbing up a slip-and-slide, and they might find nothing at all.

To aid their cause, Jones rummaged through the trunk and found a heavy-duty flashlight, a tire iron, and some rope he wrapped around his shoulder and waist. 'You never know.'

Payne nodded, realizing the unexpected should always be expected on a bad-weather mission. Even more so with an inexperienced crew. Common sense told him that they should postpone their climb until tomorrow, but he knew it was only a matter of time before someone spotted them. So he said, 'OK, ladies, time's a wastin'. We got us a mountain to conquer.'

Of course if Payne had known that two of them wouldn't be climbing back down, he wouldn't have been so glib.

69

If not for the weather, Payne would've picked up on the ambush a lot sooner. The paths carved into the side of the mountain were covered with a layer of white powder, similar to coarse talc, which had been there since mining had stopped. As they strode up the path, their footsteps appeared briefly like they were walking along a tropical beach before they were whisked away by the tide. One moment they were there, the next they were gone, thanks to the downpour.

Each droplet that fell on the path splashed onto their legs and shoes, making them look like ghosts from the shins down. It also made the footing treacherous, forcing them to tie the rope around their waists in case someone started to slide. But even if that happened, the farthest anyone would've gone was about a hundred feet, because every time the path zigzagged in the opposite direction there was a sturdy stone barrier that acted like a guardrail. On the other hand, if someone slipped sideways off the path, the fall would've been a lot messier.

With that in mind, Payne led the charge up the hill, hoping his body weight would serve as an anchor. He was followed by Boyd, Maria, and Jones, who was the last line of defense. They were about halfway to the crest when Payne saw the first sign of trouble. Lightning flashed in the distance, lighting the sky just enough to reveal movement on the peak above. A thin layer of fog hindered his vision even more than the rain, so he dismissed it as an optical illusion.

'Can we stop at the next turn?' Boyd shouted through the storm.

Paranoid, Payne yelled back, 'Why? What's wrong?'

'Nothing's wrong,' he said through labored breathing. 'I want to look around.'

Payne got the sense that Boyd needed a break more than anything else and decided it was a good idea to stop, even though they were only two zigzags from the top. Accidents tended to happen when people got tired. And Payne was tired, too. He tested the sturdiness of the rock guardrail before leaning his back against it. Meanwhile Boyd and Maria turned away from Payne, leaning their chests and arms over the precipice while looking for ruins in the landscape below. Jones waited until they were absorbed in their search before he spoke to Payne.

'I'm not liking this,' he whispered. 'These grounds are well-maintained, and this powder seems fresh. Someone's been digging up here recently. The question is, for what?'

'Only one way to find out.' Payne tugged on the rope to get Boyd's attention. 'Time to go.'

The last few paths were the toughest to climb, not

only because their legs were tired but because tiny rivulets were flowing on the path. All of them lost their balance at least once, covering them with white mud. It got so bad that Payne had to drop to all fours in order to make it up the last gradient. He used his hands and fingers like claws, burning every ounce of energy he had. When he reached the top, he flipped over, braced his feet against a large rock, and pulled on the rope like he was in a giant tug-of-war. Hand over hand, biceps burning, using his legs, back, and butt to finish the job. Boyd got there a minute later, followed by Maria, and finally Jones, who no longer looked black because of the mud.

Payne wanted to tease him, but that required energy, and he had none to spare. So he just lay there in the mud, eyes closed, mouth wide open, trying to drink enough rain to soothe the burning in his throat. Seconds later that pain drifted to his chest and the pit of his stomach because when he opened his eyes, he was staring down the barrel of several guns. They were being held by soldiers in winter camouflage, which blended in perfectly with the chalky terrain.

'Ah, shit,' Payne cursed while gasping for air. 'Hey D.J., you should take a look at this.'

'At what?' he bitched. Slowly he lifted himself into a half pushup, using his knees for support. When he locked his elbows, he saw all the soldiers that surrounded them and decided it wasn't worth getting up for. 'Tell them to leave,' he groaned. 'I'm resting.'

'Who?' Maria demanded, her vision blurred by the mud in her eyes.

'Us,' answered the only man standing without a gun. He'd been hiding behind the soldiers and used this opportunity to show himself. 'He's talking about *us*.'

Maria flinched, practically jumping to her feet at the sound of his voice. Payne thought it was because she was startled. Moments later he realized there was something else going on, something more significant. 'What are you doing here?' she demanded.

'Father sent me to fetch you.' The man was wearing a clear plastic poncho over his suit and black mountain boots that went up to his calves. 'You've been a baaaaaad girl.'

Shocked, Boyd looked up and tried to see who was there. 'Dante? Is that you?'

Things started to make sense to Payne, albeit a little late for his taste. They were staring at Dante Pelati, son of Benito and Maria's half brother. She'd mentioned Dante in passing when they confronted her about her other brother, Roberto. Later, Boyd gave them further information about Dante, telling them that he was the one who'd given them their digging permit for Orvieto.

'Charles,' Dante answered, 'I've wanted to talk to you all week. How have you been?'

Payne had no idea why he was being so friendly, whether he was thankful that they had delivered Maria and Boyd to him in one piece or whether it was just a facade. Payne wanted to find out, so he said, 'I don't think we've been properly introduced. My name's Jonathon Payne.'

Payne reached up to shake Dante's hand. But Dante looked down on him with disdain.

'You'll have to excuse me, but shaking your hand would not be in my best interest.'

'Is it because of the mud?' Payne wiped his hand on his ass, even though it didn't make any difference. 'Is that better?'

'It's not the mud, Mr Payne. It's the fact that I know who you are. I'm guessing if I were to grab your hand, you'd pull me to the ground and have me as your hostage before my men could even shoot. Not an appealing proposition.'

'It is for me.'

Dante ignored the comment and spoke to his soldiers in Italian, practically grunting his commands. Next thing Payne knew, they were dragging everyone to their feet and marching them in a single-file line to a large clearing at the center of the plateau where the soldiers had recently been digging. The giant pit was surrounded by a series of floodlights, none of which were on at the moment, and covered by a massive tent that kept the site dry.

As they walked toward it, Payne considered overpowering one of the guards and stealing his gun but decided against it since the rope was tied around all their waists. Any quick movement on his part would've resulted in a knot that even a boy scout couldn't untangle. Besides, Payne had a feeling that there'd be a better opportunity to strike in a little while.

The soldiers lowered the tinted visors on their helmets as they entered the tent. Once inside they forced everyone to their knees, then turned on the floodlights. It had been pitch-black outside except for the occasional flash of lightning, so the sudden glare was too much for them to take. Payne shielded his eyes for several seconds, blinking and squirming until he could see shadows, then shapes, and finally enough details to function. Still, due to his vantage point near the ground, he wasn't able to see what was in the pit, although he could tell it was several feet deep.

Dante said, 'I must admit I'm surprised you made it this far. My family has taken great pride in protecting our land and the secret it possesses. In fact, *I* wasn't even aware of this site until recently. And that probably wouldn't have happened without Mr Payne's assistance.'

Jones gave him a look that said, *What is he talking about?* But Payne shrugged, unsure.

Thankfully, Dante explained. 'If you hadn't killed Roberto, my father never would've told me anything. That's how it works, you know. The eldest son keeps the secret alive.'

Secret? What secret? They had stumbled onto this place through a combination of good luck and timing. Nothing more. Yet Dante assumed that they had figured everything out. And Payne wasn't going to shatter that illusion, not with so many questions running through his mind.

So he said, 'Man, your brother loved to talk, especially when I was torturing him. He was like, *my father this, Orvieto that.* Just one secret after another . . . Isn't that right, Maria?'

As if on cue, she said, 'He couldn't shut up. It was embarrassing.'

Dante studied her face to see if she was lying. 'You mean, you watched Roberto get tortured and didn't stop it? How could you? He was your brother.'

'My brother? He *stopped* being my brother the moment he tried to kill me . . . Just like you'll no longer be my brother after *this.*'

The comment hurt Dante, Payne could see it in his eyes. A mixture of shock, heartbreak, and betrayal. Payne wanted to tell her to take it back, that she had said the wrong thing, but it was too late. Any chance of playing the family card had just been eliminated.

'Cut her loose and put her on the chopper.' Dante practically spat the words as he said them. 'Same thing with the professor. I need to debrief them before we visit my father.'

One guard cut the rope in two places, while the other guards kept an eye on Payne. The severed end fell against Payne's leg when the guard yanked Boyd to his feet. The same thing happened to Jones when they got Maria. An engine roared to life outside the tent, and Payne watched as Boyd and Maria were marched through the storm toward the waiting helicopter.

Meanwhile, Dante stood still, staring into the pit, contemplating what he should do next. 'Wait until the weather clears then load this onto the next chopper. We can't get this wet.'

Curious, Payne inched forward and tried to see what was down there until one of the guards raised his rifle and aimed it at his head. Payne said, 'Sorry. Had a cramp.'

Dante smiled, knowing full well Payne was lying. 'It's remarkable that this is still intact after all of these years, considering all the digging that has gone on around it. In that regard I guess it is very similar to the Catacombs. Some might say divine intervention protected it, yet I know the truth. It is my family that guarded it, that did everything they could to protect this secret, including turning their backs on me and Maria . . . But all of that is about to end. It's time to tell everyone the truth about Christ, whether they're ready for it or not.'

Payne hoped that meant he was about to show them what was in the pit. Instead, he grabbed a black tarp and covered the hole like a father tucking in a newborn.

'Keep it dry and safe,' he told the guards. Then almost as an afterthought, he motioned toward Payne and Jones. 'And you know what to do with them.'

His men nodded as Dante left the tent and

climbed onto the chopper. Seconds later, the noise increased 300 percent as the pilot revved the turbines and prepared for a difficult takeoff. Payne knew the rain coupled with the lightning and the wind was going to make things a bitch, not only for the chopper but for the soldiers on the ground, too. The air would start whipping, and the water was going to start stinging, and before long every man on the mountain was going to be shielding their heads and eyes from the ruckus.

How did Payne know this? Because he'd seen it several times before. Even if you're wearing a helmet, visor, and earplugs, it's natural to protect your face in harsh conditions. That's just human nature. And human nature was something that could be taken advantage of.

'Jon!' Jones shouted, although it sounded like a whisper next to the engine. 'On three?'

Payne hid his hand on his hip, keeping it there until the wind and noise were at their worst. Then, when the moment was right, he counted down on his fingers so only Jones could see.

Three . . . two . . . one . . . go!

In unison they leapt to their feet and ran toward the exit. Jones was a half step quicker and beat Payne to the tent's edge by less than a yard. Still, Payne lost track of him the moment they stepped outside. His eyes had grown accustomed to the bright lights, and now that they were back in darkness, he couldn't see a thing. Combine that with the wind and rain and

534

roar of the chopper, and Payne felt like Dorothy in the tornado from *The Wizard of Oz.*

A flash of lightning proved he was headed in the right direction and Jones was still in front of him. It gave the guards the same advantage, too, so Payne immediately cut several feet to the left in case they opened fire. The chopper was now overhead, preventing him from hearing gunshots or Jones or anything else. Darkness stole his ability to see, while the rain and mud threw off his other senses. All he could rely on were his instincts, and they told him to keep running straight.

A blinding beam of light appeared in the sky and unlike before, it wasn't a flicker. This time it was the chopper's spotlight, and it gave Payne a view of the upcoming terrain. A boulder to the left, a crevice to the right, Jones directly in front. For an instant he feared that they were going to track them with the light like urban cops in L.A., but they ignored them, using the beam to get around the surrounding peaks and to slip through the storm unharmed.

As the roar faded, Payne heard footsteps behind him. And shouts. Lots of shouts. Men seemed to be appearing out of nowhere; their camouflage outfits kept them hidden until they were on top of Payne. He dodged one and then another, knocking down a third with a vicious forearm to the face. He was expecting to get shot at any moment, waiting to feel the sudden burn of a bullet tearing through his flesh, but the darkness saved him. No way they could risk shooting a target that they couldn't see, not with this many soldiers running around.

'This way,' yelled Jones from ten feet ahead. Then like magic he disappeared. First his legs, then his chest, and finally his head. One second they were there, the next they were gone, hidden by the edge of the plateau as he hit the ramp running.

Payne wanted to follow his lead but was cut off by a guard with a rifle. He pointed it at Payne and shouted something in a foreign language that Payne couldn't understand. That left Payne with two choices: he could stop for a quick explanation, *or* he could lower his shoulder and run over him. Option two seemed wiser, so he planted his head in the guard's chest and knocked him off the hill. Somehow the guy wrapped his arms around Payne and held on as they hit the ramp hard.

A crack of lightning allowed Payne to stare into his face while he surfed down the hill on the guy's ·back. The guard was young and scared – Payne could tell that from one look – but it didn't bother him. He was the enemy, and Payne needed to get rid of him as soon as possible.

He got his chance as they approached the first turn in the ramp, a turn the guard couldn't see. Payne knew it was coming well in advance and launched himself backward just before they hit the stone wall. With a sickening crack, the guard smashed into it headfirst, cushioning Payne's blow like a shock absorber. Five seconds later Payne had his helmet and rifle and was sliding down the next slope, trying to catch up to Jones before anyone caught him from behind.

The scenery whizzed by at a dizzying pace. Payne's eyes had adjusted to the lack of light, but the rain and wind and splashing mud left him flying blind. He quickly adjusted to the length of the ramps and before long he was anticipating the turns so well that he was practically running across them parallel to the ground. He felt like a swimmer in a dark pool who performed flip turns at the perfect moment even though he couldn't see the walls. This continued the whole way to the bottom, where he found Jones waiting for him in the Mercedes, the engine running.

'Need a lift?' he asked as he pushed the passenger door open. 'Please keep your feet on the mats. I don't want to get the interior dirty.'

Payne climbed in, oozing mud and blood yet feeling remarkably refreshed. Escaping death will do that to you. 'Where to now?'

'Italy,' Jones said, tramping on the gas. 'We've got a chopper to catch.'

70

Saturday, July 15
Leonardo da Vinci Airport
(nineteen miles southwest of Rome, Italy)

Nick Dial was greeted by the head of airport security, who walked him through customs and gave him a ride in an oversized golf cart. They screeched to a halt in front of the security office, where Dial was given a quick tour. The first room was equipped with dozens of screens, all of them showing different views of the airport, everything from baggage claim to the parking lots.

Marco Rambaldi, the security chief, placed his ID in front of an electronic eye and waited for the next door to unlock. He was a handsome man with jet-black hair that didn't quite match his gray eyebrows. Dial guessed him to be in his mid-fifties, probably a former cop with a background in terrorism. Someone brought in to prevent a 9/11 from happening in Italy.

'We don't talk about this room much,' Rambaldi said as the door buzzed open. 'The less criminals who know about it, the better.'

Dial walked in and saw a computer network that was very similar to security systems he had seen in

Las Vegas – a combination of live video feeds, data uplinks, and the latest in ID technology. The instant someone walked into the airport, their picture was taken, broken down into digital data, then compared to terrorist databases from around the world. If they got a hit, the suspect was tracked until the proper authorities were notified.

Rambaldi took a seat at one of the computers. 'We can focus our attention on departures, arrivals, or anywhere you'd like. Your associate, Agent Chang, told my people that the cross murderers will be arriving in Rome today. Is this so?'

'We're under that assumption.'

'Yet you're unaware of their names, what they look like, or when they'll be visiting?'

Dial grimaced. He knew his case sounded flimsy in those terms. 'You're going to have to trust me on this one. I'm not the type of cop who overreacts to –'

Rambaldi signaled him to stop. 'Who am I to argue with your methods? You're a division leader at Interpol. You must be doing something right . . . Tell me, what do you need me to do?'

Dial squeezed his shoulder, appreciative of the respect he'd given him. 'We're looking for mercenaries, soldiers for hire. Anyone with a high-end military background.'

'Why?' Rambaldi asked as he changed some configurations. Instead of focusing on terrorists, one system was now going to search for mercs. 'What's the connection?'

'The murders were done with precision in foreign locales. We suspect killers with military expertise, people who know their way across borders, people with local connections.' Dial waited until Rambaldi stopped typing. 'And since all the victims were young and strong, I'd bet we're looking for men, probably between the ages of twenty-five and forty.'

'Great. That helps a lot. The more specific you can be, the easier it is to search. If you think of anything else, just let me know. We can update the search at any time.'

Dial nodded. 'Tell me, do they have a similar system across town?' Roma Ciampino was a major airport on the other side of Rome.

'Yes, very similar. We can send them these search parameters if you'd like.'

'Sounds good. I'll let my agents at Ciampino know.'

'And what about smaller airfields? We have several scattered across the region.'

'We're sending men to as many locations as possible, but my guess is these guys will show at a major airport. With all these planes and people, it'll be easier for them to blend in.'

Payne and Jones had no choice. They had to fly to Italy. That was the only way they could catch up to Boyd and Maria. They calculated how long it would take to get to Rome and figured they could beat them there – since jets fly much faster than helicopters – if they found a direct flight that was leaving immediately. But that was just one of their problems. They were covered in mud, driving a stolen car, unwilling to use a credit card, and had no idea where they were going.

Other than that, things would be a snap.

Anyway, Jones knew they needed some assistance, so he called Randy Raskin to see what he could do for them. If anything.

'D.J.,' Raskin said, 'what a pleasant surprise!' Jones could detect his sarcasm from halfway around the world. 'You realize I'm at work, don't you? And that I *don't* work for you?'

Time was precious, so Jones got right to the point. He explained their situation – everything except the religious aspects – and asked for help. Raskin must've heard the desperation in Jones's voice because he stopped giving him a hard time and started pounding away on his keyboard.

A few minutes later, Raskin said, 'There's a Marine cargo plane leaving Vienna within the hour. I'm talking military transport. No frills, few seats, fewer questions. They're headed for Madrid, but I'm sure I could persuade 'em to stop in Rome if you're interested.'

'Very,' Jones assured him.

'Not a problem ... And I'd imagine you'd like some clean clothes waiting for you. Are you two the same size you were with the MANIACs? I can access your files and get a perfect fit. You'll look like you just came from the friggin' tailor.'

The hangar was in an isolated part of the airfield far from the public terminal. Raskin called the pilot and told him what Payne and Jones needed, probably making it sound a lot more official than it actually was. When they arrived, he had everything waiting for them, including clean boxers. The plane was still being loaded, so they had time for a hot shower and a quick meal. The weather had delayed everything – takeoffs, departures, cargo, etc. – and they were thankful for that. Planes could get above the clouds, so they handled storms much better than helicopters, meaning inclement weather was to their advantage.

As far as Payne and Jones were concerned, let it rain, let it rain, let it rain.

The flight itself was eighty minutes, which gave them more than enough time to figure out where they were headed. Jones called one of the detectives on his payroll and had her track down some information on Benito Pelati. She found an office address in the middle of Rome, two nearby apartments where he probably *kept* girlfriends (a common practice for wealthy men in Italy), and a palatial estate on Lake Albano. Dante made it clear that they were going to talk to his father, and Jones assumed that he'd want their conversation to be as private as possible. That ruled out all the city addresses and led him to believe that they were headed to the lake. If Jones was wrong, he figured they could always torture – er, *question* – Benito's staff and find out where he was hiding.

Anyway, once their plane was airborne, the pilot called in a fake mechanical problem and asked the Roman Air Authority for clearance on one of their auxiliary runways. Not only did that bump them up in the landing order, but it also allowed the pilot to taxi their plane to one of the service areas where Jones and Payne could slip into the country undetected.

Thankfully, his plan worked without a hitch. Or so they had hoped.

They were in the middle of bribing one of the ground crew to take them to Lake Albano when they heard a beeping noise behind them. A security cart drove out of the sun and into the shadows of the hangar. They did their best to look busy as the security guard listened to instructions on his headset. He mumbled a word or two, then listened some more. Finally, he pulled his cart over to Payne and Jones.

'Please come with me,' he said with a thick Italian accent.

'Why?' Payne asked, feigning ignorance. 'We just got here.'

Nodding, the guard pointed to a small camera in the corner of the hangar. 'We know.'

Within minutes Payne and Jones were herded into an airport security room where they were forced to sit at a metal table that was bolted to the floor. They'd been in enough interrogations to know where this was going. Lots of questions, lots of scare tactics, horrible coffee.

Jones glanced around the room and grimaced. 'Feels familiar.'

Payne nodded. 'If Manzak and Buckner walk through that door, I'm gonna shit.'

Well, those two didn't show up, but Payne almost shit himself anyway because he wasn't expecting to see the face that came into the room. Or the massive chin. Because that's the thing Payne always noticed when he talked to Nick Dial. That huge speed bump of a chin.

Dial walked into the room, unsmiling, and whispered something to the guard who'd been watching Payne and Jones. Dial gave the guard a moment to leave, refusing to say a single word until they were alone. The instant the door clicked shut, Dial shook Payne's hand. 'How long's it been? Five, six years?'

'Maybe more.'

'Well, you look like hell ... And so does your sister.'

Jones laughed at the jab. 'Look who's talking, gramps.'

The three of them went way back, back to the days when Payne and Jones were in the MANIACs and Dial was still paying dues at Interpol. American bars are scattered all across Europe, places for homesick tourists or overseas businessmen to get a brief taste of home. Soldiers frequented these joints more than most, hoping to stave off the loneliness that most of them never quite get used to.

One night Payne and Jones were shooting pool at a place called Stars & Stripes when they overheard a heated debate about football. One of the guys, Dial, mentioned his dad used to coach at Pitt, and that's all Payne needed to hear. Before long they were drinking beer, swapping stories, and having a grand old time. The three of them kept in touch over the years, occasionally having dinner when they were in the same town. Unfortunately, due to the secretive nature of the MANIACs, they never got together as much as they would've liked.

Anyway, the fact that they bumped into each other like this was kind of surreal. For each of them. Dial had no idea why Payne and Jones were sneaking into Italy. And they had no idea why Dial stopped them.

When they finished exchanging pleasantries, Dial got serious. 'Guys, we have a slight problem here. Right now we're flagging everyone at this airport who has any hardcore military experience, and, well, we have film of you two entering this country illegally.'

'There's a good reason for that,' Payne assured him. 'I know this is going to sound crazy, but two of our friends were just taken at gunpoint in Vienna, and we flew here to get them back.'

'You're right. Sounds crazy. Why didn't you just call the cops?'

'Couldn't. Not with these two. Too many questions.'

'How so?'

'You're already looking for them.'

'Is that so?' Dial leaned forward, slightly pissed. 'What are their names?'

'Nick, I can't. We can't.'

'Jon, if you want them to live, tell me their names. Otherwise, they're going to die while we're in this room playing Q & A.'

Dial had a point, so Payne and Jones debriefed him for the next several minutes, skipping as much about Christ and the Catacombs as they could but giving Dial all the background information he needed. Payne showed him the notes they had taken on Pelati's addresses and explained why he thought they were headed to Lake Albano and not to the city.

'So let me get this straight, the Pelatis are responsible for *everything* – the murders, the violence, the kidnappings – and Dr Boyd is nothing more than a pawn?'

'Yeah,' Payne said. 'Something like that.'

Dial leaned back in his chair and smiled, a reaction that would've been much different if not for their history together. As it was, Payne could see Dial was still having a hard time with what he had told him. 'OK, guys, here's my dilemma. I can't just call the local PD and say one of the most powerful men in Italy is guilty of something this serious. Especially without proof.'

Jones argued, 'But you *do* have proof. You have *us* as witnesses.'

'Witnesses to what? You didn't see Benito do anything. Furthermore, since you snuck into this country illegally, you guys aren't even officially here. You're persona non grata.'

'Fine,' Payne said, disappointed. 'But please do something. At the very least, can you send some Interpol agents out to the lake? I'm telling you, Maria and Boyd are in danger.'

'Jon, I just can't. Right now we're spread so thin it's embarrassing.'

The sound of Dial's phone broke his concentration. He glanced at the number, annoyed, until he realized who was calling. Jumping to his feet, he told Payne and Jones he had to take this call. 'Dial here.'

'Nick, this is Cardinal Rose. I'm sorry to call you so late, but you told me to keep you posted on any rumors at the Vatican. And, well, this is a doozy.'

Over the next few minutes, Rose filled him in on Benito Pelati's actions at the latest Supreme Council meeting – at least everything the American appointee had blabbed to Rose over a series of drinks. Very stiff drinks. Rose laughed and added, 'I would've gotten more, but I ran out of bourbon.'

Dial thanked the cardinal for the information, then returned to the table with a much different vibe. A minute ago he was grumbling about a lack of evidence and how he couldn't risk moving any of his agents. Now he had a smile on his face and a gleam in his eye.

'So,' he asked, 'have you guys ever been to Lake Albano?'

71

Villa Pelati,
Lago di Albano, Italy
(eleven miles southeast of Rome)

The helicopter roared across the calm waters of Lake Albano and settled in a stone courtyard a hundred yards from the main house. Built in the 1500s, the estate sat on the rim of a prehistoric volcanic crater and offered spectacular views of the lake, forest, and wine country.

Childhood memories came flooding back as Maria stared out the chopper's window at the place she once called home. Thoughts of her mother and the silly games they used to play filled her with equal parts of nostalgia and nausea.

'How long has it been?' Dante asked while opening the hatch. 'Ten years?'

She ignored him, not in the mood to talk to the person forcing her to walk down memory lane. In her mind he had ruined her life once before and was threatening to do it again.

The ironic thing was that Maria and Dante had been the closest siblings in the Pelati family. Even though they had different mothers and were born twelve years apart, they carried the burden of *not* being Benito's firstborn son and were forced to bear all the disappointment that went along with it. Whereas Roberto was treated like royalty, Maria and Dante were treated like second-class citizens, receiving none of the love or attention that their older brother was given. In time Benito softened his stance toward Dante, realizing that his second-born son was a capable child, and allowed him to enter the family business right before Maria was sent away to school. Not surprisingly, she linked the two together and shifted a lot of the anger toward her father and focused it on Dante.

In her mind Dante had turned his back on her in order to win their father's affection.

It was a sin that she still hadn't forgotten. Or forgiven.

Maria climbed from the chopper and waited for Boyd to do the same. The two remained quiet during their trip from Vienna, much to Dante's chagrin. He tried to interrogate them during the first ten minutes of their flight, but when they chose not to talk, he decided not to push it. He knew his options were limited, and he could be much more persuasive on the ground.

Lights in the trees twinkled as they walked through an elaborate garden and onto the stone walkway. Marble columns surrounded the shimmering water of the pool to the left while a series of statues lined the path to the right. A wide set of stairs led them to the open patio and the back entrance to the house.

Dante punched in the security code. 'Father is at the Vatican until morning. There are things to discuss before his arrival.'

Maria almost gagged at the term *father*. She had grown up without one and was in no mood to have him reappear in her life. Not now. Not if she was about to be killed for her actions. That would be a cruel way to die, forcing her to see him one last time before she was murdered.

'Do you remember his den?' Dante asked. The foyer was over twenty feet high, so his voice echoed as he spoke. 'I used to read stories to you in there by the fireplace. Your mother used to get *so* mad at me. I always saved the scariest ones for right before bedtime. I'd frighten you so much that she'd have to stay in your bed for half the night.'

Maria smiled at the memory, although she didn't want to. That was a different time, a different life, back when she was happy and things were so much simpler.

The den was just as she remembered it. An antique desk sat on the left and faced the fireplace to the right. A leather couch, two chairs, and a glass table filled the space in between. Bookshelves and paintings lined the walls, as did an assortment of relics that were displayed on marble pedestals. A colorful rug covered the floor and made the room feel warm and cozy. Maria considered that ironic, since she knew who the room belonged to.

'Have a seat,' Dante said, motioning to the couch. Then he turned his attention to the guards. 'Gentlemen, I can handle things from here. Please wait in the hall.'

They closed the door, leaving Dante alone with Maria and Boyd for the first time all night.

'I know the two of you have a lot of questions.' Dante took off his suit jacket and folded it over one of the chairs. Suddenly his holster and gun were in plain view. The sight doubled the tension in the room. 'It's been a hectic week for all of us.'

Maria rolled her eyes. She couldn't imagine how Dante could lump the three of them together. They were adversaries, not allies.

'First of all,' Dante said to Boyd, 'let me apologize for our recent lack of communication. Once you left Orvieto, I had no way of reaching you.'

Boyd's face filled with relief. 'I wanted to call, but the attack frazzled me. I had no way of knowing who was behind it. Whether it was you or someone else.'

'Once again, I apologize. I didn't know about their plans until Monday night, *after* you had left the Catacombs. If I had known what they were planning to do, I would've warned you.'

Maria sat there, stunned. Her brother was speaking to Boyd like they were partners. The conversation was so unexpected that it took a moment for things to register. 'Oh my God, what's happening here? *Professore?* You two are talking like friends.'

'Why shouldn't we be? He gave us our permits to dig.'

'Yeah,' she argued, searching for the right words, 'but he's going to kill us.'

'Kill you?' Dante scoffed. 'Why on earth would I do that? I just saved you.'

'Saved us?' she screamed. 'You just dragged us off at gunpoint. That's not saving us!'

'It *is* when you consider how many people want you dead.'

'Yes, but . . .'

Boyd patted her shoulder, urging her to calm down. 'In Maria's defense, I must admit I was uncertain of your intentions until a moment ago. Your poker face is bloody brilliant.'

Dante laughed. 'Let me apologize for that as well. You must remember that the guards work for my father, not me. If we're to succeed, I must continue this charade for as long as possible.'

'What are you talking about? What charade?' she demanded.

'The charade that I'm helping *Father*.' There was a bitterness to his tone that wasn't present before. He practically spat the word. 'You of all people should know that.'

'But . . .' she stuttered, searching for words.

Boyd held up his hand, signaling her to stop. 'You can talk about your mutual hate of him later. For now there are more important matters to discuss.'

Dante locked eyes with Maria. He wanted to say

so much but realized it wasn't the time or place. 'He's right, you know. Our itinerary is rather full. I have a family secret to tell you about.'

The chauffeur pulled the town car to the main gate of the villa. Benito sat in the backseat, mulling over everything that had happened. The violence at Orvieto, the events at the Vatican, the death of his son. Yet somehow, despite it all, he had a good feeling that luck was right around the corner, that all of his hard work was about to be rewarded.

Of course, he never imagined he'd be rewarded like this.

Boyd and Maria watched Dante as he walked over to the desk. Then, as if the secret he was carrying was too much to bear, he sighed and took a seat in his father's chair.

Dante said, 'I've known something was going on for years. I'd walk into a room and father would stop talking to Roberto right away. At first I thought they were talking about me. After a while I knew something bigger was going on.'

He picked up a trinket from the desk and stared at it, refusing to make eye contact with his guests. 'I started looking through their files, double-checking everything they asked me to do, until I found a pattern that centered around Orvieto. Extra guards, extra funds, extra everything. Something was happening there that they weren't telling me.'

Frustrated, he threw the trinket aside. 'At one point I became so curious I went to Father and asked him about it, begging him to tell me the truth about the Catacombs and all the money we were spending. But he just scoffed and told me to leave him alone. Can you believe that? He *ignored* me. Immediately I knew he would never tell me anything.'

He paused for a split second, then glanced at Boyd. 'That's when I decided to get a partner.'

'What do you mean by *partner*?' Maria demanded.

'I know this will upset you, but I've been checking up on you for years. Your schooling, your living arrangements, your lack of a social life. You're my sister, after all. There was no way I was going to forget you, even if you wanted me to.'

Maria didn't say a word. She just sat there, confused. Trying to absorb everything.

'That's how I learned about Dr Boyd,' he admitted. 'I was checking up on you and discovered his passion for the Catacombs. At first it seemed like a miracle had brought you two together. Then I realized it wasn't a fluke. You went to Dover for a reason. You went there to learn about Orvieto. You became his student because you were just as curious as I was.'

Tears fell from Maria's eyes. She tried to brush them away before anyone noticed, but Dante saw them and smiled. He knew it meant he was on the right track, that he still knew his sister after all these years.

'A year ago I was sorting through requests for digging permits when I came across Dr Boyd's. I figured this was a perfect excuse to speak, so I called him about the Catacombs.'

Maria glared at Boyd. 'You talked to Dante a year ago and didn't tell me?'

Boyd defended himself. 'I swear to you, I didn't know he was your brother. He said his name was Dante and he was your father's assistant. That's all he said to me. Ever.'

'He's telling the truth,' Dante assured her. 'I didn't want you to know because I knew you'd run in the other direction. I know how stubborn you can be. I've known that for years.'

The anger in Maria's face softened. Slowly she turned back toward Dante.

'For several months I've been exchanging information with Dr Boyd. He'd inform me about things that he'd discovered, and I'd do the same for him, all in hopes of planning a successful dig. I knew I couldn't join him in Orvieto – there was no way I could hide that – but I figured one of us could be there. That *you* could be there. And in my mind, that was good enough.'

Her tears started again. 'That's what you've been hiding? *That's* the family secret?'

Dante laughed at her innocence. 'No, that's not it at all. Father's been keeping something from both of us for our entire lives, something we should've been told long ago. I swear to you I didn't know about it until yesterday. When father learned about Roberto's death, he pulled me aside and told me everything. He told me the truth about the Catacombs, the crucifixion, and our family tree. You see, the Catacombs of Orvieto were built for us. For our family. They were built to honor *our* relative.'

'What are you talking about? Who was our relative?'

Instead of speaking, Dante pointed over his shoulder to the painting his father had commissioned shortly after visiting the Catacombs for the first time. The image was similar, albeit smaller than the one that Boyd and Maria had found in the first chamber of the Catacombs. The one Maria *knew* she had seen before but could never place in her head. Suddenly, she understood the reason why. Her subconscious had been blocking it out.

'The laughing man,' she gasped. 'I'm *related* to the laughing man?'

Dante frowned. 'Who's the laughing man?'

'Him,' she said. 'That's what we've called him, because we never knew his name. His image was everywhere in the Catacombs. On the walls, in the carvings, on a burial box. We've been searching for his identity ever since.'

'Then your search is over, because you already know his name.'

'I do?'

He nodded knowingly. 'Because it's your name, too.'

'*My* name? What do you mean? He was a Pelati?'

'No,' Dante said. 'His name was changed to protect us from his sins . . . He was a *Pilate*.'

'A Pilate?'

He nodded. 'As in Pontius Pilate. He was our ancestor. We are his descendants.'

'We're his *what*?' She stared at Dante. Then at Boyd. Then back at Dante. 'What are you talking about?'

'I mean, our family name isn't Pelati . . . It's *Pilate*. The name was altered to protect our family from persecution.'

'Pontius Pilate was the laughing man?'

Dante nodded. 'And our forefather.'

It took a moment for that to sink in. Once it did, Maria let out a soft whimper that suggested she had been blindsided. She wanted to argue, wanted to fight, but in her heart she knew her brother would never lie about something like this. That meant everything he'd said was true.

They were related to the most infamous murderer of all time.

Slowly, in an act of desperation, she turned toward Dr Boyd, who was now standing by her side. '*Professore?* Is this possible? Is any of this possible?'

Boyd closed his eyes and pondered the history. 'Yes, my dear, it just might be.'

'But . . . how?'

He took a deep breath, trying to find the words. 'As remarkable as this sounds, very little is known about Pontius Pilate. Most scholars agree that he became procurator of Judea in 26 AD and ended his term ten years later. Yet nothing is known about his birth or death, though theories abound on both.'

Some historians believe that Pilate was executed by the Roman Senate shortly after Tiberius's death in 37 AD. Others claim that Pilate committed suicide, drowning his sorrows in a lake near Lucerne, Switzerland – a lake that is located on Mount Pilatus. Meanwhile, German folklore insists that Pilate lived a long and happy life in Vienna Allobrogum (Vienne on the Rhone) where a fifty-two-foot monument, called Pontius Pilate's tomb, still stands today.

'Despite these uncertainties,' Boyd stressed, 'there are several facts about Pilate we are certain of. The most interesting involves his wife, Claudia Procula. Few people realize this, but Pilate's wife was the granddaughter of Augustus *and* the adopted daughter of Emperor Tiberius.'

'What?!' Maria blinked a few times. 'Tiberius was Pilate's father-in-law?'

Boyd nodded. 'I bet you never heard *that* in Sunday school, now did you?'

'No,' she gasped. Suddenly the thought of Pilate and Tiberius working together seemed like a probability. These men were more than just political allies. They were relatives.

Boyd continued. 'Did you know the Coptic Church of Egypt and the Abyssinian Church of Ethiopia have always claimed that Pontius and

Claudia converted to Christianity after the crucifixion? In fact, they honor them every June 25th as *saints*!'

Dante interrupted him. 'Dr Boyd, I think you're missing the big picture here. None of that is important. We should be concentrating on the crucifixion and nothing else.'

'Which is my point exactly!' he said with a dismissive wave. 'For years now I thought that *they* were nuts, honoring Pontius Pilate as a hero. Calling him a Christian. Now I know that they were right. Good heavens! He actually *started* the religion. I feel like such a fool.'

'You feel like a fool?' she blurted. 'How do you think I feel? I just found out that we've been running around Europe looking for my relative. That a painting of the laughing man was hanging on my father's wall!' She took a deep breath, trying to calm herself. 'How could we have forgotten Pilate? He's such an obvious candidate. We should've considered him.'

Boyd comforted her. 'Come, come, my dear. You're not alone in this. All of us ignored Pilate as a suspect. Cheer up! It's not the end of the world.'

'Yes, it is,' said a new voice from the doorway. Stunned, they whirled around and saw Benito Pelati and four armed guards enter the room. 'For Dante.'

Benito punctuated his statement by firing two quick rounds. Spray erupted from Dante's chest, staining the painting of Pilate and the entire wall behind him. Then, as if in slow motion, his lifeless body slid out of the leather chair and onto the floor below. The sight of this filled Maria with such a murderous rage she sprang forward and tried to knock the gun out of her father's hands. But a guard intervened, blocking her path with his body.

Undeterred, she tried to go through him, clawing at his face with a flurry of slaps and punches. The guard briefly took the punishment before ending Maria's antics with a head-butt to the bridge of her nose. Then he finished her off with a right hook to the chin, a blow that sent her crashing through the glass coffee table behind her.

Impressed with her fighting spirit, Benito stared at Maria. 'Who would have guessed it? Of all my children, the one with the biggest balls happened to be the *girl*.'

72

Maria regained consciousness, tied to a chair. Blood trickled from her nose and mouth. Gashes covered her. Shards of glass stuck out of her flesh like porcupine quills. The room was spinning.

She blinked a few times and tried to focus on the blurred figure in front of her. Fog blanketed everything. Her vision. Her memory. Her hearing. The muffled sound of her name filled her head like an echo. Someone was speaking to her. She blinked again, trying to figure out who it was.

'Maria?' her father repeated. 'Can you hear me?'

'What?' she slurred. 'Where am I?'

'You're home, Maria. After all these years, you're finally home . . . I think that calls for a celebration.' One of the guards handed a bottle of vodka to Benito, who preceded to dump it over Maria's head. The fiery liquid seeped into her wounds, causing a thunderbolt of pain to surge through her body. He laughed at her screams of agony. 'Makes you feel alive, doesn't it?'

Suddenly the details of her situation hit her like an avalanche. She knew where she was and what was happening. Worst of all, she knew who was taunting her. In an instant her longtime nightmares had become a reality. She was sitting in front of her father.

Benito said, 'I knew I'd see you again someday. Though I never imagined it'd be like this.'

'Me, either,' she spat. 'I was hoping it was at your deathbed.'

He shook his head. 'Instead, it's taking place at yours.'

Maria glanced around the room, searching for hope. A weapon. An escape route. Anything helpful. That's when she noticed Dr Boyd tied up next to her. His chin was slumped against his chest. His shirt was drenched in blood. His eyes and cheeks were swollen from repeated blows to his face. 'Oh my God! What did you do to him?'

'*I* didn't do anything. My men did quite a bit, though. They got angry when my questions went unanswered.' He studied the horror in her dark brown eyes. He had seen the same look many years ago during a similar situation, one that had happened in the same room. 'Hopefully, you'll be more co-operative than he was.'

'Don't count on it.'

He shrugged. 'Too bad. Then I guess you'll suffer the same fate as your mother.'

'My mother? What do you mean? What are you talking about?'

He smiled. He knew she would take the bait. How could she possibly avoid it? 'Come now, Maria. You don't *really* think that she killed herself, do you?

You knew her better than anyone. Did she seem like the suicidal type?'

The room started spinning again, this time from all the questions that were swirling in her head. She'd always had doubts about her mother's death. Suddenly everything started rushing to the surface. How did her mother die? What really happened? Was she killed? Was it an accident? There were so many things that she wanted to ask, she was unable to speak at all.

'I'll tell you what,' Benito offered. 'I'll trade you for information. You answer one of my questions and I'll answer one of yours ... How does that sound?'

She nodded, accepting the devil's terms without hesitation.

He pulled up a chair and sat across from her, hoping to read the truth in her eyes. 'Who knows about the Catacombs?'

'Half of Europe,' she groaned, still feeling the burning in her skin. 'People have been talking about them for years.'

Benito smirked at her insolence. Then he showed how he really felt by pushing a chunk of glass that jutted out of her thigh. Her scream filled the room, turning his smirk into a smile. 'This doesn't have to be difficult. All I'm looking for is the truth. If you give that to me, I'll give you what you're looking for ... But if you lie, you will suffer ... Understood?'

She nodded in understanding.

'Who knows about the Catacombs?'

'Just us ... Boyd and me ... We didn't trust anyone else ... so we kept it to ourselves.'

'And what of the others? Petr Ulster? Payne and Jones? What do they know?'

'Nothing,' she insisted, still catching her breath. 'They know we were looking for them. They didn't know we found them.'

Benito nodded. Unbeknownst to Maria, Dr Boyd had blurted the same thing during his interrogation, leaving Benito little choice but to believe them. At least for now. Later he'd let his men take a crack at them with slightly more persuasive methods.

'My turn,' she grunted. 'What happened to my mother?'

'You don't waste any time, do you? So I won't either. Your mother was killed.'

'Killed? By who?'

'Sorry, Maria. It's my turn now. You just used your question.'

'But –'

'But nothing!' He tapped his finger on the shard of glass, just to let her know he was in charge. 'What did you take from the Catacombs?'

'A scroll. We took a scroll. Nothing else.'

'Be more specific,' he demanded. 'Tell me about the scroll.'

'No, that's another question.'

He shook his head. 'It's not a question. It's an order. Tell me about the scroll.' He emphasized his point by putting more weight on the shard. 'Your original answer was incomplete.'

'Fine,' she grunted, hating him more by the minute. 'We found it in a bronze cylinder. In the basement.'

'In the documents room. Inside a stone chest with his picture on it.' He pointed to the painting behind the desk. 'Am I right?'

She nodded, confused. 'How did you know that?'

'How? Because that's where I left it. You don't actually think that you were the first explorers inside the Catacombs? . . . That's amazing. Women can be *so* naive.'

'What? Wait a second! You mean you've been inside?'

'Of course I've been inside. I discovered them. Or should I say rediscovered them. The Church has known about the Catacombs for years.'

'But the scroll? If they knew about the scroll, why did they leave it there?'

Benito flashed a patronizing smile. How could she be so dumb? 'The Church didn't know about the scroll *or* the lower level. The Romans sealed the entrance to the staircase two thousand years ago. It stayed closed until I ran tests on the plateau and discovered the basement.'

He grinned at the irony of the scroll's resting place. Pope Urban VI had selected Orvieto as the perfect spot to protect the Vatican during the Great Schism. Meanwhile an even bigger threat – a document that could shatter Christianity and everything that the Church stood for – sat unnoticed the entire time he used the Catacombs. Benito realized if any of the pope's men had found the hidden entrance to the staircase, the evidence of Pilate's plot would've been destroyed by the Church in the 1300s. Thankfully, that never happened.

'My turn,' Maria said boldly. 'Why was my mother killed?'

'Why? . . . Because of you.'

'What? What do you mean?'

He raised his finger, telling her to stop. 'Did you translate the scroll?'

Maria wanted to lie. Yet she knew if he sensed it, he'd stop giving her information about her mother. And that was something she couldn't risk. To her, the mystery of her mother's death was more important than the secret of the scroll. 'Yes. We translated it in Milan.'

He had expected as much. 'Then you know the truth. The hero of the crucifixion wasn't Christ. The real hero was Pilate, your ancestor. His con created the biggest religion of all time.'

She shrugged, refusing to give him a reaction. 'Why was she killed for me?'

'Didn't you hear what I said? You're related to Pontius Pilate. He was your forefather.'

'So? I'm more concerned with my mother. Why did you kill her?'

He grinned at her audacity. He decided to reward it with the answer. 'Why? Because she wanted you back. You were her little girl . . . From the moment you went to school, she became increasingly difficult to handle. She knew I wasn't going to give in to her, so she decided to apply some outside pressure, hoping to change my mind.'

'What kind of pressure?'

Benito shook his head. Her turn was over. 'When Roberto was tortured, what did he reveal?'

'I don't know. I wasn't there.'

'Maria,' he said sternly, putting his hand on the glass shard.

'I'm serious. I wasn't there. That's why Payne cut off Roberto's finger for identification. If I'd been there, I would've identified him myself.'

Benito considered this, then nodded.

'What kind of pressure?' she repeated.

'Your mother found information about the Catacombs in my office. She threatened to go public unless I let you return home.'

Finally, everything started to make sense. That's the reason her mother had called her at school and told her to pack her bags. She figured the info about the Catacombs would be enough to buy Maria a ticket home. Obviously, she was wrong. 'So you had her killed?'

'No, *I* killed her myself. Right here in this room.' He smiled, thinking back to that day. She was his wife, so he felt his actions were well within his rights. Just like putting the family dog to sleep. 'No woman was going to tell me what to do. Not in my home.

Not over Orvieto. This was *my* family's secret, not hers. She had no business getting involved in this. She deserved to die.'

73

Payne briefed Nick Dial en route to Lake Albano, warning him what type of guards Benito Pelati had on his payroll. Ex-military, ex–Swiss Guard, the type of guys that two ex-MANIACs knew how to handle. Dial realized he'd be screwed without their help, so he said a few words and made them official Interpol deputies. Somehow Payne and Jones didn't think it was very legal.

Dial called for reinforcements, too, but they managed to beat the local police to the scene. Too bad. They weren't waiting for anyone. Not with Boyd and Maria in captivity.

An iron gate greeted them at the front of the property, as did an empty guard station. Payne helped Jones and Dial over the wall before he climbed it on his own. The yard was dark and spacious. They dashed through the bushes and trees, keeping an eye out for the security staff. They weren't even sure that anyone was home until they heard a gunshot. Then another. Two identical sounds coming from somewhere inside the house. It was time to make their move. They didn't know who was involved or what they were facing, but they didn't care. Gunshots in a house were never good. So they decided to put a stop to them.

Jones led the charge to the front door, while Dial covered his back. Payne crept along the perimeter, looking in windows, trying to get a feel for the interior. He plotted escape routes, spotted weaknesses, estimated room locations and dimensions. Lives were on the line, and he knew it. The more information he had going in, the more corpses they'd have coming out. The *enemy's* corpses, not their own. Payne refused to let his guys get killed during missions.

Payne reached the front porch just as Jones had sprung the lock. Payne briefed them on what he'd seen and volunteered to take the lead. There were no objections. Dial went next, followed by Jones. A sweeping staircase went up both sides of the foyer and met on the second floor. Paintings and statues lined the walls. A chandelier hung from the ceiling, though it gave them no light. They were standing in near darkness, thankful for the faint glow that came from deeper in the house. They decided to follow it.

Noises could be heard as they moved down the hallway. Screams of agony. Sounds of torture. The crack of fist meeting face. The thud of flesh being pounded. There was no doubt in Payne's mind that it was Dr Boyd. He was being interrogated. By more than one man. The door to the office was closed and locked. A crack of light was shining around the frame. Its glow had led them to this spot like a beacon.

Jones examined the lock and realized that it was a hundred years old. A type he had never seen before. He told Payne he might be able to pick it but wasn't certain. Furthermore, he didn't know if he could do it quietly. Payne shook his head to let him know it was too risky. Payne felt the same about kicking in the door. He had no experience breaking down something that old. If it didn't shatter on his first attempt, the element of surprise would be ruined. And since they didn't know who was inside and what weapons they had, it wasn't worth the risk.

Payne turned toward Dial and whispered, 'We need a mirror. One that'll fit under the door.'

He nodded in understanding. 'Give me two minutes.'

Before Payne could argue, Dial scampered deeper into the house. Darkness be damned. Safety be damned. The only thing that mattered to Dial was meeting his objective. Ninety seconds later he returned with a chunk of glass from a broken mirror. Payne wondered how he'd shattered it in silence but didn't have time to ask. Instead, Payne dropped to the floor and slid the glass under the door. By tilting the edge back and forth, he was able to see everything in the office. Boyd was unconscious, blood dripping from his face. Maria sat next to him, being questioned by an old man Payne didn't recognize. He immediately assumed it was her father.

Armed guards were positioned throughout the interior. One stood next to Boyd. One stood next to Maria. Another stood behind the old man, watching the interrogation.

Strangely, Payne didn't see Dante anywhere. He slid the glass in further, hoping to get a better view of the far corner of the room. His boldness almost backfired when he realized he had pushed the glass between the feet of one of the guards. Unbeknownst to Payne there was a fourth guard standing next to the door. He'd been studying the room through his legs the entire time.

With his heart in his throat, Payne pulled out the mirror, then dragged Jones and Dial down the hall where he described the layout. Four armed guards. One boss. Two hostages. A couch and some chairs. A large desk. No windows or side doors. One entrance that was being guarded. Boyd was out cold, and Maria was being questioned. No gunshot wounds on either hostage.

'What do we do?' Dial asked.

Jones looked at Payne. 'Fast and hard?'

Payne nodded. It was their only choice. If they tried to draw the guards out of the office, they might summon additional guards from the lake. Or the fence line. Or somewhere they didn't know about. And if that happened, they were screwed. On the other hand, if they waited for the local cops to arrive, there was always a chance that one of the hostages could be killed.

No, they needed to attack. Right away. With lethal force.

Payne explained what he had in mind, and Dial looked at him like he was crazy. Meanwhile Jones nodded his head, impressed. Not only with Payne's idea but with the size of his nuts. Regrettably, Payne wouldn't know if he was stupid or courageous until he saw the outcome. Payne knew they only had one chance at the element of surprise. That meant they had to get through the door on their first attempt. Simply had to. And picking the lock was out of the question, since a guard was standing next to it. Not only might he hear them, but there was a chance that his ass was actually touching the mechanism that Jones would be working on, meaning the slightest vibration might lead to their deaths.

On the other hand, Payne wasn't quite sure if he had the strength to kick down the door. It was big and thick and sat on old iron hinges that looked like they were made by Leonardo da Vinci. Therefore, he had no idea what they could withstand. The same thing with the lock. Would it shatter like a modern one or could it withstand the force of a medieval battering ram?

Either way, Payne didn't want the entire success of this mission to ride on his right foot, so he decided to stack the deck in his favor. Instead of attacking the door alone, he told Jones to fire a round into the lock a split second before Payne's foot made contact with the wood, hoping the gunshot would weaken the bolt. Of course, if Jones fired too late or the bullet ricocheted back toward Payne, the odds were pretty good that he'd lose some toes.

Oh well, Payne joked, there was always a chance that they would grow back.

Without delay Jones positioned his gun while Payne measured his approach. He had room for three steps before he hit the door. Three strides that would determine everything. Dial stood behind Jones, ready to charge into the room and take out the guard by Boyd. Jones would get the one by Maria. And Payne would take out the one behind Benito. The fourth guard, the one by the door, was the wild card. Payne was hoping he would eliminate him on impact. If not, one of them would have to pull double duty. And the odds were pretty good it would be Payne. Not that he was complaining. Situations like this had always been his specialty.

Anyhow, since Dial was the one with the least to do, Payne put him in charge of counting.

Three. Jones pointed his weapon at the door lock.

Two. Payne anchored his foot against the back wall like it was a starting block.

One. He burst from his stance, ready to strike.

Jones fired his gun a split second before Payne made contact with the door. Metal groaned and wood cracked as the door slammed into the back of the fourth guard, knocking him to the floor. Somehow Payne kept his balance, allowing him to lead the charge into the room. Jones and Dial followed, bursting into the room with their weapons drawn.

Their attack was so precise that they were able to hit the guards before they knew what happened. Payne clubbed his target with an elbow and followed it with a knee to the chin, knocking him on top of the fourth guard who was sprawled unconscious on the floor. Partially because of the impact of the door. Partially because Jones's gunshot had gone right through the door lock and into the guard's ass.

Without delay, Payne grabbed both of the guards' guns, then checked on his team. Jones had eliminated his man with a kick to the throat then had gone after the old man in the chair. Dial, on the other hand, was struggling. He was playing martial arts patty-cake with his target until Payne clubbed the guard with the butt of his gun and threw him face-first against the wall.

Smiling, Dial gave Payne a look that said, *My clients are normally dead when I show up.*

Payne gave him a look that said, *Mine aren't.*

Meanwhile, Jones was all over Benito. He dislodged his weapon before wrapping his arm around Benito's neck and giving it a tug. One little squeeze, and the old man stopped fighting. No threats. No struggle. No bribes of any kind. In Jones's mind, it was kind of pathetic. He was expecting so much more from the notorious Benito Pelati.

'Kill him,' Maria begged from across the room. She was tied to her chair, staring at her father. The crazed look in her eyes told everyone she was serious.

She wanted Jones to snap Benito's neck like a wish-bone. 'He killed my mother. He killed my brother. He deserves to die.'

'You're probably right, but –'

'But what? Don't you get it? They will *never* put him in jail. He knows too much about the Church! They *won't* press charges against him. No one will press charges! He'll be freed like you were in Pamplona.'

Payne listened to the two of them as he searched the room, making sure there were no surprises. He found one, though, behind the desk. Dante was lying there in a puddle of blood.

'Maria,' Jones argued. 'I wish I could, but I can't. I just can't –'

'Then let me do it! Just untie me. We'll say he died during the rescue. No one will know.'

'I'll know,' Dial said from across the room. 'And since I'm in charge, I'd have to stop you.'

'Besides,' Payne said as he checked Dante's pulse. 'You're wrong about your brother. He's still alive.'

The police arrived a few minutes later, giving Dial a chance to call the NCB officers at the airport. They informed him that one of the crucifixion crews had been caught and were spilling their guts about the other three teams. Dial figured with a little luck that all of them would be captured by daylight. And the whole crucifixion ordeal would be over.

'And what about me?' Boyd demanded. His left

eye was swollen shut. Gauze covered the gash in his forehead. 'When will I get my reputation back?'

Dial grimaced. 'That one might take a little longer. I'm working on it, though.'

'I should bloody well hope so,' Boyd said, only half kidding. 'So what are you waiting for? Go work on it. I've got things to do and people to meet. I'm a busy man, Mr Dial.'

Laughing, Dial gave him a mock salute and headed for the dining room.

'Good guy,' Payne said to Jones, who nodded in full agreement. 'Thank God he's gone.'

Payne still didn't know what had happened during the last few hours and was dying to be debriefed, not only about the laughing man but about the Pelati family. The last time they'd seen Dante he was loading Boyd and Maria onto a chopper. Now she was begging a doctor to save her brother's life as they loaded him into an ambulance.

Obviously, they'd missed something important.

The house was abuzz with activity, so they went out by the pool where Dr Boyd filled them in on everything from the shooting to Dante's hatred of his father. He also told them about his prior chat with Dante, which pissed Payne and Jones off until they realized that it occurred way before the events at Orvieto and had little bearing on their safety. In Boyd's mind he didn't know whose side Dante was on until they'd reached the house, so he kept that information to himself.

'Wait a second!' Jones blurted. 'You're telling me we *weren't* in danger at the quarry? Come on, I don't buy that for a second. His guards did *not* want us to leave that mountain.'

Payne agreed. 'He's right, Doc. I've got bruises all over my body to prove it.'

Boyd frowned, not wanting to talk about injuries, not with his face looking like *that*. 'The guards worked for Benito, not for Dante. That forced him to keep up his ruse.'

Jones scratched his head. 'If that's the case, why did Dante bring you two here? For safety's sake, you'd think this is the last place he'd want to bring you.'

'If he survives, you can ask him yourself. In the meantime, there are more important things to worry about.' Payne turned toward Boyd. 'What did you find out about the laughing man?'

'The who?' Boyd chuckled at his little joke. 'Ah yes, the mysterious laughing man. It seems that his identity wasn't so mysterious after all.'

74

Nick Dial was tempted to leave the crime scene and drive back to the airport. It pained him to think that one of his suspects was being interrogated by someone other than himself. After all, he was the one who cracked the geographic relevance to the crucifixions, so he wanted to be present for the fireworks. Nothing gave him greater satisfaction than getting a criminal to talk.

With that in mind, he knew the opportunity to speak with Benito Pelati was one he couldn't miss. No attorneys were present, and the local cops were too concerned with collecting evidence to be worried about a simple interview. In their minds Dial had made the bust, so he *should* get the first crack at Pelati. In fact, they even offered to watch the door as he did.

Pelati looked like royalty as he entered the back room. His clothes were flawless, and his stride was unrushed. His chin was high in the air as though he was about to address the peasants from the palace balcony. His hands were cuffed yet hidden by the fabric of his jacket, so they did little to shatter the illusion that Pelati strived to maintain. He was a national icon and expected to be treated as such.

The moment Dial saw him enter the room he knew their conversation was going to be pointless. In his mind he knew there was no way he was going to get anything from Pelati. He tried anyway, asking question after question about Pelati's family, the crucifixions, and anything else he could think of. But Pelati didn't flinch. He just sat there, unimpressed, like he was half disappointed that Dial was the best cop that Interpol could scrounge up.

Thankfully, a knock on the door changed everything. Dial was tempted to ignore it until he heard the door squeak open behind him. 'What is it?' he growled. 'I'm busy here.'

'Sir,' a cop whispered, 'there's a Cardinal Rose to see you. He says it's urgent.'

Dial smiled, realizing he'd get to thank the cardinal in person for warning him about the blackmail attempt on the Church. He also knew that Rose might have additional information that he could use when he questioned Pelati. 'Yeah, that's fine. Send him back.'

Though they had never met, Rose wasn't difficult to spot. Not only was he dressed like a cardinal, wearing a scarlet robe and a red biretta on his head, but his gait was all Texas. He strolled down the hall like a sheriff heading to a gunfight. If the circumstances had been different, Dial would've lifted the cardinal's garb to see if he was wearing spurs.

'Joe, I'm Nick Dial. It's a pleasure to meet you.' The two shook hands just around the corner from the interrogation room. 'So what's up? I was told you had something urgent to discuss.'

Rose nodded. 'I was given another update on Benito Pelati that I thought would help. But if now's a bad time, I can always come back.'

'Nonsense. I wouldn't think of sending you away. Besides, I'm talking to Benito right now, and he keeps bringing up something that puzzles me. The guy will barely say a word to me, but when he does, he keeps alluding to some secret. I've pressed him, but nothing gives.'

'This secret, has he given you any hints?'

'I wish. It'd make my job a helluva lot easier . . . Oops. Sorry about that.'

Rose ignored the profanity. Most Texans swore, too. 'Have you asked his family? Maybe they know something. I've never met the man, so I'm not sure what I can tell you.'

'Actually, I think his son knew. That's the reason Benito put two in his chest. To keep him from telling anyone else.'

Rose made the sign of the cross for Dante 'Did he?'

'Did he, what?'

'Tell anyone else. One of the cops told me there were several witnesses to the shooting.'

Dial nodded. 'His bodyguards were nearby, bu none of them spoke English. I get the feeling tha was one of the requirements for his staff. It allowed him to conduct his business in private.'

'Smart man. That's the best way to do it. No fear of listening ears.'

'Speaking of smart, why do I get the feeling that you're aware of the secret? That's why you're here, isn't it?'

Rose shrugged. 'Perhaps. God works in mysterious ways.'

Glory hallelujah! Dial thought to himself. 'Tell me, is it something about the Church? Is that what the blackmail was about? He learned something about the Church and decided to make a few bucks for himself.'

'Nick, listen, my hands are tied on this one. I can't talk about it. I really can't.'

Dial couldn't keep from smiling. 'But . . .'

Rose laughed. '*But* I figure if I get him to talk about it without actually mentioning it . . .'

'Then I'll get everything I need, and you'll have a clean conscience.'

He nodded. 'Yeah, something like that.'

Dial looked at his watch and knew that he was running out of time. Pelati's lawyers would arrive any minute. 'Fine. But we've got to make this quick.'

Rose put his right hand in the air. 'Don't worry, I will be.'

Still smiling, Dial went in first, followed by Rose, who closed the door behind them. Rose had seen Pelati at the Vatican several times but had never spoken to him, mostly because the two had nothing in common. Rose was willing to give everything he had to the Church without expecting anything in return, whereas Pelati was the complete opposite. This mansion was proof of that. Rose was a giver. Pelati was a taker. It would stay that way until the end.

Pelati watched the duo enter the room and seemed to come to life. His eyes focused on the man in red who was staring at him. 'Tell me, Mr Dial, who's your friend?'

'This is Cardinal Joseph Rose from the Vatican. He came to talk to me about your case, and I decided to let him join us.'

'Oh? Why is that? Wasn't I good enough company for you?'

'Actually, you have it backward. I didn't think I was good enough company for you. You see, you kept talking about something that I knew nothing about, so I decided to bring in an expert, someone who could help me understand.'

Pelati grinned at the thought. 'This man is an expert? On what? *Christ?*'

'No,' Rose interrupted. 'I'm an expert on secrets.'

'Secrets?' He gasped with mock fear. 'Any secret in particular? *Mine,* perhaps?'

Rose nodded, taking a step closer.

'Oh good! Then this shall be fun. Please pull up a seat, Your Eminence. I'd love to hear what you know about me and my secret.'

Rose shook his head. 'The chair won't be necessary. I promised Nick that I'd be brief, and I intend to keep my word.'

'Suit yourself, Your Eminence . . . I admire a man who can keep his word.'

Rose moved closer. 'Actually, that's the thing about secrets that has always bothered me. People never keep their word, meaning a secret is never a secret for very long.'

Pelati nodded, all too familiar with the subject. 'Cardinal Rose, if I may be so bold, why are you telling me this? Are you trying to convince me that you *know* my family's secret? Is that what you're trying to do?'

'On the contrary, I wanted you to know that the exact opposite is true. You are *alone* in this. No one knows your entire secret but you. Do you hear me? *Not a single soul.*'

Pelati frowned. It wasn't what he was expecting. 'And you came here to tell me *that?*'

Rose smiled in the face of evil. He'd been sent here by the Supreme Council to protect the Church, and he intended to finish the job. 'No, I came here because I wanted to see the look in your eyes when I told you this . . .' Pulling a pistol from the folds of his robe, he said, 'Your secret dies today.'

Before Dial could react, Rose shoved the gun against Pelati's head and fired. A thunderous roar filled the room, followed by the splash of blood and brains against the wall.

Instinctively, Dial lunged for Rose's weapon, but the Cardinal was too quick to be stopped. Backing away to the far corner of the room, Rose pushed the hot barrel against his own temple and ordered Dial to stay put.

'Don't do it!' Dial screamed. 'Please don't!'

'I have to, Nick. It *has* to end this way.'

'Why?' he demanded as a wave of cops burst through the door. 'Tell me why!'

Rose smiled knowingly and tightened his grip on the trigger. 'Because Christ is my savior.'

75

Payne and Jones never heard the gunshots. They were out by the pool, discussing the week's events when Cardinal Rose opened fire. The sound was drowned out by a hovering chopper and all the police sirens that were migrating to the area.

Later, when they found out what happened, Payne was disappointed that he didn't get to see Benito's execution. That might sound morbid, but when you've seen as many good men die as he had, sometimes it helps to see the death of a devil. Somehow that helps balance the equation. At least for a little while.

Then again, Payne realized if he'd been inside for all the fireworks, he would've missed the biggest surprise of all. Something so unexpected that he still didn't know what to think of it.

Sitting between Jones and Dr Boyd, Payne was staring at the twinkling blue water, thinking about religion. He had learned more about Christianity during the past few days than he had during the rest of his years combined. Yet he was thirsting for more. For every question that had been answered, ten new ones had popped into his head. And each of them was more complicated than the last. Payne mentioned this to Dr Boyd, who claimed that was the paradox of religion. Boyd said, the more you learn, the less you know.

Joking, Payne said, 'Damn! Then I guess you don't know shit compared to me.'

Surprisingly, Boyd laughed louder than anyone.

Payne turned toward Jones, expecting a smile on his face, too. Instead he noticed a dazed look in his eyes that said he was still trying to piece everything together. The Catacombs, the scroll, the Pelati family secret. To him, they were pieces in a jigsaw puzzle that still didn't fit.

'You all right?' Payne asked.

He nodded, even though Payne knew he wasn't. Something was bothering him. Something big. Finally, Jones said, 'Doc, out of curiosity, what do you think happened to him?'

Boyd grimaced. 'Him? Who do you mean?'

'Jesus,' he answered. 'If Jesus didn't die on the cross, what happened to him?'

'Ahhh.' The sound suggested that Boyd had been expecting that question all week. 'I guess that depends on who you ask. Different experts have different opinions, though some of them are a little daft. The most popular theory is that Christ was a married man who shipped his family to Marseilles right after his trial in Judea. I've read many French manuscripts that refer to Christ's royal blood still living in France today.'

They had heard that theory, too. Payne knew some experts believed that Christ's wife was Mary Magdalene. Of course he had no idea if that was true or a brilliant piece of fiction. 'So you think Christ went to France?'

Boyd shrugged. 'That's what some believe. Others feel the risk would've been too great. The truth is, if Christ had been discovered, his whole family would've been slaughtered on the spot.'

Jones winced. 'Then where did he go?'

'According to Islamic traditions, he headed east, where he eventually died several decades later in the Indian city of Kashmir. Others believe that he went to Alexandria in Egypt, where he helped convert that city to Christianity. I even read one account that claimed he was killed at Masada in 74 AD when the Jewish fortress fell to the Romans.'

But none of those theories sat well with Jones. Frustrated, he tossed a stone into the deep end of the pool. The splash sent ripples in every direction. 'In other words, no one really knows.'

Boyd shook his head. 'I guess not.'

'So all of this,' Jones made an exaggerated hand movement that suggested everything they had done, 'and we still don't know for sure.'

'Not conclusively, no ... And the truth is, we probably never will.'

Dr Boyd excused himself and headed to the house. His face was swollen and misshapen, and his sterile gauze was no longer doing the trick. It was time for a bag of ice and a bottle of Tylenol.

Payne and Jones watched him go inside before their focus shifted to the helicopter that was hovering above. At first they thought it was a police chopper assigned to protect the grounds. Then they figured it was the media, possibly the paparazzi trying to get a picture of the murder scene. They continued to believe this until Jones pointed something out. The chopper was running dark. No searchlights. No taillights. No lights of any kind. For some reason it was trying to blend in with the dark sky above. Trying not to be seen. 'You don't think that's . . .'

Jones nodded. He knew what Payne had in mind. 'The second chopper from Vienna.'

Before Dante left the marble mine, he had given orders to his men to wait until the weather had cleared before they loaded his discovery from Vienna onto the next chopper. After that, they were supposed to fly to the villa where he was planning to meet his father.

Suddenly it dawned on them that the chopper had never arrived. Or, at the very least, had never landed. If their theory was correct, the pilot was still hovering above them, wondering what to do next. Jones grinned. 'Let's see if he's willing to join us.'

Payne bowed in his direction. 'After you, my devious friend.'

Dante's personal chopper was still sitting on the helipad at the back of the estate. There was plenty of room to land a second chopper in the yard. It was just a matter of convincing the pilot that it was the right thing to do. Payne suggested using a light to flash him Morse code, but Jones thought of something better. He climbed into Dante's chopper and slipped on the headset. A couple of buttons later, he was barking orders.

'What are you waiting for?' Jones screamed in Italian. 'Set her down now!'

Thirty seconds passed before the pilot responded. 'What about the police?'

'They're not here for you. There was a shooting at the house. Dante's taking care of it.'

The pilot considered this for a moment before he flipped on his running lights. A few minutes later he was landing in the middle of the backyard. 'Now what?' the pilot asked.

'Unload the merchandise, then get out of here. We'll call you when we need you.'

Like magic, a team of six soldiers hoisted the relic out of the chopper and eased it onto the grass. Payne and Jones couldn't risk being seen, so they stayed hidden inside the first chopper, although that probably wasn't necessary. The men were too spooked by the cops to even look their way. A minute later, they were airborne again. Off to Rome. Or Vienna. Or wherever they were going next. Payne watched the entire scene in disbelief.

'That went well,' Jones said, laughing. 'I hope it isn't a bomb.'

The two of them walked across the lawn, unsure of what they were getting into. The sky was dark, and the moon was partially hidden behind a bank of clouds. There were few lights in this part of the yard, and they weren't about to turn any on. Not even a flashlight. But Payne almost changed his mind when he saw the sarcophagus. It was made out of white marble and was decorated with a series of carvings that reminded him of the ones on Maria's tape. With one glance Payne knew that they told a story — he could tell that from their layout — but their meaning was impossible to interpret in the darkness.

For an instant Payne wondered if this was the reason that Dante brought Boyd and Maria here. To help explain what this thing was. Maybe to help him figure out what he should do next. Those thoughts disappeared quickly, though. And his mind went back to the stone artifact.

Strangely, Payne felt like a blind man reading Braille, running his fingers over the ancient designs, trying to understand the narrative. Just then the moon peeked out from behind the clouds, and he could see Christ on the cross and the laughing man standing nearby. A team of centurions was carrying a body to a cave. Then he saw a man walking out. Meanwhile, Jones was on the other side of the box, calling out images as he deciphered them.

He saw soldiers. A large boat. A series of mountains. The tip of a sword.

Neither of them knew exactly what the stone was

saying. And they realized they wouldn't unless they fetched Boyd or Maria for help. But where was the fun in that?

Instead they decided to examine the contents on their own. They figured, how much damage could the two of them do? They were only going to take a short peek inside, not even for a minute. They would push the lid aside, take a look, and then push the sucker back. No one would ever know. It would be their little secret.

They studied the box's construction and decided they should push it from Payne's side. Smiling, they counted to three, then heaved with all their might. The stone lid groaned and trembled, then slid five inches to the right. A wisp of ancient air filled their nostrils but they didn't care. Not one bit.

They were too intoxicated by what they found within.

76

Their helicopter hovered above the Archives for several seconds, just enough time for Payne and Jones to view the reconstruction from the air. It had been less than three weeks since the fire, but the work zone was buzzing. Bulldozers were plowing. Trucks were hauling. Workers were cutting boards and pounding nails. Things were looking great, at least to novices like them.

Sadly, they couldn't say the same thing about Christianity.

Payne and Jones had spent two weeks researching the topic, more to appease their curiosity than anything else. They read books. They talked to experts. They did everything in their power to answer the questions that were bothering them. And some of the answers left them perplexed.

For instance, they never knew that the Koran, the Islamic bible, asserts that Christ's crucifixion was faked. Yes, *faked*. Muslims view Christ as a prophet, someone who should be revered in the same terms as Abraham, Moses, and Muhammad, so it stunned

Payne and Jones that the Koran questioned Christ's integrity. Yet it comes right out and says that he *wasn't* crucified. The line reads:

[4:157] *And their saying: Surely we have killed the Messiah, Jesus son of Mary, the apostle of Allah; and they did not kill him nor did they crucify him, but it appeared to them so . . .*

Amazingly, this verse wasn't stashed away on a hidden scroll or locked in the Vatican's basement. It is known by a billion Muslims around the world. Still, neither Payne nor Jones had ever heard about a fake crucifixion until they met up with Boyd and Pelati.

How is that possible?

How could something so important be ignored by the Western world?

Whether it's accurate or not wasn't the point. Payne couldn't understand why this line was never discussed in a public forum. Why no one was curious enough to investigate it. Payne joked it was too bad Oliver Stone didn't direct *The Passion of the Christ*. Because he would've come up with a much different ending to the film – something with a conspiratorial twist.

Oh well, maybe Mel Gibson is planning a sequel?

Changing subjects, they also found several interesting facts about Pontius Pilate. The most surprising was Pilate's close friendship with Joseph of Arimathea, who played a major role in the crucifixion and Christ's final resting place. All four Gospels claim that Christ's body was sealed in a tomb on Joseph's personal property, even though Roman law forbade crucifixion victims from being buried. During this era, victims would be left on the cross for days where they would eventually be eaten by birds. Furthermore, the Romans were so adamant about this law that they actually posted guards to make sure that the victim's friends or relatives didn't touch the corpses.

Yet Pilate was willing to go against this code and gave Jesus's body to Joseph of Arimathea, even though he had no rightful claim to remove it. Unless, of course, something was going on behind the scenes, and Pilate and Joseph were coconspirators in the deception.

Stranger still is the wording that was used in Mark's Gospel. In the original Greek version, when Joseph asked Pilate for Christ's body, he used the word *soma,* a word that refers to 'a living body,' not *ptoma,* a word that means 'a corpse.' In other words, Joseph asked Pilate for someone who was still alive. This line was eventually changed in Latin and English translations of the Bible because translators used nonspecific words that failed to explain whether Christ was living or dead when he was removed from the cross. However, in the original version, even Mark says that Christ was alive when he was turned over to Joseph.

Payne and Jones came up with dozens of facts like these, tidbits that weren't talked about in most churches, even though they'd been verified by experts. Payne wasn't sure why that was – conspiracy? ignorance? something else? – but they intended to keep digging until they were satisfied. In fact, that was one of the reasons that they came back to the Archives.

To get the answers that they were looking for.

As soon as Payne and Jones landed, Petr Ulster greeted them with a hug. The stress that had been evident in Vienna was no longer there, replaced with a twinkle in his eye and a warm smile. All in all, he looked even happier than he did when they'd first met. And that was saying a lot, because Ulster was one of the happiest people Payne had ever come across.

'Jonathon! D.J.! It's so wonderfully great to see you! I'm so glad you could return.'

'Wouldn't have missed it for the world,' Jones replied.

Payne nodded in agreement. 'Looks like you've been busy.'

'Very!' Ulster said. 'But it's been wonderful. I've always been tempted to expand the Archives, and this gave me the perfect excuse. If the donations keep pouring in, we'll be able to double in size.'

Payne whistled, impressed. 'And what about the artifacts? Did you lose anything in the fire?'

'Nothing invaluable. There were some personal items, things with sentimental value that we couldn't salvage. Like my grandfather's photo collection.'

Payne groaned at the loss. 'You mean the ones in the hallway? Man, I loved those.'

'Me, too. But thanks to you, I still have one of the pictures.'

'Really?'

He nodded. 'The one with the Lipizzaner stallions. Remember, you took it off the wall to show us the laughing man? Because of that, the picture survived.'

'Just like an American,' said a gruff voice from behind. 'Saving our horses again!'

Payne turned and saw Franz. '*Ja! Ja!* It's true. You soldiers are always showing off.'

Payne smiled and greeted him with a handshake. 'How have you been, Franz? Still resting up from our little adventure?'

'Adventure? That was nothing! My recent trip to Amsterdam, now *that* was an adventure.'

The thought of a naked Franz made Payne and Jones slightly nauseous.

'So, why are you here?' he asked. 'Are you here to help? We could use some more hands.'

'Franz!' Ulster scolded, laughing. 'These are our guests. They should be treated as such.'

Franz waved dismissively. 'Don't start with me, Petr. Even the woman is working!'

'What woman?' Jones asked.

'*Your* woman,' Franz said. '*Ja, ja!* She got here yesterday with Dr Boyd.'

'My woman? You mean Maria? She's here?'

Payne loved the look on Jones's face. A mixture of bliss, confusion, and total shock.

'Oops!' Payne said. 'Did I forget to mention that? Sorry. It must've slipped my mind.'

'Wait a second! You *knew* about this?'

'Duh! That's the only way I could've planned it.'

'But I thought she was in Italy, taking care of her brother and her family's estate.'

'Not anymore,' Payne said. 'By the way, when did Maria become *your* woman? Does she know about that?'

'No, but . . .'

'But what? Women aren't possessions, you know. You can't just run around claiming them.'

'I realize that, but . . .'

'Maybe you'd have a little more luck with the ladies if you treated them with the respect that they deserved. Besides, before you run off and plant your flag in Maria or *whatever* you're going to do to claim her, we have some business to take care of.'

'Business?' He looked at Payne, confused, until he realized what Payne was talking about. 'Oh, that's right! Our business. I almost forgot about our *business.*'

Ulster and Franz stared at Payne and Jones like they were crazy. Which, of course, they were. They didn't call them MANIACs for nothing.

Payne said to Ulster, 'When D.J. and I were in Italy, we came across an item that we thought would look great in the Archives. It's one of those things that we think everybody should get a chance to study, not just a few old priests at the Vatican.'

Jones added, 'If you don't want it, we'll completely understand. I mean, it is kind of cumbersome. But since you're building a new wing and all, we figured you'd have the room.'

'What is it?' Ulster asked.

'We can show you if you'd like. We brought it with us.'

'You did?'

Payne nodded as he opened the back of the chopper. Ulster and Franz peered inside and saw the stone sarcophagus, hermetically sealed in high-grade plastic. 'We didn't want to expose it to the elements, so Dr Boyd showed us how to protect it. Hopefully you can figure out a more permanent solution for its upkeep.'

Struggling to see through the plastic, Ulster frowned. 'I'm sure I could if I knew what I was looking at ... Please tell me there isn't a body in there.'

Jones laughed. 'I was worried about the same thing when we opened it. But as luck should have it, it was filled with something more, um, shocking.'

'Shocking?' Ulster asked.

Instead of answering, Payne pulled several pictures from his shirt pocket and handed them to Ulster. They were taken from a variety of angles and showed the sarcophagus both opened and closed. The final few photos focused on the object that was inside, an artifact that had survived the last two thousand years intact. Evidence that had been saved by Pilate to tell his side of the story. At least part of it. The other part would be explained on a separate document.

Ulster gasped when he saw the item. 'Are those beams from a cross?'

They nodded. The stipes had been sawed in half, but the patibulum was still intact. And best of all, they had scientists in Pittsburgh test a sliver of wood, and it was first-century African oak.

Just like it should've been.

'You mean,' Ulster stuttered, 'this is *his* cross?'

Payne shrugged. 'That's what we're hoping you can prove. That is, if you have the time.'

'Yes,' he gasped. 'I have the time.'

'But that's not all.' Payne reached into the chopper and pulled out a small storage case. 'There was one more item inside the sarcophagus, something we haven't opened yet. We figured it would be best if we left that to you, Boyd, and Maria.'

With shaking hands, Ulster opened the case and saw a bronze cylinder, similar to the one that had been found in the Catacombs. Yet instead of Tiberius's seal, the cylinder was stamped with Pontius Pilate's official symbol, an emblem that hadn't been used since the days of Christ.

'I have no idea what's inside. But if we're lucky, it might just tell us what happened.'

And as luck would have it, it actually did.

*

As far as Payne could tell, only six of them (Dante, Maria, Boyd, Ulster, Jones, and himself) knew everything. And by *everything* Payne meant the truth about the Catacombs and the identity of the laughing man. Several others – everyone from Franz to Nick Dial to Randy Raskin, not to mention everyone at the Pentagon who monitored Raskin's calls – knew bits and pieces of the tale. Still, Payne realized it would be difficult for any of them to put the whole story together, simply because none of them had enough information to go on or the proof that they possessed.

No, as far as Payne could tell, only six of them knew the secret that Cardinal Rose thought he'd silenced forever when he killed Benito Pelati. Thankfully, Rose was a poor detective, otherwise Payne knew he would've heard from Rose's bosses by now – in one way or another.

Speaking of which, Payne wasn't really sure what the Vatican knew (and didn't know) about their adventure. And he had no intention of asking them. Ever.

Why? There's an old adage that says there's no such thing as a stupid question. Well, that might be true, but Payne knew there *was* such a thing as a dangerous question.

Especially if the wrong person wanted to know the answer.

Or wanted to keep it a secret.

Epilogue

The scroll was in remarkable shape considering it was penned by Pontius Pilate on his deathbed. Buried in the hills of Vindobona, the parchment stayed undisturbed for nearly 2,000 years, protected by a bronze cylinder, a stone sarcophagus, and a family with a secret past.

Generation upon generation of Pelati men went to the grave thinking that their forefather, Pontius Pilate, was a hero. That he was the true founder of the Christian faith. That Tiberius had called upon his noble servant and asked him to fake the death of Christ for the betterment of all things Roman. That Tiberius was so impressed with his heroics that he honored his achievements in stone, immortalizing Pilate's image and amazing deeds in the Catacombs of Orvieto. Yet none of the Pelatis – not Benito, Roberto, Dante, or any of their ancestors except Pontius himself – knew the full story of the crucifixion until Maria broke the seal on the cylinder.

As she translated Pilate's final words, she gasped at what she learned, because she held a document that proved what she had always believed: God works in mysterious ways.

Pontius Pilate to my sons and heirs.

I sit on the threshold of death, ready to be judged for the things I have done and those I had hoped to do, yet that does not mean I have not already seen the glory of God, for I have witnessed it firsthand, and its magnificence has changed me into the man I am today.

I knew of the Nazarene long before I looked upon him, word of his flock and his miracles spread across the desert like a plague, one that threatened the peace and prosperity of the land placed in my charge. In time I knew word would reach across the sea, as it always does, and I would be asked to place my boot upon the Nazarene before his followers had grown into a mob that Rome would struggle to crush. Yet the opposite occurred, for when I heard from my liege, he spoke to me in hushed tones, asking me to stoke the flames of the fire until we could use the heat for our betterment. I knew not of what he meant but allowed the fire to burn until it heated the walls of Jerusalem, at which time I received the guidance I had been lacking and the steps I had to follow, for they had been sent by Tiberius himself. I was to place the Nazarene on a pedestal, high above the false Messiahs that had preceded him, and give the Jews the proof they needed that this was their true God, that this was indeed him.

It was decided that this could be done only through death, or the appearance of such, for this is a miracle that cannot be faked and one that would assuage even those who did not believe. In time the Nazarene was brought before his peers and for a mere pittance I was able to ensure the outcome, completing the ruse by washing my hands of the events as though I had no part in the verdict. This angered my Claudia, for she felt that I should exert the power of my rule to protect the holy man whom she had seen in her dreams, yet this could not be done, for fear of angering the Roman throne, the one who whispered to me and encouraged my deceit.

To guarantee the illusion of rebirth, the Nazarene was forced to endure brutality on a public stage, for at the end of the day there could be no doubt that this man had been through hell yet survived solely by his station in heaven. I kept apprised from afar since my place was not near the cross, for a man of my status would care not of a common criminal, one of many that was silenced every day under my rule. Instead, members of my elite guard were put on his watch and asked to complete the task that had been laid out before me, and for this they were promised property in a distant land, though they would never enjoy their bounty, for their silence could only be guaranteed with the tip of my blade. The Christ was given a drug that would result in the illusion of death while inducing no more than a heavy sleep that he could arise from at a distant time, yet the dose was too great or his condition too weak, and word came to me that the Nazarene, the man we had chosen as the Chosen One, was no more. I went at once, inspecting the Nazarene for myself, hoping upon hope that his sleep was but deep and his state was but temporary, yet this was not to be, for as I had been told, this man had indeed left the land of the living.

Far from the eyes of Tiberius yet still within his reach,

I knew what must be done or I would suffer the same fate as the Christ, only my life would be ended without the peace of mandrake or the glory that is achieved in battle. My allies were few and options limited; thus after a night of no sleep I knew I must flee as this was the only way to ensure my continued life. My preparations started in haste, with me telling no one, not even my Claudia, knowing that word could not leak or I would surely be questioned by those who served the position that I intended to abandon. This continued until the third day, the day I was to leave, when I was greeted by one of my men, a man whom I trusted, one I could count on in the most dire of times, and he gave me word that could not be explained, news that forced me to open my eyes to a new way of life: the Nazarene had risen and walked from his tomb alive.

I knew not how this could be, for no man could wake from the slumber of death from which I bore witness: I felt the cold of his skin, saw blood not weep from his wounds, heard no sound when I rested my ear upon his rib. Yet two days later the holy man from Nazareth, the man I murdered for the betterment of Rome, found the heavenly strength to discard the yoke of death and emerge from the tomb in which he was forever sealed.

Looking back with the wisdom of my many years, the latest of which I have spent repenting in this distant land while living on Roman treasures given to me for the secret task I didn't achieve, I do regret, after his emergence from the cave, not searching for him in the streets of Jerusalem and falling to his feet and begging his forgiveness for what

I had done. I despise myself for not joining his flock and spreading his word, for my presence as a Roman, bearing witness to the death he had risen above, would surely have aided his cause and saved the lives of many of his disciples. But instead I did the worst and most cowardly thing that I could possibly have done: I sent word to Rome that all had been accomplished, that his death had been faked, and his return had been revealed to members of his flock – though unforeseen events prevented it from occurring on the great stage that Tiberius had hoped, for if it had been done as planned, the religion of the Christ would have taken hold at once, and the people of Judea would have sung his praises to the world, and the world would surely have listened, believing that the Messiah had returned as prophesied, and everyone in all lands Roman would have joined hands in unity, and the benefits to the Empire would have been immense.

In retrospect, some might ask why I write this now, why it has taken so long to share my story with those who must hear it, and for that my answer brings me no pleasure, for it means I lived my life as a coward and not as the hero that Tiberius was led to believe: the approach of my death has given me courage I did not have in life, and with this courage, I beg of my sons, and their sons as well, to honor the life of the Christ, for he was the true Messiah.

Author's Note

The concept for *Sign of the Cross* first came to me in 1998. I was teaching high school English at the time and had just started to outline my first published novel, *The Plantation*. I loved both concepts equally well but chose to keep *SOTC* on the back burner since I knew it would require the type of research that I couldn't do in a rural community.

Looking back, it was the best decision I could've made as a writer. Not only because I had access to several world-class libraries when I moved back to Pittsburgh, but also due to the explosion of the Internet. That allowed me to scour documents from the Vatican, view the Dead Sea Scrolls from the Qumran Library, and read letters that were penned by Tiberius himself. All of which allowed me to expand my story beyond the concept that I had originally planned.

Amazingly, *SOTC* could've been a thousand-page book. My agent urged me to stop my first draft at the 711-page mark, even though I had more than enough research to keep it going. In hindsight, I'm glad he stopped me. Otherwise *SOTC* would've killed half the rain forest. Of course, the sad part in all of this is that I saved some of my best research for the end of my original story line and was never able to squeeze it into the shorter version. Oh well, if *SOTC* ever gets made into a movie, I can include my research in the bonus material on the DVD.

In the meantime, if you're interested in the non-traditional history of Christianity, there are many nonfiction books that explore the final years of Christ. The most infamous is *Holy Blood, Holy Grail* by Michael Baigent, Richard Leigh, and Henry Lincoln. Published in 1983, it reveals many theories about the crucifixion of Christ that I chose not to include in my story. Other books that I saw mentioned in my research (but haven't necessarily read) include: *The Templar Revelation* by Lynn Picknett and Clive Prince; *Rosslyn: Guardians of the Secret of the Holy Grail* by Tim Wallace-Murphy and Marilyn Hopkins; *Jesus and the Lost Goddess: The Secret Teachings of the Original Christians* by Timothy Freke and Peter Gandy.

A complete list of books can be found on my website: www.chriskuzneski.com.

Changing subjects, I'd like to address one final issue. After reading *SOTC*, several people have asked me to point out which parts of my book are real and which are fiction. Obviously I take that as the ultimate compliment because it suggests I have blended things well enough to create a plausible world. That being said, I have no intention of telling anyone (including my mother) which details are true and which are make-believe. I mean, that's one of the reasons I chose to become an author. I longed for the opportunity to blur the line between fact and fiction without ever having to explain myself.

In other words, everything you read is the way it *really* happened in my universe.

Besides, Jonathon Payne won't tell me anything else. The bastard.

Don't miss *Sword of God*, the next
gripping thriller from Chris Kuzneski –
read the first chapter here . . .

Praise for *Sword of God*:

'This globe-crossing action thriller . . . evokes
the spirit of Dan Brown, with welcome doses
of Lee Child's ex-military tough-guy grit'
Publishers Weekly

I

Saturday, 23 December
Jeju Island, South Korea
(60 miles south of the Korean Peninsula)

The boy could smell the blood from fifty yards away. It was a strong, pungent odour that made him gag yet piqued his curiosity. Common sense told him to turn around and get some help. His father. His mother. One of his neighbours. Anyone who could protect him from what he was about to discover. But common sense rarely mattered to an eight-year-old.

Especially when he was somewhere he didn't belong.

The valley to his right was lined with camphor trees, many seventy-five feet tall and a hundred feet wide. The path in front of him was rugged, made of black volcanic rock that dominated the subtropical island and formed its very core. The temperature was cold, in the low forties, but would climb steadily as the day wore on, a by-product of the nearby Kuroshio and Tsushima currents. The sun was still rising over the Eastern Sea when he made his choice. He zipped his jacket over his nose and inched forward, following the stench of death.

For years his family had warned him about this place, claiming it was built for evil. It was a story that wasn't difficult to believe. Sometimes, late at night, he could hear the screams – bloodcurdling shrieks that ripped through the hillside and jostled him from his sleep. The first time he heard them he assumed he was having a nightmare, but the sounds didn't stop when he sat up in bed. In fact, they got louder. This went on for days, weeks, until he could take no more.

He had to know the truth.

Ignoring his family's wishes, he sneaked into town and asked one of the village elders about the sounds from the hill. The old man laughed at the boy's audacity. He, too, had been a curious child and felt this trait should be rewarded – but only if the boy could understand the truth.

'Look at me,' the old man ordered in Korean. 'Let me see your eyes.'

The boy knew he was being tested. He stared at the old man, refusing to blink, hoping to prove his courage even though his palms were sweating and his knees were trembling.

Tension filled the hut for several seconds. The entire time the boy could barely breathe.

Finally, the old man nodded. The boy was ready for the truth, if for no other reason than to keep him afraid of the place on the hill, to keep him alive. Sometimes fear was a blessing.

With a grave face and a gravelly voice, the old man whispered a single name that was known throughout

Jeju, a place that sent shivers down the boy's spine and woke the hairs on his neck.

Pe-Ui Je Dan.

The boy gasped at its mention. The place was so infamous, so ominous, that other details weren't necessary. He had heard the stories, just like everyone else on the island. Yet until that moment he had thought they were just a myth, an urban legend that had made it across the Sea of Japan for the sake of scaring children into doing their chores. But the old man assured him that wasn't the case. Not only was it real, it was close. Just up the path.

At that moment, the boy promised that he'd never venture up there. And he meant it, too. It was a vow he intended to keep. Not only for his safety, but also for the safety of his village.

Unfortunately, all of that changed on the morning he smelled the blood.

As strange as it seemed, there was something about the scent that attracted him. Something magnetic. Animalistic. One minute he was walking to the store, the next he was tracking the scent like a wolf. Crunching up the rocky path, looking for its source as if nothing else mattered. Sadly, this happened all the time in the world of children – courage and curiosity taking them places where they didn't belong – yet rarely did it lead them into so much danger.

The boy didn't know it as he trudged up the hill, but he was about to kill his village.